One HUNDRED percent Mine

A novel

EMMA AISEMAN

Contents

To my daughter and all the other superheroes out there living with Type 1 diabetes

1

Prologue

Claire

I am not one to kiss a stranger. Most definitely not. No, this kind of admirable bravery is reserved for Kate, my sister, who takes what she wants and says what she thinks. And although most people claim they can barely tell us apart, we're very much different.

Kate is a year younger. And I don't even think we look the same. Maybe just a little, with Kate being the supreme version. But that's about it as far as being alike goes. She is fearless, and happy, and loving, and outgoing. Her little apartment is always filled with friends, and delicious home cooking scents, and sounds of laughter. And she always knows the right thing to say, or when to throw her arms around me and pull me in for a hug when I need it the most. Even when I don't say a word. And not just because she's my sister and knows me best.

Like the night Ryan and I broke up. *"It's not me, it's you,"* he said, uncreatively, and I was mostly annoyed that even our breakup was uneventful. Unoriginal. Bland. Pleasant almost, if it weren't for my dripping heart. And dripping, not bleeding because—really—we both knew this thing between us had ended long before Ryan decided to put both of our collective thoughts into words, or rather—actions. Packed his stuff, and disappeared.

Maybe disappeared is a bit too dramatic, given his office is right across the street from mine. So okay, not the most devastating breakup on the Richter scale, but it still felt like a part of me had been taken away. So I took myself and just ran, despite not typically being a runner. And before I knew it, I was on Kate's couch, still embarrassingly breathless—from running—head leaning on her shoulder, a cup of hot cocoa in hand while she was busy plotting how to bribe Ryan's hair stylist to give him an ugly haircut and shave his eyebrows. And it took a long time to talk her out of it.

So when it comes to kissing strangers, like I said, Kate would gladly rise to the challenge. If she hasn't already. But not me. I'm the shy one. Or maybe just an introvert, but anyway—I don't typically jump unknown guys, no matter how handsome or attractive they may be, and no matter the circumstances.

Except... Ryan. He's coming out of the elevator, at the mall, of all places, and although he hasn't spotted me, I get this uncontrollable urge to prove that I've moved on. That I enjoy life without him, party animal me. Even though it's only been a couple weeks since our uneventful breakup, and I haven't really left my apartment—except for the occasional showing of my face at work and being dragged to dinner at Kate's place every other night, just to *"get you out of your own head."* Her words.

And kissing a stranger would not typically be the first option on my how-to-make-your-ex-think-you've-moved-on list, but my brain is working overtime, struggling for an original comeback as quickly as possible. I usually pride myself for thinking on my feet, but I guess there's always an exception to the rule, a first. And this guy, whom I've never met before, happens to be in my line of fire, while my head is turned the other way. His head is probably turned away too, because our bodies collide, quite literally, and then our eyes meet.

Well, it takes a while to lift my head because he's about a foot taller. Gorgeous eyes. Bad-boy pretty face. And a wall-of-muscle body. Just throwing it out there. And I can definitely attest to that because I'm pancaked into his pecs and his arms steady me reflexively, turning this whole embarrassing situation to something that feels more like a tight embrace. Something I was not aware that I needed, until now. And I'm not sure how it looks from the outside, but let me tell you—from the inside, it's sizzling. A verb I'm not quite familiar with outside of the culinary aspect. And it's totally flooring, the length one would go to prove a point.

I lift my head to his ear, mumbling something that has to do with "my ex..." and "kiss," and maybe a few more nonsensical combinations. Would I have said that if this stranger wasn't so incredibly... HOT? Probably not. But without even blinking, he pulls my chin up and then his lips are on mine. "You have to make it convincing," is what I hear, and it has to be me chanting because it's definitely my voice in there, muffled by his kiss and some hitched breathing—also me. Tasting him and liking every moment of it. A complete unfamiliar guy and an even more unfamiliar sensation. And I am not sure what compels me to lose all reasonable inhibitions, but I let my tongue go free between his parted lips and in response he slides a hand to my butt, pulling me even closer. A bold move that has my entire body tingling in a matter of seconds. I would have pushed him away if it weren't for the fact that in the full two years of my miserable relationship with Ryan, I hadn't felt this way. Not even once. Not even close. Heck, I don't remember feeling this way before, ever.

"You think he's convinced?" asks this handsome man. His raspy voice rumbles through my bones.

"Huh?" For a second there I can't even recall the *he* we're talking about. Or where I am.

"Not yet," I hear myself say. "Got to go the extra mile to make it believable." Me again? *Where did my brain go?*

"I got you," his whisper floods my veins. His scent blurs my senses completely as he deepens the kiss.

And oh. My. God.

This guy can kiss. My body is plotting to pull him into a dark closet right now and not let him out until I get my fix. And I don't even know if Ryan is still there. More importantly, I don't even care.

But eventually my new knight in shining armor pulls back. He lets his eyes peruse my face for a few seconds. Maybe assessing the damage, or wondering who's the crazy woman who has so desperately kissed him at a mall. Then our eyes meet again, and I can't quite grasp it—it's almost as if he's seeing right into me. As if he really sees *me*.

My heart is pounding like the time Kate convinced me to hold her hand while, unbeknownst to me, she was about to jump off a cliff into a deep, icy lake, our hands still attached. And it wasn't such a high cliff, but the world slowed down as we were jumping, or rather... falling, and my heart was pounding so hard I thought it might explode. As it is now. Plus, my entire body is on fire, and detaching myself from his body feels a bit like that shot of icy water.

"That was..." I say, as I try to catch my breath, "pretty convincing."

"Damn right. I think the coast is clear," he announces, his voice still a rasp.

"Thank you for that ... kiss," I say. Sometimes you don't know how much you need something until that *something* comes bursting into your... hmm... yeah.

And he just nods. Like it was no trouble. Like he's just helped me pick up a stack of books from the floor. I take a long look at him, absorbing as much as I can as he turns and walks away. A short gray T-shirt with the sleeves folded in that way that shows off his muscles, interesting tattoos on both arms. Ripped jeans that fit to perfection. Tousled hair. And I can still feel those traces of his prickly stubble on my skin. He definitely owns that bad-boy look and wears it with pride. Sexy as hell. I wonder if he lives nearby, or if I'll ever be lucky enough to see him again, or match a name to that scent, and that voice and the taste of those lips.

2

Cube-shaped world

Claire

"I'm so proud of you!!!" is what Kate has to say when we meet for lunch a few hours later at the park near my office. "Finally taking what you want and showing that lame excuse of a boyfriend—"

"Ex," I cough-correct her.

"Showing that lame excuse of an *ex*-boyfriend of yours what real men do." She wiggles her eyebrows. The wind ruffles her hair, blowing it over her face. Kate's smile grows wider. The fall weather is in full swing, making every corner of the park a mixture of new and distinct combination of bold yellow and orange and red. Kate loves this season. But for me, the cool breeze and scent of cinnamon and cider everywhere somehow make loneliness more pronounced. Ryan or not. Although it's not this specific moment, because when Kate's around, it feels like the world smiles back at me too.

It's thinking about the after.

After I get home from work.

After the day turns into night and the night turns back into day. And keeping my head in the game and my feet in the race.

And it's not about not having Ryan in my life anymore. Because being with him actually felt lonelier than just being alone.

It's just life, I guess.

Except for when I go to work and it's all fine again. Because the noise around me is much louder than the noise inside my head. And not just that; being a scientist is my comfort zone, and developing new medicines for patients with incurable diseases is my calling. Yes, I am one of those workaholic-by-choice people. And in the past few years, and mostly since embarking on a relationship with my (now) *lame excuse of an ex*, as Kate so eloquently dubbed him, work has become my favorite pastime too.

Well, excluding any and all interactions with the esteemed Harriett Wallington. VP of Clinical Development at Amarinex Bio, and best known as *the Dr. Wallington*, of course, because God forbid someone forgets her title or affiliation. If life was a fairytale, she'd definitely be the evil witch. Actually, she'd be the witch regardless of any fairytale. A universal witch. And for some obscure reason (except, of course, for her unwavering success in the field), everyone else pretends to like her.

Well, I'm not fooled.

But I'm determined to not let her ruin work for me. Despite the fact that my one source of pleasure has become tinted.

"I'm so excited you'll be taking time off on Thanksgiving!" My sister clasps her hands. I can already see her mind forming plans of us cooking and baking together in her tiny—yet extremely well stocked—kitchen.

And I don't want to sound like a party pooper, but I'm really trying not to flinch. While my three-day vacation request has been approved by Steve, my manager, Dr. Wallington has already expressed her displeasure. I wish I could care less. And I mean it literally.

My phone pings. Loud and disrupting.

"Oh-uh," is my knowledgeable sister's interpretation. "Sounds like lunchtime's over," she giggles as she jumps up to her feet, collecting our sandwich wrappers and empty box of fruit salad.

"Yep," I confirm as I scroll through the *Need saving in the conference room ASAP, please!* text message. "Sorry..." I go for an apologetic look even though Kate has already moved on to her next adventure.

"See ya, sis." She blows an air kiss in my direction, disappearing into one of the antique stores.

"Oh Claire, thank God!" Charlene, the executive assistant to Joe Denman, our CEO, welcomes me back as I walk into the Amarinex offices. She fixes my wind-blown hair quickly with a motherly stroke of her hand while leading me in the direction of the conference room. "Dr. Copeland is already here, and the executives are still at the board meeting."

"Dr. Copeland is early?" I ask.

"Like two hours early," Charlene huffs, on the verge of freaking out.

"And where's Derek? That's *his* pet project." Not like he's been talking about it every day for the past month...

"He's MIA..." Charlene gives me a desperate look. Derek likes to disappear around lunch time. A known fact.

But since I go by the live and let live approach, plus I like Charlene, I say, "Don't worry, I've got this," and I smile sweetly at her, because she always has my back. As a matter of fact, Charlene always has everyone's back. She's the kind of person who leaves lunch on my desk when I'm in back-to-back meetings just to make sure I don't forget to eat. The kind who gifts me a corporate jacket when I forget mine at home. The kind who calls me every day when I'm sick just to make sure I don't run out of chicken soup and that miraculous cold and cough medicine you mix with hot water and pretend it's tea. So yeah, when it comes to helping her out—I'd be first in line.

"You're a life saver." She gives a sigh of relief. "Just stall him until Joe comes back. He's a scientist, here to hear about our pipeline, I'm sure you'll find plenty of topics for discussion." She fixes the collar of my blouse. "And he's handsome too! What you young people may call *hot*." Charlene brings out her signature wink. "He's thirty-three years old, already checked." She winks at me. "Just four years older than you, a reasonable age gap."

"Thank you for the additional info," I chuckle, and not in an enthusiastic way. "I've heard about him, Derek is like his best friend and biggest fan, hasn't been shutting up about him since this project started. Also heard he's quite opinionated when it comes to science, which probably means this is not going to be an *open* scientific discussion. Didn't know he's hot though." I sigh-smile, because what good would a hot-stubborn scientific consultant be? Other than adding a whole bunch of trouble to the daily routine I call life. Some people may find it entertaining.

I don't.

"Now, let's not let Prince Charming wait." Charlene opens the heavy glass door to the conference room and nudges me in.

"Claire, please meet the distinguished Professor Copeland," Charlene announces as I enter the room. "Dr. Copeland, please let me introduce you to one of our most brilliant clinical development scientists, Dr. Claire Bellingham." I hope I'm the only one noticing her matchmaker voice. "The rest of the team will join you two shortly," she promises and disappears back into the hall, closing the door behind her.

"I'm the babysitter," I deadpan.

This is before my gaze meets his. Before my brain is able to establish the inevitable connections to produce the important conclusion that Dr. Copeland is a bit more than just young, handsome, and an outstanding academic professor brought in to advise us on some scientific strategy. Along with his well-respected academic credentials, he also happens to be the name behind the pretty bad boy's face. None other than the owner of those lips that completely took over my common sense this morning, and made time and space and Ryan disappear.

OH. SWEET. GOD.

I was kind of hoping to see him again, sure. But this isn't exactly what I had in mind.

It takes incredible willpower to pull my jaw back into a more neutral position and get my breathing back in order, while the handsome man on the other side of the long table just nods politely. Completely unfazed. As if he has no recollection of this canon event. As if these few short moments that rocked my world never existed.

I know I had a pretty wild imagination as a kid, maybe even made up a few imaginary friends. But none of it rolled over into my adult life. Unfortunately, because an imaginary perfect boyfriend would have been nice.

"Pleasure to meet you," he says nonchalantly, as I let myself wonder whether there's a reasonable explanation. Maybe he has a brother who happens to be an incredible kisser, and looks like an exact replica of him.

Same eyes, same build.

Great build... Just throwing it out there.

Same chiseled jaw line, clean-shaven now. Same lips.

God, those lips...

The only exception are the clothes—he's wearing a suit and a tie.

Well, people change clothes.

And the glasses. Dr. Copeland has glasses, adding a sophisticated edge to his looks. The incredible kisser from this morning didn't have glasses, but did have the same molten amber-honey eyes. And suit or no suit, glasses or no glasses, he still looks like a bad boy to me.

"You alright?" he inquires.

Same voice.

Something I don't easily forget.

He gets up to shake my hand.

Same undeniable presence. Intoxicating smell. Same spark-provoking touch.

He's waking up all kinds of butterflies that weren't meant to be awoken. This can't be a brother, not even an identical twin. This *is* him.

But unlike yours truly, Dr. Copeland is still completely unperturbed.

Which I can't quite understand. Because I'm all electricity inside. This morning's incident clearly didn't leave the same mark on him as it did on me.

The wishful thinker in me wonders whether this guy may be suffering from short-term memory loss, because a moment like the one we shared this morning—that's not something one could wipe off their brain that quickly. Or pretend it never happened. One being me, of course, if I haven't made that part clear enough already. Maybe it was a typical morning for him. Coffee, two-hour workout, then kissing random girls senseless at malls. It certainly wasn't a typical morning for me. Not the kissing part, nor the mall. Yes for the coffee, although I'm not sure what compelled me to stop and get one there.

He sits back down, and I'm committed to putting as much distance and a large, conference-room-sized table between us. Because—God help me—the things I might do.

"So, Dr. Copeland," I say, trying to remind myself that besides drooling all over him I am also a fearless leader, a scientist with a PhD in molecular biology, and a creature capable of logical thinking and holding decent conversation, or at least used to be one before this morning. "I'm so glad you were able to join us today." I let the words out as I glance to the impressive set of world clocks we have on the wall, hoping this will prompt him to admit he's massively early.

He nods. "Christian," he says.

"Christian," I repeat, liking the sound of his name on my lips. "I'm Claire."

"Claire," he repeats and I hate how much I enjoy watching his lips move as he says my name. "I'm glad Joe has finally decided to pursue Type 1 diabetes as a potential therapeutic indication," he says in this deep voice of his.

Wait, what? Did he just say *pursue*?

I wasn't aware.

And to be more precise, I vocally objected to this idea at our last board meeting. It's a very high-risk project, and based on the gloomy precedent of finding something that could actually cure this disease, I voted to focus our efforts on an indication we have a higher likelihood of making a dent in. The decision was to explore different options. We haven't honed in on any disease in particular.

"I don't know about pursuing," I say. Because, if we are, no one has bothered to update me that a final decision was made. But clearly the man is here. I'm getting tired of Harriett and others' desire to keep loading on outside advisors when we have the best talent internally.

"Very well," Christian says, not sounding too content. "What's holding you back?"

"Me? Holding me back from doing what exactly?" The wide range of vivid images going through my out-of-control mind is unbelievable. I could really use a cold shower right now.

"From pursuing Type 1 diabetes in full force," he clarifies.

Oh... right.

"Let's begin with the fact that there's no path." I cross my legs. His gaze is way more intense than it should, given we've barely even started this discussion.

"No path?" he challenges, eyes studying me carefully.

"No regulatory path. It's almost impossible to get anything approved for this disease."

"Almost impossible. Still possible. And there is also an approved drug to prevent, or at least delay the onset of the disease."

"Well, you're technically correct," I cut him off. "But it's a one-off." Plus, I'm not convinced it's that much helpful. It's not really a cure. My tone is clipped but he seems to be enjoying the exchange.

"A one-off?" He lifts an eyebrow at me, making me question my line of arguments. "As in—that's how some of the greatest discoveries in the history of science came about?"

This does go in line with his stubborn reputation, at least from what Derek has been telling us. Plus, he has a point.

"Okay. But even if we follow the same path, I don't think any of our drugs could disrupt the development of Type 1 diabetes. Especially since we don't even know what to target."

Just me being honest. And afraid to fail. But also unusually feisty. I suspect this part is mostly about him not giving two shits about our little spicy moment this morning.

"I couldn't agree more," he says. Agreeing, with me? I've just trashed his idea... "That's why I'm not going to propose that we go for prevention of this disease." His eyes have this incredible spark as he rolls the idea in his head. "We're going for long-standing diabetes."

"Patients with long-standing Type 1 diabetes?" I am slowly digesting his words. Although, admittedly, I kind of like how he uses the word *we*. "But there are some things you can't re-verse. It's not just about quieting down the immune system, you can't bring back lost pancreatic beta cells. We know that at least eighty percent of insulin-producing beta cells in the pancreas are already dead at time of Type 1 diagnosis. Has the key to beta cell regeneration been discovered and I missed it?" I'm not fully aware that I sound a bit spiteful until the words come out of my mouth. But I don't feel bad about it either. Even if upsetting a well-paid academic consultant is not something one should be doing—putting my tad-too-passionate tone aside—my state-ments are based on science.

"That's a common misconception," he says, sounding like my words have just sparked a new channel of conversation entirely. "The basic assumption is flawed, and is based on animal data, not human data. There's no compelling evidence in humans for such an extensive beta cell destruction. The cells may be shutting down, become quiescent, but are not dead. I do believe that once we remove the stressors for a long enough time, the cells might recover, maybe even start secreting insulin again. We might not need regeneration."

"No compelling human data, you say?" Dr. Copeland's temporary amnesia may extend to his professional life as well. And he thinks my assumption is flawed? He's delusional.

"Yes. That's what I said. And actually, there's evidence for insulin gene transcription in patients with long-standing Type 1 diabetes. In some patients, even after twenty or thirty years, you can still find insulin mRNA." His enthusiasm is contagious, I'll give him that.

"No compelling data for beta cell destruction in human?" I ask again, a bit dumbfounded. Just pure scientific disbelief. Well, except for my overly harsh tone that is still hanging around from this morning. "Because there are papers. Hundreds of them. And reference after reference, talking about beta cell destruction. Eighty percent of beta cell loss, I believe is the number I saw, at time of Type 1 diabetes diagnosis." I know I'm repeating myself, but this guy is not making any sense.

"Show me one," he challenges. His voice unwavering, eyes staring into my soul. "But make sure it's based on human data, not animal models," he says as the door to the conference room opens.

"What do I get out of it?" I challenge right back, realizing, only after the words leave my mouth, how inappropriate this sounds. Which is in complete synchrony with what's going through my body.

"You'll get to prove me wrong," he answers, matching my tone.

"You've got yourself a deal, Dr. Copeland," I say, noticing Harriett Wallington walking in.

Just when I was finally having some fun.

"Oh, Chris, so good to see you!" The esteemed Dr. Harriett Wallington practically throws herself at the handsome professor across from me.

"It's Christian," he corrects her. His face unreadable, but he certainly doesn't look happy to be reunited with this *old colleague*—the title Harriett insisted on grouping the two of them under when Derek mentioned his name. And pretty much at every other opportunity thereafter. I hadn't given it much thought, honestly—my list of life concerns has better things to preoccupy my mind with. But now I'm intrigued, because it looks like her majesty might get nominated for the overstated-of-the-year award; firstly because Christian isn't old or nearing an age that could remotely be considered as old, seeing as he's only four years older than me, based on Charlene's research—so definitely not *old* friend—and secondly, he doesn't seem to know who she is.

A fake.

That's who she is.

But then again, this could also go along with my theory of Christian's short-term memory loss.

Yes, we're back to square one.

Now that I'm not busy debating pancreatic beta cell destruction or lack thereof, I can let my—extremely high maintenance and working very well, thank you—short-term memory go back to processing my latest canon event.

How can he not remember me?!

Harriett elegantly ignores the chilly tone of the encounter and takes the seat closest to the handsome man I kissed this morning. *Devoured* is probably a more accurate term.

She's such a simp.

"Christian, my man!" Derek finally emerges, inflicting a 180-degree change to the ice-cold atmosphere. Whatever Derek does during his lunch breaks, I could use some of it too.

"Derek!" The handsome professor gets up for a bro shake, and for the first time since stepping foot in this conference room, he smiles. Not the polite, politically correct kind. An actual relaxed, comfortable smile. According to Derek, they've been friends for like forever. I think for the purpose of avoiding conflict of interest he may have downplayed it a bit, since they certainly look like best buddies. And there's no doubt that Christian's longer-term memory does work.

Derek rounds the corner and takes the seat on the other side of this man. "Sorry I'm late," he says, although we both know that Derek isn't sorry, and actually isn't even late, it's just that this molten-amber-honey-eyed bad-boy professor, who's locking gazes with me right now, was massively early.

"Okay, let's get this party started," Big Boss Joe says as he enters the room, bringing a breeze of optimism with him. Behind him, head slumped, face gloomy, is Steve, my manager, who used to be a bit less insecure and have a tad more spine before the evil Dr. Harriett Wallington punched a hole in his tires. Not literally, although I wouldn't put it past her.

The people around the room exchange greetings and handshakes and start the slide deck. If we do go forward with it, this would be Derek's project, which means he would normally be the one leading the discussion, but Harriett—"*sorry to steal your thunder*"—Wallington jumps in just when things get exciting. "So," she tries her best polished smile at Christian, making it seem as if this whole thing is her idea rather than Derek's, "we are going to present a few of our leading assets in hope to find the one that is best situated for development for Type 1 diabetes. Please feel free to stop us for questions or comments. We want to hear your thoughts." And it's only when Big Boss Joe clears his throat that she finally says, "I'll let Derek start with how he's envisioning this project."

"It's finicky at best," Harriett protests before Christian has a chance to weigh in. "We need to de-risk whatever it is you came up with." She turns a fake-sweetened blaming glare at Derek. The way he's *envisioning* this project, it appears, does not seem to be in line with her majesty's vision. And despite the fact that we usually try to show a united front when speaking with outside advisors, she adds, "I assume you were hoping for a cure, but frankly we all know that once these poor patients are diagnosed with Type 1 diabetes, it's already too late."

Now although she sounds like the condescending asshole that she is, for once I can't judge her for it, since I had been living with the same notion until Christian challenged it about twenty minutes ago. And even now, I still need to do my homework to dispute his theory—or better—dispute the status quo—which is where Harriett belongs. And I never want to belong to any kind of group Harriett is in.

"Harriett," Steve rubs his forehead, looking almost resigned, "the team hasn't even seen Derek's study design. I suggest we move on with the agenda and make the decision on the study population after this meeting."

Go Steve!

"Stevie," Harriett doesn't waver for a second, diminishing him with a pet name he hates with a passion, her eyes narrowing as she turns her sharp teeth in his direction. "We have many topics to discuss today, let's not waste Dr. Copeland's precious time. We're going with individuals with high risk of developing Type 1 diabetes, not patients that already have the disease. It's non-negotiable. We all know there are no pancreatic beta cells to salvage after diagnosis."

"Technically, that's not..." Steve tries, but from his glistening complexion and dissipating conviction, I can already tell he's starting to back up. That 'Stevie' nick name is like a bad spell, turning him so small he almost disappears.

Talk about team spirit. Harriett definitely enjoys shutting people up. And mostly shutting them down.

Christian shakes his head, pushing away from the large table. The spark in his eyes could light this entire conference room on fire. "This perception is based on studies done in animal models, not human," he says with an admirable conviction. I can already and unequivocally say, he might not have the best short-term memory, but he's definitely not one to back down from an argument with this devilish woman.

Harriett does her typical cancelling hand wave at him, trying to kill any idea that does not conform to her theories, albeit with a saccharin smile, meant to soften the blow. At four-hundred-dollars-per-hour-consulting-rate for Dr. Christian Copeland's opinion, she sure has no shame. Christian ignores her and presses on. "The greatest unmet need is with long-standing diabetes," he says. "Patients who have been living with the disease for years," he adds, eyes gleaming with enthusiasm as he takes the group through his reasons to believe, commanding the room and showing us all how we can make a difference. How we can bring a real change into the life of patients already living with Type 1 diabetes. He shares his theories and some of his latest data, and I'd be lying if I said I wasn't convinced. It's a whole new side to the story I never considered. Never even thought existed. And of course I'm going to fact-check every single detail in his theory when I get home—I'd like to think of myself as the *question everything* kind of scientist, although clearly I missed a spot—but for the time being I am awed. And from the looks on most of the faces in the audience right now, I am not the only one. "Now, if you don't mind," Christian's eyes narrow as he looks straight at Harriett, "I'd like to hear the rest of what the team has prepared for discussion today."

"Alright," Harriett finally relents, batting her eyelashes and perusing Christian's chest with no shame. "Take us through what you had in mind, Derek."

"With pleasure." Derek gets up and finally takes back control over the slide deck.

When the team starts trickling out of the room after several intense hours of brainstorming, pipeline exploration and high-stakes discussion, I can still sense Christian's gaze studying me.

Is he getting his memory back?

I linger in my spot, slowly picking up my laptop and cell phone, giving him a chance to say something on his way out.

"Don't forget our deal," is what he has to say, even though I'm not the one with memory issues.

"Can't wait to prove you wrong, Dr. Copeland." I try to go for a mischievous vibe but there's still feistiness there too.

"Christian," he corrects me, a small lopsided smile forming on his lips.

"Christian, this was outstanding." Harriett appears between us, leaning over to block my view. But he doesn't return the sentiment, just nods back at her. His almost-smile—the one he was about to give me—morphs back into an unreadable expression. The one I'm slowly learning is his business look. His handsome-serious resting face.

We all leave the conference room with a sense of optimism. No decision made yet—but right now it feels as if the sky's the limit. And somehow, I have a feeling that as far as my treacherous body is concerned, this is not limited just to science. Or at least the kind of science I'm supposed to do at work.

But also, there was another strange thing happening in that conference room. Harriett's typical non-negotiable list of *must haves* was somehow toned down into the *nice to have* list. And while she usually finds the team's ideas *visionless* and *doomed to fail*, she eventually conceded and nodded her head enthusiastically when Christian said that our ideas were "novel," and "fearless." This handsome bad boy could probably argue that the world is cube-shaped and Harriett would agree.

Like I said. She's a simp. An evil witch and a sycophant.

And let me just stop right there, because watching Christian tame the mighty Dr. Harriett Wallington felt almost as good as that kiss from this morning. Already two things that this man does better than anyone else in *my* world. Cube-shaped or not.

3

Some kind of day

Christian

My mind is reeling as I walk down the small street leading to Derek's favorite bar. Today's been a fucking roller-coaster, starting with Jake needing a site change for his insulin pump first thing in the morning. Note to self—kinked cannula is an actual thing, typically appears without any advance warning, except for the pump's alert system that insulin is not being delivered (if you're lucky). Alternatively, you learn about it the hard way when blood sugar starts creeping up, causing a slur of undesired hyperglycemia symptoms (less lucky), or ketoacidosis (much less lucky). And unfortunately, kids are not spared from this dubious pleasure, not even at five years old. Plus the timing always sucks—like today—when Jake's mom is away on business travel.

And although I should know better and always be prepared, it definitely threw me off because, as far as I can help it, Jake's time with me should be fun, not painful. And even though he claimed he didn't feel a thing, pretending I was a natural with needles while I was struggling to find some fat tissue on his tiny abdomen to get a new cannula in—something this skinny little guy barely has—I didn't miss that small tear he quickly and masterfully swiped away. Breaks my heart into pieces every time.

And honestly, given the fact that insulin was discovered back in the 1920s, one would think we'd have a better solution for Type 1 diabetes by now. Or at least more sophisticated insulin pumps than the current old-fashioned bulky boxes... Which is where my mind was going when I suggested we play some basketball at the court near his school. There's nothing like basketball to cheer this kid up, especially when he accidentally knocked off my glasses with the ball that then bounced straight down for a full smashing effect. It would have been a disaster if it weren't for Jake's worried gaze that I dismissed with a "I didn't like this pair anyway," and his carefree laughter that followed and made my heart swell. And the fact that his school is steps away from the mall, where they just so happen to have same-day replacement glasses for skillful fuckups like me.

Which was where I headed right after I dropped the little guy at school. And that's when I saw ... *her*. She came out of nowhere, the most beautiful woman I've ever seen in my life. Full disclosure, I wasn't wearing my glasses and I'm half blind without them, but there are things you just know. And I didn't need glasses to know that she was stunning. The kind of woman who takes your breath away. Which is exactly what she did when she, without much warning, decided to jump me. Asking me to kiss her, make her ex jealous or something, with the added challenge of making it look convincing.

Who does that?

Not my typical go-to activity at the mall, but my body decided to oblige. And for some obscure reason, my mind seemed to think that making it look convincing—fulfilling her request to a T—was a good idea. There was something about her—her scent, her touch, the way her grip on me tightened and her breath hitched as if she'd never been kissed like that before. And for a moment I almost forgot where we were, forgot what the hell it was that I was doing, or the fact that I had no idea who this girl was. Until my common sense struck back. So I let her go, despite my body's vivid objection, turned on my heels and went to get my goddamn replacement glasses, helplessly trying to take this new surge of energy a few notches down.

Then I showed up two hours early to my meeting at Amarinex Bio just because I could, and mostly because I forgot that the meeting had been pushed back to the afternoon—hey, I had a lot on my plate this morning—but I quickly realized it when I saw the terrified look on the poor admin's face.

Then came this beautiful feisty woman, Claire Bellingham, to keep me company and mostly challenge my scientific notions, while we waited for the rest of the team to come back from lunch. It wasn't so much what she said but the way she said it. She was polite, and composed, I'll give her that, but I could see the steam radiating off her. The way she gave me those looks, as if she couldn't determine whether she was pissed off with me or intrigued. I'd be lying if I said I didn't enjoy our little exchange. And although some of her arguments were based on dated scientific notions, she put in a good fight. And I can't really blame her because she represents the common knowledge, the unfortunate status quo. Something I need to change. A perception I've been trying to challenge and battle for my entire academic career.

And on another—very different—note, there was something about her that reminded me of that gorgeous woman from the mall. But what are the odds that the sweet whispering voice, those soft lips that kissed me, that body that clung to me so tightly, all belong to no other than Dr. Claire Bellingham, the fearless scientist at Amarinex Bio? Not a goddamn chance. Plus—unfortunately, I would never be able to recognize that woman from the mall even if she stood right in front of me. That is, unless she took my glasses off and kissed me again.

"What's up with you, man? A girl broke your heart?" comes the voice of my asshole friend and eternal bachelor, Derek, as he hands me a beer and positions himself on the stool beside me at the bar.

"Long day." I try to shake that woman out of my mind. Well, actually both women. Great, as if one wasn't enough.

"That chick Harriett made you lose it?" He goes for an easy out.

"Chick? There are lots of adjectives I could give Harriett Wallington, chick is not one of them, believe me," I drawl.

"*I* think she's hot," he says.

"You think every woman under the age of fifty-five is hot," I remind him.

"What did I miss?" asks my new buddy Aiden. His wife Ellie recently got her own lab, just across from mine at GERI, which stands for Gene and Epigenetic Research Institute. A relevant detail because Ellie introduced me to Aiden, and before long he started joining Derek and me at our traditional Wednesday beer night. Derek has been my best buddy since elementary school. And with him and Aiden, despite Aiden being relatively new to our little group, it's that kind of friendship where you can't even recall a time when you weren't part of each other's lives. Even if they tend to get on my nerves most of the time.

"Christian here was alluding to the possibility that I think every woman under fifty-five is hot," Derek pouts.

"I wasn't alluding to it, I straight-out stated a fact," I explain.

"I hate to break it to you man, but he's not wrong." Aiden, obviously, is quickly becoming my favorite here.

"That's beside the point," Derek says, handing a beer to Aiden. "Our boy here is suffering."

"I'm not suffering, just deep in thought," I try to fend for myself.

"Which is how we got to discussing my co-worker Harriett Wallington," Derek gloats. "She agreed with everything our boy Christian said today. Unheard of. I think she likes him."

"Or maybe she just knows good science when she sees it. This has nothing to do with liking me," I say. Because really, Harriett is the last person on my mind right now.

"Want me to put in a good word for you?" Derek keeps at it.

"God no," I sigh. "You're relentless."

"Well, there's clearly a girl involved," Aiden determines helpfully, scanning my face with his gaze. "But it's not Harriett."

"Thank you."

"Oh, you know something I don't?" Derek wiggles an eyebrow at him, taking another sip of his beer.

"I know he was whistling to himself this morning in his office, long before he showed up in *your* office," Aiden supplies. "That's what he gets for having his lab right across from my wife's lab." Should have seen this one coming.

They both look at me. Waiting. These assholes are impossible.

"Okay," I sigh again. "A girl at the mall this morning asked me to kiss her." I can't hold back the smile as I watch their faces transform to my nonsensical whereabouts. "She wanted to make her ex jealous—"

"You lucky fuck!" Derek chuckles.

"That explains the whistling," Aiden deadpans.

"Fast forward to now," because I'm not really the guy to kiss and tell, "I can't get her off my mind."

And then there's Claire, who kind of rocked my afternoon, but I'm not going to mention that, it's way too confusing. Plus, Derek will never let me live it down. Him, Claire and I will need to be able to work together like goddamn mature adults.

"I don't think I've ever seen you this excited. Not even when Stephanie pulled you into the janitor closet back in high school," Derek says smugly, recalling memories from our shared high school time.

"Has to be true love," Aiden deadpans but Derek nods enthusiastically.

"So, Prince Charming, what are you going to do about it?"

"Nothing," I say, my words accompanied by their vocal disappointed reactions. "I don't know who she was and I wasn't wearing my glasses, so I won't be able to recognize her even if I wanted to find her." And I do.

"Sounds like a Cinderella story to me," Derek laughs, taking a copious swig at his beer, emptying his bottle. She didn't happen to leave her glass slipper behind?"

"Modern Cinderella story, sure, PG version," Aiden scolds, already seeing where Derek is going with it. At least I have one reasonable friend.

"So," Derek toys with the idea, a big smile on his face. "Your only option is to go house to house, kiss every girl who vaguely fits the description your half-blind self recalls, until you find your one."

That's just fucking great.

4

Beta testing

Claire

I spend the next few days fervently researching Type 1 diabetes. Exploring discoveries, theories, scientific paper after paper, following each and every lead I can find. Each place I look has pancreatic beta cell death mentioned as the process leading up to Type 1 diabetes diagnosis, confirming everything I'd already known. But to Christian's point, not a single one of these scientific manuscripts explicitly states that this is the mechanism leading up to disease diagnosis in human patients. In my defense though—many of them don't state otherwise either. So I follow the trail, pulling out the original papers. It's like little rabbit holes, each citation referencing a previously published paper, most of which eventually trace back to several common archaic publications, sending me back in time. I never liked history, but

I find it extremely annoying that authors reference citations of citations instead of the actual original publication. Especially if they misinterpret or take it out of context, and before you know it there's a whole new piece of common knowledge that is based on some misrepresentation or blown-out-of-proportion information.

Well, it turns out Christian was not wrong—or rather, and it does pain me to admit—Christian was right. I come across studies in a spectrum of animal species backing up the eighty-percent-beta-cell-death theory. The only solid human evidence I'm able to dig out is based on a handful of very extreme cases. And actually, there is evidence supporting the exact opposite in humans—but I'd been too hooked on what I thought was right to even see it. Living my happy scientific life and building towers on the foundations of misinformed theories. Like finding out your entire childhood was a lie, and then suddenly have all these small pieces fall into place, finally making sense, even though up until that moment, you had no idea. Not in my case though—as much as I would have liked to believe in some fairytale version of what preceded my childhood, my mom is way too grounded, way too honest. I've had all my facts laid out since day one.

Breaking an established common notion, even if based on false or misinterpreted information, is extremely difficult. Although it still begs the question—how have I lived my life accepting something so readily without feeling the need to challenge or question it? Outrageous. Embarrassing.

But of course, I'm not going to admit I was so profoundly wrong. Not to Christian, that is. And I'm also not going to admit that thinking of Christian brings about small shreds of excitement that I've been trying to rein in.

"Okay, that's enough." My sister Kate attempts to pull me out of my laptop. Yes, I have this way of working late without making it show. I leave the office just like everyone else. Grab my stuff, shuffle my way home via the metro, change into my flannel pants and T-shirt, grab something to eat, then hook myself back up to my laptop. I usually change my status to *offline*, even though I'm very much online, just so people think I have a life. I don't really have a life, but that doesn't mean everyone has to know about it. "Come on, put that laptop to hibernate," Kate instructs with her kindergarten teacher determination. "And put something nice on." She gestures to my stained T-shirt. "We're going out."

I know better than to argue with my sister. So I sigh deeply while closing the lid on my best friend, putting that little electronic device to rest, and get up from the sofa that has already taken my shape.

"Where are we going?"

"Just put something nice on." So bossy. "I'll brief you on our way there."

"Two Coronas," is my sister's drinks order for us as we settle in our booth at the local bar.

"One Corona, I'm not into drinking tonight," says me, the party pooper.

"Okay, so Corona for me and white wine for the lady here," Kate chuckles.

"Just peach iced tea for me," I tell the waiter. The thought of getting alcohol into my system at the moment makes me sick. I can see Kate shrug in my peripheral vision. "I haven't been feeling too well the last few days, maybe alcohol is not a good idea for me," I explain, and pull out a menu from the center of the table.

"Too bad, because we're here on a double date. You might need some to take the edge off," she jokes, but I can see the hint of concern forming in that forehead of hers.

"Double date?" I sigh. "As in you're playing matchmaker again?" Can't say I'm surprised though. My sister has been patiently waiting for me to drop Ryan so she could match me up with someone "more suitable." Her words, not mine. But at this point, really, any guy within my age range who's not Ryan and not married would probably fit the definition. At least in her view. "You know Ryan and I broke up like two weeks ago, yes?"

"I'm aware," she says calmly. "But at the age of twenty-nine, it's time for you to have some fun. This has been long overdue." She gives me a mischievous wink and I brace myself, because the last time she tried to match me up it ended in a boring, tired, sad relationship that stretched out way longer than it should have, with a side of potential other keepsakes I don't want to think about.

It's not like Ryan's a bad guy, or disloyal or checks any of those flat-out negative boxes that would have made it clear and easy to up and leave. He's a good guy, good-looking too. But somehow the combination of him and yours truly was lukewarm. And for some reason we both found ourselves sinking into a relationship that brought about more boredom than excitement. Made both of us feel more alone than together. And maybe I'm crazy, but in my mind, feeling lonely in a relationship is a thousand times worse than when you're actually alone. Well, thank goodness I didn't have to make that hard decision. Ryan made it for the both of us. And so—looks like I'm on the market again.

"Time for me to make it right," says my sister, chiming in on my conversation with myself. I wish my gene pool contained a fraction of her optimism. But it's possible mine carries a rare pure pessimism mutation. And let me tell you—it's a dominant mutation. Or maybe I'm just a homozygote. Most likely the case. It just hasn't been formally characterized yet. The mutation, I mean. My lack of optimism is a well understood trait.

"I'm actually happy alone," I tell Kate. Even though she's the one person in the world that I can't bullshit.

"I can see…" She rolls her eyes. "But this is different."

"Okay," I deadpan.

"No, seriously Claire-bear." She uses her childhood nickname for me. Her go-to approach when trying to dig out my lost traces of impulsivity. "I'm developing this app." She sits up straighter, taking my hand in hers. "It's a matchmaking app, but not what you think." I should probably shut down the conversation at this point, but her eyes are sparkling with enthusiasm, and I just don't have the heart to be the one to break the charm. "And I really need some beta testers." She makes the face that I can never say no to.

My sister is a computer science geek, dreaming of having her own start-up one day. Her brain constantly brews up solutions to mundane problems—like dating. But she believes inventing can't happen when you focus on inventing alone. Plus she also loves kids. So she leaves her tech superhero prodigy self to the evenings and weekends, and spends her days undercover as a kindergarten teacher. These little creatures love her and make her incredibly happy. And in a world like ours, where happiness is so hard to come by, going through life with a smile on your face is an incredible achievement. So if it means that I need to hear potty training stories during the day—aren't they supposed to not have any more of these accidents after they turn five?—and be a beta tester for her prototypic dating app at night—so be it.

"Sure, I'll be your beta tester," I chuckle. "What do I need to do?"

"Glad you asked," Kate says, pulling out her pre-prepped response faster than light. "You'll need to fill out a questionnaire about yourself, what you're looking for in a life partner or in your near future in general."

"Okay, I assume you've already taken care of that part." I roll my eyes, seeing as we're here waiting on our double dates.

"Nah uh. I kickstarted it, but you're going to have to do some reflection," she laughs. "It's about *you*."

"Well, you know me better than anyone," I'm already backing up. Answering questions about myself is a known form of torture. At least for me. My argument is legit.

"True, but only you know what you really want. I don't want to match you up with another Ryan."

"Yet we're on a double date today and I haven't answered any questions yet," I challenge.

"Today we're using a special app feature called—surprise me."

Great...

"So we are both going to be surprised?" Can't really say that I'm surprised though, my sister has always had a very creative mind. This is very much in line with her unique competencies.

"Yes, we're actually testing two special features today: "*Surprise me*, which allows you to jump in and try, just based on very basic demographic information—age, gender, sexual orientation, stuff like that. And the second feature we're testing today is called *double trouble.*" She pauses to evaluate my reaction. I'm already *not* liking it, but I let her proceed. "Also known as—*bring a friend.* In case you don't feel like going alone to a *surprise me* blind date and prefer to have a friend tag along."

"You mean looking for *double trouble,*" I cough.

"Right. As long as the friend is also signed up to the app, you can both go. A double blind date."

"A double-trouble-surprise-me-bring-a-friend double date?" My eyes are already searching for the nearest emergency exit.

"Correct!" Kate marvels at my incredible conclusion-making skills or the fact that I haven't yet bolted. "This feature also helps in getting more app subscribers—peer pressure!" She clasps her hands together.

The waiter is finally back with our drinks. "Would you like to eat anything, ladies?" he asks, checking my sister out.

"We're waiting on our dates," Kate says proudly, knowing this entire night is the result of her own invention. We'll see about that soon... The waiter nods politely and disappears.

"One issue, though." I'm not done with my line of questioning. "Don't you think it's kind of misleading to go on a date when I literally just broke up with my boyfriend?"

"Thought you'd never ask!" Kate jumps happily in her seat, taking a sip of her Corona, waiting for my plummeting expectations to build up again. "That's why I developed the *rebound* option."

"The *rebound* option? So people can actually sign up willingly to be a rebound?" My sister is definitely creative, I'll give her that.

"It's a double-sided rebound—your match might be coming out of a breakup as well, so you won't be in it alone. Someone to pick at your wounds with." This makes me scrunch my nose. "You could wipe each other's tears away, have some much-needed post breakup sex, and maybe live happily ever after."

"I hate to break it to you, Kate," I cough. "This is called a hook-up. A more sophisticated, nicely wrapped sort of hook-up, but still."

"This app is *not* meant for hook-ups!" Kate exclaims. "But yeah, if all that comes out of it at the end of the night is you having a good time—then I'm all for it."

And before I have a chance to object, two men appear at the entrance, heads scanning the tables. Kate does this funny thing with her eyes. It's the same gesture she's been doing since we were teenagers whenever good-looking boys were around. "So your guy is Paul, thirty-eight. Mine is Andy, thirty-two," she whispers and waves to them.

"Why do I get the old guy?" I laugh and she elbows me gently.

"You always had a thing for older guys."

They walk over, making sure we're indeed Kate-twenty-eight and Claire-twenty-nine. We shake hands. They are both good looking and polite. And while Kate used our true ages, the guy I've been matched up with seems more like Paul forty-nine rather than thirty-eight. And he also has a light untanned strip of skin on his ring finger, as if he's been wearing a wedding ring for many years and has just recently taken it off. Recently as in earlier today. Some kind of rebound.

"Recently divorced?" I ask before he has a chance to order a drink, making him choke. I know, I'm direct, what can I say? And while I may agree to be someone's rebound for the sake of some *good time,* as Kate eloquently stated, I have a very strict rule against dating or hooking up—or whatever sophisticated app definition Kate has for it—with someone who's married, or on the verge of getting a divorce but is still technically married. Or even just recently divorced. I don't want to be that woman Dad brings home when the kids are still hurting and dreaming of a life in which their parents get back together. Not when the wounds are still bleeding.

"Almost divorced," Paul-thirty-eight admits. At least he's not trying to deny it, I'll give him that. But I know for a fact this wasn't Kate's intention when designing the app, so my first comment as a beta tester will be to ban married people from it. And mostly ban Paul from it.

"I don't think it fits the *rebound* definition," I say kindly, prepared to splash his face with my iced tea.

"You're right, I'm sorry," he says all too quickly. "But—" of course there's a but... "Andy here really begged me to tag along." His eyes turn to his friend. My eyes follow, and seeing as Kate is enjoying the conversation with her self-made app-date, I decide to hold off kicking my married date out. For the time being.

"Is your friend also married?" I jab. "I mean, *almost divorced?*"

"No, his girlfriend broke up with him over a month ago, and he's so heartbroken, I thought it would be good for him to go out a little. Meet someone new. And beta test this cute app."

"Does your wife know?" I ask. Because she really should.

"No," he says quietly. "She wouldn't care, anyway. But just so you know, I did not come here with the intention of ... doing anything."

"I did not come here with *any* intention, really." I sigh. Didn't even know I was going on a date until mere minutes ago. I decide to give Kate about an hour to check out Andy, for the sake of this beta testing session, before I drag her back home.

"This app needs some fine tuning," I tell her under my breath when this hour is finally over. Even if Andy isn't married, what kind of friend drags his married buddy to a double date? Not one who should go out with my sister, that's for sure. And besides, I'm not sure I should be going on blind dates when this confusing guy I met a few days ago is pestering my mind.

5

Professional assholes

Claire

"I've been going through the beta testing comments log. I assume *CB* is you?" Kate asks as she sets down her little plastic box of fruit on the metal bench when we meet for our weekly lunch. It's a double-period break from her role as a kindergarten teacher. Not from her fearless app developer job, though.

"You assume correctly," I say, plopping down beside her with a bag of Cheetos, the only thing my stomach has been finding appetizing lately.

Kate eyes me suspiciously but then brings her mind back to the task. "Could you please walk me through the unique logic behind your comments?" She opens her laptop and squints her eyes at the screen. "Especially your interesting request for additional features..."

"Yes," I oblige, crossing my legs. "It would be great to have a check box for users interested in finding a match with someone who won't break their heart, or make them sad. Can you make a feature for that?"

My sister gives me a funny look. "Let me think about it," she says rolling her eyes, then honing in on my bag of Cheetos again. "Claire-bear, is that what you're having for lunch?"

"Hmm-mmm," is my response while I noisily munch away on my nutritional orange meal. "And a feature that will screen out liars and married people," I add before fishing for another Cheetos from the bag, recalling our less-than-successful double date.

"Ooohh!" I can practically see the lightbulb going off in Kate's head. "Maybe I could get them to connect their vitals measurements from their smart watch to the app while they answer their profile questions. Unusual spikes in heart rate or skin temperature could mean they're lying!"

"Sounds more like a lie-detector-assisted-interrogation than matchmaking to me, but I can't say I hate the idea." I keep chewing.

"Or link it to their tax forms. Married-filing-status people, I'm on to you." Kate's contagious laughter fills the air.

"Or ask them to provide photos of both their ring fingers. I'm sure you could design a sophisticated algorithm that detects hidden tan lines, like the one this douchebag had. What was his name?"

"Paul—"

"Oh yeah, Paul-thirty-eight."

"I'm so sorry about that, Claire..." Kate's eyes fill with guilt and I almost regret bringing it up.

"It's all good, but I hope you won't be seeing his friend again. Letting a married guy tag along on his double date..."

"Andy felt really bad about it, they're just co-workers, he claims he didn't know..."

"Right," I almost choke on the singular Cheeto in my mouth. Kate has such a big heart that she always sees the best in everyone. And has miraculously managed to stay this way through adulthood. Maybe that's why she enjoys her day job as a kindergarten teacher so much, spending time with naive, optimistic, un-ruined little people. But I can't really complain, because her positive view of personas extends to mine too. She always insists on seeing my good qualities, for some reason.

"Drink up," she instructs and hands me a water bottle. "Now, why haven't you filled out the app's questionnaire? How am I going to find you the best match?"

"You know I don't like this kind of stuff." Don't like to answer questions about myself. Don't like to dig deep into what excites me or what makes me tick. Just don't.

"Exactly, that's why I'm developing a feature just for you, sis."

Great. Another feature. I try to hide my impending sigh, but this just makes my little sister snort.

"The matching tool I'm working on can curate free text. It's still under development. Still far from being perfect, but instead of answering a gazillion questions about what you want and don't want, you can just give it to me in a few words." Her face beams with excitement as she describes it. "Think about it, instead of an app trying to put words in your mouth or limit the possibilities to the templated questions, you get total freedom to describe your dream person. Your one!" Kate literally squeals. "You just speak your mind, I'll type."

This clearly means a lot to her. "What, *now*?"

Kate nods, so I stop myself from rolling my eyes and say in earnest, "Someone who just wants *me*. You know? Likes me the way I am." Kate tilts her head, listening and typing at the same time, so I go on. "I hate feeling like I'm in some kind of competition all the time. I know I'm not the most interesting, most beautiful person in the room. But it would be nice for a change to feel as though in this person's eyes I am."

"Go on," my sister encourages me. "I need at least eighty words."

"That's like an entire essay," I try to joke but Kate's face tells me I need to come up with more or I won't be able to go back to my Cheetos.

"A person who sees me. And sees through my bullshit. Prefers actions over words. Who knows what I need even when I don't say it, and especially when I don't know it."

"Claire-bear, I hate to break it to you. This is quite specific, yet doesn't tell me a lot about this potential guy."

"I think I've made it through the eighty words, didn't I?"

"Well yes... with some fillers," Kate sighs. "Once we find this guy—ask him if he has a brother, because I want one too."

"Will do," I laugh and pop another Cheeto into my mouth.

My sister's face falls when her eyes narrow on the screen. "From the current pull of beta testers there seem to be zero match...."

"Well, yeah, I didn't think this person exists, not a shocker."

"Which is why I'm going to have to pick from the pool of people outside." She gestures to the world around us.

"Oh-uh, I don't like the sound of it."

My phone buzzes, shaking the little bench we're seated on. I take a sip, hand my sister her bottle back and reach for my trusty device to turn off the alarm. Yes, I'm the kind of person who sets an alarm during lunch breaks. Time is important to me. Whether late or too early, I dislike both options. Which is why I have my system. Timers at the end of short breaks or meetings, alarms for longer ones. Helps reduce the stress around keeping track of ... time. Exactly.

"Wow, that felt like two minutes," Kate packs up her picnic basket, a smile never leaving her face. My idealistic sister treats time in a more romantic, fluidic way. And really, her kind of tardiness is the only kind I tolerate.

"Sorry," I say as she pulls me in for a hug. "I have another meeting with this confusing man..." I've been spending way too long thinking about his pretty bad-boy face, and his lips on mine, and Dr. Jekyll and Mr. Hyde personality.

I may have failed to prepare myself for the fast heartbeat that strikes me when Christian Copeland so much as looks in my direction. Okay, I was trying to tone that sensation down the first time we were thrown into a room together alone. Telling myself it's aggravation (not attraction), blaming it on my impatience toward people who disagree with me when it comes to science, and also on the fact that he was so unfazed by the kiss. Right now, I can still associate my cardiac thumping and the heat washing over my body to this short maddening history here, but as his gaze meets mine, burrowing yet again into the most guarded parts of my soul, I feel myself tripping. Metaphorically speaking, of course. But to be on the safe side, I quickly grab the closest chair I can find and take a seat at the large conference table. And only when I'm seated, not very comfortably, I realize the proximity I've inflicted on the situation at hand. Too close.

"You're early, again," I can't help but point out. Because this insufferable man seems to aspire to getting on my nerves. Can he not see my issue with time?

"And it bothers you?" He arches an eyebrow.

"How observant of you."

"Last time was not intentional," he admits, unapologetically. "This time was. I was hoping we could touch base before the meeting."

"I see." I let my eyes peruse his handsome face. Still breathtaking, unfortunately. "And what exactly is it that we need to touch base on?"

He chuckles, clearly not taken aback. The sound of it does something unfamiliar to my lungs, which seem to have forgotten how to let air in. "Your last homework assignment." His eyes study me as he talks. "And discuss your findings."

I shift uncomfortably in my seat and glance at the large series of world clocks on the wall above him. All of them, unfortunately, indicate we have plenty of time. When my alarm interrupted my lunch with Kate, I was hoping to go back to my cubicle to read over the plans for discussion today, and the abundance of notes I took while uncovering how misguided my status-quo knowledge was. I was also planning to come up with a plan of how to admit that to Christian. But when Charlene said he was already here and asked me, yet again, to keep him busy while we waited for the rest of the team to come back from lunch, giving me that mischievous wink of hers, I had to change course and skip the preparation.

"Discuss my findings?" I swallow. There are so many things I don't like doing. Admitting I was wrong is a big one.

"Yes," he says. "What did you find out?"

"I found that I'd been pretty much living a lie, scientifically," I admit on a sigh. Might as well say it now rather than in a room full of faces, or specifically—Harriett's gloating face.

"And it annoys you," he smirks. And despite talking about my shortcomings here, his gaze makes my treacherous body flutter.

"Very much," I scoff. "*You* annoy me," I say it like I'm joking but I really do mean it. And it's not just about him being right, or the fact he enjoys it. I'm still stuck on that hot, steamy kiss at the mall—sorry, I can't help it. I know Kate is the beautiful and easygoing one, I know heads usually turn after her when we walk down the city streets together. But this Dr. Copeland person doesn't seem to suffer from memory issues in any other domain of his life. Which begs the question, am I really that forgettable?

"*I* annoy you?" His eyebrows crush together, making his pretty face even more attractive, if that's possible. But he doesn't waver.

"Let's just stick to the task," I say, turning my body back toward the large conference table to open my laptop.

"Agreed, Dr. Bellingham." He does the same, going into all-business mode. "I've made some slides," he says, giving me the opportunity to move away from describing in detail how right he was—which I do appreciate—and back to more neutral ground. But before I get a chance to respond, a little pop-up message appears on the right lower quarter of my screen, indicating I have an incoming email. From him. And from the little red circle by his name, I can see he's already gotten access to Amarinex internal systems. Which means I can see him on the company chat, see when he's online, or in a meeting, or when he's idle... and even worse: he can see all that about me too.

About an hour into our lively discussion, I'm doing anything in my power to discuss my newly learned facts without admitting, again, that I was completely off-base before, blaming my misinformed knowledge on the dated common notion in the field. Which is true but is hardly an excuse, especially for a scientist. While Christian is sitting back and listening to my words intently, studying me, a small tilt to his head, a content expression on his face. Reading me so completely. And I hate the twist in my stomach that his molten-amber-honey eyes and his full undivided attention create, but at the same time, I'm loving every moment of it. I've officially gone insane.

"Chris! So good to see you again," comes Harriett's devilish voice as she struts into the conference room without a warning, invading our little bubble. As if I wasn't annoyed enough.

"It's Christian, Harriett," he says, his tone is reprimanding as he lifts his eyes from the laptop, apparently not liking the nickname, or the fact that she uses it despite him already correcting her last time. And maybe it's my wishful thinking, but he seems to not like the interruption either.

"Yes, yes," she says, taking the closest seat on his other side. Which means I'm going to have to hear her voice from up close for the next hour. Dammit.

"My man." Derek walks in, all smiles and freshly showered, judging by his wet, tousled hair. And from Christian's knowing smile, I can already guess he knows exactly what his friend is up to during these lunch breaks. He gets up for a bro handshake, and a whiff of his cologne makes its way into my nose, provoking the annoying heart thumps again, this time with a side of cheek blushing. Urgh. I can't see how I look, but I can definitely sense it. And when Christian settles back beside me, his quick glance at my face indicates he is aware too.

We go through some slides, plans, more reasons-to-believe and lots of sticky points, on which Christian and Derek seem to unequivocally agree. And now that I've seen the other side—of the scientific literature, that is—I can't help but agree too.

"Okay, kids," Harriett finally says. She has this weird smug expression on her face, as if she's about to break their spirit any minute now. "Our legal department is not crazy about the potential conflict of interest here," she says. Oh yes, have I mentioned that in addition to her MD degree, she's also a trained lawyer? And although I bet she hasn't discussed this alleged issue with anyone in our legal department yet, she takes the initiative and says, "We're going to need to distance you boys from each other."

"What?!" Derek is definitely not liking the idea. "What conflict of interest?"

"You're best buddies." She splits a glare between him and Christian. "That much is obvious. You can still be in charge of this project, Derek, but the day-to-day work between you and our expert here, is going to go through Claire."

"What?!" That's me pitching in now with an instinctive reaction. "Don't I get a say? I hardly have any bandwidth." It's not that I'm not interested in diabetes research, just that I have so many other projects already. Plus, this confusing man is an-noying, and exciting, and the last thing I want to do is spend more time around him and get myself even more... excited. And confused.

"We pay you enough money to expand your bandwidth." Harriett says shamelessly, quite content with my objection. "This is your first priority now, Claire, and you are to work closely with Dr. Copeland and keep him happy." She gestures to Christian, who doesn't seem at all upset by the new prospect.

"*Keep him happy?* Are we back into the eighteenth century now?" I say, trying to hide the slight split in my voice.

"*You are*," Harriett smirks, seeming to find this all entertain-ing. She can clearly see my growing aggravation, and it only seems to increase her satisfaction.

"Does Steve know about this?" I remind her I have an actual manager, a decent person who should be fencing off unwanted interruptions that prevent me from doing my job. I wish I could vocally share my line of thinking to a better extent in this current forum without posing an imminent risk to my position.

"He does, and has agreed this is the best way to avoid the op-tics of a potential conflict of interest. Derek can't work directly with his best friend. So you will, and report back to Derek," she says as if she didn't come up with the idea just now. "Steve is still your line manager, but that's about it." Steve's name rolls out of her with such disdain that makes the room dark and chilly, like a whole thunderstorm has just settled upon us. And then she gets up, struts back towards the door, and leaves us to it.

"Derek?" I turn my head to my colleague, but he doesn't seem bothered at all.

"Like Harriett said, make the man happy," Derek chuckles and wiggles his eyebrows.

"Derek!" Christian scolds. Then, turning his gaze to me. "Please don't pay attention to this idiot. I'm surprised about this whole idea as much as you are," he says in earnest. "And I don't need you to keep me happy. This partnership is strictly scientific." Finally someone is making some sense here. "I need you to keep me honest, and I expect you to challenge and question every single idea I bring to the table. I'm guessing Harriett is concerned that Derek would not be able to stay objective. Well, we've already established that *you* can."

I wouldn't call my spite objective, but... "You can definitely count on me to cross you at any chance I get," I say, my face dead serious. I'm still a bit shocked that we're going to need to work together. Closely.

"Good," Christian says. "And I'm sorry about the insinuation that your immature team members have made here." He gives Derek another reprimanding look. "This was unprofessional," he gestures to where Harriett was sitting, "and out of line. Definitely shouldn't have been part of the conversation."

"Looks like there's one thing we agree on," I say and get up from my seat, slapping Derek on the back of his head as I pass.

"Ouch!" Derek gripes. "I'm sorry, Claire, I was just joking." His good-natured laugh makes it hard to stay mad at him, but I persevere.

"Apology not accepted," I huff. Disappointed—but not surprised—to learn that my colleague and my skip-level manager are two professional assholes. Okay, maybe Derek isn't so bad, but I still make a point by storming outside.

6

Partnerships

Christian

"Dude, what was that for?" I ask Derek, because being a dick is not typically one of his signature moves.

"She needed a little push," he chuckles, giving me a side wink.

"A little push?" I raise an eyebrow. "She's already feisty as it is, especially toward me for some reason. Now we're supposed to work together, and you're not helping."

"Yeah, she has been kind of hard on you. What did you do to upset her?" Derek gives me his man-whore stare.

He does spend quite a big chunk of his time with women on his arm and in his bed, but as far as I know, he's always been a hundred percent transparent with each of them, and they all somehow accept not being the only ones in his life.

"I didn't do anything, you dickhead." I throw my pen at him. "At least, not that I'm aware of." I close my laptop and push to stand. "But kicking someone when they're down? You can do better." Because the hurt I saw in Claire's eyes, fending for herself against Harriett, and then Derek, that's not going to work for me.

"Yes sir, Dr. Copeland!" He salutes. "Anything going on between the two of you that I should be aware of?"

I wish I knew. "I need to go pick up Jake from school." I go for a legit diversion.

"Hey, maybe teaming you up with Claire isn't such a bad idea after all," Derek calls after me.

I feel like I've missed an entire episode of a new series everyone's talking about, and no one—absolutely no one is bothering to bring me up to speed.

"Uncle Christian!" I hear Jake's excited voice as I step into the kindergarten hallway. I bend down and he sprints toward me, little hands wrapping around my neck as I scoop him up and into my arms. This guy's hug is the highlight of my week, every week.

"Hey bud!" I ruffle his hair and throw him on my shoulders. "I missed you!"

"I missed you too!" Seated snugly, legs dangling from each side of my head, he ruffles my hair too. "Ms. Kate asked to see you," he says quietly.

"Uh-oh, am I in trouble?" I ask, and he gives me his contagious laugh in return.

Jake has had a few clashes with classmates over his insulin pump. Kids can be cruel at any age, especially toward anything different or out of the ordinary. And I have tried to put a positive spin to their insults—like maybe being called out as different is a good thing. He's been taking it like a champ, but my stomach twists and churns as I brace myself for some potential bad news. Whenever something happens at school, it has to be reported at pickup.

"Christian, good to see you," she says with an easy smile when we peek our two heads—Jake's and mine—through the door frame of his classroom. "Come on in," she welcomes us, looking relaxed and positive, as always.

"Good to see you too, Kate." I shake her hand politely and remove the little guy from my shoulders, letting him settle into one of the bean bags on the carpet. "What's up?" There's never a good time for bad news; I prefer to get that part done with and push the issue to its resolution stage.

"Nothing bad, I promise," she reassures me, seeing my worried face. Okay, I can take an actual breath now. "Jake is such a pleasure to have in class, we're so lucky to have him." And of course I agree with that.

"Thanks for the reassurance." I give the little guy a wink.

"I wanted to ask your sister," Kate goes on, "but I haven't had a chance to see her in a while, I hope I'm not too late. Do you guys have plans for Thanksgiving?"

"Thanksgiving?" I came in here expecting to get my heart ripped open over some kids bullying my nephew. Kate's reassurance took it down a notch, but it still takes me a minute to shift my mindset and tuck away these thoughts. "No, I don't think we have any special plans." My hand goes to rub the back of my neck. I always spend Thanksgiving with my sister Julia. Even before Jake was born and before his asshole of a father decided to disappear.

"Great!" Kate squeals. "In that case, my sister and I would love to invite you all to Thanksgiving at my place. Julia and I talked about it, but we haven't actually formalized our plans. She warned me you might not love the idea, but I really hope you can make it."

Might not love the idea? Is there a particular reason I shouldn't? Has my sister decided to play matchmaker? Kate just mentioned her own sister... It does smell like a set-up.

And again, still feeling like I've missed an episode on some new show everyone's talking about. Still waiting for the "*Previously, on...*" to help get me up to speed. But seeing Jake's hopeful face as he leans over from his beanbag, I nod politely, planning to take this one up with my sister later.

Two and a half hours later, after one tiny kids' soccer practice accompanied by another one of Jake's hypoglycemic episodes that I resorted to resolving with a pack of gummy candies and a juice box... and sure, okay, *over-resolved* and said yes to a big scoop of chocolate ice cream—I get overprotective like that when I see his shaky hands and that lifeless-helpless look on his face—and we're finally back at my sister's.

"Ice cream again?" She gives me the stink eye. I did remember to clean his face afterward, but the chocolate drips on his shirt must have given it away.

"Mom, don't be mad at Uncle Christian, he was trying to cheer me up," Jake sticks up for me. He's such a mature little guy, growing up way too fast, having to act as his own pancreas at the age of five. It's been almost a year since his diagnosis, and I still can't wrap my head around it.

"You, shower." Julia ruffles Jake's hair and gives him a noisy kiss, then raises an eyebrow at me. "Cheer him up?"

"From the hypo," I explain before she starts worrying about potential school issues—as if hypoglycemia isn't bad enough. This seems to settle it for now as she jumps into another potential issue. "Did Kate talk to you?" she asks.

"About Thanksgiving?"

"Uh-huh," she says with a conspiratorial smile.

"Care to elaborate what this invitation entails?" I return the question. Something is going on here.

"No," Julia chuckles. Getting information from my sister is like pulling teeth, but I've had years of practice.

"Then I'm not going." Of course I'll go, I'd never leave my sister and Jake alone on Thanksgiving, but this is my foolproof interrogation method.

"Urgh! You're impossible." Like I said. Foolproof. Works every time.

"She's been dying to introduce you to her sister for like ages," Julia starts and I roll my eyes in response. Ignoring me, Julia goes on, "But she, the sister, had a boyfriend. Now that they've broken—"

"Hold up, Jules. *My* sister, my own flesh and blood wants me to be a rebound?" I clutch my heart in feigned shock.

"Rebound? She'll take one look at you and realize you're the one she's been waiting for her entire life." Being quite familiar with my sister's relationship sarcasm, I just sigh.

"Does the sister know she's being summoned for a Thanksgiving blind date?" I push my fingers through my hair. I haven't figured out all the details of this vicious plan, but I don't like it already.

"She doesn't. And we're going to keep it this way, otherwise we'll have a no-show."

"You might get two no-shows."

"Jake will not let that fly." She's smart, my sister. Unfortunately. And knows all my weak spots. "You're going to dress nice, make your signature gluten-free mac and cheese dish and join us for an awesome dinner at Kate's house. Who knows, her sister might just be your one and only."

"Not possible." The words slip out of my mouth before I can help it.

"Why not? I'm telling you, I have a good feeling about this one!" Zero sarcasm this time, which is rare for Julia. She says it as if Kate's sister and I have been destined to be together, and it's just a matter of technicality to help us realize it. I could tell her that the only woman on my mind these days is that incredible, stunning girl from the mall who took my breath away with a single kiss. But that would sound insane. And then ... there's Claire, who fascinates me on a completely different level. And if I'm honest, has also kind of lodged herself into my mind. Two. Two unforgettable women came into my life on the same day, and that's already too much for me to handle. But I'm a weak brother at heart, and an even weaker uncle, and so unfortunately, Thanksgiving blind date it is.

I get home, kick off my shoes and settle on the couch with my laptop. For some reason, since this new partnership with Claire was announced this morning—with the exception of the couple of hours I spent with Jake—I've been constantly checking my emails, trying to see who's going to break first and schedule a regular working meeting series. Or at least see if Claire has had a chance to give my initial slide deck a thought.

Why do I give a damn about what she thinks?

One of the perks of being added to the Amarinex systems as a collaborator, with the rationale of keeping internal conversations to a more secured level, is to be able to see who's online at any given moment. Something I uncharacteristically decide to use for my advantage right now as I go into the company chat to check on Claire. I'm curious to figure her out, is she a nine-to-five kind of person? An all-nighter? How dedicated is she to this project? If I find out she regularly logs off by 2 p.m. to go to the gym and never picks back up, like a less-than-bare-minimum kind of person, I might mention something when I see her again. Working with dedicated people is important, especially when it comes to stuff that means so much to me.

I type the letter C and Claire's name and picture are the first to appear on my screen. There's a little yellow circle next to her serious-gorgeous face, indicating she's offline. But before I have a chance to exit the chat, I see the three dots appear by her name.

"Working late, or spying on your team members?" she types.

"Both," is my comeback. There's no point denying it. "Thought you were offline," I type. The little circle is still yellow, despite her online presence.

"Not that it's any of your business, but I set my status to automatically switch after hours to offline."

"So no one will know you're working?" I take a wild guess.

"You're correct, Sherlock."

"People usually have it the other way around, you know." I chuckle to myself as I type.

"Yeah... don't want people to know I have no life."

Wow, had no idea this serious girl had a sense of humor.

I send her a laughing emoji.

"I wasn't joking," she types when she sees it.

Interesting.

"So, no life?"

"You got it. But if you dare yap about it to Derek, I'll deny."

"I don't tell my friends everything. And I certainly don't yap."

"Just so you know," she keeps at it, "I am as unhappy about this partnership between us as you are."

She's unhappy. Okay, that part was pretty clear.

"I'm not unhappy," is my best rebuttal. Especially now that I realize that I'm dealing with a workaholic.

"O-kay," she writes. Does she not believe me? "Well, *I* am." Honesty is an important trait, even if it kind of stings.

"May I ask why?" I try, because it would be nice to know what I've done to make her so feisty. Or maybe she's like that toward everyone?

"No, you may not."

"Well, I hope I'll be able to change your mind."

"We'll see about that."

7

Too sick to talk

Claire

I'm not sure why it affects me like that, but it does. It's Harriett's *"Who do you think you are?"* morning greeting as I step into the office, barely able to hold myself up after my recent morning repulsion for coffee.

Caught off-guard I say, "Excuse me?" Even though I should really know better by now. I'm not surprised by the audacity of this woman or the level of her bitchiness—these are well-known traits and certainly not new. She's been finding novel ways to spite and provoke me every day. It could be about an idea I suggest that doesn't conform with her line of thinking, or my tone of voice. Sometimes it extends to the font or color palette I use for my PowerPoint slides. Or the size of my bullet points or whether I use periods at the end of each sentence—formalities she changes so often that even an eager follower could lose track. When she's not busy fussing over aesthetics, she's rejecting my requests to take days off, even if I plan them weeks in advance and line up my back-ups. Even when it's actually backbone-less Steve, my manager, who should be the one approving these and sticking up for me. Nothing gets past her, and no one likes to cross her. I regard the three-day-off request around Thanksgiving, the one I was able to secure, as a sort of miracle. Dr. Harriett Wallington is a next level micromanager, with a special affinity to yours truly, I've come to realize. But she's also known for her very high success rate when it comes to clinical trials, so I guess she'll be sticking around.

I'm just not sure what it is this time. Because for the past week I've been working closely with Christian, exactly like she asked. And we've been making good progress. I search my memory for a slide deck I sent that she would want to butcher. Or a word out of place? Had I slashed her tires in my distracted state and forgot?

I look down to my clothes to make sure I didn't accidentally show up in my pajamas and flip-flops, or my favorite cropped T-shirt with the *I hate my boss* logo. No, and no. Nothing comes to mind. So I pull my head high and give Harriett a confused look.

"It's 9:05," she admonishes, looking at her watch, tapping her foot like my high school math teacher.

"It is," I agree, not sure where she's going with it.

"Our office hours are 9 to 5, at a minimum. You are expected to be here on time."

I look around—most of the cubicles are still empty. Our offices are always open, but we are exempt employees on a flex schedule, so while I may have showed up to work a tad after nine this morning, I always work over forty hours a week. I actually work over seventy hours each week. I may change my status to offline after hours, but I do submit my true hours to Steve at the end of each week. If she really wants to know how many hours I put in, I'm sure she could check the system. Or ask Steve. Plus, I usually get to the office by seven thirty each morning. I can't sleep anyway. This morning, my nausea kept me attached to the bathroom floor for way too long. But I doubt she would care that there's an actual reason.

"I work hard," I say. "I don't think you need to—"

"That's for me to decide," she cuts me off. "And I don't care what you do outside of work. I expect you to be here by 9 a.m. Sharp. Every morning."

Wow... talk about motivating employees. I heard this phrase once—*"People don't leave their jobs, they leave their managers."* And even though technically my manager is Steve, I am so close to saying something stupid right now—yet extremely satisfying given the circumstances—like *I quit.*

"She was in a meeting with me," I hear Christian's voice behind me, deep and confident. There was no such meeting, and I never asked him to jump to my rescue. But the pace at which Harriett's ugly scowl morphs into a fan girl smile is just so fascinating that I take it.

"Oh, Chris." She turns toward him, completely forgetting about me.

"It's Christian, Harriett," he reminds her again. I doubt she needs a reminder though, she just enjoys doing everything her way.

"Yes, Christian, I'm sorry." Her eyes travel down his body before she finds his face again and fans herself. He's hot, I give her that. But no need to be so obnoxious about it.

I give him a curt nod as he comes to stand beside me, and excuse myself to my cubicle, before Harriett regains her memory, in which I inevitably exist.

And it may be the annoying encounter with this witch-bitch, or something else entirely, like the recollection that I have another—not made-up this time—meeting with Christian in his office soon, but something is making me restless. I'm nervous, walking back and forth, down the hallway, in and out of my cubicle, back to the kitchen area where a spread of bagels and coffee has been set up. My stomach is churning. I can barely keep my breakfast down and the sight of food is making it so much worse.

What is happening?

Uncharacteristically, Christian managed to talk me into a regular-frequent meeting schedule. With him. He actually made *me* create a recurrent series of meetings. And once on my calendar, there's no way for me to escape. To his defense, I've been assigned to work with *him* on this project, and we have a monstrous timeline and a deadline from hell. Well—a deadline from Harriett, but that's just one and the same.

Long story short, we need to come up with a complete first-in-human clinical trial design and a long-term plan leading up to phases two and three clinical trials, and a full-blown strategy that will hopefully lead to drug approval—we're talking several years down the road here, seven at a minimum, and that's if all goes well—when in fact we haven't even agreed on the patient population we'll be targeting, or the endpoints...

Which means we're going to see a lot of each other for the next several weeks, until we have it all fleshed out and ready to be presented to Amarinex stakeholders. And working at risk—because they might turn this entire plan over and send us back to the drawing board. What's more, in order to facilitate all that,

Christian has been assigned a temporary office in our building, one with a window and an actual view overlooking the Potomac. While I'm still sporting a cubicle! Just another one of a long list of reasons to resent this insufferable yet handsome, short-term-memory-lacking man.

Now I need to convince my body to align, because staying mad at Christian is not working very well for me. Not when he shows up to work in a pair of suit pants that hang from his waist in such way that makes my head turn, and a pressed button-down that's stretched over his wide chest, unbuttoned at the top and rolled up at the sleeves, exposing a set of attractive, ink-decorated forearms. The same ones I had my eyes on back at the mall. He looks like an elegant, classy bad boy. Someone should lock this guy in his office, because this is clearly creating a distracting work environment. For me. The plan was to file my thoughts into the *I don't like this guy* compartment, but then he goes and stands up for me like he just did, and my brain decides that it would much rather have its neurons misfire from lusting over Christian versus fussing with Harriett's bullying.

"Good morning," I say, as I enter Christian's temporary office—yes, the one with the view—a short time later.

"Good morning." He lifts his eyes from the notepad on his desk, gesturing for me to sit. The man has a goddamn corporate laptop with two giant screens, yet he'd rather use an old-fashioned pen and paper. And unfortunately—I like it.

Stay strong.

"Congrats on the office," I say, not bothering to smooth out the edge in my voice. I don't care if he notices. Or rather—I want him to notice.

"Thank you," he says, checking off the politeness box. "I've been looking forward to hear more details about your findings."

"My findings?" I stall, hoping we were past that stage already. I still hate to admit that I've been walking around for days trying to forget the fact that I was wrong. Yes, I already admitted it to him once last week, but I didn't really go into details. "About the unfortunate misinformed and outdated status quo surrounding the field of Type 1 diabetes?" I choose to take the guilt and admission off my shoulders and blame it on the collective world of science.

"Yes, *those* findings." A slight smile climbs up his pretty face. I'm still expecting a gloating reaction but, yet again, he seems genuinely interested. Okay, with a side of a smirk. But a modest one.

Dammit, he's not giving me enough fuel to maintain my vendetta. The one that's supposed to keep him out of my mind and me out of trouble.

"Okay, you clearly know your stuff." I say. "We can move on, we're on an extremely tight deadline." Just yours truly skipping ahead. I doubt there's anything I've recently learned that Christian doesn't already know.

"Thank you, appreciate the kind words," he chuckles and turns his screen in my direction so we can work on our slides. At least he's giving me an out, not asking me to come up with the embarrassing *you were right* kind of direct admission just yet. Thank goodness. Because I really don't have it in me right now.

"There's one thing I'm not sure about." I go back to a point we've been avoiding. "Why don't you want to go for Type 1 diabetes prevention?" My eyes scan his face for signs of resistance, which is what I'm trying to provoke. Fuel. I am looking for fuel. Fuel to keep me from liking this guy. "I think we should." I know I'm kind of late to the game, because this past week we've been working on a different plan entirely. "Instead of trying to reverse diabetes in patients that already have the disease."

Christian looks disappointed. Yet he humors me for a second, and with a slight tilt to his head, he says, "You want to focus on Type 1 diabetes prevention?"

"Yes, it's our best option, and there's already a path. There's precedence." I bat my eyelashes at him, sensing some resistance but appreciating his patience. And his full attention.

"These patients need it more," he says. "We have an opportunity to do something novel here. We can make our own path." The handsome professor puts down the pen that he was apparently holding—I hadn't noticed it up until now. My entire being is still stuck on that canon event that involved his lips on mine. "Plus," he goes on, "I believe it was you who predicted that the mechanism of action of our drug of choice here would not work for prevention. And now that you have your scientific facts straight," he pauses for impact, glancing straight into my soul, "you know that this same mechanism of action gives us a plausible basis to aim for disease reversal."

And now that I've done my homework properly, and know what I know, I also know he might be right. The plan we came up with is adventurous, bold, and possibly, maybe… could actually work. I don't usually shy away from giving a good fight, so at this point I would normally come up with a witty remark or a rebuttal. But like I said, he's not wrong. Plus, for some unknown reason, this one discussion is getting physically challenging. I feel my heart beating slightly too fast and my stomach doing some weird somersaults, and not in a good way. I know I said I don't like to be wrong, but this is unusual even for me.

"I don't think going straight into patients is the—" I have a well-thought-out sentence already crafted in my head as a strange burn rises up my throat. "Excuse me..." I can barely bring myself to my feet, though somehow I do—because retching all over this guy's carpet is not exactly the charm I'm going for—and make a run for it.

Awful. Repulsive. Disgusting. Just a few words to describe the way my throat and stomach feel right now. I'm beginning to suspect that this is no longer about admitting that I wasn't right. Note—I did not say *wrong*.

I wash my face, dab at it with a paper towel, get my hair into order and go back into my cubicle. No, not into Christian's office. I need some breathing room. That and the toothbrush I keep in my drawer.

I take deep breaths that mostly make me dizzy, drink some icy water, read a paper or two, ignore my emails for a bit. And around noon I start feeling better.

"Hey," I hear Christian's voice behind me. "How are you feeling?"

"Had better days," I say, turning around, surprised by his concerned expression and the to-go box with food he's holding up. For me?

"Got me worried. Hope it's not something I said," he tries to joke, handing me the box.

"Thanks. Maybe it was," I huff and turn my attention back to my laptop. Can't bear the smell of food, or the thought of getting nutrients into my body right now. I go in for a distraction. "Your study design is very optimistic," I say, opening our collaborative deck on my screen. Anything to break the intensity of our eye contact. "A small positive twist to the likelihood of it to fail." And that's a compliment, coming from me.

One time. The guy brings me lunch one time and I go all soft on him? Come on...

"It's bold," he agrees, "but it does have multiple check points where we could pivot." Then he rests his hand on the back of my chair and bends over to point at the screen.

My vision blurs as my body focuses on the proximity of his scent. Each one of my treacherous cells make it their personal goal to line up against him, bit by bit, until I find the back of my shoulder tucked close to his chest.

"Sorry," I say, surprised by how my body actually physically made its way there. But I'm clearly not sorry as I make no attempt to move back, and he doesn't either. His lips are somewhat close to my ear as he keeps sharing his thoughts on whatever it is my screen is showing. I need to focus my attention to hear what he's actually saying, because his warmth and his gravelly voice transport me to that moment at the mall. I must be going crazy.

8

One inhale

Christian

One inhale. One inhale is all it took—in the proximity of Claire—to bring my mind back to that moment at the mall. The moment with that girl who melted in my arms and held on to me so tight. And that's all I can think of the entire day, and night, and as I drive to work the next morning.

The thing with having bad eyesight is that you learn to rely on other senses. Other inputs. Like sound and smell. Without my glasses, I might not be the best at recognizing someone's face, but the sound of their voice and the way they speak help the recognition.

I haven't been around that girl from the mall long enough to know her voice, or her way with words, but my body seems to think it remembers. And my mind is playing tricks on me.

Because it clearly confuses Claire with... her. And this one inhale made my olfactory system think this gorgeous spitfire scientist also smells like her. This flowery scent I haven't been able to bring myself to forget. And now I can't stop thinking about her. That girl. *Or is it Claire?*

And if it's not bad enough, they've both been inhabiting my dreams too. There they've been the same person so many times that I can no longer tell them apart. It's all mixed up. In this dream, I go into Claire's cubicle, lay my hand on the back of her neck. I can feel the sparks going off as I touch her skin, starting at my fingertips and spreading through my veins. She turns her head, looking at me over her shoulder. Only instead of the serious-feisty gaze of hers, she has this wild gleam in her eyes, like that girl from the mall. Or at least that's what my glasses-deprived self remembers. I had known her in my dreams, it seems, before ever knowing anything else.

"I've finally found you," I tell her, in my dream, because my sorry ass wouldn't speak this way in real life. And she turns around, pulls me in close and asks me to promise I'll never let go. I'd happily agree if I stopped waking up at the same exact point every goddamn night.

And then I go to work, in real actual life now, to my lab at GERI, and every few days I show up at Amarinex offices, positioning myself at that temporary office they've allocated for me, and count the seconds until Claire struts in, with her beautiful, serious face and her fearless attitude. I'm not sure how I'm supposed to be able to focus, when my body is convinced that these two gorgeous women are now one, and my brain needs to work overtime to shut it down.

We've been meeting almost every day now, in person or online, to work out our study design and plans. I might be delusional, but I swear her sad resting face lights up a little whenever she enters a conference room and spots me in it. Then she typically thinks better of it and tries to shove that trace of a smile away, but the damage is already done. My heart is already swelling, and I can't help it to save my life.

She's smart and tough, keeping me constantly impressed and mostly on my toes. She makes sure to give me a hard time. Our conversations have taken on a routine. I suggest something, Claire plays devil's advocate. I explain my rationale, she agrees to some but never stops looking for holes in my theories, asking uncompromising questions when others would usually back down. She challenges me, and I like it. A whole freaking lot. I may even throw some daring ideas out there in anticipation of these little scientific debates.

"I think we should," I say again, because this time she hasn't really expanded on our difference in opinions.

"I don't agree to that."

"Why not?"

"Why do you think?"

"I think you just enjoy disagreeing with me," I challenge.

Claire shakes her head, and I'm drawn to the way her hair bounces and how her little hoop earrings swing gently from side to side. I'm a complete goner for this contentious woman at this point.

"Not true," she denies, and I know she's lying by the slight twitch of her lip. But she won't let up or let her smile show. And between these small invigorating discussions and these sparks of energy she throws at me, I'm slowly learning her unspoken language. Learning to anticipate her reactions and trying to decipher these little shades of sadness in her expression. For the most part these are untraceable, she hides them well. But I see it; when she leaves my office, or when she walks down the hall, when she has no idea I'm looking. I can't help but notice that something is bothering her. It's almost like she's sinking. Right in front of my eyes.

Claire

It takes me a few more days of this inability to focus, the constant nausea, barely eaten breakfasts that end up going up faster than down, weird exhaustion as if all energy has been sucked out of me, and this new unfathomable dislike for coffee and alcohol—my two old friends, especially since Harriett decided to join Amarinex—to realize that something might be off. Which is why I find myself here, at my local grocery store. Far enough from the office to reduce the chance of running into anyone and everyone I know.

I walk between the long busy shelves, collecting food items I don't really need and would probably not be able to get myself to eat. Procrastinating as much as possible. Plodding up and down one specific aisle I'm trying to avoid. I like these grocery stores that arrange items in an associative or task-oriented manner. The peanut butter is near the jelly and conveniently located near the sliced bread. The steak rub is just next to the—you guessed it—steaks. The tampons and pads are organized neatly by the colorful boxes of condoms, conveniently located next to the...

pregnancy tests. And despite the high order of organization; by topic, color, size, usage. I feel lost.

I could really use a sign right now. My mind is reeling as I pull one of these little test boxes off the shelf. And then a couple more, one from each brand, because if it turns up positive I might want further confirmation before I let my mind jump to conclusion and go on an endless spin. Reproducibility is an important component in any observation—when it comes to repetition, I mean. My hands are already full of giant Cheetos bags—my continued dietary predilection. Yes, I'm the kind of shopper who underestimates their shopping list to the point of not picking up a cart or a basket until one of the workers forces one into my hand. Not this time though, not when I'm in the aisle of privacy. So when I walk back without looking and crush into someone, I'm not terribly surprised that everything falls to the floor.

"Sorry," I say, as I nonchalantly bend down, trying to pick it all up as soon as I can, focusing my eyes on these little packs of pregnancy tests that somehow landed face up on this someone's shoes. Nice shoes. So I'm hopeful I've bumped into a very busy individual who could care less about a fellow shopper's selection of items. But it's false hope, because I know these shoes.

Christian

On the way home from work, I decide to stop at the grocery store near my apartment building to get Jake his favorite brand of cereal—which happens to also be gluten-free—my sister is being proactive here, reducing his wheat intake in hope of avoiding future celiac diagnosis, something that patients with Type 1 diabetes are at higher risk for developing, as if one autoimmune disease is not enough. But regardless of gluten, or lack thereof, or whether Julia's methods are based on solid scientific evidence, these cereals are admittedly good—taste-wise, at least—so I am all for showing my support.

I mindlessly fill my cart up with groceries, letting my thoughts drift between the two women that somehow stormed into my life on the same day. I'm strolling through the aisles, looking for cereal, when I spot her long chestnut hair in my peripheral vision. I slow down for a double-take, making sure before I get closer. She has her back to me, and seems quite focused on some boxes, reading the labels, comparing different brands in utmost concentration, then piling several up in her arms. But before I have a chance to make my presence known, she backs up quite abruptly. Into me. Dropping everything to the floor.

"Sorry," she says, bending over to pick up her loot without looking up. Her eyes hone in on my shoes, where a few items have somehow landed.

"Claire," I say, kneeling next to her, picking up a few large Cheetos bags and what seems like endless supply of... pregnancy tests. At the sound of my voice, and her name, her head lifts hastily and her eyes shoot up to me. She looks alarmed.

"Wha— What are you doing here?" she asks, confused.

"Getting groceries." I try to sound reassuring while I pick up her stuff, then offer my hand to help her up. "Here, you can use my cart." I make some room in it with my free hand.

"No, thanks, I'm— Good." She sounds hesitant as I hand her the pregnancy test boxes.

"Oh, that's not ... mine," she mumbles. "For a friend... who might be... pregnant." Her face a cute shade of crimson, decorated with a shy smile that doesn't quite reach her eyes. This may very well be the first time I've seen her lips turn upward, but it's more an embarrassed smile than anything.

"Sure," I say, reluctantly letting her hand leave my hold. "None of my business."

"You're right, it isn't." Her regular feisty expression snaps back into place as she shakes off her thoughts. "Well, good night Dr. Copeland," she says in a formal voice, stepping back and putting a distance between us.

"Good night, Dr. Bellingham."

9

A possible revelation

Claire

Still recovering from dropping a generous supply of pregnancy tests—which I still haven't gotten myself to use—on Christian's shoes, I spend the next day hoping his short-term-memory-loss will play in my favor. The team is scheduled to go out to dinner with a vendor who's trying to land a fat contract with us. I usually like these—fancy restaurant, expensive wine and nice work-related conversation kind of events. That is, on a normal day with reasonable appetite and craving for alcohol. The kind of normal that hasn't been happening for me in a while. So I would have passed if it weren't for Derek mentioning that this company may end up being our partner of choice for the clinical study Christian and I are trying to develop.

Harriett is being the professional witch-bitch that only she knows how to be, and somehow other people find it funny. Or just don't notice these traces of venom she infuses into it. Typical. Not that I need them to. But how can so many people take her daily jabs as innocent humor? Or genuine kindness? Seriously, how blind does one have to be to not see through her layer of fake loveliness? She's a corporate bully, and it makes me sick. And that has nothing to do with the fact that I'm already feeling sick as it is.

"Get yourself together," she tells me in a low tone, lips barely moving, when I position myself at the table. I am not anywhere near her, it's a large space and we are the first ones there—so I got my best pick—as far away from her claws as physically possible. I look down at my outfit again—I went for an elegant, simple-yet-classy look, a tad of makeup, I've even done my hair. So what's the deal with her? My dress might be showing a little cleavage, but that's not something Harriett should be concerned about.

"What now?" I ask.

"You look miserable. No one likes sad, petty, party poopers." Such words of wisdom and encouragement are sure to bring back the sunshine and rainbows and chase away my dark clouds.

"Okay," I say, because I'm so exhausted that I have no fight left in me.

Harriett, probably hoping for an argument, is clearly not happy with my lack of response. "And stop trying so hard." She goes for a brand new, albeit contradictory, tactic.

"Trying so hard to do what?" I ask, confused, because really, right now all the trying I do is aimed at keeping my last meal—be it a bag of Cheetos as it may—in my stomach, and keeping myself awake.

She lowers her voice as a few team members join us at the table. "To impress Christian."

"Was I? If anything, I've been trying for the opposite," I say honestly. I mean, yeah... He's hot, and admittedly the best kisser out there—at least by my standards—judging by that one sizzling kiss at the mall. But with this little short-term memory loss thing he's been pulling off, I kind of got the message that for him it was completely meaningless. And while I may not be a social genius, I can certainly take a hint. I have dignity. And I don't do players—which based on all of the above facts, I assume he is one.

"What did I miss?" I hear Christian's voice closing in. Assumptions are a funny thing. *Never assume*—something I learned quite early in my career as a scientist. Yet I still do it in my personal life, having been under the impression that Christian wasn't going to make an appearance tonight.

Harriett's expression lights up at once as she gestures to the seat next to her. Could she be any more obvious? But Christian is already committing himself to the seat closest to him—which happens to be just next to mine, greeting me with a light squeeze to my shoulder that has this magical effect of calming my nerves. Only to light them all on fire.

"I was just telling this silly girl here," Harriett points at me, her gaze taking on some degree of disappointment from Christian's choice of seating location—too far for her reach, "that she's being pretty obvious, trying to make you like her."

Oh. My. God. Did she really just say that?

I can feel my face heating up with a combination of terror and annoyance. My pulse is reaching my ears way too quickly. I would go for a witty insult right now—I live for these moments, usually—but I'm afraid that if I open my mouth I might throw up all over the table. I take a small breather and a sip of cold water—thankfully the waiter filled my glass a moment ago—and before I have a chance to say anything, Christian jumps in.

"She doesn't need to, Harriett," he chides. His tone is kind but is also reprimanding. A warning. I like him so much right now. Short-term memory loss or not. "Claire has been challenging my knowledge since day one. She stands for what she believes in, she questions everything I say. She's a professional. Your comments *are not*."

Look at him. Seeing right through the witch-bitch and her distasteful humor.

Harriett's smile dies a little, but only for a second, until Big Boss Joe walks in and takes the seat beside her, making her feel significant again.

The waiter comes back with two bottles of wine, offering the attendees the option between red and white. My heart speeds up as he closes in. "For you, miss?" he asks.

"Just water, thanks," I say quietly, hoping to avoid Harriett's radar. I can see Christian's head turn toward me, eyes searching mine, but I don't reciprocate. He has this tendency of gazing into my soul and there are things in there that even I'm not sure I want to know.

"I have to say, Claire, I'm surprised. No alcohol tonight?" Of course Harriett's antennae picked that up. She'd never miss such an epic moment. She knows I never say no to free alcohol.

"We have a lot of work to do, planning to continue working later, we both need to stay sharp." Christian's voice comes to my rescue, again. "No wine for me either, thanks," he tells the waiter.

Hmmm. Let me just put it out there right now. My plans for later, up until a second ago, included waddling to the metro station on these malicious heels, getting myself home, shedding this uncomfortable dress and crawling into bed. Nothing more, nothing less. None of that, unfortunately, had anything to do with Christian. But now that he's stuck up for me so impressively, for a second time in five minutes, I am officially reconsidering my decision of not liking him. Heck, I might even consider putting aside that whole pretending-that-kiss-never-existed act he's been playing. He might be a playboy who couldn't care less about women he casually kisses at malls, but I'm willing to look past it if he keeps putting Harriett in her place like that.

We spend the next couple of hours having normal civilized conversation with the people around us. Harriett moves on to frying bigger fish and sucking up to Big Boss Joe. I focus on ordering the smallest portions on the menu with what I hope will have the least distinct smell, pushing my food around the plate to make it seem like I've eaten a reasonable portion, until it's finally time to leave.

And just to make it believable, Christian and I go back to the office. It helps that the restaurant is a walking distance away. It doesn't help that my stilettos are pinching my toes. Since when have these heels been so tight on my feet?

"Thanks for the save back there," I say to Christian, who notices my struggle and offers a hand. But I persevere.

"You don't like each other too much," he chuckles.

"Harriett? She's a science suppressing, creativity killing bitch. I don't think I ever disliked someone as much as I do her," I admit.

"She's a bully, very unprofessional." He noticed...

"Well, I've had my share in it too," I release an embarrassed laugh, because things have been said.

"I'm sure you have," he snickers. "But she shouldn't be speaking to you the way she is, regardless."

He walks me to my cubicle and I sit down with a sigh, ruffling through some scientific papers. I expect that now that he's got me safe and sound back to work, he'll vanish. Instead, he enters my little cubicle space, dragging a chair for himself, and takes a seat. A smug smile on his pretty face. The nerve this man has. Unbelievable.

"Do we have a meeting?" I challenge him. I know he'd said that to Harriett, but that was for face-saving purposes.

"I don't need a meeting to see how you're doing," he says, clearly not deterred by my reaction as he pulls my chair to take a closer look at me.

"Thanks for the cover up." I try to hide the hitch in my breath. "Now I have some work to do, so if you'll excuse me." He should really stay as far away from me as possible. He shouldn't like complicated. And I'm all that. I also can't handle the piercing eyes that are looking into mine right now. It's doing all kinds of things to me.

"Sure," Christian says and stands up. But it's when he steps aside, about to turn on his heels and leave, that I feel that urge to run into the restrooms again. Only this time Christian is right behind me.

I'm perfectly capable of throwing up all by myself, but can barely walk straight with these ridiculous heels. He pulls on my waist and ushers me into the largest stall in the ladies' room, still supporting my body as he shuts the door behind us. "You better leave now," I warn, dropping to my knees and letting my face hover over the toilet. "It's gonna get ug—" I barely manage to finish the sentence before the first violent stream of my half-digested dinner decides to come back up. But Christian doesn't seem interested in rushing out of the stall. Instead I feel his hands smoothing my hair back and away from my face, as I go in for seconds. "I'm a mess," I heave, taking shallow breaths, not sure whether a third round is coming. And as I lean back into the wall, the man gets up and disappears. "I did warn you," I call after him but he's back in half a second with a wet paper towel, situating himself on the floor next to me and cleaning my face gently.

Wow.

I had no idea men like that exist outside of romance novels.

"You're not a mess," he says with certainty, following the trail of the wet paper towel with his palm. "Just maybe a little pregnant."

"What?! How—" I did a pretty lousy job pretending last night at the grocery store did not actually happen in real life. As lousy as my cover story of getting all those home pregnancy tests for a 'friend.'

"None of my business, but I'm guessing your significant other is not thrilled about it," Christian tries to read my less-than-content expression. And he's right, it's none of his business, but since he's the only person in this world—other than myself and a smaller-than-pea human creation, apparently—who are aware of this possible revelation, my brain chooses to let him in. At least for this moment.

"You could say that."

"No thrills?"

"No significant other," I wince. "And definitely no thrills." My throat burns, my eyes sting, welling up with unwelcome tears. I want to say I'm terrified, but that might just qualify as too much information.

"Hey," Christian says, his expression softening as he wipes a sneaky tear off the corner of my eye. I try to come up with a snarky remark, to remind him—and mostly myself—that I'm still angry about his lack of short-term memory. But then he has to go and do something unexpected. He pulls me into his chest for an oh-so-comforting hug. And I'd be lying if I said that being in his arms again felt anything less than where I should be. And for a while, the clouds above my head seem to clear. Despite having thrown up and feeling like shit a moment ago. I breathe him in for a second before I pull away.

"Everything will be okay." He slides a finger under my chin, letting our eyes connect. "I promise," he says, as my treacherous body, without taking my common sense into account, connects with his chest again.

Promise. And despite knowing clearly well that this one promise is beyond anyone's ability to keep, it still makes me feel better. Magically erasing my tears and lighting up my darkest corner, even if only for a few moments. Until we break the hug, and Christian helps me back to my feet.

10

Maybe baby

Claire

"Kate, I think it's time for me to retire from my career as a beta tester for your dating app," I tell my sister as we walk to our regular booth, before I have to come up with an excuse for not ordering alcohol, again. And before our up-and-coming, surely unsuccessful, new attempt at a double date commences.

Memories of last night are still running through my head. "*I'll take you home,*" Christian had tried to insist.

Even after the little sparkly hug inside the tiny stall in the ladies' room, he still wouldn't mention that kiss at the mall. Admit that it was at least... memorable. That maybe *I* was a bit memorable? That I had left a speck of impression? No. This rock-muscle-bodied-bad-boy-pretty-face-kind-hearted man still insisted on not letting up on his amnesia issues, despite the fireworks exploding around us for the short moment he held me in his arms. Vomiting or not, the sparks didn't care. That's why I decided that letting him take me home, or comfort me, or be in my business—was a bad idea. So I pulled it together, refused politely and booked myself an Uber.

I have a talent for being alone even when surrounded by others. That's how it's always been, and I had no plans on changing it last night, even if it meant sitting by the toilet in the middle of the night, home alone, with several positive double-lined pregnancy sticks looking at me. Yes. Christian's inference skills are, unfortunately, spot on. And admittedly, finding out that all my latest symptoms are due to pregnancy and not some scary incurable disease—I may have spent some unreasonable amount of hours consulting Dr. Google—was sort of a relief. But a very short-lived one, once I realized I have an official excuse to worry for two.

"Retire?!" Kate's loud protest brings me back to the moment and to the bar we're at. "Why? You're my best tester!" she exclaims.

"You're just saying that because you're my sister," I chuckle.

"Maybe. But doing it with you makes it so much more fun," she says, as if double dating is some sort of a sisterly bonding activity I'll now be depriving her of. "And how will this app ever rise above the rest without your quirky comments and unusual spec requirements?" She makes her funny face and I can't help but laugh. "What can I do to change your mind?" She doesn't really mean it as a question, already bracing herself for a negotiation in which my sister almost always comes out on top. Not this time though.

"Not much you can do." How do I break the news to her without making her fall off her seat? "Except maybe add a feature for men interested in dating single pregnant women—"

Her face transforms at once as she releases a squeal. "Claire Marie Bellingham! You wouldn't!" Despite knowing my sister for my entire life, I'm not sure whether she's more surprised right now or impressed.

There's a short speechless moment that feels like forever, before she finally says, "I'm impressed!" Putting an end to my back-and-forth. "You're not joking, right?" She does a double take, letting her eyes bounce to my not yet visible pregnancy belly while I shake my head. Kate responds with something between another one of her squeals and a cute happy scream. She jumps out of the booth and pulls me over to an exhilarating hug, this time exceeding even her own Kate's typical excitement. I can literally see the adrenaline rushing through her as if we've just robbed our local grocery store of their entire candy stash—yeah, well, we had an interesting childhood—and climbed Mount Everest at the same time. The latter being a speculative scenario, although Kate would never turn down such adventure if I was willing to give this a go.

She pushes my shoulders to arm length and takes a good look at me. "My all-business, all-serious, never-a-plan-out-of-place sister! And just when I thought you couldn't surprise me."

"I know," I mumble in stark contradiction to my breathless, ecstatic sister. Well, maybe we're more alike than I had been brought up to believe.

Kate pulls me back into her embrace. "Who's the lucky guy? Please say he's handsome, I want my little niece or nephew to have the finest gene pool," she speaks into my hair. Her hand on my stomach, searching for a bulge which I clearly don't have yet given the advanced pregnancy stage of... probably a bit over a month. Then she draws back to take a closer look into my eyes. "Wait... you don't look too happy about it," she determines.

"It's Ryan," I say. My voice is a squeak and I hate it. I should own it, given I opted out of conventional contraceptives, thinking these kinds of things happen to other people, especially after almost a year of no activity in that domain. I mean the chances of getting pregnant over one-time-a-year sex using the rhythm plus withdrawal methods are not high, but not zero either, and it could actually be significant if that—apparently miscalculated—one day lands within your ovulation window. Especially if your partner—or ex-partner for that matter—is not well-versed with the latter component of said combined methods.

"What?!" Took her a minute. Kate releases her hold on me, and I take the opportunity to go back to the booth. "This was your one chance to break free from that boredom."

"I'm not bored anymore, I can assure you," I try to joke, but I really don't feel like laughing. "Anyway, he doesn't know. Yet."

"Oh," Kate says, as if my downhill-snowballing life is still salvageable. "So don't tell him. Are you even sure it's his?"

"Yes, *I'm sure*. And no, I'm not going to hide a baby from him."

"I thought you guys stopped having sex like um months ago." Yeah, that was part of the problem. Even us having sex stopped being exciting. Well, honestly, that had never been exciting. Not with Ryan anyway. Always had been. Guilty for fretting about it to my sister.

"Kind of. This was our one attempt to see if there was something worth saving." After which we both came to the conclusion that—no. Probably not even worthwhile staying friends. But apparently Baby here had a different plan.

"Not trying to judge you, older sis," my one-year-younger sister jabs, "but unprotected sex with a guy sounds more like a me thing, not yours."

"Well—" I'd checked off all my out-of-character boxes that night, apparently— "we were both so drunk." Had to be in order to go along with the stupid attempt. "And I didn't think he'd... finish anyway."

"Did *you* at least?"

"I was too drunk to remember."

"Then no—you didn't," Kate says. "Please don't marry Ryan, you deserve to spend your life in a more exciting relationship. With someone who will swoon you away and love you like you deserve. Or at least make sure you climax—"

"Don't worry," I chuckle. "There's no risk that Ryan'll want to get married." Not to me anyway. Baby or not. "And I wouldn't want to marry him either." But I find it hard to believe that I can get swooned by anyone. This word doesn't even belong in one sentence with me in it. Although that kiss at the mall... My body was clearly reacting to that confusing man.

Still does. Dammit. Must be the pregnancy hormones.

"But just so we're clear. You are still coming to Thanksgiving dinner."

"What Thanksgiving dinner?" I ask, because when it's only Kate and me—we don't even bother giving it such a formal name as *dinner*. It's more like a whole day of lazily cooking and watching movies while sprawled over her couch.

"The one I'm hosting," says my brilliant sister.

"Okay, spill it," I sigh, because when Kate gets elusive like this, I just know I'm in for trouble.

"Remember Jake?"

"The cute little boy in the kindergarten class you teach?" This kid must have left quite an impression on my sister, because she mentions his name a lot.

Kate nods. "He's the sweetest kid ever. He lives with his mom, Julia, she's a single mom. I couldn't let her and Jake spend the holiday all by themselves. You should have seen those cute boy's eyes when I invited them to join us, my heart just melted on the spot."

"And?" I ask, because something in my sister's tone sounds suspicious. I know her too well to tell I'm only getting half a story here.

"Okay, sure," she relents. "She has a hot brother that I think you—"

"I knew it!" I bang my hand on the table so hard I almost knock off the fake center piece candle between us. "I think that now, pregnancy and all, I should be exempt from your match-making attempts."

"You'd think," Kate smirks. "I need to ramp up my game—I have a future niece or nephew on the way, so I only have about... How many months?"

"Eight?" I shrug, guesstimating.

"Fine. Eight months to find the little pea a daddy, and make sure you don't get back to Ryan," she determines. "You should see how her brother is with Jake. I can tell he's going to be an amazing father!"

"Okay, hold your horses. I don't think that in my condition I should be going on dates," I try, although I already know I'm losing this battle.

"Nonsense," Kate dismisses my concerns. Like I said, losing this battle. "And you're going to fall head over heels for each other. You're going to love him. And he'll love you. Love at first sight. I just know it." Am I the only one uncomfortable with this L word being thrown around so many times it's practically being abused?

"If he's so great, why don't you date him yourself?" I am curious now.

"Because you two are meant for each other. Julia and I have it all planned out already," she says with confidence only Kate has. "We've been patiently waiting for you to break up with Ryan."

"And now I'm pregnant," I say. Not that this is supposed to stop her, but I try anyway. "And we're about to embark on another double-blind date with other people."

"Enough with the lame excuses, I'm not taking no for an answer."

11

Ten signs you no longer like your job

Claire

Because one sign is not enough. I need at least ten very thick signs to finally admit that I don't like my job anymore. And I say *'anymore'* because I used to love this place and this role that accounts for my annual income. Once upon a time, before Harriett joined Amarinex Bio and turned it into the dark dungeon that it is today, under her dictatorship regime, it used to be my happy place. My escape from my overly think-ful brain.

But lately, I realize, I've been taking the longer way to work. Deliberately choosing to get off at the more distant metro stop. And no, I'm not into expanding my daily step count or increasing my fresh air intake. Breaking a sweat does not sit well with me. It's more of a gradual office dread that I've developed. A very specific dread that has to do with running into *The* Harriett Wallington, or hearing her voice, or dealing with her sophisticated insults and her fancy stink eye or eye rolls.

I've also been counting the days till Thanksgiving. And no, not because of my sister's matchmaking plans. And double no, I'm not your typical cheerful holiday lover, nor am I a person who enjoys days off from work. On the contrary. My leisurely activities during vacations normally involve reading scientific manuscripts and work emails. Urgh. The pre-Harriett good old times. And don't think for a second that it has to do with that little stick that yielded two pink lines when I peed on it. Or the additional repeats that followed, with the combined count of six blue and pink lines. Yes, I had to repeat the pregnancy test to make sure it wasn't a false positive, or an outlier. Several times. Using multiple kits by different manufacturers. I'm thorough. Yes, the results were very consistent. But this is beside the point.

This Harriett Wallington dread developed long before the conception of Little Pea here. All it took was an introduction made by Big Boss Joe and a dead-fish handshake from Dr. Wallington. She then flashed a nausea-worthy saccharine smile toward said Big Boss, accompanied by *"We're going to be the best of friends, I already know it."* And a big-ass fake smile that morphed into what looked more like a twisted, teeth-baring snarl when we were left on our own. I'm still not sure what compelled her to say, right there and then, without knowing a single thing about me: *"Wipe that stupid smile off your face, drug development is a serious business, not summer camp."* A 180-degree turn in a span of less than three minutes.

Her show for Joe was obvious, but what made her dislike me with a passion since day zero hadn't been fully clear. Not to me, at least. I'm sure she's capable of some sort of positive feelings toward other people. Some. People who are not me. And I do know my history. Dr. Wallington and one of my past PhD advisors had been ex-lovers. Married, to be precise, and arch-enemies following a pretty ugly divorce story. Based on some top-level grapevine intel, he found out she was cheating on him with more than one man. Several. But I only worked in the poor guy's lab. I never conspired to ruin her academic career thereafter—she was able to accomplish that entirely on her own. Therefore, I did not expect to find myself at warfront.

And I'm pretty sure that Joe's introductory words—*"Claire is our youngest and brightest scientist,"* he had said, *"and impressively productive,"* only added oil to the fire, infusing the conversation with some air of competition. Seriously, why would he introduce me like that? Or was it me, nurturing her resentment by apologetically admitting that science made me happy? I was trying to bring the compliments one notch down after I saw her expression shift. I never liked her either, but really wasn't looking to acquire a hater. Harriett's newfound hobby since that day, it seems, has become—as she so eloquently put it—*"Making sure science will no longer be your source of joy."*

News flash, science will always be my source of joy, even Harriett can't take that away, but practicing it at Amarinex Bio is certainly isn't anymore.

As much as I hate to admit it, Christian showing up has made the place bearable again. Seeing his name on calendar invites has had the unexpected byproduct of lightening up my mood. And having Harriett assign us to work together is counterproductive to her wishing upon gray clouds above my head. But that's just a temporary fix. Once we complete our study design task and get senior leadership endorsement, Christian will go back to his academic life in his lab at GERI—the Gene and Epigenetic Research Institute, the place of dreams for scientists—and I'll probably need to start looking for a new job, because this witch-bitch vs moi thing is not working too well for me. To the point that I'm seriously considering a career change. Anything to get me as far away from her and as soon as possible. Especially now with Baby on the way. And I can't believe I'm speaking like this, even if just to myself.

But the benefit of having Christian around extends beyond softening the blows. It also softens Harriett's blows. Even if she's just pretending to be nice. Unfortunately for me though, Christian is at GERI today, despite it being one of the days he'd normally be at Amarinex offices. And as I pass by his empty temporary office, I feel a pang of disappointment. And I don't like it. Don't like the fact that he's not here on a day he should be. Don't like that it has a say over my mood. Don't like that I care.

I sit in my cubicle, dwelling on my misfortune, trying to eat my lunch and finish a slide deck on a very stretched deadline of thirty minutes, assigned to me by... well, that's an easy guess. Lunch break is for the weak, it seems. Food makes me sick anyway.

Something flickers in the corner of my eye. It's a little camera icon flashing at the bottom of my screen. I click it.

Christian's handsome face appears on the large computer screen, making my heart stumble for several beats. This has become our tradition on days he's not here, with the excuse of getting more work done. But my visceral reaction to it is only getting stronger with every call. I might need CPR if I keep going at this pace.

"Not eating today?" he asks as his eyes spot my abandoned lunch.

"No time to eat in this place," I utter, moving my lunchbox out of sight.

"Not if I have a say," he determines. His eyes studying mine as if reading into my unspoken words.

"Harriett promised Big Boss Joe some competitive analysis slides in thirty minutes. Guess who needs to make them on a last-minute heads up?" I huff.

"She did what?" His eyebrows shoot up protectively and I'm liking it too much. "It's just the teaser," I explain. "The full thing has to be ready by Monday." As if I have no life, no plans for Thanksgiving and own a magical wand that can make me cough up an entire analysis over a single weekend. Truthfully, she's not completely off. I have no life. But I actually do have plans for Thanksgiving weekend, I've made a promise to Kate. And even if I were to cancel said plans, it still wouldn't solve the absence of a magic wand. And since the use of AI-based technologies is strictly forbidden at Amarinex, the only thing I've been coughing up these days are my half-digested meals.

A reasonable manager would sound somewhat apologetic when dumping work on me last minute, knowing very well I was planning to be on PTO. Or at least give her subordinate—Harriett loves this word—a realistic timeline to complete the task. Like one-plus day upon my return. Or maybe, out of courtesy, check with me whether I could fit it in during the days off I'd requested *months* in advance. But no. Not Harriett Wallington. Though I decide to spare these petty details from Christian and just sigh quietly. He doesn't need to know I was planning, for a change, to not work during a weekend. He doesn't need to know about Kate, or her plans to spend the coming holiday with me, cooking and baking cookies in her little kitchen, in preparation for *the dinner,* at which she's conspired to match me up with her idea of Prince Charming.

"How are you feeling?" Christian pulls me back from my internal rant session. If I were to attempt to answer that honestly, I wouldn't even know where to begin.

"Pretty good," I lie. I know he's asking about my inability to keep food down. Or the less than a pea-size human I'm nurturing while barely able to process any of it. But I choose to focus on the task at hand. And I'm pretty confident that if I push my next few meetings to the afternoon and spend the evening reading all my missed emails, I can get the annoying slide deck to Harriett in time. So, all things considered, I do feel pretty good about it. And although I would love to keep staring at Christian's handsome face through the camera and delve idly into the possible reasons this man can't remember that kiss we shared, I really need to get back to work. So I apologize for rushing the conversation, decline his offer to help because this one task has nothing to do with our shared project, even if his consulting agreement with Amarinex is wide enough to cover it, and hang up the call. The sacrifices I'm willing to make for Dr. Wallington just don't feel like me anymore.

That's why, when I wake up the next morning, after finishing up my slides and spending most of the night catching up on my relatively urgent backlog items, more exhausted than before I had made an attempt to get some shut eye, I don't have the energy to deal with the witch. I also don't recall any meetings with Dr. Forgetful-Pretty-Face, so, ignoring his emails, I decide to call in sick for the first time in like ... ever. I let my head sink back into the pillow, pretending it's one of those sweet early morning moments when you let yourself drift back to sleep, snuggling really good, not having a care in the world. My past teenage self would have thanked me immensely if it weren't for the nausea that has me running to the bathroom twice and the feeling that the world is closing in on me. But at some point, a new kind of exhaustion takes over. And despite being well-aware of my adult responsibilities, I drift back to sleep.

I wake up to loud banging sound on my front door. I don't remember ordering anything. Thinking I must have made Kate worried somehow—maybe I'd missed some calls while dozing off—I open my eyes. I'm still not the least bit less exhausted, yet somewhat disoriented. It's still light out, but I have no idea what time it is. I somehow manage to climb out of the depth of my blankets, can't care less that I have nothing on other than a tank top and a pair of underwear, and open the door.

But it's not my sister.

Nope.

Not even close.

"For Christ's sake," I hear the gravelly voice that's been hunting my dreams lately.

I could run and put some clothes on, but for some reason my tired brain decides to play it cool as I step aside—bra-less, pant-less and all—and let the man connected to the voice come in, closing the door behind him.

"Do you normally do house visits to your collaborators?" I ask.

"I was worried about you," he says, sending a hand through his hair, his molten amber-honey eyes darkening as he takes me in, desperately trying to focus on my face. The concerned expression he came in with is quickly taken over by a heated one.

"Nothing to worry about," I say, liking that I at least have some effect on him. "I took a sick day. Just tired."

"You weren't responding to my emails. Or phone calls."

Phone calls. "I don't recall sharing my number with you."

"It's in your email signature."

"I was asleep," I say. The man is not lying. He did email me last night. I saw it. But chose to ignore it. "And I'm going back to sleep now." I gesture toward the door, hinting for him to leave but not quite convinced it's what I want. And from his un-nudged expression, I can tell this little uncertainty does not escape him. There's a tiny tinge in me wanting him to stay. "What?" I ask.

"Can you please go put some damn clothes on?"

"I'm fine like this," I challenge. "You're the one who decided to come here, deal with it. Or leave."

"That would be too easy." There's some hitch to his breath but he perseveres. "You don't let anyone get close to you, do you?"

"Sure I do," I protest, confronted by how this man can so effortlessly read me.

"Name one person at Amarinex who knows a thing about you. Other than your name and job title." He takes a step closer. My heart thumps so loud I'm afraid he might hear it.

"Charlene," I say, although she takes care of everyone, whether they ask for it or not, so maybe I'm not playing fair.

"Not including Charlene," he growls. Yep, he's on to me.

"Steve," I answer, not able to take my gaze off Christian's burning eyes.

"Steve? Your boss?" An incredulous expression stretches across his pretty face.

"Yes, he knows my address." The intensity of our interaction makes my cheeks hot and my stomach flutter. This is what he does to me every time he's around. I have no control over it. And seeing him here, standing in my apartment, exuding massive amounts of testosterone, is making me weak in the knees. I hope it's one of the many pregnancy symptoms, because any other explanation would be much more challenging for me to deal with at this point.

"It's on your HR records, smartass." He releases a slow smile.

"Kate knows everything about me," I say. Although we both know she doesn't work at Amarinex, so I'm not adhering to the rules of his question very well.

"She's your sister." He takes another step closer.

"Still," I stand my ground, inhaling the scent of his cologne.

"Does she know?" he asks.

"About..." I pat my still-flat belly, can't bring myself to put it in words. His eyes drift to my mid-part for a fleeting moment, before he brings them back to my face and shakes his head. "That you're ... sad."

Sad? Am I sad? This comes a bit unexpected.

"So now you're a psychologist too? I'm not sad." My first instinct is to deny, but seeing his insistent expression, I concede. "Just not particularly happy."

"Why not?"

I shrug. "Happiness is in Kate's department. Not mine. Always has been. And besides, I doubt that anybody other than my sister gives two shits about how I feel." And I'll make sure to do a better job hiding it carefully from now on.

"Well, *I* do. And I can tell you were feeling this way before you found out you're pregnant." Obviously, he sees right through me.

"Moods are just the result of our environment. Hostile environment, gloomy environment, annoying people who decide to grace us with their presence," I say. Or a load of crappy tasks with an overnight turnaround. It's a well-known fact. How does he not know that?

"No, they're our *reactions* to our environment based on our own perception, something we have control over."

"Not all of us apparently, Dr. Copeland," I chuckle.

"You've become so proficient at keeping people away that you don't even know how to not do it."

"What are you talking about? Keeping people away is a great skill, I have it on my personal development plan." Now it's my turn to take a step closer. "Why do you care anyway?" I rest my hand on his chest and rise to my tiptoes, trying to look deep into his eyes to retrieve my answer, like he does to me. The effect on my heartbeat though, is unexpected. And having my hand so close to his heart, I think he may be suffering similar consequences.

"I just do," Christian says, before he takes a step back, walks into my kitchen and opens my mostly empty fridge.

"What are you doing?"

"Making you something to eat."

"Okay then, gonna go brush my teeth," I state.

"You might want to put some pants on," he comments as I reappear in the kitchen and pull myself up to sit on the countertop next to him.

"Not really," I tease. Must be the pregnancy hormones getting the best of me.

12

It starts with a fight

Claire

L etting someone into your life is not an easy thing to do. Maybe for some people it's easy, natural, exciting. Not when it involves yours truly, though. These fun adjectives don't come along on my journey if I don't actively and forcibly pack them up in my oversized travel bag and drag them out the door. Okay, maybe I'm exaggerating, I barely even own a travel bag. Oversized or not. My travel is mostly limited to work-related travel, so it's really just a tiny trolley.

But regardless of the simile, it is an incredible effort for me to even consider allowing Christian in. To let him join in on the journey. Or as he has just coined it (while I'm still insisting on staying in my underwear and bra-less T-shirt), let him be my *"someone to run with."* And by *run* I hope he was referring to the esoteric term of life and not literal running. Mostly because I don't run, nor do I engage in any activity that increases your blood flow, or your pulse, or make you break a sweat. With the exception of lovemaking, of course, but I haven't done much of that in the past two years. If Christian was referring to that I'd be all in—another one of the many side-effects of pregnancy, I assume—although I doubt anyone calls that kind of activity *running*. And I also doubt that this is what he's after at this point.

I sit on the countertop right next to him, watching him engage in improvised cooking, due to the unfortunate lack of coherent ingredients in my fridge, speaking softly to me as he goes, but not making any actual moves. None. He has to be the perfect gentleman. Why can't he bring back that bad boy from the mall? How do I make that side of him reappear? And why do I spend my time lately trying to figure out ways to complicate my already complicated life?

I have to admit, though, Christian's cooking skills are superb, making me consider giving up Cheetos as I munch on the early dinner he whipped for us in less than thirty minutes while limited to the meager variety in my kitchen repository. I even catch myself laugh at something he said. I can't even recall what it was, I am so dazed by his presence, so amazed by what a couple of hours in the proximity of this man can do to me. But I'm very well aware that my IQ probably drops a mile a minute when these molten amber eyes gaze straight into mine.

Life is almost sweet again, until my phone rings. My screen indicates "Witch-bitch"—the one and only, making me snap back into reality in a matter of seconds.

"Hello?" I answer, seeing Christian's eyes search mine in my peripheral vision. Harriett Wallington doesn't typically call me after hours. A passive aggressive or purely aggressive email usually suffices when executing her devilish attacks. I can feel my hand nervously shaking as I hold the phone to my ear. It's not fear. It's rage. And it's obvious even to the non-observant eye. I press the little speaker sign and put the phone back on the counter, choosing to let him hear the conversation over noting my tremor. Anger is taking over, I just hope Christian is busy enough not to notice.

"Don't worry, I'm not calling to ask how you're feeling," her annoying voice fills the room. "Because I don't care."

"Wasn't suspecting it for a second," I assure her, feeling Christian's presence nearby, his hand on mine in a supportive squeeze. Of course nothing escapes him.

"Although I do hope you have a good reason for missing our board meeting today."

"What board meeting? I had nothing on my schedule..."

"It was ad-hoc. And that's beside the point. The board doesn't like the idea that your study design targets patients with long-standing diabetes. So let Dr. Copeland know and change it back to a prevention study, like we originally talked about. Prevention in people at high risk for developing Type 1 diabetes. Not already diagnosed patients, and definitely not patients with long-standing disease." She says the last few words slowly, like it might be too complex for me to comprehend.

Christian tenses besides me. I can feel his grip tightening.

"But we've talked about it and the team agreed. Christian and I have all the details down already. And you know the mechanism of action is just not going to work for prevention." My words make sense but my voice is weak, small, lacking conviction. "And there's already one approved drug for prevention, which merely delays the disease by a few months, it's not true prevention."

"Exactly. There's already a path. And we're going to follow it." I hate how Harriett takes my own arguments and twists them to support her side.

"But…" I feel so tired, and all at once—drained. So not in the right head space to protest right now.

"Enough arguing, for once in your life just do what you're told." And that ends the one-sided discussion. Her signature finale before she hangs up the call.

"Well, guess we're back to the drawing board." I let my shoulders slump.

"You're giving up? Just like that?" Christian's hand leaves mine.

"Harriett is a science-killing bitch, we know that already. We'll just have to come up with a different design. We're not married to this one specifically, we have to keep our heads in the game." I try, wincing at my own choice of using the M word in a sentence. But Christian just shakes his head. And not in the pleasant-warm way of his. He looks a bit angry, and mostly—disappointed. "We can come up with something she'll eventually agree on."

"Why didn't you speak up? I thought we'd agreed on our approach. You could have voiced your disagreement."

"There's no use fighting her, I've already learned it the hard way."

"I still think you should have objected," he insists.

"Let me just remind you, Dr. Copeland—while you're a tenured professor at GERI, which means that worst-case scenario you might lose this collaboration with Amarinex, *I* might actually lose my job. I have to choose my battles here, and I'm not going to light an entire fire over an insignificant detail."

"*Insignificant?*" His expression changes at once to some combination of surprised and... hurt? It's as if I personally offended him.

"Jesus, you're taking it way too personally." I'm just making an observation here. "It's drug development, that's what we do. You can't let this disease get to you like that, it's messing up your judgement. We're part of the study design team, we must stay objective." But Christian just shakes his head again, not looking at me. "Why is it so important to you, anyway?" I press, thinking back to the original team presentation he gave at our first meeting with Big Boss Joe. The passion in his tone. The spark in his eyes.

"It just... is," he sighs. I feel like I might have hit a nerve there. "You should fight for what's important to you." Yep, definitely hit a sensitive spot.

"Maybe I should first figure out what it is that's important to me," I say.

"Maybe you should," he scoffs.

And despite knowing he's referring to the study design and Harriett-related businesses, I stop to consider it with regard to my miserable life. How unfortunate is it that I actually think he has a point?

"Well, maybe you're right," I growl at him, choosing to take it as an insult. Still busy kicking the conversation into the personal realm. "And if this," I gesture between us, "is what having *someone to run with* means," I air quote, "then I am withdrawing myself from the race." I don't know what race I'm actually talking about, but how have we gone from warm and friendly to mutually kicking each other in a span of ten minutes? My anger decides to gear up and the words leave my mouth in an auto pilot kind of mode. "So thanks for the offer, but no thank you. I barely know you, and I don't think I can trust you. And from the little bit that I do know, you're either a liar or a coward or both. Either way you're a total ass. Or you have a terrible memory disorder."

"What are you talking about?" He looks puzzled.

"See? You're doing it again," I snap. "You can go now. This conversation is over. If you have anything else to say, you can call Derek. I'm done here."

"Fine," he says, not even trying to argue. So I get myself off the kitchen counter and show him the door. Because I'm so pissed at the world right now, and Harriett, and work plans going down the drain, and failed relationships, and unplanned pregnancies. And although Christian has nothing to do with the puzzle pieces that make up this thing called *my life*, at this moment he is and generally has been in my line of fire. And I'm still mad about that kiss that did nothing to him, while, for the life of me, I can't get it out of my head.

Christian looks at me with fire in those molten amber-honey eyes, already halfway out the door. And even though we're both furiously mad—misdirected fire from my end as it might be—I can't help but think how gorgeous this man is.

13

Thanksgiving dinner

Christian

I don't know what it is about her that messes up my brain so completely. I know I shouldn't have pressed her so hard to voice her objection to Harriett, especially since it's not her fight. She doesn't even know what I'm fighting for. Or *who* I'm fighting for. But it was the words she chose—"*insignificant detail*" that hit a sensitive spot. I should have stopped to tell her about Jake. Share that what she may regard as insignificant, has to do with the most important person in my life. And the life of so many other patients living with Type 1 diabetes. That it's so much more than just a corporate debate or a mere scientific disagreement. That for me it *is* personal.

But I didn't. I closed up instead. Despite my promise to help, to be there for her. To be her person to run with. Why did I even use that analogy? Maybe running sounded less intimidating at that moment in time. An activity that doesn't necessitate talking, especially if you're new to the sport and still work on adjusting your breathing. Although, admittedly, I *am* a runner, and breathing has long stopped being an issue. When I run, that is. Not when I look at this woman. Or exist anywhere within five miles of her.

So of course I wasn't really talking about running as a sport. I was talking about going through life. And sharing moments. Good and bad moments. A much more challenging aspect than physical running. And as Claire made that comment, I suddenly realized this can't be one-sided. But I was too mad; at Harriett's lackluster management of a project that could have had the potential to transform so many lives, Jake's included. At the way she treats Claire. And at myself—for not being able to protect her. The way Harriett so effortlessly—over a goddamn phone call—was able to turn off that spark in Claire's eyes, wipe off that beautiful smile of hers and make her sink further into this bottomless frustration. And mostly let her take it out on me. *A liar or a coward...* I'm still trying to figure out where that came from.

But instead of saying something, I just let it all get to me and did exactly as Claire asked—I left. And so the one step forward we were finally able to take was overshadowed by a giant step back. An entire marathon's worth of running in the opposite direction.

And now it's Thanksgiving night and I'm pretty sure we're not really on speaking terms. Pretty sure she's gone to Derek and asked to reassign someone else to work with me on this project, or better yet, remove me altogether, as Harriett's plan doesn't go hand-in-hand with mine anyway. Not sure why they needed me in the first place if Harriett is on a mission to obliterate every goddamn plan we come up with.

But as I said, it's Thanksgiving night, and I'm expected to put on a smile and a reasonably polished appearance for the sake of Julia and Jake. Find my civilized side and hold a freaking conversation during a blind date masked as a family-friendly dinner. I'm not sure why, in my right mind, I agreed to this matchmaking attempt concocted by my sister and Jake's kindergarten teacher. They've been elusive about the whole thing, but Julia had to reveal some of the details, to make sure I shaved and *"dressed to impress."* Her words. Plus, Jake's teacher, Kate, has been so kind to Jake, and so supportive. Hurting her sister, who I know absolutely nothing about, is the last thing I want to do. But it's bound to happen. I have no interest nor room for romance in my life. Especially now when Claire—unknowingly and unintentionally— has taken control over most of my brain cells. And some other essential organs. And if that's not enough, I have this woman from the mall to thank for taking over the rest of my—used to be—common sense.

Jake, I remind myself. I do it for Jake. And Julia. The two most important people in my life. I repeat it in my head like a mantra as I shave my couple-days-old stubble and as I button up my dress shirt. Did Kate mention her sister's name? Probably not. I'm going to try to make a reasonable, friendly conversation but keep it at that. I keep reminding myself of that as I follow the directions to Kate's place, still repeating it in my head when I ring her doorbell, holding the bowl of mac and cheese my sister talked me into making, and a bottle of pinot noir.

The door flies open and Kate appears. "Christian, I'm so glad you could make it." She gives me a happy, carefree smile that immediately puts me at ease. This is, hands down, one of the most important skills a good kindergarten teacher could have, just saying.

"Uncle Christian!" Jake's voice warms up my thoughts as he quickly appears. Thankfully Kate is quick enough to take the wine and food off my hands before Jake leaps into me. I feel my heart swell as I squeeze him close. I love this kid so much.

"Made your favorite dish, kiddo," I tell him.

"Ms. Kate's sister is here!" he says excitedly, not giving the food the time of day. "She's really nice, you have to meet her!" He jumps off my arms and pulls me out of the kitchen and into the living room. Even my own nephew is in on this matchmaking plan.

I try to shove my unfortunate lack of emotional availability at the moment and pretend to play along.

And I would have kept at this family-friendly front for the rest of the night. Easy. If it weren't for her. The sister, standing with her back to me. I take in the long chestnut hair, her soft curves. The air about her that steals my breath away as she spins toward us. Eyes I could drown in. The smile that slowly turns into a puzzled expression when her mind registers it's me, while my heart misses a beat. Multiple beats. It might have stopped altogether. We've seen each other almost every day in the past few weeks, yet this thing she does to me only keeps getting stronger.

"You're everywhere," she mutters under her breath, in a way that only the two of us can hear. She's obviously still mad, and I'm pretty sure I'm the last person she wants to spend a family meal with. I should be frustrated as well, but I find it impossible. "And now you're in my Thanksgiving too," she adds.

"Sorry," I say. Just because she's Kate's sister and the last thing I want to do is mess up the positive connection with my nephew's kindergarten teacher. But that's really the only thing I'm sorry about.

"Claire," she introduces herself in her outside voice. Then her eyes narrow and her voice lowers, "in case you have trouble recognizing people out of their usual context." And as I try to process what she means, Kate and Julia walk over to us and Claire's fiery expression softens.

"This is my brother, Christian," Julia says proudly, and I try to put everything aside, tamp down the thrashing of my delusional, confused heart, and slap on a smile for my sister's sake.

"Julia and I have been secretly conspiring to match you guys up for ages!" Kate reveals, then fixes Claire with a sidelong stare. "But looks like you two already know each other?" She definitely knows her sister well.

"We do," Claire speaks without letting her eyes leave mine, it's like a warning. "We work together." Her tone is sweet for the unsuspected observer.

"That's an insane coincidence," Kate says and I can see from the look in Claire's eyes—she's not happy about it, to say the least.

Claire

Argh... I want to strangle this handsome, frustrating man. But that doesn't sound like a very family-friendly thing to do. Definitely not when his nephew is around.

Since that kiss at the mall, he seems to be everywhere. At my workplace. In my house. At my sister's for Thanksgiving dinner. And if that's not enough—he's constantly in my head. It must be the pregnancy hormones. I used to wake up to anxiety. And stress. Just thinking about the day ahead, about work, about Harriett. Not that I miss this churning sensation in the pit of my stomach by any means, but now the only thing I think about when I close my eyes at night, or open them again in the morning, is Christian fucking Copeland. About peeling his clothes off and jumping his bones. Running my hands across his bare chest, along the contours and ridges of his ab muscles, those muscles I crushed into at the mall. I have this constant buzz building up in my body. For this man I can't stand. The man who kissed me breathless and won't even give me the time of day.

And of course our sisters sat us next to each other, close enough for his cologne to wrap itself around me, for his body heat to draw me in. For his thigh to accidentally rub into mine. By the look on his face I know he didn't mean to, but for the life of me I can't move mine away. I also need to consciously remind my hand that it can't follow. That I'm still mad. And that this dinner has to be kept at a kid-friendly level, as his nephew keeps looking at us with heart eyes.

"Do you like working with my uncle?" he asks me. He's a smart boy, I can tell.

"I do," I say. Although 'like' might not be my first word of choice. I can feel Christian's eyes flicker in my direction, studying me.

"He likes you too," Jake happily supplies. He has this one dimple that appears when he smiles, just like Christian's.

"Oh, I do?" Christian's gravelly voice sounds beside me and I have to turn my head in his direction, only to see this heartwarming smile appear on his face as he looks at his nephew.

"Yes, you do, I can tell," Jake giggles but tries to keep a serious face. This wordless exchange between them makes my earlier anger and frustration melt away. Sometimes it's the things not said that are so much more powerful than words.

And Christian has to do this adorable thing; in one smooth motion he gets up and scoops the little kid in his arms, then lets Jake wrestle him to the ground, faking a defeat as Jake announces himself as the strongest person in the room. They're both laughing out loud. The wrestling match quickly turns into a tickling battle while Julia is trying to remind them that we're about to have dinner. It's probably the first time I hear such a carefree burst of laughter coming out of Christian. And I have to mentally slap myself for switching from being mad at this man to completely swooning in a span of five minutes. The pregnancy hormones must be messing with my head. Although the swooning part must have been there all along.

The boys are back at the table and Jake pulls out a beeper-looking device from his pocket, gently punching some buttons on the screen. I can see it's connected to some kind of plastic tubing extending from under his shirt.

"How many?" he asks Christian.

"Thirty is my best guess," Christian answers simply.

The kid nods in approval and turns his gaze to my sister. "Forty-five?" Kate gives out her guess in a game I'm still not familiar with.

Then it's my turn, I assume, because Jake's eyes flicker to mine. "Do you want to guess?" he asks playfully.

"Sure," I feel the corners of my mouth curve up to a big smile, because this boy's charm is irresistible. "Just give a number?"

"We're trying to guess the carb count for the mac and cheese on his plate," Julia explains. I'm a little puzzled as to our rationale but I go with it.

"Fifty?" I try, taking a quick scan of his kid-sized plate and portion. I don't know how much five- or six-year-olds are supposed to eat, and I'm more used to thinking in calories than evaluating food based on its carbohydrate content. A whole new aspect.

Jake nods in approval. "Mom?" He turns his head to Julia. "Who was the closest?"

"Your uncle." She smiles, but there's a sad shade to her tone as she speaks. As if this isn't just a fun guessing game. Which I'm beginning to realize isn't.

"I had an unfair advantage," Christian gives him a wink. "I made the mac and cheese."

Jake smiles back, then turns to his little device. "It's my insulin pump," he explains patiently as his big eyes look up to meet mine. "Want to see?"

"Of course," I say, although it feels like a total invasion of his privacy. I give Christian a quick look, seeking some sort of approval, which he returns with a reassuring smile. Making this whole quarrel between us seem so immature and stupid now. I get up and walk over to the little boy's side of the table. He turns the screen of his insulin pump to face me, showing me how he sets the amount—0.75 units, Jesus Christ, are kids this young supposed to know how to use decimals?— and gives himself a dose of insulin. All by himself. A five-year-old kid. Realization slowly sinks in as the shoe finally drops. Jake has Type 1 diabetes.

Christian

"I'm so sorry," Claire says when the two of us are alone, out for some fresh air on her sister's porch. Her words are almost muted, trying to keep the conversation to ourselves, but fly out of her mouth so quickly. "I'm sorry I gave you a hard time for taking things so personally," she says and I can tell she means it by her blushed cheeks and the strain in her voice. "I didn't know Jake has Type 1 diabetes. That's why it's personal for you. Why didn't you say anything? This changes everything."

I'm not sure what she means by *changes everything.* But I feel relieved to have this one detail out in the open, floating in the air between us. As if sharing that piece of information about this little guy who means so much to me, unloads some of the pain and the worrying. And there's something else. The look in Claire's eyes. I was expecting pity, which is my usual rationale for keeping stuff to myself. But it's nothing like that, not even close, as she takes a step closer, walking straight through my walls, and lets her palm rest on my chest. She sees me.

14

Fine tuning perceptions

Claire

I did not expect Thanksgiving dinner to go this way. After several hours of food, family and fun conversation, dish washing, game watching on TV, board games playing with Jake and Christian—I had no idea Apples to Apples and Monopoly could make me laugh so hard—I feel like a new person. Or at least in much better spirits than how I came in, which in itself is an achievement. Christian, it turns out, is the dream uncle any kid could wish for. But somehow this doesn't surprise me. It fits perfectly with the image of him that my mind has been sketching. The only piece that seems to be out of place, at least in my head, is—

"So when did your brother start suffering from short-term memory loss?" I ask Julia when the boys are out of earshot, as casually as my tone will let me, because these things might benefit from early intervention.

"Christian?" Julia laughs. "He has perfect memory. He remembers things I've forgotten long ago." We're standing in Kate's kitchen, washing and drying dishes.

I glance over to the living room, where Christian and Jake are turning Kate's couch into a fort. "Yes, long-term memory. But does he have issues with his short-term memory?"

Julia gives me a bemused look, shaking her head mischievously. "Not that I'm aware..."

"Hmmm. So it's not him. It *is* me," I mumble. I was planning to say this last line in my head, but by the way both sisters—mine and Christian's look at me right now, I realize it wasn't just an internal thought.

Julia puts down the plate she was holding and dries her hands with a towel. "I'm sensing you two have some past? Unfinished business?"

"Not really, just..." I stumble on my words. And there's a pang of disappointment there too. Because it's not memory loss. Just indifference. My throat burns for some reason and I try to cough it away.

"What did my brother do?" Julia asks. Her expression wanders between intrigued and concerned.

"No, I... shouldn't be making a big deal, really, it's a stupid thing." My voice feels small, and the words are out before I can help it. It's an abbreviated, steamy—details-reduced—version. And now it's out in the open, and I try to lighten the weight by throwing a few smiles in, not showing how much this really gets to me. But turns out my execution has a more serious impact than vouched for, judging by the looks on their faces.

"Christian is *him*!" My sister is excited about this new revelation, especially the prospect of being able to put a face to the man I haven't really been able to shut up about. Admittedly, not all details were shared in a positive way, but she has years of practice reading between my lines.

"At first I wasn't sure it was the same guy from the... mall, because he wasn't wearing his glasses, but—"

"Wait," Julia stops me in my tracks, hand propped up dramatically. "*Wasn't* wearing his glasses?" She emphasizes the *wasn't* as if this tiny little detail clears her brother of all douchebag-related accusations.

"Shouldn't contact lenses work just as well?" I ask, because, believe me, there's not a single person in this kitchen that would love to get to the root cause here more than me.

"He doesn't wear contact lenses. And he's half-blind without his glasses," she chuckles, a big understanding smile spreading across her face. "He's definitely not that kind of guy."

"Who?" We all turn our heads abruptly to see Christian, now leaning on the door frame, waiting to be brought up to speed on our conversation. His hair is tousled now from another wrestling match with Jake and some pillow fighting, his tie undone, hanging from both sides of his collared shirt. I hate to admit it, but my heart is skipping some beats over him. Again.

"Girl talk," I say, hoping we drop the subject. I can feel my cheeks heating up.

"You!" Julia throws the dish towel at him, hitting his chest with a thud. She has a pretty powerful arm. "I expected more of you!"

"Ouch! What did I do?" Christian looks surprised. A bit confronted even. Well good, maybe that will help refresh his memory.

Julia glances toward the living room, making sure her son is deep into TV watching before saying: "Kiss a girl and pretend it never happened?!" Her tone is teasing, but there's some big sister vibes in her posture, hands on hips, scolding eyes. "And since when do you walk around without your glasses? Please tell me you don't attempt driving like that."

Christian steels, hyper-focused on me like no one has ever before. There's a ghost of recognition that begins to cross his face. Or is it realization? Then very slowly, he takes off his glasses. His molten-amber honey eyes look at me with such intensity and... awe. As if he's spent a lifetime searching for me. "It *is* you," he mumbles huskily, half to himself.

Everything else from this moment on is a blur. There may have been some discussion, some apology from Christian, and lots of joking and knowing looks from Julia and Kate. But all I can really feel is the intense eye contact. The sound of his voice. His presence around me. As if that one little piece of information closed some sort of an electrical circuit. And my heart beating takes on a whole new intensity scale. And I give up trying to make it calm down.

Christian offers to walk me home, and we find ourselves taking the long way, wandering the streets, enjoying a rare warm and breezy fall night. The built-up anger and frustration I'd been nurturing have been completely replaced with understanding, which gives way for a whole slew of other sensations, and the feeling is overwhelming. Our hands gravitate together, fingers entwined, as we walk side-by-side. The cool air helps get my breathing back in order. It's the middle of the night at this point, but we can't break the spell—sleep is overrated. So instead, we stroll idly, chatting the night away. I tell him about my childhood; laughs and hot chocolate, movie nights with Mom and Kate, the absence of a father figure that I never actually felt I was missing. Well, except for maybe when I watched other kids get picked up by their dads or thrown over their shoulders. Christian tells me about his childhood and growing up with a single mom—something we apparently have in common—but his story gets sucked into a darker turn, taking on too many responsibilities at a young age when his mom was dealing with a mental health condition, caring for her, sharing the burden with Julia, his sister. "The fear of dying can kill a person so many times before their actual death," he says wistfully. I squeeze his hand, waiting for him to continue, but he fast-forwards to the present, trying to lighten up the mood. And I'm beginning to realize there is so much more to this man than I'd thought, and I'd love to get lost finding out everything about him.

At some point, we land at my doorstep. The sky is starting to show little streaks of morning, dark giving out to small speckles of light. Now that the dark clouds of anger and disappointment are gone, I'm amazed by the growing feeling inside me. I am well-aware the raging pregnancy hormones may be contributing to it, but I just can't help myself as I let my head lean into this man's chest, let his arms wrap around me. His warmth is comforting, melting away layers of ice from my frozen, tucked-away feelings. My muscles relax instantly in his embrace. It's something about him, I realize, recalling how he pulled me into his chest on the floor inside the restroom stall at work, chasing away my demons. It feels so much nicer, though, without that throw-up aftertaste and the burn in my throat.

"I feel so tired," I muffle into his chest muscles as a big yawn escapes me. I don't want this night to end, afraid this magic will be gone tomorrow, but exhaustion takes over. Must be one of the secret joys of pregnancy, right beside the regular urge to down a bag of Cheetos and morning sickness.

"Let's get you to bed," Christian says softly, as if tucking me in and telling me a bedtime story are on his list of responsibilities. He takes the keys off my hand, unlocks my apartment door and then I'm in his arms. Chivalry, is where my brain goes, as he effortlessly carries me to my bedroom, lays me gently in my bed and helps me out of my shoes. This would have been such a fine romantic moment if it wasn't for my bladder, reminding me there's one more stop I have to make before finally resting my eyes.

A few more minutes and a few less clothing items and I'm snuggled in my bed, letting Christian smooth the hair off my forehead and spread another blanket over me.

"Get some rest, okay?" Christian's lips press lightly onto my temple, his hand closing softly around mine. He's about to let go but I hold on, not ready to say good night, or good morning, or whatever time it is, I've lost track. I just can't bring myself to let him go.

"Can you stay?" I ask, yawning again. What am I saying? Needy is not my modus operandi, yet those words were mine. And the intention behind them... also mine.

"What?" He does a double take. I honestly can't blame him. We weren't even on proper speaking terms up until a few hours ago.

"Just take these off." I pull at his pants, yawning again. "I need to cuddle." I swear I've lost control over my own voice. Okay yes, and my own thoughts. But I'm a grown person, so I brace myself to accept that I will eventually have to let go of his hand, and his pants.

To my surprise, he obliges. My eyes are half-closed, my vision already blurring with impending sleep. But I hear some shuffling in the background and can feel the blankets move, and the mattress dips behind me. I sense his body heat as he lays close, but not close enough to touch me. My body—from a half floating-into-sleep vantage point—deems the distance unacceptable, so I scoot back until my shoulders fit themselves snugly and perfectly against Christian's warm chest. Funny, I never thought spooning was actually a worthwhile thing. Then I pull his free arm over me, letting his fingers spread around my still-flat belly. And this is where I find my inner peace. Christian's breath hitches and he steels, growing hard behind me. I would love to do something about it, I think to myself, as the sweetest slumber gets the better of me.

15

Holidays

Christian

"Hmm..." Claire says in a sleepy voice as she stretches gently beside me and goes back to the same position we both woke up in. "So what's your backstory?" Her hand and head are resting on my chest, her legs tightly tangled with mine. She escaped from beneath me to run to the bathroom as I was debating whether I should get up and put on some clothes, but now she's back and I can't find a single good reason to move away.

"Backstory?" I try to play it cool, when really all I'm able to think about is the flowery scent of her hair and the warmth of her body gently pressed to mine. And that kiss. That one kiss at the mall. I'd do anything to taste her lips again. I've been up almost all night, spooning her like she asked, trying to calm down the lust as she snuggled sweetly into me. Reminding myself she's pregnant, and asleep, every time her body shifted slowly against mine, feeling like a teenager again. Gosh, what this woman does to me is unbelievable.

"Yes, your backstory." She shakes me out of my reverie. "Why are you single?"

Talk about being direct. "I guess I was looking for my one," I admit, and then kick myself mentally as I realize I've just used the past tense. Because even though we haven't known each other long enough for it to be a reasonable thought, my stupid mind seems to think I've actually found her. Twice. On the same day. And now I just need to accept it, and make her realize it too.

"How about you?" I ask, despite knowing about her recent breakup which left her... pregnant.

"Same," she says simply, taking me by surprise. "Someone to excite me. Ryan and I, it wasn't... that." She doesn't elaborate. Her body shifts a tad closer if that's even possible. Her hand travels down my abs. "No matter what," she says quietly, "I never felt like I excited him. Or he, me. Physically or emotionally. I guess these things probably go together." Her fingers stop at the waistband of my boxers. Last night she asked me to take off my clothes and snuggle close to her. I obliged, but knowing she was in nothing but her underwear and a tiny T-shirt—her go-to outfit at home, it appears—I intended to keep my pants on, not trusting myself enough. But she insisted I take them off. And now she's upping the challenge.

"I suggest you don't move any farther, because unlike your ex, I'm way too excited right now." And pretty much every time I so much as think of her.

"Oh," she says, surprised. Why is she surprised? Her eyes travel to my boxers and her cheeks redden. Guess she was too passed out last night to feel my torture.

"Me too," she admits openly. Then she takes my hand and rests it on her heart as proof. It's pounding almost as wildly as mine. "I always wondered how sex feels," she muses.

"Well, you should know, seeing as you're already pregnant," I chuckle.

"Not that kind of sex," she sighs. "That was an attempt to fix things between Ryan and me. Like a one last chance at seeing if we could have wild sex after not sleeping with each other for like a year."

"A year? Jesus." I could barely last this one night next to her. A whole year? I would die.

"Yes. And was it wild, you ask?"

"No, I don't want to hear about wild sex with your ex." A tinge of jealousy takes over me and I don't like it.

"Well, you're in luck, because wild is the last word I would use to describe it. It was cold and technical. Mechanical."

"Sounds like a carpentry workshop," I say. And I can't help but feel a bit angry that this ex of hers was not capable of loving her like she deserves.

"Oh, don't hate on carpentry. Carpentry workshops are fun and exciting. Nothing like that." She laughs, melting my heart away. And although I've had my fair share of wild sex in my life, I have a feeling that taking Claire would be a whole new level of wild. Redefined. But before I have a chance to dismantle this idea, she stretches one leg over my hip. Her core now presses tightly against a painfully hard part of me, and she rocks herself gently, to my pure torture.

"Hmmm," she releases a soft moan, content with the result of her doing. "I feel like you're more turned on right now than Ryan ever was with me." She sounds pleased. "And seriously," she teases, "I'm more turned on right now than I ever was with him, and you haven't even touched me."

I appreciate that she shares every bit of detail that crosses her mind with me, not even bothering to stop between her sentences. Less so when her ex is involved, though. And although I should probably remind myself that we're supposed to be able to work together, professionally, I'm also more turned on than *I* have ever been. So the idea of making her forget all about her ex seems much more appealing at the moment. "I bet I can make you come without even taking your clothes off," I helpfully pitch in.

"Aren't you full of yourself?" she chuckles.

"Aren't you doubtful."

"Just a healthy degree of skepticism, until proven otherwise," she challenges me. And to make her point she pulls off her T-shirt, revealing her full breasts. It's such a bad idea but I let my hand slide up her ribcage and over her right nipple, gently pinching it with my fingers. She squirms and rubs her warm core against me. I can feel how wet she is even through the fabric of her underwear. And mine. Damn. I lower my head, taking her nipple into my mouth. She gasps, then smiles at me. We're laying on our sides, buried in each other, her leg still wrapped around me. I smooth my palm over her soft skin and pull her knee higher, then let my hand trail down her thigh, angling her to just the right amount of pressure in all the right places. My fingers trace her cheeky underwear, resisting the urge to take it off, teasing her through the thin fabric. My mouth finds her nipple again and she moans softly, writhing against me.

Her breathing quickens as she starts picking up speed. "Oh my gosh, Christian, yes!" I didn't take her for the vocal type. Another turn-on. The long-lost teenager in me is trying to break out. I know I promised to make her come without taking her clothes off but I'm hanging on by a thread. "Holly... shit," she can barely catch her breath. "I'm gonna—" She brings a hand to her mouth, surprised, trying to muffle her voice, but I move it away.

"I want to hear you," I assure her, upping the friction.

A loud moan escapes her as she gives in, shuddering in my arms over and over again. I'm so turned on by the way her body reacts to mine.

"That—" she says on a breathless note, stopping for air. Her voice is coarse and sexy, a content smile crossing her face. "That must be a world record, Christian Copeland, making a girl come in under two minutes." There's a hint of embarrassment in her gaze before her eyes turn dark again. "Now I'm intrigued." Her hand travels back to the waistband of my boxers.

"Let me take you out to dinner first," I say painfully. And I mean *painfully* because I don't think I've ever wanted anyone as much as I want this woman right now. But she is way too important for me to fuck this up over a one-night stand. Or morning.

"Dinner?" She glances at the alarm clock on her nightstand. "There are so many hours until dinner. Plus, I can't go out to dinner with you. We're supposed to be working—"

"We are," I agree. "And you're right, it's unprofessional," I deadpan, but am also studying her reaction carefully, contemplating an apology for crossing the line, despite being well-aware that two are playing this game here.

"I mean, we're supposed to be working on our proposal to Harriett, it's due tomorrow," she reminds me, not taking the dinner idea off the table but not quite taking it seriously either. "And *it is* unprofessional," she teases, "but no one has to know." I love the smug smile on her face as she whispers the last few words.

"Okay then," I settle it and pull us both off the bed. It's incredibly inhumane torture to stop at this point, but I want to make sure I do this right. "Now let me make you some breakfast, Dr. Bellingham."

"This sounds like a good idea, Dr. Copeland."

16

Avoiding him much

Claire

"You," Christian says when I enter the large conference room at Amarinex headquarters.

"Me," I admit, not meeting his eyes, guilt creeping up my spine as the memories of the feel of him start trickling down. It's been a few days since Thanksgiving, the night we shared, and the morning after, when I got my fix without even shedding my underwear. Christian certainly lived up to his word, but broke the spell for a homemade breakfast he insisted on cooking for me. We spent the rest of the day working on the slide deck for Harriett, then he went home, still awaiting my response about that dinner.

Well, it's been a few days since, and he's still waiting. Why? Because now that I can't stop thinking about our all-night conversation, about sleeping in his arms, about wanting him so SO badly then, and now, and anytime in between. I feel like a liar. I know that hiding the truth and lying are not exactly the same thing. But I should probably tell him that I'm a little out of my depth here. That those moments we shared, that were really only meant to satisfy my curiosity, don't even begin to scratch the surface. A whole sea of curiosity that now threatens to drown me.

And now I'm terrified. Scared of losing control. And I'm not worried about the physical aspect of it—that was a VERY welcome loss of control. I'd do that again, that's for sure. And again. It's these feelings I'm worried about. The butterflies. The pattering in my chest. The way my heart squeezes when I recall how sweet Christian is with Jake. How he so naturally and selfishlessly took care of me. I'm scared of how much I want him around me. All the time. The nagging, needy feeling, like I could depend on him. I'd been with Ryan for two whole years and never felt any of it even once. I'm an independent person, so where is all this coming from? And then there's the professional side of things—I'd been assigned to work closely with Dr. Christian Copeland to avoid the potential conflict of interest of him working with his best buddy Derek. And instead of being the professional I'm supposed to be, I jump his bones. Some professional I am.

Hence why I haven't returned his phone calls. Or opened his texts. Which is why he's giving me a bit of a pissed look at the moment. Is it weird that I find his scolding expression sexy?

"Do you make a habit out of luring innocent unsuspecting guys home then never calling them back?" he deadpans, but there's some ruefulness in his voice. I can see why he's not crazy about the way I'm handling it.

"I don't know..." I go for a counterattack. "As far as I could tell, you had a very active part in it too," my female organs jolt happily as I conjure the vivid image of him in my bed, "and there was no innocence involved."

"I have no regrets," he supplies.

"Me neither," I say, despite myself.

"Yet you're avoiding me."

"I am," I admit. "Guilty as charged." I'm at a loss for words. I know ignoring him wasn't one of my brightest ideas. Neither was getting him in my bed, getting half-naked and rocking against him with the hope of a wild one-night stand (or one-morning). I acted on my impulses while trying to get him out of my system, potential consequences thrown aside. But now that he's right in front of me again, I can't believe I thought I'd be able to stay away from this man. "Despite what you might think, there isn't some master plan here. I'm just scared." I must have drunk some truth serum this morning with my water.

"Of Harriett?" Christian's head tilts in understanding. He thinks I'm worried about losing my job. It's up there on the list, but there are much bigger concerns topping it.

"No. Of my own... feelings." I'm a simple gal, what can I say. I tried to go for elusive but I just don't possess that kind of talent. His surprised face speaks volumes, and I feel compelled to explain this sudden honesty. "If I need to lie to everyone else about us, I should at least tell *you* the truth."

His molten amber eyes darken in response. "This makes the two of us," he says, his voice a raspy whisper now that the team is rounding the corner, dress pants and shoes already visible through the bottom of the decorated glass wall. I open the slide deck we've worked on and click the button to share it on the large conference-sized screen, quite nervous that the team is going to kill our idea. My eyes turn to Christian and he gives me a *"you've got this"* nod and a wink that melts away all traces of insecurity. And I know he has my back. That no matter what—we're running this marathon together.

But like I've said before, I'm no runner. And despite Christian's heroic attempt to match my pace, Harriett Wallington has this tendency of making me leave her meetings deflated. I go in as a reasonable person with a reasonable presence and I come out as an extremely diminished, insignificant, air-less blob. She just has that effect on me. It's always a seemingly positive phrase, coupled with a *"but"* and a very elaborate reason as to why the first supposedly positive phrase is really meaningless, overshadowed by what comes after that *"but."* And even if her words and the tone of her voice didn't really make me seem small around other people in the meeting—because they already know me and I'm well-prepared with a response—it still makes me feel this way. I'm not sure where her poison comes from. I mean, people get divorced, and other than having worked for her ex, I absolutely had nothing to do with it. Especially since she's the one who cheated on *him*. And it's not like I'm competing for her role either, or trying in any way to steal her thunder. I'm really just trying to do my job. Get these patients the best potential chance at a possible cure.

A good clinical trial design can prove whether a drug works or not. But a poorly designed clinical trial could kill even the best drug. With Harriett, I'm not sure how it's going to be. But now that I know about little Jake and his life with Type 1 diabetes, I'm even more motivated to fight.

Christian and I were very well prepared. We had answers to every single question, we had a plan for every potential complication. We even got Big Boss Joe impressed. Until Dr. Harriett-evil-Wallington, the science-killing witch came in and had to flip this entire thing upside down. Bring out the big gray clouds and start raining on our parade.

"Welcome to my life at Amarinex for the past ten months and twenty-one days," I tell Christian when we're finally out of the butchery. Which is how long it's been since Harriet-fucking-Wallington joined the company. Everything before her seems like rainbows and unicorns.

"Sounds like you're actually counting," he says, holding his office door for me.

"Oh, trust me, I am."

There's a ninety-five-percent chance our plan is about to get killed, but this time we're in the fight together. And so at least Big Boss Joe was not ready to let our design go. Not just yet. He wants two additional alternative solutions or mitigations to some of the potential *"holes"* that Harriett thinks she found, by next week. Come up with something that will put him, and mostly Harriett, at ease.

"How about that dinner?" Christian asks, handing me a bottle of water as I position myself in one of the chairs in his temporary office.

"I can't even keep my breakfast down, let's not talk about dinner right now," I digress. Because thinking about our project and study design, and even the evil Harriett, is so much safer than encouraging my swooned heart. "Now get to work," I command.

"Whatever you say Dr. Bellingham," he chuckles. I try to push aside the lust-filled memories of Thanksgiving night and the morning after. The only half-explored wants and needs. And now that I know Christian better, there are so many more moments I need to push aside.

17

Appointments

Claire

"Mom, I think I'm following your footsteps," I say into the FaceTime call. My mom looks sun-kissed and gleaming, and content. I wouldn't usually have this type of conversation at the office, but phone calls with my mom are rare these days and I need to make the most of them, so I get up and enter one of the empty huddle rooms, closing the glass door behind me.

"How so?" My mom tilts her head to the side with an intrigued look. It doesn't take a genius to notice how different we are from each other. She's a brave, strong-willed woman, who stands up for herself and fights for what she wants. And now that Kate and I are grown-ups and can fend for ourselves, she's finally living the dream. I mean—her specific dream. Mountain climbing and extreme trekking in South America. I've lost track of where exactly. Kate and I get postcards once in a while—Mom likes physical mail. We do sometimes get emailed photos she takes with her phone, but that's only when she gets to places that have cell phone reception and an outlet for charging. I think it's probably been a month since we've last spoken, and as her smile spreads wider I realize how much I've missed her.

"I'm pregnant, Mom." I just drop the bomb. My mom doesn't need prep talk before cutting to the chase. She'd much appreciate a bucket of ice over slowly adjusting to the waters. It's one of the many things I love so much about her.

"Congratulations baby!" she says but I can see she's laser-focused on my expression through the screen, trying to read between my lines. Moms can do that sort of stuff. Even through time and distance and FaceTime. "Is it Ryan's?" she asks with much-diminished enthusiasm. She never liked him. Said he was "*turning my fire off.*" I don't really know what fire she saw in me to begin with, but maybe that's a mom thing too.

"Yes." Unfortunately.

"Well, I hate to break it to you, honey, but those are not really my footsteps. You know who the sperm owner is, you're in a relationship. Although the latter is a different discussion to be having..." Then she quiets down, deciding that maybe trashing Ryan's character right now might not be helpful. But she's right, I know who my unborn baby's father is. And technically this baby was conceived while we were still in a relationship. Already two things more than I can say about the man who's responsible for half of my DNA. Maybe one day I'll take one of these DNA ancestry tests and try to find out, but as of right now the only thing my mom remembers from a careless, fun night on an overseas vacation is that he was very handsome and her best one-night stand. She left in the morning, before he had a chance to wake up and pull her back to bed. She wasn't looking for a serious relationship, not knowing she'd find out a few weeks later that this one unforgettable night had left her with a keepsake. Pregnant. With me. And no chance for the guy to choose whether he wanted to be in my life or not. Because she hadn't even asked for his phone number. Or where he was from. Or his last name.

Now Kate's dad's story is a little different. That guy was meant to stick around. But not every guy, unfortunately, is capable of reasonably raising or liking a child who's not their own. And so it was either him or little one-year-old me. I guess I wasn't much of a picnic, but thankfully, to my mom, the choice was clear—and so as the story goes—he got kicked out, right there and then, a week before Kate was born. We haven't heard from him since. Kate knows all the nitty-gritty details because my mom doesn't know how to tell half-truths, or idealize memories, or beautify cold, sad facts. Kind of like me, come to think of it. Maybe there is some similarity in our stories after all. And at least from the outside, Kate never gave it a second thought, just deleted him completely. Never once wondered—out loud—what it could have been like to grow up with a dad. That's how my sister is, you better not mess with the people she loves. But I do wonder sometimes.

"Claire-bear, you're awfully quiet in there, are you okay?" My mom jolts me out of my brain fog.

"So, Ryan and I are not really in a relationship. Not anymore." I pull myself back to the *now*, which is not much better than the *then*. "He broke up with me. Before I knew about the pregnancy."

"And you're sure the baby is his?"

"Mom!"

"Just asking. Wishful thinking."

"Yes, Mom, unfortunately I *am* sure."

"Does he know?" she asks cautiously. Easily sliding herself into my thoughts. Would she have said anything to the man that fathered me had she had the opportunity?

I shake my head. "And I'm not sure I want him to know. I don't want him to think I want something from him." Because I don't. I don't need him. And I sure as hell don't want him to come up with some crazy-ass idea of trying to get back together out of pity. He is certainly capable of proposing something like that.

"I understand you completely, I would feel exactly the same," she says, even though I only voiced half of that out loud. The rest was in my head. "Do you want to keep the baby?"

Do I?

I haven't really given it a serious thought yet. More so I've just been trying to avoid dealing with this decision. But as I mull it over, I say, "Yes. I can do this."

"You can certainly do this," my mom proudly agrees. "You're a strong, independent woman," she says, and I wish that much were true. "But that's not what I was asking. Do you want to?"

"I'm not sure I like kids," I say. I really don't. This part of the family genetics belongs with Kate. Could be the paternal difference, although her dad didn't leave much impression there.

"Oh honey," Mom chuckles. "Don't worry about that part. I never liked kids until I had my own."

"So becoming a mom made you like children?" I ask hopefully. And as I say it, an image of Jake summons itself. I've only spent a few hours with that kid, and I already like him.

"No. I still didn't like other children. Only you and Kate," she chuckles.

"Okay, that's something I can work with, I guess." I suck in a breath. "Mom, when are you coming home?" I can't help myself as nostalgic thoughts wash over me.

"How far in are you?" she asks.

"Hmmm." I try to count back. "About eight weeks maybe?" Do you count from conception or your last period? I probably need to get myself one of those pregnancy books. Oh gosh.

"So around July?"

"What?" I'm losing track of the conversation.

"The baby. About seven? Eight more months? A summer baby!" my mom says helpfully. "Wouldn't miss it!" she promises. There's some noise in the background and I see her turn hear head with a smile. "I'll join you guys soon," she says to her fellow travelers, pointing the camera to them while they're all waving enthusiastically at me. "Now I'll let you go back to work honey," she tells me, "but do text if you need anything."

"Kay. Love you Mom!" I say as reality slams into my face all at once and anxiety starts to build up.

I'm going to be a mom.

Me.

A MOM.

Do I even want to be a mom?

And as if that's not enough, an alarm pops up on my phone. OB-GYN appointment.

Today.

And of course I knew that, but somehow managed to shove it aside and forget.

I'm so not ready for this.

My stomach is churning, my vision blurring, my last eaten meal, though wasn't much, is threatening to come back up. I kick off my heels under my desk—I should really start wearing something more comfortable to work given how often I find myself needing to run lately—and rush to the nearest bathroom. Which happens to be right around the corner from Christian's temporary office. But there's no time to worry about that right now as I get into a stall and say goodbye to a perfectly good, nutritious lunch.

I lean back into the wall, sinking to the floor, trying to catch my breath but my body refuses to calm down.

I hear the door swing open. "You okay?" Christian's voice follows. It's phrased as a question, but he somehow knows the answer. Like this sixth sense he has for me. And then he's in my stall. "Let's get you some fresh air," he says, pulling me up with one hand. His other has my heels dangling from two fingers, and my jacket. "I figured you'd need these." He hands them to me.

"Thanks," I mutter, noticing the jitter in my hands.

Oh no...

I know where this is headed.

"Talk to me," Christian pleads once he's able to get me outside, away from the office environment and into the little park where Kate and I have our little weekly lunches together. He ushers me onto a bench where we're now seated, side by side. The cold breeze does nothing to calm down my nerves.

"Believe me, you don't want to know," I manage, trying to get some fresh air into my lungs, but my breath is so shaky I regret even trying.

"Try me," he says, molten amber eyes staring straight into my soul. Whether I put it in words or not, he already knows.

"It starts with a thought," I let out. "And a little voice in my head warns me that I might not want to go there, but I can't really help it or stop it. And before I know it, my mind is reeling, my heartbeat speeds up like I'm running a marathon I never trained for, and my hands start shaking." His eyes flicker for a moment to my hands before he takes them in his. "Then everything starts spinning out of control and I don't even know where it started or where I'm going with it. My rationale is left at the starting point of a crazy race that has no finish line. Or maybe it does, but I'm certainly not running in the right direction."

I stop for a shallow breath, trying to remind myself that I'm not actually experiencing it now, just retelling my deepest, most guarded childhood secret to no other than Christian. The—no longer insufferable— very handsome guy who somehow became my only source of fresh air lately. I expect his expression to take on critical, judgmental features. Like any reasonable person would get before letting you know that you've officially lost it. Or worse—rush you to the nearest mental health facility, leave you at the entrance and frantically drive away.

I squint my eyes tight, because I don't really want to see it. Or even know he thinks it. And I'm about to take it all back, say I was kind of joking, but before I have a chance to open my mouth, I sense his body heat closing in and his hands around me in the most comforting, warm hug that has ever existed, at least in *my* world. I lean into his chest and he holds me tight, not letting me go or escape or collapse or whatever would have happened if he wasn't here with me right now.

"It's not the first time," he half-asks, half-knows.

I shake my head. "Not in a long time, though. Used to happen when I was a kid."

"How did you make it stop?" His voice is even, pulling me out of my reeling.

Make it stop.

I once knew how to do that too.

"There was this grounding exercise I used to do to focus my mind on the present," I recall. "Focus on the actual rather than the might be; five things I can see, four things I can touch, three things I can hear, two things I can smell, one thing I can taste. But I'm not a kid anymore. I doubt that would—"

"Do it," he commands in a tone that doesn't leave any room for arguing.

I look around, naming five random items. "It feels ridiculous," I say.

"It isn't. Your heartbeat is already slowing down." And he should know, my chest wall is still sandwiched against his. "Now four things you can touch," he says.

"This bench we're on," I say, moving my hand across it, trying to focus on the metal cooling my skin. "My sweater." I try to look for things I can touch without having to get up or leave the warmth of Christian's body. "Your arms," I slide my fingers across his biceps. The fact that he's not wearing a jacket comes to mind. "Your neck," I say, letting my hands slide up to his nape, sensing the skin bristles under my touch. This is definitely taking my mind off everything else. Focusing on Christian. I move on to naming three things I can hear, his voice being one of them. Then his intoxicating scent comes up as one of the two things I can smell. The Mexican food truck behind us is the other.

"One thing you can taste?" he remind-asks me.

Trying to think within the confines of his hold, I lift my head and let my lips meet his. It's a small chaste kiss. Or at least meant to be, I think. But he tastes exactly as I remembered.

"Looks like you're feeling better already," he rasps.

"I am," I say. "I don't recall this method working so well before." My hands are no longer shaking. The heavy brick weighing on my chest is finally letting some air through. My heart is still racing, but this time for a different reason. A truly welcome one. "Thank you."

"Glad to be of service," he says, smoothing a strand of hair off my face and tucking it gently behind my ear.

Christian Copeland.

The man who's just averted a potential anxiety attack.

Must be magical.

"That hasn't happened since I was twelve." I feel the need to explain. "I thought I'd gotten over it through the years. But now with the pregnancy... my first prenatal appointment is today and there are so many things that could go wrong. And I'm... worried and scared and—you probably think I'm crazy right now," I say into his chest.

"I don't," he says in a soft voice, as if this is the most natural reaction in the world. His face still serious as he asks, "Is the baby's dad going with you?"

It takes a few seconds to register.

"To the appointment," he clarifies.

"Ryan? NO!" I shake my head. Maybe a tad too vigorously. "He doesn't even know I'm pregnant."

"Okay," he just says. Not so much in agreement, more like shelving that thought for an easier time.

"What? I am planning to tell him, just haven't found the right moment." I don't like that there's something he wants to say and doesn't.

"That's your decision."

"But?"

"None of my business."

"Okay, let's make it your business. Don't hold back when you're talking to me," I insist. "It makes me feel incompetent."

"*I* would want to know," he says simply. "If I were the father, I would want to know. To have the opportunity to be part of my unborn kid's life."

I think of my father, whoever this person is, who was denied of that opportunity so completely. Or maybe he wouldn't have considered it an opportunity. Maybe he was spared.

"I will tell him, but there's no *being part.* The last thing I want is for my ex to come back into my life out of pity. He already made his choice—which did not include me in it," I say, thinking back to the day Ryan broke up with me. In retrospect, I'm kind of happy he did. It saved us from living a life of boredom out of some sense of responsibility.

"Like I said, it's your decision." There's more between the lines. That much is obvious. But this topic goes back to storage, for now, since the clock is ticking.

"So anyway, the appointment is—" I glance at my watch, "in less than an hour. I better get going." I peel myself away from his warmth.

"Do you need a ride? Want me to come with you?" Christian offers and I shake my head.

"I need to do this one on my own, but thanks," I decide, not sure what book of rules I'm basing that on, and head toward the metro station.

"I can't," I blubber over a string of text messages to Christian once I'm seated in the wait-room of my OB-GYN clinic. "I can't do this on my own." Screw that invisible rule book. Took all but twenty minutes for me to throw the metaphorical thing away. "I thought I could but I can't."

"You can," the man in shiny armor writes back in between my text attacks. "But you don't have to." And then, "Text me the address."

"I know I worry more than I should and that it's totally out of proportion and counterproductive, but I just can't help it," I say when I see him emerge into the hallway of the clinic. I stepped out of that place, couldn't bear the sight of all the excited, expecting couples who came in together, while really all I have to offer this baby is—me. And mostly, I couldn't deal with the thought I'd have to walk in there alone. And somehow my worries that bad things might happen have taken over, for the second time in one day, as if I'm on autopilot—a very lousy autopilot program, if I may say. "This is where my scientific brain hasn't been able to be put to good use. I think I took one too many pathology courses in graduate school." I stop for a breather. "It was a required course and I've pretty much memorized all the things that could go so catastrophically wrong..."

"Hey." Christian pulls me closer, entrapping me in his arms as if to protect me from my own disruptive knowledge. "Statistically speaking, there are way more things that could go so incredibly right. Why not focus on them?"

"Historically speaking, bad things can happen to everyone, so might as well be prepared."

Christian shakes his head. "I refuse to let you live this way."

"Right," I say, as if he has any control over the mess I call my life. "Go ahead, admit it. I'm out of my mind."

Christian closes the last few gaps left between my trembling body and his, holding me tighter now. I let my head rest on his chest and release that pent-up breath I was holding.

"I only have one thing to say," his gravely voice reverberates through me, my body nestled protectively in his arms. My heart changes its anxious thrashing to its Christian-is-around kind of thumping, making breathing feasible again.

Like I said, this man is magical.

I lift my head up in question. "That I need meds and lifelong intensive psychotherapy?"

Christian shakes his head, letting our eyes connect. "That you don't have to go through this alone."

Christian

"Any medical conditions?" Dr. Efron asks and Claire shakes her head. We've been sitting in the doctor's office for the past thirty minutes, talking through how the next seven and some months are going to look. Now we're into the details of Claire's family and medical history.

"How about baby's dad?" The doctor turns her gaze toward me, catching me off-guard. "Any medical conditions?" I could see how she would mistake me for the father. Claire and I are seated close together, her hand in my lap, tightly holding mine. She hasn't let go since we walked in.

"Oh, he's not the dad," Claire replies ruefully. This shouldn't strike me as a surprise, we haven't even had sex. Yet the effect it has on me is unexpected. Those few words make my stomach churn. As in, I kind of wish I were. Kind of wish there wasn't this ex of hers, unknowingly looming over us. Is it crazy that I barely know her but already want her to myself?

"My apologies." Dr. Efron smiles kindly. Recalculating. Non-judging. "Do you have any information on the biological father's medical history?

"I don't recall anything noteworthy," Claire replies with a cynical tone. Then quietly to me she adds, "Including our entire relationship." This makes me chuckle.

This woman.

The doctor goes on explaining the different medical exams and lab tests. Ultrasound. Transvaginal for early pregnancy, abdominal in later stages as the baby grows bigger. Risks of alcohol, smoking, raw seafood. And recommendations for healthy pregnancy: start prenatal vitamins, sleep more, relax, exercise, reduce caffeine intake. The list is long, on the verge of overwhelming. Claire listens and nods. Her grip on my hand tightens with each topic being covered. She's given a gown and is asked to undress from the waist down for the ultrasound. The doctor splits a smile between us and leaves the room.

"You okay?" I ask as Claire gets up.

"No." She starts to shed her pants with one hand, the other still holding mine.

"I think that's my cue." I gesture with my head to the door.

"You're not leaving me here!" She grabs my shirt with her free hand.

"I'm not, I promise. I'll wait outside, give you some privacy?"

"If you're leaving, I'm leaving," she says half joking, half clinging to me for dear life.

"Okay then." The look in her eyes says I'm staying. So that's what I do.

Claire

Overwhelmed. That's a word I underestimated. A word I'd used before when starting a new job or when dealing with *novel*—whether welcome or unwelcome—life situations. Technically, this word still qualifies here, but then all those other situations should have gotten much smaller words. It just never felt quite so real or big before. Perceived pressure vs you're now completely in charge and fully responsible for the growth and development of a whole person. An embryo. A fetus. A baby.

My baby.

My little father-less baby.

I always thought things would be different. *My* kid would know their father. *My* kid would grow up with a father. *My* kid would have both parents come to school parties, and birthdays. And concerts. And sports games. And dance recitals. Spend time with both parents on weekends, maybe even grandparents. A big family. Now, as I'm covered in a pink paper gown, holding Christian's hand, staring into the screen, trying to make sense of a little blob in a black and white ultrasound image of my uterus, the only thing I can think of is that if I could give this child a minuscule fraction of the love and happy memories my mom has given Kate and me, that alone would be a raving success.

Then my mind drifts back to all the possible things that could go wrong. Again.

As a kid, a therapist had once told my mom that I understood much more than what my life experience allowed me to comfortably cope with. That my anxiety was temporary. A matter of filling in the gaps. And sometime into my early teenage years, it indeed resolved. But now that we're talking about pregnancy and another human being, there's an entire new pool of concerning scenarios to choose from, and a whole lot of novel life experiences to accumulate. *Just need to stop these automatic thoughts*, I unsuccessfully remind myself.

"Five things," Christian leans in and whispers in my ear, sensing my reeling. His hand brushes some stray hairs off my face and his lips follow with a soft, chaste kiss. I don't even need to go through the entire rundown; the sound of his voice, the touch of skin, the taste of his lips on mine. He just knows what I need, even when my wordless jumble of a brain doesn't.

We stay quiet, staring at the screen in fascination.

"I can see a pulse. Here," the tech says jovially and points to a tiny beating dot. It's incredible. This is when I realize I've been holding my breath. And Christian has been doing the exact same. We both release a sigh mixed with wonder and relief. My head turns to the man beside me. I look into his eyes, those gorgeous molten-amber honey eyes, and he sends back a glassy gaze. And an incredible, heart-swelling smile. A shiny little tear is nestled in the crinkle of his eye. I let go of his hand, just for a second, and reach for his face, letting my fingers travel up that little drop and swipe it away.

And now I finally understand Christian's running analogy; someone who shares your joy, but also your fears, and your pain. It's the one person you can lean on when things get too hard.

The one to help you back up when you fall, help you find your way when you feel lost. And the one who makes sure you know you're not alone.

18

My feet won't listen

Claire

My feet won't listen. They just won't. I've told them not to make a total fool out of myself. Not to walk down that one specific street and wander into Christian's apartment building. When he dropped me home that day, right after he'd held my hand and calmed down my nerves while we watched this little pea-size baby on the screen, he mentioned his address, just as an FYI. Why did he have to tell me where he lived? Why does it have to be a reasonable walking distance from where *I* live? And why on earth does this stupid street—the same one I've walked down so many times before—look so much more enticing, or actually breathtaking, now that I've found out Christian lives here?

I don't know everything, which is why I can't answer any of these stupefying questions. Nor do I know the reason I find myself strolling off into the little path leading to his building and walking in. The security guard doesn't even give me the time of day. I guess I either don't look suspicious, or I have a girl-next-door face. I take the elevator to the tenth floor, where I assume Christian lives based on his apartment number. A number I committed to memory once mentioned. Why? This has to be another one of those challenging questions. And now I'm officially a stalker.

I stare at his door, pleading with myself to stop, turn around. Go home. Not make a fool of myself. I'm still not sure what I'm trying to achieve here. There is not a single scenario that would make this situation any less complicated. Or my feelings any less confusing. But my feet refuse to stop, and my hand insists on pressing his doorbell.

I wait silently, trying to calm down the heart thumping. I can feel the blood rushing through my veins, my face heats up, my palms clammy despite the cool weather outside. A small part of me hopes he won't answer. If I can't control myself, maybe the world will. I'm about to turn on my heels when the door swings open and my world reduces itself to this guy standing before me. His handsome face, his molten amber eyes. He's wearing a T-shirt, a beat up—sexy—pair of jeans, barefoot, tousled hair. I feel like I might be interrupting something.

"Hey," he says, surprised, a warm smile appearing on his face.

"Hey." I blink. "I... don't really know what I'm doing here," I admit. Why can't I keep anything to myself around this guy?

"Come in." He steps aside, opening the door wider. I hesitate, taking a quick glance into his apartment. There are two plates on the counter, two forks, two cups. A dinner for two, set on his kitchen island.

"You have company." I try to rein in the disappointment that's quickly settling in.

"I do," he says, eyes not leaving mine.

"Sorry for showing up unannounced. I should have called."

"I'm glad you came," he says, despite my stumbling words.

"Really?" I'm not so glad. "I mean we never said we were exclusive, so it's not like you're doing anything wrong, but I'd rather not know."

"I'm gonna stop you right there," Christian chuckles.

Oh, he thinks this is funny? My throat is burning. "I should go—"

"Claire!" There's a little voice behind me and my brain moves into rewind mode when I turn around to see—

"Jake?" I hope the incredible relief in my voice is not as obvious as I feel. "I'm so glad to see you!"

"Me too!" Jake chirps and gives me a big hug. I know Kate does this thing for a living—being the beloved kindergarten teacher that she is, getting so many hugs every day—but I don't think a kid has ever hugged me before, except for maybe when I was a kid too. I also don't know how it is with other kids, but Jake's hug is so carefree and simple and unconditionally affectionate that my almost broken heart is slowly starting to put itself together. I like this boy.

"I thought..." I begin to say to Christian, but then—realizing I need to keep it to a kid-friendly level—I just stop there and shut up.

"I know exactly what was going on in that creative head of yours." The man is cracking up beside me. It's embarrassing—jealousy, possessiveness, these are not adjectives typically used to describe me. But Christian's laugh is so contagious I can't keep a serious face.

"No, you don't," I try to deny, grabbing a pillow off his couch and sending it his way. Jake seems to like the idea and quickly joins in, throwing one of his own at his uncle. This kid is smart in his choice of sides.

"Yes, I do." Christian catches the pillows, and before we have a chance to reload, he charges forward and pulls Jake and me onto the pile of pillows on the floor, holding us down in a group hug. And just like that, I find myself laughing out loud. I'm so far gone for this man.

Jake, being the tiny kid that he is, easily releases himself and comes to stand beside us, while I still struggle to find where Christian's feet begin and mine end.

"Uncle Christian, can Claire stay for dinner?" Jake flickers his big amber can't-say-no-to eyes to us.

"That's up to Claire." Christian turns his gaze to me, his body still close to mine, with the same kind of can't-say-no-to look on his face. In what world would I ever want to say no to this irresistible guy and his adorable nephew?

"Who's cooking?" I ask as Christian rises and pulls me back up with him.

"All of us." Jake motions for me to follow him back to the kitchen.

"Sounds like a plan," I approve, stepping closer to see what's brewing. "Hmmm, meat sauce? Smells delicious."

"Not just any meat sauce, it's called Bolognese, and we're making spaghetti too, my favorite!" Jake explains. "And gluten-free chocolate chip cookies. They even taste like *real* cookies." Then he runs off, mumbling something about a drawing he needs to finish.

"These *are* real cookies," Christian chuckles.

"Gluten-free? Does he have celiac?" I ask.

"No. I mean not that we know as of yet," Christian responds. "His last screen was about six months ago, but it is more common in patients with Type 1 diabetes. Julia has made it a target to reduce his gluten intake to fifty percent, thinking it may help reduce the risk. I don't think the science behind it is completely clear, but I try to support my sister where I can. Plus, if he ever does get diagnosed with celiac, at least the transition will be smoother."

This man makes my heart swell.

I'm still standing by the stove, my back to Christian, as I brace myself for a much-needed explanation for why I'm here, that I'm not usually a stalker, possibly contemplating an apology for interrupting Christian's quality time with Jake. But what happens next takes me by surprise. Actually it takes my breath away, literally, as Christian steps closer and scoops me from behind into a hug. As if me being here is the most natural thing in the world. My body certainly thinks so, as it chooses—without consulting me first—to lean into Christian's embrace. And it feels good. Too good. The kind of good that blunts your senses and runs the risk of disabling any and all defense mechanisms and common sense.

"Thank you for saying yes to this little guy," he rasps into the side of my neck, lips almost touching my ear. It's a small gesture, but I can't seem to remember how to properly breathe while I'm basking in his scent and the welcome proximity. "It's the first time I've seen him smile today," he admits as I turn to face him.

"Really?" This kid seemed like the happiest boy alive back at Thanksgiving dinner.

"Yes, something happened at school today and he won't talk to me about it."

"Do you want me to call Kate?" I ask. There's an added benefit to being the sister of his kindergarten teacher.

Christian shakes his head. "We have to respect his wishes."

And I like this about him. A whole lot.

Jake is a bit quieter than he was at Thanksgiving while we all sit around the kitchen island and munch on his favorite food. I am no children expert by any means, but he seems way too reflective for what I'd imagine a five-year-old boy should be. Christian and I exchange unspoken looks when Jake mentions he misses his mom, who's away at a medical conference in New Orleans. One of the downsides to having a mom who actually nails it on the career side is the travel aspect. Much harder to do when you're a single mom, take it from mine, but I'm sure having a doting brother and uncle like Christian in her corner makes it a bit more bearable. My mom didn't have that kind of support system, but she still nailed it. Slowly perhaps, but surely. My mind wanders to my near future and how that might look for me, replicating the single mom aspect, but I chase it away quickly. I'll have plenty of time to worry about it later.

"Did you finish the drawing, bud?" Christian asks as Jake and I clear the table. I try to help with the dishes but am turned away by a very capable and convincing host.

Jake nods noncommittally. "Want to play Uno?" he asks me. Wow, this kid is a master at segueing.

"That's my favorite game," I say. Kate and I used to play it all the time as kids. The memories of Kate's creative cheating attempts bring a smile to my face. Some great stories to make Jake laugh over but since my sister is also his kindergarten teacher, she might not appreciate being known as an Uno cheater.

"Can I start?" he asks, pulling me by the sleeve into the living room, where cards have already been dealt for two players. They're face down, but I suspect some tampering may have been involved.

"Sure. Which stack is mine?" I ask, going along with his preplanned game.

"This one," Jake says, positioning himself on the carpet. I plop into a pillow, facing him, and take my pre-curated stack. I'm surprised to see I have four wild cards, two draw-two and one skip card. Looks like I've been dealt a winning hand. Jake looks at his cards. "Do you want to switch hands?" I give him an out, as he probably meant for my stack to be his.

"Nope," he says with a big smile.

"I might win," I warn him. Kate as a kid used to get emotional and quite vocal over losing, and I'm certainly not looking to upset this guy here, especially after what—I suspect—hasn't been an easy day at school. Jake's smile widens and he shakes his head with an impressive confidence. "Oh, you want me to win?" That's an unexpected twist.

"Yes," Jake nods enthusiastically. And here I thought he was planning to cheat for his own benefit. But no... He's made sure I'll win, not leaving anything to chance—or not giving me much credit on the Uno side of things. I find it adorable.

"You sure?"

"He's sure." I hear Christian's voice closing in as he settles next to us on the carpet. My heart flutters happily. "He's taking it easy on you. Next round you're on your own." He winks at Jake. "This kid is an Uno prodigy."

I certainly nail the first round. After that, Christian shuffles the cards and deals, and Jake wins almost every time. As expected.

At some point Jake gets up, disappears into one of the rooms and comes back with a piece of paper, which he lays carefully on the coffee table in front of us. The drawing he was working on earlier. It's cute and colorful. I thought kids his age drew stick figures, but maybe I underestimated them. There are four pretty elaborate figures, with hair and clothes and even fingers.

"This is Mom," he says, pointing at a figure with long yellow hair, a colorful dress, and—I'm guessing—a stethoscope, hanging from her neck. "This is Uncle Christian and you." He points at two figures holding hands. This kid, it appears, seems to know stuff that I still haven't figured out. "And this is me." He points to... I'm not sure. This fourth figure is smaller than the rest, but doesn't quite look like a person. Not the way Jake draws his people, at least. It's colored gray and is more square-shaped than anything, sprinkled with what looks like red and green buttons. But it does have legs and arms, one of which is holding Christian's hand on one side, the other holding his mom's.

"Thanks for showing us your drawing, bud," Christian says. His voice is laced with concern.

"Nice drawing," I add, afraid to say the wrong thing. But the kid has talent.

"Thanks," Jake says quietly. I think he may be waiting for us to ask why he drew himself this way, but Christian doesn't prod, giving him space to share if he wants. And I do the same because—what do I even know about kids?

"Do you like how I drew myself?" Jake turns to me. Oh boy, why do I get the tricky question? My eyes look up to Christian for guidance, but he seems just as lost.

"I like your hair more in real life," I choose to say. Because this box thing he drew has no hair, and I'm not sure what else to say.

Jake laughs in response. Thank goodness. "Obviously! Robots don't have hair."

"Oh, you're a robot?" Christian takes the opportunity.

"Yes," Jake confirms.

"That's a very cool robot," I chime in. "Is that what you want to be for next Halloween?"

"Not really. But Tommy said I'm a robot and then Hanson said that too. And now everyone thinks I'm a robot." And by the way he says it, I'm guessing that being a robot outside of Halloween is not considered a good thing.

Christian pulls the little guy into his arms. "Why did they say that?" he asks protectively.

"Because," Jake's eyes fill with tears all at once. He pulls out his little insulin pump from his pocket. "This," he says. "It has buttons, and wires."

"It's tubing, not a wire," Christian pulls the little guy closer, gently wiping a tear off his cheek.

"And this," Jake pulls up his shirt, revealing something that looks like a port on his little belly, where the tube connects to.

"That's how insulin is delivered into your body." Christian patiently explains what I'm sure Jake knows all too well.

"And this." Jake pulls up his sleeve, exposing another little device on his arm that looks like a coin-sized chip, circled by adhesives.

"That's your CGM. It monitors your sugar levels continuously and tells your pump if less or more insulin is needed." It's subtle, but Christian's voice cracks a little with every word.

"I know, Uncle Christian," says Jake. "But *they* don't know."

Continuous glucose monitor. Insulin pump. Tubing. Ports. I feel a pang just trying to wrap my head around how a five-year-old kid needs to have these terms in his daily usable vocabulary. Go through life with these devices tethered to his body. Be his own pancreas 24/7 in order to stay alive. And if that's not enough, having to take shit from his peers for that.

Christian remains pensive for a long moment, holding his nephew in his arms, ruffling his hair. I can see the incredible pain in Christian's eyes as he glances at me, deep in thought. Until something shifts in his gaze, an idea, or maybe a decision. He lowers his face to Jake, letting their foreheads connect. "Well then," he says with an admirable confidence, "we're going to make sure they do."

"Should you call your sister?" I ask once Jake is sound asleep in the other room. It's a spacious apartment with two large bedrooms. One of them is Jake's, "*For when my mom works nights or has to travel,*" Jake had explained. It has a cute, elevated twin bed with a slide, a bookcase filled with colorful children's books and a huge toy chest. But Jake's favorite activity, it seems, is building forts out of chairs and blankets. Which happens to also be *my* childhood favorite activity, and so that's how we spent our time together until Jake's bedtime.

"No, I don't want Julia to worry, she'll drop everything and take the next flight home. She's presenting tomorrow. We can handle it until she's back."

We.

I wish I had an uncle like him growing up. Or any other fatherly figure in my life as a kid, for that matter. "I can't believe Jake has to deal with these meanies on top of everything else... So what do we do?" It does not escape me that Christian's eyes brighten as I choose to embrace the *we*. As in *him and me*. Something that—outside of conversations with Kate and my mom—I've never been fond of. Yet for some unfathomable reason, coming from Christian, I like the sound of it. Way too much.

"We make it cool. And fun. Instead of unfamiliar and scary," he says, confirming our new partnership, eyes glimmering as he tries to think this through.

"Fun?" I double check that my ears are still functional. He nods. "Christian, I don't mean to be a party pooper, but needles and medical devices *are* scary. And not just for five- or six-year-olds, for adults too."

"Did you say, *party*?" He chooses to focus on a different part of my sentence. There's some lightbulb going off in his head. Not sure how he chose to pick this word out of everything else.

"As in *party pooper*..." I clarify.

"We're going to throw him a party. *A pump party*," Christian says, a smile slowly stretching on his handsome face.

"I hope you're not planning to rely on my inadequate, or rather non-existent, party planning skills." I give him a serious look to make my point. "Please tell me you're good with party planning or know someone who isn't me who can—"

"There's a blog called 'Overprotective Mom,' written by a parent of a kid with Type 1 diabetes. It's an old blog, she hasn't been active in over ten years. But now that you mentioned parties it reminded me. One of her posts was about throwing a pump party to mitigate the exact same issues we now need to deal with."

"You read an over-protective mom's blog?" I lift an eyebrow at him. This man doesn't seize to amaze me.

"She called herself that out of sarcasm, citing her kid's first endocrinologist who had the nerve to tell her she was neurotic and over-protective for not letting her daughter's glucose levels be on the lower side at bedtime. Fear of severe hypoglycemia. Her kid grew up before continuous glucose monitors were trustworthy, and before they could formally work with insulin pumps in a closed loop. It's not a perfect system now either, but back then, they had to wake up at night, prick their kids' little fingers to check their blood sugar levels and fix it; make them drink some juice if too low or inject insulin if too high. Which is pretty much what we still do now, minus the finger stick, for the most part. I get why she'd feel over-protective, losing sleep over it, having to constantly worry. I can barely sleep when Jake spends the night here. Can't imagine what Julia has to live through every single day. And night," he sighs. "Insulin injections keep people with Type 1 diabetes alive by lowering their blood sugars. But believe it or not, the most common and dangerous side effect of using insulin is hypoglycemia. Having low blood sugar, too low for too long—and we're not talking days, we're talking hours. Or less. Could lead to loss of consciousness. Coma. Even..." he shudders, "death."

"Do you wake up at night? To check Jake's blood sugar?" I ask.

Christian nods. "I still find myself checking the app on my phone multiple times a night, making sure he's not running low. But that's an improvement. I used to stay up all night before he had his CGM. Now he wears one. It's set to alert us, pretty loudly, if his glucose levels drop too fast or too low. And many insulin pumps nowadays work in a closed loop system and would suspend insulin delivery if that happens."

"That's good." I find myself trying to hang on to these small sprinkles of positivity. I'm not usually the cheerful side in a conversation, but seeing Christian's pain makes me want to grab those sunbeams from between the clouds and hand them to him.

"It is. Much better than it used to be. But it's not a perfect system. And sometimes suspending insulin delivery is not enough to bring his blood sugar up."

"What do you do if it's not enough?"

"I wake him up, give him juice and sit with him until it goes back up," he says somberly. "But, I mean, he's only here like a night a week. His mom has to live with this fear every night. So a physician that calls an overwhelmed parent "*neurotic*" or "*overprotective*" for trying to protect their kid from an actual, real risk of hypoglycemia, instead of helping them come up with a plan to reduce that risk, I think should revoke their medical license and never see a single patient again." I think it's the first time I see signs of real anger on Christian's face. He's been quite calm in his scientific rebuttals with me and even with Harriett. But this is an entirely different story.

I take Christian's hand in mine and give it a squeeze. "I'm sorry again for giving you such a hard time at the beginning. I didn't know you had personal connections to this disease. And honestly, I had no idea what patients with Type 1 diabetes and their families are dealing with. I still don't know, actually. I'm just beginning to understand a small fraction of it."

"These kids are superheroes, I can tell you that." There's a short pause before he adds, "And you're already making it up for me by helping me plan Jake's pump party." He slaps a smile back on.

"Oh, am I?" I chuckle, and he nods. "So then, let's read the blog post together, get some ideas," I offer, pulling out my phone.

I open my eyes to find myself cuddled in Christian's arms, on his big and quite comfortable sofa, in the living room. The sun is already up and as my consciousness gradually snaps back into place, I realize the sweet dream I had is actually a memory. Reading through the blog post, brainstorming and making pump party plans and supply lists with Christian until the early hours of morning. Resting my head on his chest when my eyes became heavy and my body sleepy.

"I should go home," I recall yawn-rambling, without much conviction.

"You're not going anywhere like this," came Christian's protective voice rumbling through me.

"Like what?" I asked, eyes already half shut. Yawning again, louder.

"You can have my bed," he offered generously.

"It feels so comfy like this, I just don't want to move," I'd said, cuddling deeper into him. My sleepy state of mind must have gotten the best of me as I sank into the sweetest slumber. Again. Breathing him in, not letting this man move an inch. We did eventually move into a horizontal position, covered up by a blanket. And I do recall Christian trying to give me the entire sofa to myself, but I held onto him tightly. I can't be held accountable for what I do when I'm half asleep. And with Christian.

But now that I'm awake, still wearing last night's clothes, not wanting the kid sleeping in the other room to get the wrong idea, I peel myself off Christian's enticing warmth and drag my tired body to the bathroom, trying to make my hair slightly more presentable for other people's sake. And yes, despite the sweet awakening, I can't get away from my recent morning sickness routine, which is what woke me up in the first place. A quick glance at the clock shows it's 7 a.m. At least everyone else is still asleep.

I brush my teeth swiftly with the one adult toothbrush I can find—assuming the red and blue Captain America one is Jake's—and wash my face. Then I decide—not sure what has gotten into me—to make pancakes. Not my brightest idea, I'm like the world's worst cook. But I'm hoping said world will be on my side today, as I'm really trying to cheer these guys up.

Christian is still deep in sleep on the sofa, handsome and peaceful, when Jakes struts into the kitchen, a bit surprised to see me there—which I take as a good sign. One that possibly means that Christian doesn't often bring women home. At least not when Jake's around. Jake smiles widely and gives me a hug.

"I'm making pancakes!" I announce.

"Yay!!!" he whisper-shouts, eyes beaming. "Can I help?"

"You actually came right in time, because I really do need help." And I'm dead serious, because despite my good intentions, I have zero experience with making breakfast. This part is up Kate's alley.

Jake joyfully takes on the batter stirring role and double checks my ingredients list, offering helpful reminders; I may have forgotten the eggs and vanilla extract. Good thing this kid knows his way in the kitchen.

"Good morning." Christian's raspy morning voice sprinkles goose bumps over my skin. He walks up to us with a sleepy gaze and tousled hair, scooping Jake into a big hug and giving him a loud kiss. Then he comes for me. I can feel my heart tumbling and my face growing hot as his arm wraps around my waist from the back and his lips lightly press a kiss to my cheek.

"Good morning," I say on a breath, trying to bring my pulse under control.

"We're making pancakes!" Jake announces.

"Hmmm, my favorite!" Christian says, backing up from us and turning on the coffee machine. "We have some time before school." He winks at Jake. "Should we challenge Claire to a basketball match?"

"Yes!" Jake jumps up, fist bumping the air, then disappears into the bedroom area to get dressed. The way Christian cares for his nephew is mind-blowing to me. I'm all gooey inside when I see these two interact.

"Thank you for staying," Christian says quietly to me. Somehow I hadn't even considered not staying as an actual possibility.

"Sorry for not letting you leave my side and making you sleep on the sofa last night," I offer.

"Anytime," he chuckles. "Although it's the second time you've fallen asleep when I'm around. Should I take offense to that?"

"Offense? No, not with me," I laugh, because if it were up to me, I would have jumped his bones back in my apartment, right after my power nap. Or at any given moment really. "You have this incredible ability to disarm me, calm down my misfiring nerves," I say.

"You mean bore you?" he deadpans.

"NO! It's only when you're next to me that I'm finally able to relax." I want to say *breathe* but that might sound a little strong. "Plus, pregnancy makes me unbelievably tired. I know this baby is still pea-sized but according to this—" I pull up the pregnancy book I've started reading on my phone and show him. "It says it's normal. Doesn't feel so normal, but who am I to argue with *America's #1 best-selling pregnancy guide*?"

"Ok, then, I'll take it as a compliment," Christian settles it, giving me a lazy, just-woke-up-with-you-next-to-me grin.

"You should," I say, feeling a smile with that same exact nature taking over me. I don't normally smile like this. Don't normally smile. Don't normally talk about myself or feel the urge to help others, or particularly care much about anyone who's not my sister Kate or my mom. I don't normally like kids or spend time around them. I don't like to sleep on sofas and certainly not cuddle tightly an entire night in a guy's arms, wearing yesterday's clothes.

Or at least that's what I had grown to think about myself. Or what I thought I wanted other people to think about me. *Before* Christian came into my life and turned my world upside down. To the sunny side. I feel like a totally different person around this man than I am with anyone else. It's like with him I can finally be... *me.*

19

Pump Party

Christian

"Take the day off," I tell Claire. She's still blushing a bit after seeing Kate's surprised-impressed face when she spotted us together, dropping Jake off at school, holding his hand on each side. It's an adorable look on her. "Spend your day with me. I just have a few things to do in my lab, then we'll go get supplies for the party." There's nothing suggestive in my words but her eyes dip to my chest and she makes no effort hiding it, sending my mind into other places.

"Already taken the day off," she confirms. "We've committed ourselves to a party today," she says, excitement emanating as she speaks. So different from the way she is anywhere else.

This woman. I can't seem to get enough of her. Challenges me with science all day, cuddles in my arms all night, made pancakes with Jake (not edible, I should probably label the sugar more clearly to better differentiate from the salt... but it made her and Jake laugh so hard it was totally worth it), and then crushed us both in basketball. My kind of girl.

We've pitched the pump party idea to Kate who excitedly hopped on it, added a few extra details and promised to clear her class's afternoon schedule. We also ran it by Julia (without the background details at this point), who gave it a raving green light. Which means the pump party is on. Today. Because why not?

Back in my Land Rover, I catch Claire staring at me, a contemplative smile on her face. And I can't help but pull her chin up and bring her mouth to mine. It's a small kiss, just a brush to her lips, but she makes this cute sound in the back of her throat and grabs my neck, parting her lips and pulling me closer. I've only ever really kissed her once, as an unsuspecting bystander at the mall, and I'm dying to know if the taste I remember and that spark I felt were real or just a wild idealization in my memory.

Our tongues connect in a greedy dance. I let my teeth gently pull on her bottom lip. Her hands move to my hair, tangling us further. Yep... these memories were VERY accurate. And right now, I'm on fire. I try to remind myself we're still on school grounds. Last time I made out with a girl in a parking lot was in high school, some fifteen years ago. Different girl, different time, different car. But despite being an eager teenager back then, raging hormones and all, it was nothing, not even a fraction of the way I feel right now. The way I want Claire, the way I *need* her.

"I would love to explore that thought further," my words come out raspy and breathless as I ignore the protesting voices in my head. "At the after-party."

Claire

I feel intoxicated. By his touch and his taste. And the feel of his lips on mine. There's an unspoken promise in the air between us. Like it's just the beginning. Of what exactly? I don't know. It's also probably not my best idea to let my life tangle with someone new so soon after a breakup. And while pregnant. Not to mention he's a colleague and we're supposed to work together. But it's Christian. How can I not? My body and mind seem to have conspired against me. I stopped having a say when I bumped into him at the mall, glasses-less, clueless to who I was. The man kissed me like I'd never been kissed before, obliterating the recollection of any kiss preceding that moment. Ruining any future kiss with anyone else.

A pleasant buzz runs through my veins, my body feeling hot in so many places. We broke the kiss and now I'm playing with the air vents as we quietly drive away, trying to cool off what feels like my very flushed face. It's early December with a chilly breeze outside, but we're blasting the air conditioning on the lowest possible setting, both still burning.

A twenty-minute drive later, Christian pulls over by a huge metal gate. The entrance to *The* Gene and Epigenetic Research Institute—GERI. A research hotspot for scientists. The campus is located in Washington, DC, but attracts talent from all over the world. I've always been curious about this place. Now I'll get to experience the magic from the inside. I tried to convince Christian to stop by my apartment and let me change clothes, but he said that except for him, no one from GERI saw me yesterday, so they won't know I'm wearing the same outfit. He also said he didn't trust himself alone with me, and that if we stopped by my house we might never leave. Both were pretty compelling arguments. And since we're on a mission of planning and throwing a pump party today, I relented.

"Good morning," Christian says to a big scary security guard through the rolled-down car window, displaying his employee badge. The guy takes the badge and scans it with his eyes.

"Good morning Professor Copeland. You have a guest?" the guard asks, lowering himself quite a significant distance to glance at me through the window.

"Yes, Dr. Claire Bellingham," Christian introduces me, matching the solemn tone. It feels like a TSA moment at the airport, so I wipe my smile and settle on a poker face.

"Do you have an ID?" The guard is down to business.

"Sure." I pull out my driver's license and hand it over with a jittery hand. Interactions with authority make me nervous: MVA, passport appointments. I'm always worried I'm missing some essential documents in my pre-curated stack. I never am, but the thought of being turned away is somewhere up there with being late to meetings or deadlines.

"Do you have an invitation?"

"I invited her. She's my guest," Christian reminds him, keeping his calm.

And just when I think I'm going to get denied, maybe walk myself to the nearest bus or metro station, the guy cracks a little smile. "Ah, yes, my apologies." He turns for a second and produces a visitor badge for me. "Have a good day, Professor Copeland." And with a press of a button, the heavy gates open, and we're in.

It's like entering a different world entirely. A sacred science haven. The campus grounds are vast and beautifully maintained. Geese and deer are walking around leisurely through the large grassy areas. A few of them decide to cross the road just in front of us, and a line of cars stops and waits patiently for them to clear. Each of the many buildings we pass by is decorated with creatively trimmed bushes, and the trees here seem to still bear some of their foliage colors. The hustle and bustle of the city is completely taken over by a surreal sense of calm and an inspiring academic atmosphere. I open my window and take a lungful of this air of research freedom. Why did I ever decide to leave academia?

"Want a tour?" Christian's tone matches my excitement.

"Would love one," my voice sounds dreamy, "but we have a pump party to organize."

"Well, then, you'll have to come again." He squeezes my knee and I feel heat spreading from his hand through my entire body.

We stop at a large parking garage and walk side by side to his building. The breeze smells like colorful fall leaves and crisp December air, and Christian. Our hands gravitate together, fingers interlocked, and my heart forgets how to properly function. Christian scans his badge, leading me through a staircase that opens into a large corridor and into a spacious, fully equipped, open-plan laboratory.

"Welcome to my lab," he says, trying to sound modest, but I can feel his sense of pride. And I love that about him.

He introduces me to his postdoctoral fellows and interns as Dr. Claire Bellingham, only letting go of my hand so I can shake theirs, citing some of my work from the time I still worked in a lab. Their respect for him is palpable and admirable. But, I mean, I can't say I'm surprised—everything about this man is admirable.

We enter his office, which is located at the end of the large open space. He closes the door and walks behind me to take my coat, looping an arm around my waist and landing a small kiss to the back of my neck. I can't help the smile that takes over me, or the little hitch in my breath.

"I have a short experiment to run," he explains, which is the reason we're here in the first place, "and then I'm all yours." *All mine.* I think I like the sound of it way too much.

"Need another set of hands? I may be a bit rusty but—"

"I'd love another set of hands. Especially yours." His tone is chaste and deep in science, but my mind is going to so many places right now. I can barely remember my name, let alone how to follow an experimental protocol. But I follow him back into the lab and busy myself with a clean lab coat and a pair of gloves.

We work together, bumping into each other once in a while. His students watch us with fascination from their desks and lab benches and stay out of our way. I'm surprised by the sense of joy that holding tubes again gives me. The noise of a centrifuge, the dial of a pipette. I've been working in an office for the past few years, completely forgetting how much I liked doing this stuff.

"You're smiling," Christian observes, "unprovoked." He's grinning at me, ear to ear.

"You're saying it as if I never smile."

"Not like this, not to yourself while you're busy doing stuff." He may be right. It's been a while since I actually enjoyed my work, thanks to her majesty—Dr. Harriett Wallington. I've been secretly—so secretly that maybe I haven't even noticed—craving my old life in the lab. Plus, lusting over Christian is pretty much overpowering every other sensation.

"Hey man, do you have time next week to join my lab meeting?" I hear a deep, serious male voice coming from the lab entrance. "Yan has interesting data, wanted to get your take." The owner of the voice appears right when Christian and I finish loading our plates into the machines, but stops in his tracks when he spots me.

"Claire, this is Aiden," Christian says. "Aiden, this is Claire." Something registers on Aiden's face as he hears my name. As if—Christian has been talking about me? The thought makes something in me flutter happily before I have a chance to shut it down.

"Very nice to meet you, Claire," Aiden says. He looks a touch too serious, sort of grumpy, but his kind eyes say otherwise. I do wonder, though, if he ever smiles.

"Nice to meet you too, Aiden," I say and take my gloves off to shake his hand.

"Aiden is a professor here at GERI, his lab is focused on epigenetics research. And my new best friend. Right alongside Derek, but Aiden—" Christian turns a warning gaze toward his friend, gesturing with his head to me, "I swear if you say anything to Derek, I'll kill you."

Aiden nods, complete poker face mode on. Looks like this guy would withstand torture before revealing even the most mundane detail about whatever topic.

"And why are we keeping essential information from Derek?" asks a cute voice with an accent I can't quite place. The owner of the voice is a beautiful woman with a big warm smile that fills up the space with bubbling energy. She's sporting a pregnancy bump. Me in a few months—minus the beauty, the happiness, and the confidence. At the sight of her, Aiden's face lights up, his features brighten, and what do you know—he *does* smile. For the right person. And if this girl isn't his person, there must be something wrong with this world.

"Claire, this is Ellie," Christian says, taking his gloves and lab coat off, signaling for us to move into his office. "And we're not going to mention anything to Derek because Claire works at Amarinex. *With Derek,*" he explains to a pregnant Ellie. I assume they already know that Christian is under a professional consulting agreement with Amarinex. I'm not sure, however, whether they know we were tasked to work together due to the potential conflict of interest with him and Derek being besties. Which is funny, seeing as I'm becoming queen of judgement lapses where Christian is involved.

"Oh! *You're* Claire," Ellie says excitedly, and before I have a chance to confirm, she pulls me in for a warm hug. "I've heard so much about you!" she says into my hair. The fact that Aiden and Christian both are giving her *tone it down* looks does not escape me. And I have to admit I kind of like it. I also like how she waves them off, not giving a care in the world, and pulls me to the side, ready to expose Christian, her laugh filling the lab.

"Ellie is Aiden's wife," Christian adds. So apparently there's something very right with the world. I'm relieved. Seriously. The way Aiden and Ellie look at each other warms my heart. There's no other way I could see this one go.

"You mean Aiden is Ellie's husband." Ellie gives Christian a chiding-goofy look. "Since you met *me* first." Then turns her head to me. "My lab is just next door," she explains. "And if it weren't for *me*, matching these guys up as best buddies," she splits a stare between Aiden and Christian, "you would have never even met each other."

"She has a point," Aiden confirms, and Christian nods.

"So Claire, you're the one who's studying microRNAs in autoimmune diseases," Ellie says enthusiastically. "I read every single one of your papers, love your theories."

Wow... "Yes, I *was*," I admit, surprised that someone is actually interested in my research—because publishing in this space hasn't been easy—and even more surprised to hear that Ellie is so enthusiastic about it. "I kind of shifted gears when I moved into industry," I say, sounding more wistful than I want to.

"I sense reluctance." Aiden makes the observation, putting on what I'm guessing is his academic mentor hat.

"No, I love my job. I love working in industry. Just not loving the lack of academic freedom." More like scientific suppression and dictatorship, all induced by one witchy person named Dr. Harriett Wallington. But up until the moment she strutted into the Amarinex offices, that part of my life was pretty complete.

"Well, if you're ever interested in making the switch back to academia, talk to me," Ellie says warmly. "My research is focused on epigenetic factors in autoimmune diseases. We've been looking into microRNAs lately, which is how I came across your papers." And I just know that landing a job with someone like Ellie could make my work-life so much brighter. Like an immediate professional click if you will. That is, if I were one of these brave people who take professional leaps with a baby on the way.

"Now, what are you guys up to?" She switches gears.

And since Ellie looks like the perfect person to plan a celebration, I just throw it out there: "We're planning a party."

"What party? Count me in!" So much energy packed into one person, and it's contagious. But Christian's face grows serious as he probably recalls last night's conversation with Jake. I kind of regret saying anything. Maybe they don't know about his nephew? I'm starting to craft an apology in my head, but Christian cuts in.

"Jake has been having a hard time at school," he explains. "His classmates are making fun of his insulin pump. Calling him a robot or whatever because they don't understand." The room grows quiet all at once. So they know Jake. They know about his Type 1 diabetes. Maybe letting them in on the plan was not so bad after all.

"I'm sorry, man," Aiden says. The unsmiling, serious expression returns to his face.

"Kids can get mean sometimes, especially when they spot something that's different or unfamiliar," Christian explains with an admirable sense of patience.

Ellie releases a string of expletives in a foreign language. But I can understand context clues. So do the others.

"Uh oh," Aiden warns. "You've awoken my little tiger here." He seems like the kind of person who can make everybody laugh out loud while keeping a dead serious face.

"I don't think I qualify as *little* in my current gigantic state," Ellie says, gently rubbing her baby bump.

"Watch it, that's my wife you're talking about," Aiden teasingly admonishes, making her laugh playfully.

"So where does the party aspect come in?" She comes to stand by her husband, looping her arm into his.

"We're throwing a pump party for his class. To make the unfamiliar become more familiar. And hopefully give it a positive twist."

"When life gives you lemons…" Ellie agrees.

"Exactly, and since you're already here, you might as well make yourself useful," Christian offers, walking up to the whiteboard on his wall with a marker in hand, making us all face him as if we're in a scientific brainstorming session. "Okay." He lifts his hand and writes TYPE 1 DIABETES in big, bold letters in the middle of the board. "What does it mean to you?"

"Needles. Checking blood sugar. Counting carbs. Insulin injections. Fingertip pricking." The words fly out of our collective crowd. "Hypoglycemia. Being your own pancreas 24/7." It's overwhelming. Spending some time with Jake has made me realize what a long way the drug and medical device industry still has to go to improve the lives of these patients. Saying this disease already has treatment and settling for that is the overstatement of the century, and simply just doesn't cut it. Yet so many people in this industry keep saying it. My past self included.

"It's all true. And accurate." Christian writes every single item in separate bubbles, connected by lines that come out of the name of the chronic diagnosis his nephew has to live with for the rest of his life.

"But I doubt these are the kinds of things Jake would want us to focus on," I add. I've only spent two evenings and a morning with this little guy. But his sunshine personality tells me that instead of all these sad items we've listed, he would want to bring out the positive.

"I think you're right. We need to focus on the good parts."

We just need to figure out what those are.

Jake's party is a raving success. I doubt these kids will give him a hard time now that the unfamiliar has become familiar, with a positive twist, thanks to some tips from the *Overprotective Mom* blog, Ellie's funny additions and Christian's flawless execution.

We had to divvy up the prep work; Ellie and I were in charge of getting the supplies, Christian and Aiden got the treats. We then met again at Christian's office to cut little pumps out of colorful foam sheets and draw buttons on them to look somewhat like Jake's insulin pump—one for each kid to decorate with stickers and shiny glitter glue. I had to text Kate to find out headcount and allergy information, which she quickly and happily provided.

Then we made it into a game, the rules of which were simple. Jake's class listened excitedly to Christian's instructions and to Jake, who was standing proudly by his uncle, giving tips to his friends that only an experienced 'pumper' would know. Like—"*if your blood sugar is too low, you need to eat some gummy bears,*" holding up a bag of sugary candies, while Kate and I walked around the class and gave one bag to each kid. Or—"*if your blood sugar is too high, you need to take some insulin,*" pretending to punch some numbers on his pump, while his trusted helpers—again, us—handed the kids the colorful makeshift foam pumps and gave them plenty of time to decorate.

To Jake's five- and six-year-old peers, it was a fun game, and they giggled their way through decorating the pumps and chomping through their bags of gummy candies. But for Jake, this is life, unfortunately. *"Eating sugary gummies or drinking juice might seem fun,"* I recalled Christian's words from our late-night conversation, *"but not when you have to be woken up at 2 a.m. to do it, with extreme exhaustion and shaky hands, because your blood sugar had dropped to a dangerous low."* And checking blood sugar, counting carbs, giving yourself insulin multiple times every day, and changing the infusion set for your pump every three days or less—certainly not fun. But we'd chosen to shed positive light on this party, so all the other aspects were tucked away. If Jake decides to share any of the cold, hard truths behind it with a friend at some point, that's up to him. Today's party was about making lemonade, not rubbing flat-out lemon juice onto his wounds. And it was a raving success. Sometimes, it seems, tackling challenges with a positive spin can do the trick.

These parents raising kids with chronic diseases, coming up with creative ideas of how to make their children's lives easier and more appealing, are amazing. And brilliant. And the kids who actually have to live these lives, never able to take a break, are just pure superheroes.

"We have a few hours until pick-up," Christian says as we leave the school parking lot. "Jake has after-school soccer today." He turns on the radio, and a song I haven't heard before pumps excitement into the air. The kind of song you just know you're going to love even before you hear the half of it. "How about a late lunch?"

"Can we stop at my place first?" I ask, seeing as I'm still wearing yesterday's outfit. "I need a shower and a change of clothes." Plus, it sounds a little like a date, and I still haven't figured out that part just yet.

"Anything for you," he says. Then, stopping at a traffic light, his eyes flick to mine as he adds, "Thank you. For being there for Jake. And for me."

"Christian," I take his hand, letting our fingers interlace, "you're the best uncle a kid could ever wish for. What you did for Jake today was amazing. Thank you for letting me be part of it."

20

After party

Claire

"Make yourself at home," I say as we enter my apartment.

Christian takes a seat on the couch, a glass of cold water—the only drink I have in my fridge other than milk—in one hand. His phone is in the other, with the pretense of reading work emails, but I spot the small glances he takes at me as I cross the room, pretending to organize some stuff, enjoying the attention. The way his molten-amber honey eyes follow me behind his glasses while I walk from the kitchen to my bedroom, and back again, because I *forgot* I needed to drink more water. I can see him smile under his breath, inwardly calling me on my bullshit.

I take a quick shower. Wrapped up in a towel, hair still dripping water, I walk back into the living room. Christian lifts his head from his phone, eyes darkening as he considers me, trying to decide whether to let his gaze roam my towel-clad body or pretend to still be on his phone. He seems a bit surprised by my somewhat bold move.

He has no idea.

I don't either, actually. I don't typically do *bold*. Or have *moves*. But I find myself asking if he could help with something. So he follows me, playing along.

"Can you reach the top shelf?" I point to my closet, deciding I want to wear, out of everything I have in there, the one blouse I can't reach. Why is it so high up there? Well, for starters, it's a summer blouse, not something qualified for DC's almost-winter temperatures, not usually. And also, this was Ryan's least favorite blouse. It's teal, like his least favorite basketball team. Does that mean no one in his life can wear teal? Well, yes, if you ask him, but he's not in my life anymore, and it happens to be my favorite color, so I get to wear teal whenever I want. And now is a perfect time.

Christian chuckles at the lame, made-up task but comes over to stand behind me, effortlessly reaching for the top shelf as I drop my towel to the floor. *Intentionally*, of course. And we both know it. I take a step back, closing the gap between us, turning my head to look at him over my shoulder. His molten amber-honey eyes are dark with need and I can feel his warm breath on my neck.

"Does last night's dinner count?" I ask, referring to his "*Go out to dinner with me first.*" I had no idea that I have a seductive voice, but apparently I do.

Christian swallows hard, letting one hand skate up my rib cage, fingers grazing the underside of my breast while he's mulling the idea over. My skin is on fire, willing him to continue.

To not stop now. I don't know if it's the pregnancy hormones, me, him, us. "Don't stop," I plead. Because if he does, I think I might explode. But he does stop, for a second, weighing the possibilities, or maybe potential consequences. Then he removes his glasses slowly, resting them on my nightstand before he lets his stubble gently slide across the back of my neck, followed by his lips.

"It doesn't count as me taking you out to dinner, no," he rasps into my ear. His hand climbs up, cupping my breast, his fingers toying with my nipple. His body wraps around my backside. He's all woken up for me and hard, pressing through his clothes against me. A loud moan escapes my lips, a sound so unfamiliar it takes me by surprise. "You may want to put that towel back on before I lose control," he groans. His other hand travels slowly down my stomach before stopping.

"Show me how you lose control," I whisper.

Christian exhales, letting his hand slide the last bit of distance.

"*Yes,*" I breathe.

"You," he chants almost to himself, resuming his exploration. Waves of heat and pleasure take over. "The things I want to do to you..." he rumbles, turning my chin to him, bringing his lips to mine, kissing me hard.

"Show me," I beg. My body is so hungry for more of him. I turn in his arms, unbuckling his belt with trembling hands. I can barely contain myself as he pulls his shirt over his head, revealing his massive chest. I let go of his lips only to let my tongue explore the grooves of his ab muscles as I remove the rest of his clothes and let them land in a pile with my towel. I'm already breathless as I set him free, greedy hands wrapped around his length, wanting more. I honestly don't know what I'm doing, Ryan never liked that kind of stuff, not with me anyway, but I let Christian's wild breathing guide me. He brings my lips back to his. Our kisses are impatient, needy, fighting the urge to come back for air in between steamy mouth attacks that are impossible to stop. Until Christian pauses. He gives me one dazed look, then sweeps me off my feet and lays me gently onto my bed, but he doesn't follow. My body burns in all those spots we were connected a second ago, begging for his touch again. "That's your chance." His voice is strained.

"Uh?" I don't have any words in me right now. Other than potential descriptions of what I'd like to do *with*—or rather *to*—this man.

"To stop me," he clarifies. His husky making-out voice is so sexy, and his molten amber-honey eyes are making me melt inside.

I give him an incredulous look. Because on account of all things I would never consider doing, stopping what we have going right now is at the very top.

"I think it might actually kill me if you don't come closer," I admit, surprising myself with the admission. It's a whole side of me I haven't met. I let my legs wrap around his waist and pull him over, his length pressing against me. "Don't stop," I plead, hardly able to hear my voice over my thumping pulse, finding his lips again like this is my sole air supply. I rock my hips against him, back and forth, a form of torture, driving us both insane.

"I'm clean," he grunts, slowly unraveling.

"Me too. And also already pregnant," I laugh. I pull him closer, tightening my grip as he sinks into me, connecting us in so many new places. I lift up to meet him. I know he's trying to be gentle, considerate, but right now I have no room for that as my body embraces this unfamiliar feral side. Christian slows us down, taking his time with me. His lips leave mine, kissing my neck and down my breast. He takes one nipple in his mouth, biting it softly.

"Don't slow down," I beg, rolling my hips faster.

"I've been dreaming about you for so long." His gravelly voice is a whisper. "I want to savor it."

"You can do that later," I say between thrusts. "Can't hold—" I start, but my body is already flying off that cliff. Free falling.

A sexy, mischievous smile spreads across Christian's face as he angles against me for the most delicious friction. My groans get louder as he now controls our collective movements, thrusting and driving us wild, and I let go completely. As he lets go completely. As we bring each other to a blissful-sedated state I don't think I've been to before.

The best one-night (or rather day) stand of my life. But I don't think I can stop at one. And from the way Christian turns and pulls me over him, sliding my thighs up his sides and pressing me to him, I don't think he's going to stop at one either.

21

Confessions

Claire

I'm aware that keeping truths locked away is lying, in a way. The right thing has been pretty clear, hovering over my head, dropping annoying reminders that there is something I have to do. Yet it takes a few more weeks until I finally call Ryan and summon a conversation. And now we're seated across from each other at the local coffee shop. From our lukewarm body language toward each other, it's hard to guess that we once—and not very long ago—were in a relationship. And impossible to guess that he's the father of the little plum-sized fetus I'm carrying inside. I try to dig deep into my memory, recall a time we once were head-over-heels in love. *Were we?*

I can't seem to recall.

Ryan looks happy. Happier than he ever was with me. Like he's started a whole new and improved chapter in his life. Sort of like I have too. I feel a little guilty, knowing that what I'm about to say might wipe that boyish smile off his face. Complicate whatever it is he has going for himself. But I've come this far, there's no going back now.

"You look good, Claire," he says, splitting his one slice of lemon pound cake into two. He drops one half onto the paper bag it came with and pushes it over to me like he used to when we were still together. A cute gesture. That is, if you like lemon cakes.

"No thanks," I say, pushing the paper bag back to him.

"Not hungry?"

"Not into lemon cakes," I say.

"You're not?" He's taken aback. Surprised, hurt even. "You never said."

And he's right. I might have not consumed anything with lemons in the two years we were together, or even drank lemonade. But I never mentioned it directly. Not even when he ordered a layered lemon cake—which is his obvious favorite—for one of my birthdays. Didn't want to hurt his feelings. I'm not big on cakes anyway. But now that I'm in confession mode—and currently possess strong aversion to most foods, yes, Cheetos is still my go-to sustenance—I let myself.

"Sorry," I say, grimacing a little when he apologizes too, for never actually taking notice. He's a nice guy. Oblivious at times, but I don't think he means to be.

"You look good too." I put the conversation back on track.

"Thanks." His familiar bashful smile decorates his features. He's quiet, for a moment, slowly sipping his coffee before he says, "You look happy."

"I am," I realize, "happy."

"I don't think I've seen you like this before. Gleaming." That's because I wasn't. Gleaming. Or happy. It wasn't him, just the subpar combination of life and... us. But with all due respect to honesty and to this decisive confession mode, I'm not looking to hurt Ryan's feelings. So I settle for a quiet *thank you* to match his tone, and cut to the chase.

"I'm pregnant." I just throw it out there. I'm so bad with delivering messages in a mellow, empathetic way. I'm better at not delivering messages at all, or doing it the blunt, bomb-dropping way.

Ryan's face morphs into a big question mark, but he's too busy choking to ask anything, so I just get on with my execution, afraid that if I stop I might lose my courage. "Yes, you're the father. That one night when we tried to fix things between us." Things that had already been lost long before. "Probably not our best attempt."

"Are you sure?" Is the one thing the man chooses to ask when he partially regains his voice.

"Yes, I *am* sure," I scoff.

"But you're seeing someone. I'm pretty sure I saw your tongue deep in some guy's throat at the mall right after we ended things."

So he did see it. "That was two weeks after *you* had ended things, and I wasn't sleeping with him." At least not at the time.

"Didn't seem like it to me." Yeah, I can see where he'd get that idea. That kiss was HOT.

"Well, not until about a month later, I wasn't," I say, "and by that time I was already a few weeks pregnant."

"Oh." Ryan sinks deep into thought. "If it's about money—"

"I do pretty well for myself, thank you very much, I'm not here to talk about money." And I'm honestly quite offended by the direction his mind is going.

"Are you planning to keep the ba—"

"I am," I say faster than he has a chance to finish his question, surprising us both.

"There are other options—"

"Shhh! Babies can hear you, you know?" I stop him, covering my still-coverable belly with my hand. It's instinctive, but at the same time, I can't believe I just said that. Didn't even know I had that kind of motherly thing in me. Coming into this conversation, I think I might have still been on the fence. Basking in the comfort of stalling my decision. But now, hearing Ryan hinting about the alternative feels like someone is trying to rip my heart out. And suddenly not keeping it doesn't feel like an option anymore. How has this unborn baby become a part of me so quickly?

"O-Kay," Ryan drawls, smiling a little. I pull out the little ultrasound image that I seem to be carrying along now, like a proud mama bear. He takes a painfully long look, then gives it back. We both fall into silence, then revert to sipping our drinks, each of us in our own head. I should make it known that drinking herbal tea is not my forte, and not having an intense aversion to coffee is definitely something I look forward to. When our mugs are empty, we get up and head outside, still not a word between us.

We cross the road toward the large building of the public library, once our favorite hang-out place on a too hot or too cold or gray and rainy day. Or maybe just Ryan's favorite. As much as I like reading, I don't like quiet places. Or anything less loud than the noise in my own head.

Ryan stops and settles onto the large brick stairs leading to the entrance. "I'm not sure what to do with this information." His head lowers between his knees. "I'm in a relationship," he mumbles. Then pauses to lift his head back to look at me. "With someone I really like."

"Me too." I say, surprising myself a bit. I've been avoiding labels like the plague, but am growing comfortable with Christian's running partner analogy. With benefits. "I don't expect you to do anything. In fact, I didn't even want to tell you about the baby, but Christian insisted you needed to know. And Kate too. And my mom."

"Christian?" Out of everyone I've just mentioned he chooses to focus on the one he doesn't know. "That's the guy from the mall?" There's a tinge of jealousy in his voice. Didn't he just say he was in a relationship?

"Yep," I say, kicking my shoe into the brick stairs.

"He looked kind of... rough," he says. That's Ryan's slang for someone who spends his spare time getting into fistfights and seeing them through.

"He really isn't," I say, chuckling. Although I can see where Ryan is coming from. "He's an endocrinology professor at GERI."

"Professor? With these tattoos on his arms? And those muscles?" Wow, and I thought he barely even noticed us.

"Hot guys can be professors." The words just slip out. "And anyway, that's not the topic of today's conversation."

"Right," Ryan sighs. Then, "I don't think I can be someone's father right now. I don't think I want to."

My tone is even when I say, "You don't need to either." Then I turn away and leave. I had no expectations coming into this conversation. None. Zero. I even said I didn't want Ryan back in my life. Which is why I'm so confused right now, trying to figure out why I feel the way I do. I'm honestly relieved that he doesn't want to get back together. But there is also disappointment and frustration brewing in my hodgepodge of feelings. What exactly was I hoping for? Am I offended on behalf of an unborn baby?

Christian

I get a "Gosh! I'm so mad right now!" text from Claire, and then radio silence. I write back, I call, I wait and then re-attempt all of the above. I try to think back to every single thing I may have said or done in the past twenty-four hours. She seemed quite content this morning when I kissed her goodbye and dropped her off at work. I know she was planning to meet up with Ryan sometime this week, but as of this morning she wasn't yet set on an actual day and time. Still, I'm worried. Worried enough to drop everything in the lab and drive over to Amarinex offices. I take the stairs two at a time, not having patience for the elevator, then try to talk myself into looking unbothered as I walk across the hallway. But she's not at her cubicle, or the bathroom. Or any of the meeting rooms. Has she gone home? I storm out of the building and back on the road, headed to Claire's apartment.

"Where's your sister?" I ask when Kate appears at Claire's door. I know she doesn't need a special reason to visit her sister, but doing so in the middle of the day does strike me as a bad sign. "Is she okay?"

"Oh, hello to you too." She smiles kindly at me, alleviating some of my worry, but I can tell her smile is laced with concern. "She's in the spare bedroom, building shelves," Kate steps aside and gestures for me to enter, pointing in the general direction of where shelves apparently are being assembled.

Seriously? Is that why she can't answer her goddamn phone?

"She could have said something, I would have built her shelves," I say.

"I suggest you don't say that to her." Kate stops me, blocking my path.

"What? Why?"

"She likes carpentry. It helps calm down her nerves. Since we were kids. But especially now," she lowers her voice.

"So she doesn't really need shelves?" I ask, lowering my voice as well. She did mention some carpentry fondness, coming to think of it.

"Not really," Kate whispers.

Noted.

"Ryan?" I ask, realizing the meet and greet might have taken place sooner than I thought. Kate nods somberly and lets me through.

I follow the sound of hammering. Claire is on her knees, wearing a pair of heavy-duty gloves and a somber expression, hovering over a shelving unit that's lying sideways on the floor.

"He wants nothing to do with his own baby. Nothing," she says as she spots me leaning against the doorframe. "What kind of a father says that about their unborn kid?" Her eyes focused on the intense hammering.

"I'm sorry," I say. I don't even know the guy and already don't like him.

"It breaks my heart," she says.

I know I shouldn't ask. On a scale of the worst possible timing, this could be even worse. I may be falling for Claire, but that doesn't give me any right to expect the same of her. Yet the words are out before I get a chance to stop them. "Do you still love him?" I brace myself for her response.

"What?!" She lifts her head only to give me an incredulous look. I hold my breath before she says, "Of course not. Love has nothing to do with it. And by the way, I don't think I ever loved him." I know it shouldn't, but there's this little ball of hope climbing up my chest.

"Claire," I take a step closer and bend down so our faces are level, gently removing the hammer and her heavy-duty gloves. "Will you let me help?" Her skin bristles as I take her hands in mine, gently smoothing my thumbs over her wrists.

"I'm perfectly capable of building these shelves on my own," she scoffs, almost offended.

"I'm not talking about the shelves," I sigh. "Will you let me be there for you?"

Her eyes lift up to me, lost and gloomy. "Why on earth would you want to get yourself into something anyone in his right mind would steer away from?" she asks. Her bottom lip quivers. It's a minuscule shift but I see it. "Even this baby's dad is already running away. You barely even know me."

But that's the thing. I know it hasn't been long, but I feel like I *do* know her. I know how she looks when she wakes up in the morning. The cute little sounds she makes when she's asleep. The little worry in her bottom lip when she thinks she cares more than she should, or the shake to her hands when she's upset. Her reasons. Her worries. Her fears. Her eyes tell me everything I need to know. I want to tell this gorgeous, incredible woman that since meeting her for the first time, seeing her smile has quickly become the best part of my day. That there's nothing she can possibly say or do, nothing I could possibly learn about her, that would change how far gone I am for her, or how bad I freaking want her in my life. That I don't know everything, but this is the one thing I've known for sure since the moment she came into my life. How do I tell her all that without scaring her off?

"I'm not going anywhere," I finally say, closing the distance between us and throwing my arms around her. "Whether you like it or not." I could go on a full monologue, but I'm aware of her apprehensive skepticism, aware of how tense her body feels against mine. So I just focus on keeping her close to me, hoping my thoughts and feelings will somehow absorb through her walls. Her muscles relax as she melts into my arms, finally letting me through.

22

Honey, I'm home

Christian

In the weeks that follow, we're inseparable, stealing kisses whenever we're alone. We work, we cook, we eat, we chat through the nights, my place or her place, and wake up tangled in each other's arms. We read pregnancy books together, go to Claire's OB-GYN appointments together, and with Ellie and Aiden's recommendation, even sign up to prenatal yoga classes as a couple. Claire's morning—or rather whole day—sickness is gradually subsiding. Her cheeks fill with this adorable blushed color, and the signs of fatigue are almost gone. Her baby bump is starting to show, and sliding my hand over it is possibly at the very top of my favorite things. Right after another very favorable effect of her pregnancy hormones, which pretty much makes this gorgeous woman insatiable, wanting me all the time. And

I'm very happy to oblige. Claire looks radiant, glowing. Happy. And she's all mine. Or at least I hope she is as we lie in her bed, snuggled tightly under the sheets. Her fingers are playing with the hairs on my chest, my fingers splayed across her belly in watchful anticipation, excited by each little butterfly flutter under my palm. I know the books say you don't actually feel the baby move until later in the pregnancy, but we're both convinced we already do.

"Did you feel that?" Claire chirps, her eyes bright and gleaming.

"I did!" I say excitedly, lowering my head to her little bump. "Hey Baby," I whisper, letting my mouth hover over Claire's belly button. We are probably the most unoriginal pair of adults in the world, naming an unborn baby "Baby," but somehow between kissing Claire and letting my heart swoon over her and this baby, I can't bring myself to care about the rest of the world.

"Will you go baby shopping with me?" Claire asks in this sweet, lazy post-sex voice of hers that I can't resist. She stretches ever so slightly and then cuddles back into my arms. I let my lips trace small kisses along her naked body until our mouths connect again.

"I'll go anywhere with you," I promise.

"Hmmm…" she sighs sweetly, letting her leg wrap around me. "Christian Copeland, what have I done to deserve you?" Her words end on a moan as I slide my hands around her hips, hugging her tighter into me.

"That's the exact question I've been wanting to ask, only with you as the subject," I say, pulling my head slightly back to look into her eyes. I feel lucky and grateful and— "Move in with me," I say, surprising us both. I know it's fast, but I've never felt so clear about what I want. For years I'd been so busy taking care of Mom, and then helping Julia around with Jake. I don't regret any of it for a second, of course. But for the first time in my life there's something, someone, I want for myself.

Claire looks at me with wonder, weighing the possibilities. "There's... Baby," she says on a warning note.

"I'm very much aware," I say softly, letting my hand find its way to her bump again. Would it have been easier if she wasn't pregnant? Sure. Do I wish this unborn child was mine? Every fucking day. But part of falling for someone so completely, I'm beginning to realize, is accepting them as they are, and everything that comes along with it. I wouldn't change a thing about Claire, and that includes this baby too. "I was asking both of you," I clarify. There's another little flutter under my fingers, making us both smile. I swear this tiny baby growing inside her is reacting to my touch.

"I think Baby is saying yes," she notifies me.

"What about Baby's mom?" I prod. I don't think I've ever wanted anything in my life like I do this. Her. All of her. Us. Along with anything and everything that the prospect of *us* has to offer.

There's a noise coming from what I think is the front door to her apartment. Some key shuffling, accompanied by the sound of a man's voice from somewhere in the living room. "Honey, I'm home."

Claire

I am about to consider Christian's proposal to move in with him. This man has bewitched me. Taken me by storm. I don't even know the proper words to describe the way he makes me feel. I just know that for the first time in like forever, I'm happy. And this is a kind of happy I haven't felt before. A sort of happy that overshadows every other noisy or scary thought that likes to occasionally pop into my head. The kind of happy that can lower the volume of that constant rumble and rumination in my head. And it's fast, and scary, but I think—or at least hope—that these feelings are here to stay, and although I haven't voiced any of it out loud yet, I hope Christian is here to stay too.

But our little quiet haven is disturbed by a noise coming from my front door. Followed by that familiar, unmissed, "Honey, I'm home," as if the past few months never happened. As if Ryan and I hadn't actually broken up. As if we hadn't actually agreed that I'd keep the apartment until the end of our lease. Right before Ryan packed up his stuff, moved out in a swift and—did he give me back his copy of the key?

"Stay here," Christian whispers, jumping off my bed, wild-eyed and ready for war. Ready to protect me. And I love this about him. Although I really shouldn't be using that word with him in the same sentence. It's way too soon.

"It's Ryan," I say quietly, before Christian hits someone for real. This does not ease his battle-ready face, which now looks to be shifting back and forth from the need to protect me to the need to fight over me. But at least he decides to put on some clothes and helps me find mine. While in the meantime, it sounds like the intruder has opened the fridge and turned on the TV, like it's a regular day getting home from the office, pre-breakup. I try to bring my sex hair under control and make the short way to the living room. My heart is pounding at the thought of having my past and my present collide.

"Ryan, what are you doing here?" My eyes narrow even before they register his image. He's seated on the sofa, remote in hand. He's in his suit and loosened tie, straight out of a day in court. He looks good, content. And while he looked good when we were together, he never seemed quite content as now. But it's fleeting, as his eyes grow wide and his posture tenses when Christian appears behind me.

"I'm home," he says. "I'm back. I'm here for you. For our baby." And yet he says it as if he never actually left. Never actually told me he didn't want anything to do with either me or—later on—with "our" baby. In fact, this specific combination of words coming from him makes me feel sick. Literally sick. So after a few weeks of quiet, I get that oh-so-familiar burn in my throat. My hand flies up to cover my mouth as I make a run to the bathroom. Me throwing up is definitely not a pleasant sound, and I can hear Ryan muttering from the living room as my dinner comes right back up. I can't blame him, but the striking contrast and irony are not lost on me when Christian appears in the small bathroom almost instinctively and smooths the hair back from my face, whispering calming words in my ear. Yet despite the loss of my earlier dinner, and Christian's soothing voice, the knot that's forming in my stomach is not going away. And unfortunately, Ryan isn't either. So when I get back to the living room, I decide to make an introduction.

"Christian, this is Ryan, my *ex*." Yes, I do put some emphasis on the 'ex' part, in case Ryan is having memory issues. Rare for the seasoned lawyer that he is, but still.

"Ryan, this is Christian," I say. We haven't really gone through relationship definitions yet, not outside of our own heads, that is, so I leave that part blank, noticing how Christian's jaw clenches. They acknowledge each other with a slight nod. Neither of them says a word.

"Are you here to give me back your copy of *my* apartment key?" I prod, narrowing my eyes at Ryan, really just going for two questions in one.

"No, I'm back, I..." Ryan gets up from the couch and I somehow instinctively find myself closer to Christian.

"Who said I wanted you back?" I snap.

"Can we talk? Alone?" Ryan pleads.

Christian turns his gaze to me, "I can go," he offers, searching my eyes for confirmation. That I'm okay. That we are still okay.

"No," I answer them both, speaking through the loud thumping of my heart, brought on by what I'm about to say. "Christian is part of my life now." It's the best I can do without using any titles. "If you want to talk, you'll need to talk to Christian too."

Out of the corner of my eye, I spot the slow smile forming on Christian's lips as his arm snakes around my waist protectively.

"Are you sure?" the incredible man beside me inquires quietly, while Ryan looks at us, rolling his eyes and slapping his seasoned lawyer expression back on.

"Never been so sure."

Christian

I know this conversation should probably happen without me there. It's their child, their life, and they have a lot to talk about. But Claire won't let me leave, and I can't say I don't like it. Her hand is nervously clutching mine as her body rests as close as physically possible to mine, and as far as living room-size-possible from Ryan. I'm an observer in what feels like a high-stakes legal discussion more than anything, I think. My mind goes to so many places at once that I only hear bits and pieces of their words.

"You said you didn't want anything to do with the baby," Claire argues.

"I said I wasn't ready to be someone's father," Ryan tries to explain, maintaining some kind of professional poker face composure.

"Oh, right. And now you are?" Claire is not having it.

"I want to be," he says honestly. He looks like a good person, I'll give him that. Just lacking a great deal of passion. I don't know if he's like that all the time—a mask he's used to wearing, carryover from work—or is it just part of their dynamic?

"You wanted me to..." Claire's voice splits at the edges, she pulls our entwined hands to cover her baby bump protectively, letting my fingers sprawl over as much surface as possible before saying, "You were hinting at having an abortion." I can feel her pulse rising dangerously. Her hands tremble.

"I was just alluding to the fact that you have options," Ryan says.

"Hey, watch it!" I can definitely take this guy down in a second, and that's all I can think of when I point my finger at him, ready to leap off the couch and into his face, but Claire pulls me back.

"I'm sorry," he says, as if we misunderstood his intention. "That was then." I notice the tiniest crack in his demeanor. "I want to be here for the... baby, take care of whatever you need."

Claire looks even more annoyed by this last sentence, ready to punch him herself. "I don't need anything from you. Thank you for stopping by, you can leave the key on the counter," she says.

"I want to be part of this baby's life." Ryan's voice takes on a higher pitch in what sounds like a plea. "I want to move back in, be there for you, be there with you every step of the way. I shouldn't have left to begin with."

What exactly does this all mean? I don't like it one bit.

"Ryan, you broke up with me," Claire tries to keep her tone even, losing her breath mid-sentence. "We both fell out of love. Honestly, I don't even know if we ever were in love to begin with."

"You can't say that," he tries, starting to list events from their relationship. This is where my mind tunes out. I can't sit here and listen to all the ways another man loved *my* girl.

"I moved on, Ryan," Claire interrupts, her voice pulling me back from my agony. "And us breaking up was actually a good thing, because—" she turns her head back to me, letting our eyes connect, "I met Christian. He's been here for me, for Baby, since day one."

"But I'm the father," Ryan responds without much conviction.

"You can visit, you can get involved, but we're not getting back together." Her eyes search mine again, as if seeking confirmation. That I'm still here, still on board. I was not prepared for this conversation. Not prepared for this forum. Not prepared to share Claire and Baby with someone else. A baby who isn't even mine. And even though it definitely feels that way, I have no right claiming ownership here. These are not my decisions to make.

"I don't think that's going to work." The lawyer in Ryan makes his appearance again. "I'm not going to be a 'weekend dad' while you're spending your life in someone else's arms." He splits a stare between us, lips forming a tight line. "I'm either all in or all out. It's an all or nothing proposition."

Proposition? Fucking asshole.

Claire doesn't even hesitate before she gets up and says, "Then it's nothing."

23

The kid who once was me

Claire

I know having Christian here to witness this painful discussion with Ryan is the lifeline I needed, my support to lean into as I shut Ryan out of my unborn baby's life. But this is only part of the picture, I realize, as I watch Ryan quietly return his copy of the key and walk out. Christian is quiet, glued to the same spot on the couch for a long moment. Deep in thought.

"I'm sorry," I say as I sit back down, turning my body to face him.

"*You're* sorry? Why are you sorry?" He finally breaks the silence.

I take his hands in mine. "For dragging you into this. I was so focused on how I felt, what I was experiencing, that I wasn't paying attention to how this must be for you."

"Claire, don't apologize. I'm here because I want to be. And I'll support you in any capacity you need or want from me." His words are in such contradiction to Ryan's 'all or nothing' approach. "Love, especially for a child, should be unconditional," he says, making my heart swell. "He should want to be in his child's life regardless of whether he has you in his arms or not."

"I'm sorry you got caught in the middle of all this." I wince, worried that this acidic rain might break the special bond that has started to form between us. My eyes fill with tears and I try to blink them away, still trying to determine the meaning of all this. "I think—" I take a deep shaky breath, "I've decided," I say, even though these thoughts—that have been there all along—are only now forming into what feels like a decision, "that it's easier if you let me go."

"Easier," he says, studying me. "For you?" I don't miss Christian's melancholic tone and the big dark cloud that quickly settles between us.

"For *you*," I clarify, letting my eyes drop to the floor. Because it's definitely not the easier option for me. And I'm probably going to regret this moment for the rest of my life. But not everything is about me. And making Christian stay in the middle of this jumbled mess called my life is not fair to him.

"You've decided?"

"Yes."

"Without asking me what I think about it?"

"Precisely," I say. It's a confident word, but my voice is so weak, as if about to break any moment. I'm holding my breath, holding myself together before shattering into a million pieces. I can't fall apart now.

"And what if I say no? That I don't want to let you go? That I'm not going anywhere, unless you make me?"

There are emotions one holds inside sometimes without even being aware. The kind you only realize you're capable of feeling when it floats to the surface. And once there, it's impossible to bottle back up. Or pretend it hadn't been there all along.

My entire being shifts from mournful to relieved, and grateful. And there's more—inside what I'd thought was my frozen heart—feelings I don't even dare try to unpack.

"I was hoping you'd say that."

"I know how important it is for you to have Ryan in this baby's life. And he's an ass for making you choose," Christian says, sliding a gentle hand over my bump. I nod, and this one simple movement makes my unshed tears roll down my cheeks. Childhood memories decide to wash over me, now of all times, and he sees it. Of course he does. "Tell me," he pleads, wiping my tears gently with his thumbs, his eyes asking for permission to see those guarded places of my heart.

So I tell him about the kid who once was me. The kid who used to daydream about finding her dad in a faraway land. Making up stories about reunited families and happily ever afters. And not just in my dreams. Despite being an anxious kid who worried herself a bit too much over apocalyptic scenarios and lethal epidemics, to the point of sometimes not being able to breathe, happy was important. My mom made sure of that, in our little old apartment with its peeling wallpaper and its narrow kitchen that could barely fit Mom, Kate and me. We spent so many nights on the carpet around the coffee table, playing board games or munching on dinner. Snuggling through the evenings with a good movie on our yard-sale couch, or a book in each of our hands. Kate liked adventures, I liked medical mysteries, feeding my disease obsession—to my mom's dismay. Mom would read whatever we would, like a book buddy, to share the experience, but I think her favorites were non-fiction travel books. She never complained though. About the books or anything else. Nothing was ever too hard or too overwhelming or too impossible, even as a single mom, raising two girls all on her own. Anything Kate and I would dream of trying, she'd be there to support. As she does now. Except for maybe finding that one-night stand from her past who happens to be my long-lost father. And that dream eventually dissipated, along with that hopeful, optimistic dreamer version of me.

"It's not that I'm not optimistic now," I conclude my little biographical sketch. "Just maybe more cautious, and realistic. And sometimes on the wrong side of statistics. And now *I'm* about to have my kid going through life without ever meeting their biological dad," I sigh. "Is it worse having a father who never wanted you, or one who never knew you existed?" I ask, not expecting an answer. He hugs me then, quiet and warm, and I lean into our comfortable silence.

"I honestly don't know," Christian finally says, responding to my rhetorical question. "At least I can beat the shit out of the former, if I ever see him again." The pain in his eyes makes me realize he's not just talking about Ryan anymore.

"Tell me about your dad," I ask.

"Not much to tell," he huffs. I give him an insistent look so he adds, "Left my mom to raise three kids on her own." I had some idea about his dad but—

"Three kids?" Besides Julia, he never mentioned another sibling.

"Brianna..." He rolls the word slowly, as if not wanting to let go. There are endless shades of sadness to his tone when he says her name. "That's a story for another time."

"Tell me?" I plead, every Ryan-related thought completely pushed out of my mind.

He hesitates for a moment. "My baby sister. She was not even six months old when my dad left. Brianna was crying for days and—probably unrelated to the fact that he was gone, but as a kid I was convinced it was—she got really sick. Mom never said much about it. Some infection, probably treated with the wrong antibiotics, if at all. I was too young to understand the details. Anyway, she died. It all happened so fast."

I want to say something, but I have no idea what I could possibly say to make him feel better. So I just remain quiet. Looking into his eyes, I plead without words for him to continue, as I begin to assemble the puzzle pieces that make up this man.

"Mom spent every waking moment blaming herself for not having enough money to take her to better doctors or get a second opinion. Blaming herself for Brianna's death. She started having panic attacks every time Julia or I would get sick. Stressing over worst-case scenarios. Every fever became a deadly virus, every headache a terminal brain tumor, every fall a catastrophic accident. Then she started worrying about her own death, about the what-if, *her* worst-case scenario—that something bad would happen to her, and Julia and I would be left alone in the world. She worried so much about death that she forgot how to live. She'd been falling apart for years, and we had no idea how to take care of her."

I think back to my little anxiety attack before that first doctor's appointment, the way Christian knew exactly what to do, what to say. The way he so quickly made me feel grounded, the way he disarmed me from my own intrusive thoughts. And my mind is already running a thousand miles a minute. If this baby is a girl, I decide, I'm going to name her Brie, after Brianna.

And to Christian, I say, "I'm so sorry."

"Don't be. My aunt swooped in at some point and took us all under her wing, so I did get to have a reasonable childhood. And for that I'm grateful." He coughs, as if trying to hide the emotions in his voice. "Funny thing is," his eyes fall to his feet as he mulls it over, "to this day, I blame the asshole who called himself my dad for everything. Every.single.thing. For leaving us. For not being able to separate between what he had or didn't have with my mom. For not choosing us. I'd be happy to break Ryan's face any day. Just say the word."

24

The right thing

Christian

"This is not easy for me to say, and don't get me wrong, I would much rather kick your ass," I grate the words out. I know I'm going to hate myself for doing it, but I had to do the right thing. For Claire. For the baby.

The key Ryan left on Claire's counter had a keychain with his law firm logo. So I looked it up and called him. A few days later, I'm sitting across from the guy at a local bar, busying my fingers with the coaster that should have been resting under my beer, not able to bring myself to drink. I'm here on a mission. Well, two, apparently. The side mission—trying to stop myself from breaking Ryan's teeth—is unplanned but forms as we keep hitting a wall in our conversation. The main mission, however, is to convince him that his *"all or nothing"* is a shit approach when it comes to family. That his kid should be his everything regardless of where his relationship with Claire stands. And that "*nothing*" is just not an option. It's what I wish someone had said to that lame excuse of a person who used to call himself my father.

There's been more silence than words in this exchange. More jaw clenching (me) and beer drinking (him). Ryan doesn't say he's going to give it a try, but eventually he does call Claire with some sort of amended proposition. He has good eyes, I notice, and I'm hoping also good intentions. Claire is surprised, quite pleased that this is somewhat going her way—not knowing I had anything to do with it of course—I made Ryan swear it was going to stay that way.

But then Claire comes up with *this* plan.

Ryan has no idea what he's getting himself into.

Neither do I.

"So you're here for family therapy?" Doctor Levine splits a friendly gaze between Ryan and me. We're both sitting across from him, sharing the only sofa in his office, where Claire—we'd both assumed—was supposed to join us, but she had a different plan. Apparently.

"Do we look like a family to you?" Ryan sighs in exasperation, crossing his arms tight across his chest.

"You tell me." Our newly appointed therapist smiles warmly.

"Claire didn't give you the backstory?" Ryan asks, almost literally pulling his hair out.

"No, she wanted to keep me 'unbiased,' her words, and I respect that." Dr. Levine pauses for a meaningful moment. "I'm here to help you find common ground, equip you with tools for getting along better, and mitigate potential issues in your relationship."

"We're not in a fucking romantic relationship," Ryan spits out. The man has no patience. I lean back, trying to resist the smile forming on my face. Can't say I'm not enjoying Ryan's torment. Dr. Levine never mentioned anything about a romantic relationship. We're both in the same room, speaking with the same person, yet each of us is hearing completely different things. "We're in love with the same woman," Ryan adds tersely, not able to take it anymore.

"Are we?" I question, not smiling anymore. The man needs to get his facts straight. "Last time I checked, you broke up with her."

"But I came back. I apologized, admitted I was wrong. Said I was ready to become a dad."

"After you had told her you wanted nothing to do with her, or the baby. And brought up abortion as an option, twice!" Okay, so maybe I'm losing my calm a bit too.

"People can change their minds," Ryan insists, turning his head away from me to look at Dr. Levine, hoping to get a sign of agreement there. But Dr. Levine is experienced enough to appear neutral and non-judgmental.

"Problem is," I jump in, "while you were busy seeing someone else and not giving a fuck about Claire or the baby, I've been there for her. Throughout doctor's appointments, blood tests, ultrasounds, holding her hair when she was throwing up. Falling for her." The last part slips out so naturally, as if it's a known fact.

"Thank you very much for filling in for me," Ryan says. "But I'm here now."

And I know that what he really means to say is 'you can go now,' but this option is off the table. I can't believe I actually talked him into coming back to Claire's life. If we were still at that bar, drinking our beers, my hand would now be wrapped around his neck, and not in a friendly manner. But we're here, sitting in a therapist's office, because stupid naive me thought it was a good idea for Ryan to be in his child's life. And since it turns out he doesn't think there's room for me there too, it certainly seems to have backfired.

"Okay boys, let's not forget that there's another side to this story," Doctor Levine intervenes. I can't blame him for calling us *boys* given the way we look right now, ready to rip each other apart. "Her name is Claire. She has her own free will," he reminds us calmly.

Let's face it, we're both here for Claire. She said that if we're going to make it work, we're going to have to find a way to get along. I thought she was mainly talking about Ryan. He's the one who needs to work on himself. But here I am, willing to kill the guy. Or rather—willing myself not to kill the guy. Which is a big enough hint that he's not the only one who has work to do. The room around me is getting hot. I fold up the sleeves of my dress shirt, loosen my collar, trying to rein down my frustration.

Dr. Levine straightens in his seat. "Before we begin, I'd like to hear from you what you're both hoping to achieve. Christian, why don't you start?"

I think back to my mom, to all those days she couldn't get herself out of bed. To the dark cloud that surrounded her, all the time, no matter what. To the past and the fear, burdening her every breath, every thought, not letting her move into the present or have a glimpse of hope for a long enough moment to think about the future. Yes, she lost a child, but she also had two still living, two who needed her, needed her presence in their lives, needed her smile and her comfort. Had therapy been more common, more known at the time, had we had the money to afford it and the sense to seek it, maybe she could have been saved instead of willing herself to die. "I think sometimes people need help to make things better and should not be afraid to ask for it," is how I choose to summarize this trip down memory lane. Then thinking back to the actual question I add, "I hope we can come to a reasonable understanding. Some sort of balance, for the sake of Claire and the baby."

"Well, aren't you Mr. Perfect," Ryan grumbles low enough that only I can hear.

Dr. Levine nods. I can see he senses there's more to it than what I chose to put into words, but he doesn't press. Instead, he turns his gaze to Ryan.

"Claire said that if we want to be in her life, we need to learn how to get along with each other," he says matter-of-factly.

"And how do you feel about it?"

"I can't see why I need to get along with another man in order to be with this woman." Ryan blows out an exasperated sigh. "I don't believe in therapy or in spilling my guts and digging deep. It only brings about more sorrow, makes darkness climb out of its tightly locked Pandora's box and show its ugly face. Adds more fuel to the fire. Gives people more things to fight about. Makes couples break up." His voice breaks at that last note. There's a backstory there, that much is obvious. "Sorry, nothing personal, Doctor Levine," he adds. "Therapy completely fucked up my parents' relationship. I wouldn't be here wasting your time if it weren't for Claire's insistence."

"Noted," the doctor says, still offering a genuine smile despite the apparent criticism. "I agree with you."

"Good," Ryan sighs. Then does a double take and frowns. "Did you just agree with me?"

Dr. Levine nods again. So I say, "Doc, this is a strange choice of career for someone who doesn't believe in therapy."

"Well," he chuckles, "therapy is not a one-size-fits-all. Digging deep into the past is not always the best option. Sometimes we need to focus on the present, and the future. And I believe in doing things differently. Which is why I'm here. I think people know deep inside what they want and how to get it. They just need to ask themselves the right questions. Make the right plans."

"Right." Ryan looks unconvinced. "And this is going to take hundreds of weekly therapy sessions stretched over several years, to pay for your sports car, or vacation home, correct?" Ryan's sarcasm is palpable, but given what he's just shared, I can see where he's coming from.

"Not with me," the doc says. "We're going to settle for two to three sessions, short and sweet, to help you build the tools you need to go where you want to go," he says, reiterating the tools piece. "And like I said, we're not going to delve into the past, I promise. We're going to focus on the present and the future." He pauses. "And I'm not into sports cars."

"I don't mean to sound financially focused, Dr. Levine." Ryan's serious face cracks a bit. "But it's not a very good financial model, for you."

"Well you're right." The doc smiles honestly. "If you're looking for a more traditional therapist I can recommend—"

"I prefer your approach," I jump in before he gives Ryan new ideas and we end up in long-term relationship with another therapist.

"Good," Dr. Levine approves, turning his gaze to Ryan who decides to nod in somewhat reasonable agreement. "So you've come to the right place." He leans back.

He lets us each tell a bit about ourselves, just general "fun facts," he calls it, and asks us what we're hoping to achieve, giving Ryan a chance to try again, this time without the sarcasm. He doesn't ask about Claire—past, present, or future—but Ryan volunteers the info. Maybe better to just rip off the Band-Aid. Ryan's little monologue is one-sided, yet fair, I'll give him that. Dr. Levine lets him speak without interruption, all while paying attention to my face as if looking for cues. Or clues. And probably finding a bunch of them, despite my attempt at a poker face. Because fuck, I'm jealous as hell.

Then it's my turn to speak but I get pretty self-conscious about the fact that Ryan had a full two years' worth of shared experiences with Claire, while all I have is a few short months. Yet they pack so much feeling into them, I don't even know where to begin. Unconventional therapy at its best, I guess. But Ryan and I need to fix things between us if we want to stay in Claire's life. To "*do our best to create a positive environment for the baby,*" were her exact words.

"I met Claire a few months ago," I say, and Ryan tries to hide his smirk. I feel like a teenager recalling the exact moment when my life collided with this stunning woman, the day she asked me to kiss her at the mall—to make the guy who's currently sitting next to me jealous—and took my life by storm. I know exactly how many days have passed since that moment that changed my life, but I purposely omit that part, trying to sound like a responsible adult. It may sound ridiculous—that in such a short period of time I've become so close to and so smitten with this woman, I'm well aware—but as I say the words, I realize I don't care about time anymore. And Ryan doesn't either. He looks jealous as hell when I'm finally done talking. And so consequently, after executing Claire's plan and completing our first therapy session, Ryan comes up with a plan of his own. The most atrocious idea. Far worse than couples therapy.

"This is some next-level bullshit," is what my friend Aiden has to say when he stops by my lab the next day and drags me to the small nameless coffee spot on GERI campus. Someone should really give this place a name. It's too iconic to just be known as "that coffee place," (GERI jargon) or "the Good Coffee," (Ellie's jargon). It's also the place Ellie persuaded me into going to meet Aiden for the first time, insisting we were meant to become best friends. Well, she wasn't wrong. The place is mostly empty, as it typically is. There's free coffee in the kitchen of almost every floor in every building at our institute, so that's where most coffee-deprived people go, but this conversation calls for something more. Definitely better coffee, and a higher degree of privacy. "Abstain from sex? Really? Is this what the therapist wants you to do?" Aiden gives me an incredulous look. And this time, I suspect, it has nothing to do with him being a brilliant scientist, just my friend, and a reasonable guy. "Where did you find this goddamn therapist?" he demands.

I haven't even gotten to the end of the story. I only mentioned that Ryan and I have started—I can't believe I'm admitting it—*family* therapy. At that point Aiden was still maintaining his poker face. I then went on to tell him about Ryan's latest and greatest idea. Hence why we're here, waiting for the *better* coffee, while Aiden is questioning Dr. Levine's credentials.

"No, actually, Dr. Levine was against the idea. But Claire's ex insisted this was the only way he would get a fair chance at having an equally active role in his unborn baby's life and fix his relationship with Claire," I explain. Although it doesn't make any more sense to me when I say it out loud, and actually only makes my frustration grow thicker.

"You mean a fair chance at getting back together with her?"

"Fuck, I hope not," I grunt.

"And you're okay with all this?" my friend asks. His already serious face takes on a broodier shade as he considers me.

"Of course not. I fucking hate it." I throw my hands in the air. "But he said he needed some room in Claire's life to have an opportunity to get involved." Aiden knows I grew up without a father. Knows how protective I am of Jake, who had his scumbag dad walk out on him too. There are just so many complicated families in this world. Maybe this one doesn't have to be. "This is an opportunity for Claire's child to grow up with both of his biological parents around. Something I can't have her give up just because of... me," I sigh. "And as much as I'd love to give a good fight and claim her and the baby as mine, I'm not sure I'll be able to live with myself knowing that I was in the way. That because of me this baby would never get to know his or her biological father," I try to explain what seems like rational reasoning in my head. "I can't guarantee Ryan will stick around, but I can't be the reason he decides to leave either."

"This is so fucked up." Aiden empties his espresso cup and pushes it aside. "I'm sorry, man. You're going to have a tough discussion with Claire, I assume?"

"Hmmm, that's another thing." I finally pick up my cup of coffee. "I told her everything last night."

"Oh, you did?" My smartass friend grabs my jaw with one hand, slowly turning my head to the sides, as if looking for bruises.

I chuckle. "She actually found it funny. Hilarious, to be exact. She thought that us keeping our hands off each other for the next few weeks was—and I quote—*actually hot.*" I laugh, recalling how Claire blushed when I listed all the things that we won't be able to do. And how she wanted to do all of them yesterday.

"Enlighten me, please. How does the two of you abstaining from sex have anything to do with making room for this guy?" Aiden's not really asking, more like sharing his skepticism, which is extremely valid.

What I failed to mention to Claire and now also to Aiden, is that Ryan had actually proposed I take a step back, get out of Claire's life for a bit. And since that was not going to work for me—not after I promised I'd be there for her, and because there's no way in hell I'm willing to give her up for this dumbass—I settled for us temporarily acting like friends. Give Claire an opportunity to choose. And all I can do is hope that she'll choose *me.*

25

Not a pissing contest?

Claire

I'm all wrapped up in what started as a pissing contest. Contestant one is the person responsible for half of the genetic material of my unborn child—also known as Ryan, my ex and maybe Baby-dad-wannabe. I still haven't forgiven him for his lukewarm response, for not wanting his own kid in his life, for bringing up *other options*. But with a baby on the way, I can't possibly be thinking about just myself anymore. When my child asks about their biological father one day, I want to at least be able to say that I tried.

And then there's the man who's stolen my heart, who's owned every single promise he's made so far, who takes responsibility, who's always there for me. Who helps me up when I lose my balance and holds me close when I feel lost. Who makes me feel found. My *someone to run with*, as he so eloquently said. The man of my dreams. Christian, who's so far been everything I ever wanted, and probably everything I didn't even know I wanted and am only just finding out. But who's to say he's planning to stay my *someone to run with* for the long run? Pun intended. I'm seriously awed by how this incredible man puts me and Baby first, before thinking about his wants and needs, or anything else really.

I was about to tell Christian that this was a ludicrous idea, that Ryan doesn't get to control who I do or do not sleep with. But then giving it more thought, I realized that maybe this wasn't such a bad idea, for an entirely different reason. The thought of keeping Christian to myself carries an unbearable amount of guilt. Part of truly caring for someone is wanting them to be happy. Wanting what's best for them. And maybe what's best for Christian is being with someone less complicated. Someone who isn't pregnant with another man's child. Someone who isn't... *me*. Maybe a temporary attempt at a platonic relationship could be Christian's chance to consider his options, while I still get to keep him in my life. I need to do the right thing for him, even if it's incredibly, unbelievably painful. And I hope that he chooses me all over again. Now that he has a better idea of what that might entail. Same goes for the moving-in-together piece. A statement that may have slipped out of him in a post-sex blissful moment. He hasn't mentioned it again since Ryan came barging in, but now that we're temporarily friends *without benefits*, moving in together would make everything infinitely more complicated. So I don't bring it up either.

Part of this crazy agreement entails giving each of the men in my life an opportunity to get involved. The lawyer in Ryan tried to insist on *"equal visitation rights"* but I had to remind him that Baby hasn't been born yet, and as flattering as it may sound, he does not get to decide who I spend *my* time with. Or when. There's also no such right for him to spend time with me. At least not that I'm aware of, but I relented to his plea to meet up for catch-up dinners once a week. And I did agree to let him come to one of my doctor's appointments and one prenatal class in a few weeks from now, but only because Christian will be presenting at a scientific conference in Boston. Needless to say, Christian was not happy about any of it, but after just one more session with Dr. Levine, my man and my ex have magically become almost... buddies, bonding over sports games, and me... Something shifted between them, and now we have a tri-member WhatsApp group—they were debating whether to include me, thank you very much—and the three of us even went out for dinner together last night. So now I'm thinking, maybe what started as a pissing contest is actually turning out to be just fine?

But now, I need to deal with another pissing contest. And I don't think Dr. Levine's magic powers can have any positive effect here. Because this one involves me—and I truly believe I'm a worthy contestant—against the science-crusher witch-bitch, her majesty Dr. Harriett Wallington. Yes, life tends to be interesting that way. Unfortunately.

And this has nothing to do with pregnancies or parenthood. Although you never know where her original frustration might have stemmed from. But it does involve doing the right thing and taking responsibility. And of all days and of all weeks, this cage fight has to happen when Christian is away.

Before Joe Denman became known as Big Boss Joe and moved up to the glass corner office, he was my line manager. He was the one who hired me, naive and experience-less, into industry, the one who gave me my first chance and spent innumerable hours coaching and mentoring me for the role. I will forever remain grateful to Joe for seeing potential in me and giving me that opportunity. Which is why I still think very highly of the man, despite him being the same person who thought it would be a good idea to hire Harriett Wallington as his CSO when he moved up to the CEO position. People make mistakes. It's part of human nature, even if your name is Dr. Joe Denman and you run a billion-dollar start-up company. Had I been there on Harriett's interview day, maybe I could have stopped the avalanche. Harriett, Chief Scientific fucking Officer? You have got to be kidding me.

Anyway, as CEO, Joe became way too important and busy to have so many direct reports, and we all had to move down the ladder. At least I was spared there—since Harriett didn't care for us lowly level scientists, I moved further down the corporate ladder, reporting to Steve. Who, by the way, had never had direct reports before, but at least has a heart, so was much better suited for the job. What Steve doesn't have though, is the guts to stand up for Harriett Wallington. Even when she metaphorically beats the shit out of his team members. Ahem... me. Even when she's making decisions that are so scientifically and morally wrong. And although I'm known for picking fights with her, this time the witch has outdone herself, and I don't mean it in a positive way.

As with any other team discussion topic, this one starts out mundane; a piece of data from our animal model. At a first glance, this should not be something to risk my career over.

"This does not need to go into the report," Harriett unequivocally concludes once Emily and Jean, two of our best preclinical scientists, are done showing their latest findings in mice, which just happen to include some weird trends in their animals' wellbeing shortly after receiving our drug. I know it may be meaningless, and I know mice are not the same as humans. But the whole point of doing this experiment with our drug was to identify potential safety signals that could translate into risk in patients. And when designing a clinical trial, understanding what one needs to watch out for is important.

"I don't think we can ignore these findings—the mice are less active, their food consumption is decreased, this needs to be included in the report," I chime in. My eyes are focused on the team, but I can already feel the rage being sent my way from Harriett's direction. I'm in for a fit and I know it. In the face of personnel turnover or just changes in team assignments, a finding that is not included in a report will simply not be remembered, and eventually—disappear. Just one of the many things I learned from Big Boss Joe, when he was still just Joe, but nevertheless an excellent manager and an outstanding clinical trialist.

"This is a minor issue," Harriett argues, her tone condescending. "Claire, I'm sure you can tell the difference between spurious findings to actual ones. And these are mice for God's sake, there are so many unspecific reasons that could impact their activity and feeding behavior." And she's not wrong, it might be spurious or unspecific, but it's nevertheless an important sign in mice since they can't talk, can't tell us what's bothering them or what hurts. I let my eyes travel in Steve's direction. He's shrinking in his seat, as if becoming smaller will erase him from existing in this conference room. I try to telepathically coax him to speak up, but he gives me an apologetic look of *I agree with you, but can't possibly start a front against Harriett.* And I think he's mostly regretting the moment he got out of bed this morning to attend this meeting, or the moment he was promoted to be my manager. Steve is a good guy, but he doesn't like conflict. Especially conflict that involves Harriett.

"Of course, Harriett," I say, trying to remain calm despite the fast beating of my heart and the sound of my pulse in my ears. My body is at the point of flight or fight already, and I have a feeling it's going for the latter. "Only I think we'd be making a big mistake if we don't look into it further. Plus, it seems to be dose dependent," I try to reason with her, a sign that this finding may actually be a real thing.

"Claire has a point, it is more pronounced with the higher doses," Jean says cautiously, considering who she's dealing with. Harriett's raging eyes shoot to her direction.

"This is not going into the report, were you not listening? We can't rely on an artifact in a poorly performed experiment." Harriett shifts her approach from diminishing the importance of the data to questioning the validity of the entire experiment.

Jean and Emily exchange offended looks. *Poorly performed experiment?* Seriously?

"We could repeat the experiment..." Emily offers.

"This is a waste of time. And money." Harriett sighs in exasperation, like she's the only reasonable person in this room dealing with a bunch of fools. "You are making a big deal out of nothing. I'm the CSO and I put my foot down. And Claire, I'd appreciate it if next time you can keep your insights to yourself, or you'll be removed from the series invite."

Drug development done right is about doing the right thing and putting patients first. Joe drilled that sentence into our heads until it became second nature. As it should. It's also our company's motto, like many other biotech and pharmaceutical companies. So by all means, it shouldn't be a new concept for Harriett. But somehow my principles aren't anything more than unnecessary insights in her mind.

"Steve?" I say, once we're the only two people left in the room. "We have responsibility to our future patients. We can't just trash data that taints our safety profile."

"But what if it *is* an artifact? A fluke?" he asks, doubting what we both know.

"What if it isn't?"

"Claire, I see your point but, I don't know…" He rubs his forehead.

"Then repeating the experiment would be the right thing to do."

"I just don't think it's a fight worth fighting," he shrugs and drops his head low. "I have no intention of getting on Harriett's bad side. She has so much experience, I'm sure she knows what she's doing. I'd rather keep my job."

"I'd rather lose my job than work in a place that doesn't put patients first. For God's sake, we're developing medicines for patients. They are our purpose. Safety is our responsibility, we can't leave a stone unturned and then hide behind *oops, we didn't know.*"

My computer beeps like it does when someone sends me a message on the company's chat. "Have a minute?" is what appears when I glance at it.

"Big Boss Joe is asking for me," I tell Steve. His apprehensive look says it all. Our morning meeting is already making waves. "Want to come with?" I try to joke.

He shakes his head vigorously. "Sorry." He then adds as an afterthought, "If you need me there I'll support you, of course. But I'd much rather stay out of it."

I nod. He does have five kids and a wife on medical leave, so it's not the best timing to go to war with Harriett. That's what they have me for. Pregnant, kind of already showing, but fearless believer in justice.

I stalk out of the room and head toward the glass-walled C-suite. Charlene lifts her head from her desk as she sees me approaching, a consolation smile on her lips. I give her my best smile back and breeze into Joe's office.

"Did you want to see me, boss?" I ask. He may be the CEO, but to me he's still just Joe, the humble mentor who trained me.

Joe turns his head from his computer. His serious expression transforms into a more relaxed one when he sees me. "Yes," he says, motioning for me to sit.

I close the door and take one of the fancy chairs that the new designer thought would match the biotech-y atmosphere of the newly renovated office. It's not as comfortable as the old worn-out chairs he used to have in his old office, but I'm feeling dizzy, so I accept.

"Okay," I say, ready to make my side of the story heard. I'm actually glad he called me in here, so I don't feel like I'm tattletale-ing.

"How are you, Claire?" Joe asks, leaning back in his chair. His eyes rest momentarily on my somewhat visible bump—I haven't really gone public with this information at work yet, I probably should, as I'm already showing—but he doesn't say anything, and moves his eyes back to mine, as if moving on.

"Peachy," I answer, and he returns a knowing smile. "Just trying to execute everything you've taught me, but it's becoming increasingly difficult with Harriett around." I try to sound as objective as possible but can't help the disdain that comes out of me at the mentioning of her name.

This makes Joe smirk. "Have you thought about trying to get along with her?"

"Sort of like—if you can't beat them, join them?" I challenge. And at the sight of him nodding his head I add, "We both know better than that. You don't really expect me to agree with everything she says, without question, when it's wrong."

"She said you were questioning her judgement. In front of a room full of people," he sighs. "This is not the first time. You two are going to need to find a way to get along. The board of directors were adamant about having Harriett here. She has an impressive track record for bringing multiple drugs into the market." He pauses for impact, or for me to digest the fact that his hands are tied. "I am very much aware that she's not making it any easier with her snarky responses, but could I ask that you take these discussions with her to your 1:1s? Without an audience."

"I see your point." I nod, letting my head drop a bit. I know he's going for conflict avoidance 101, or path of least resistance, or whatever is the new trend in executive leadership training right now. I understand where he's coming from. He has to play the part.

But I know it's still Joe in there when after a few uncomfortable moments he adds, "Okay, now tell me what actually went down."

"Thought you'd never ask." I sit up straighter, hooking up my laptop to the large screen on his wall and pulling up the slides that Emily and Jean were presenting. We go through the data, the observations, the concerns. The possibility of it being a fluke vs an actual, potentially concerning safety finding.

"Thank you for bringing all of this to my attention," Big Boss Joe says finally. "I agree with you."

"Thank you," I say a bit too victoriously.

"Not with your passionate dislike for Harriett, or the way things might have been said, but with your observation. This does look to be dose dependent, which to me is a big enough hint that we ought to explore it further. If the team can't trust it—" he says 'team' although he really means Harriett— "we should at the very least repeat the experiment. And when the results come in, please include me in the discussion. If these are true findings, they must go in the report." Just like I thought. But yeah, I get the point. I can be nicer. Well, Harriett could be nicer too.

"Do you want me to let the team know?" I offer, trying to suppress a smile of satisfaction.

"Let me speak with Harriett first," Joe says in his masterful diplomatic manner. He knows me all too well. "And Claire," he calls after me when I'm already by the door.

I turn back in his direction. "Yes, boss?"

"Thank you for doing the right thing for our patients."

26

A walk in the park

Claire

One of the benefits of becoming friends *without* benefits with Christian is getting to know this man from new angles. My *someone to run with*. Not that I'm in any way advocating for switching to a temporary sex-less relationship mode, but letting the tension build up while making sure we're not left alone to test our diminishing willpower brings us even closer together. Furthermore, it brings about some entertaining new outing ideas: mini-golf, free DC museums, the zoo. Most are very kid-friendly by definition, and so also an awesome opportunity to spend time with Jake, who's officially made me a mandatory spectator at his soccer games. Not surprising, though, as I've now become one of his most eager supporters. This includes wearing his team colors under my oversized coat, with a paper cut-out of his number attached to my back, huddled close—but not too close—to Christian, screaming at the top of my lungs, "Go Jakey!" As I am at the moment, because there's nothing I want more right now than to see this boy smile. And scoring a goal is a nice second.

"You'll make a great soccer mom," Christian whispers in my ear. I have no idea how this man can make the word 'mom' sound so sexy. But I make sure to tell him that.

Which is partially why we both decide it would be a good idea for him to do a milkshake run from our favorite ice cream place, a few minutes driving distance away—both to satisfy my desire to drink a milkshake, but mostly to cool off the urge to pull Christian to me by the jacket and kiss him. We run the idea by Jake when he jogs by, and he gives us a raving thumbs up. And as Christian walks back to his car, I fix him with a happy look and what feels like a carefree smile, for once not thinking about worst-case scenarios and bad decisions.

A big mistake.

It takes a whole of ten minutes for me to realize how stupid and selfish agreeing to this idea was when Jake stumbles over to me. His expression is shallow, like he's looking at me but is not really there, the color completely drained from his face.

"Claire." His voice comes out distant and almost ... sad.

"Jake, what is it?" I ask, lowering myself so we're level, watching the kid I know wither in front of my eyes. It's as if he's vanishing right before me. His hands shake as he brings one into his line of vision, as if trying to remember whether that signifies anything, or if it's at all a part of him.

"I..." He can't seem to recall the reason he extracted himself from the team and came over. I hand him his water bottle but he shakes his head. "Hippo..." His voice is so weak it makes my heart sink.

Does he mean hypo? As in hypoglycemia? Low blood sugar? My brain is going a thousand miles per second as it dawns on me that I don't have a single sugary thing that could help bring his blood glucose up. Worst-case scenarios quickly cloud my mind. Passing out. Coma. Death. The list of consequences starts building in my head as I try to get myself together. I have no clue how to take care of someone with Type 1 diabetes. I don't even know how to take care of kids. What the hell was I thinking?!

This is when Jake's little CGM device starts beeping with an *urgent low soon* alert, confirming my suspicion. Well, news flash—it's already low and getting worse by the second. I pull out my phone to call Christian but... no service. Of course it has to happen on my watch—me. The least competent, least experienced person with the tendency to freak out. And in a place with no cell phone reception. Sending Christian for milkshakes... I should have known better. The kid has Type 1 diabetes for God's sake. Hypoglycemia. The number one risk of being on insulin. And I have NO sugar.

"It's okay," I tell Jake, trying to convince myself too, as I look around us anxiously for anything that could qualify as a sugar source. Christian should probably be back any minute now, but what if there's traffic? We're at an isolated park with no snack stand or store in sight. My heart is beating out of my chest as I notice a mom lazily walking with two kids, holding a picnic basket. A responsible, forward-thinking, planned-ahead parent. "Hang on," I promise Jake, leaving him there on the bench as I run frantically to the unsuspecting woman and her kids. "Please, I need sugar," I say, probably making zero sense. She's taken aback for a second so I manage, "He has Type 1 diabetes, he has low blood sugar." I turn my head toward Jake who's silently sitting slumped on that bench. "Do you have any candies? Juice? Please..." A motherly understanding crosses her face as she quickly searches through her basket and pulls out two juice boxes.

"Here," she says, and if I wasn't in such terror I would have probably kissed her.

"Thank you!" I holler as my legs already rush to little Jake, who's disappearing further into oblivion. "Drink this!" I say, unwrapping the straw with trembling hands and punching it into the box so forcefully that juice sprays over my shirt. Jake holds out a hand, so shaky he can barely get the straw into his mouth. Then he sips, slowly and quietly. He doesn't say a word, doesn't complain. At—not even—six years old, already accepting how life has to look for him. Most likely forever. But this time it's on me.

He drains the box, hands still shaky, as are mine, as I hand him the second one.

When Kate and I were little, we used to love jumping from the couch to the carpet. Mom always told us to stop before we hurt ourselves, and of course we didn't, until the day Kate fell headfirst into our glass table. Her nose was bleeding and her forehead needed stitches. I remember how scared I was then. Terrified. But it's not even close to how scared I am now. I don't think I've ever felt so scared in my life.

But I have to park these thoughts. I need to focus on Jake. So I hug him, and I hold his hands, and I promise that everything is going to be alright. Then we wait for his blood sugar to come back up while we finally get Christian on the line, who reassures me that two juice boxes will do the trick and that these things happen, unfortunately, quite often. And that, sure enough, Jake has about ten packs of gummy candies and a glucagon emergency kit in his sports bag.

But it's not until the color is back to Jake's face, and his gaze comes back into focus, and he says, "I'm ready for my milkshake now," that I am able to breathe again.

"I'm sorry, I should have told you about the candy stash and what to do in case of low blood sugar," Christian says after we drop Jake off at his mom's. "I mean, his blood sugar was well within the higher range when I left, but I sometimes forget how quickly it can drop when he's active... I'm really sorry," he says again, probably feeling worse than I am.

"I'm going to make such a terrible mom," I tell him, and I mean every word. "What was I thinking? I don't even know how to take care of kids. I've never even babysat children before."

Christian redirects the car into a small outdoor plaza parking before putting it into park and turning to face me.

"I disagree. You are going to be an amazing mom," he reassures me with an unwarranted degree of certainty.

"Amazing? I can't believe I sent you to get milkshakes and put Jake at such a huge risk. I'm so irresponsible, I can barely take care of myself..."

"That's not true." He takes both my hands, giving them a squeeze. "And you did well, you took care of Jake, you managed the situation, you made sure his blood sugar went up as quickly as possible. You kept him safe. Jake was happy as can be by the time I came back."

"That's because this kid is a superhero," I say.

"He is, isn't he?" Christian smiles.

"You know," I realize. "There's this perception among people that since patients with Type 1 diabetes have insulin, they already have a solution," I say, looking down to our connected hands. "I know it's not a cure, just something to take care of the symptoms, but until I met Jake, I was one of these people too. I thought—why bother developing a cure when there's already a reasonable treatment. I had no idea."

"That's true." Christian searches my eyes. His expression somber. "Many people think it's like a daily drug that just takes care of everything for you. It's not," he says. "It's four daily injections at the very least, or an insulin pump. Each dose has to be carefully calculated based on your blood sugar, the carb content, how active you are or going to be, your health, your own specific insulin sensitivity—which also changes based on the time of day, the way you feel, and so many other factors we don't even know them all. And even if you do everything by the book—it's never going to be perfect. Or completely balanced. And then there's the long-term complications... I try not to think about that. I can only hope that by the time Jake gets to be a teen, we'll already have a cure."

"I hope so. I wish for a cure," I say, realizing I'm using that same tone little Kate and I used to use for making wishes. Real wishes. The pure ones you make as a kid that come straight from the heart.

When we talked about the erroneous perception among *people*—when it comes to dealing with Type 1 diabetes—we meant some scientists, too. And also some higher-ranking professionals who hold important positions involving policy and decision-making. Even some leaders in the field of drug development whose opinion can make or break whether a potential asset becomes a possible cure. This of course includes her highness Dr. Harriett Wallington, who decides again to challenge our proposed clinical trial design, reverting back to aiming at preventing Type 1 diabetes development rather than trying to reverse the disease in patients who are already living with it.

"There's an effective treatment for T1D," she says, abbreviating Type 1 diabetes to fit her cold, clipped tone as her glare is fixed on me. "It's called insulin," she says slowly, as if I'm having a hard time grasping her complex concepts.

There's some noise gathering in the background, provoked by this statement. Like, maybe, hopefully, some of our scientists and leaders disagree with this notion. But other than chatter, no one takes the lead. And since Christian had not been invited to this meeting—Harriett usually makes sure to single me out when she has bad news about our project—I have to speak up.

"It's effective in lowering blood sugar. Nothing more. It's not a magic drug, it's a constant struggle. It keeps them alive maybe, but there are still long-term complications. Still reduced quality of life. And—" My mind goes back to the park, to Jake's face, his slow, quiet, almost sad tone, his trembling hands. "Insulin has a major side effect, and it's called hypoglycemia."

"Sure. Hypoglycemia," Harriett shoots back. "They can eat something sweet. Who wouldn't want to be able to solve their problems with sugar? It's a minor issue compared to the benefit."

"It's a MAJOR issue! They could lose consciousness. Could go into a coma. People die from it, you know?" The words just storm out of me, I can feel my pulse in my ears, my blood reaching a boiling point. All induced by Harriet's ignorance. An ignorance I unfortunately shared until the day I met Jake and witnessed the struggle he and so many others have to deal with 24/7 for the rest of their lives. There are never any breaks.

"You are obviously emotional right now," Harriett decides to say, in the absence of any compelling argument to negate what she is supposed to know as truth. But emotional? Would she have said that if I were a man? I bet not. I look around the room, hoping for some peer support, and finally finding it in Emily, who gets up from her seat and pulls up the hem of her shirt a bit, exposing her CGM and an insulin pump port next to it. I had no idea.

"Claire is right, Harriett," she says, raising her voice for the first time since I've known her. "Insulin helps us survive, but don't mistake that for a cure."

27

A big happy family

Christian

Since Ryan came back into Claire's life in this weird capacity he's been insisting on, turning us into a one big happy family... and with his ridiculous *friends without benefits* rule I agreed to—I must have been temporarily out of my mind that day—I've been holding on to each of these prenatal yoga classes with Claire, reveling in the opportunity to finally hold her, touch her, feel like her true partner again, her person. As I do now, seated behind her, rubbing her shoulders, compliments of Janet, the instructor, who winks at me as if she knows exactly what's going on, my trusted partner in crime.

Claire stretches deeply, rested snugly between my legs, releasing soft moans as my hands work her trapezius muscles.

"That's exactly what I needed after all that exercise," she says, referring to the yoga stretches we've been doing for the past thirty minutes. Her words are followed by another, this time louder, groan, turning me on. Her hair is so close to my face, her ear grazing my jaw.

"You do that one more time and I'll make sure to engage you in a different kind of exercise after class," I whisper in her ear.

"Oh," she breathes, "you do that." And of course she does it again. Needless to say, this yoga class turns into torture every week, and it takes every shred of self-control in me to persevere. I have to remind myself that it's temporary, until Ryan becomes comfortable enough in his role as a dad in this equation, hopefully soon. Or until Claire loses her patience.

But when I drive Claire back home, she comes up with a ludicrous statement that sends my mind spinning.

"I'm okay with it if you want to see other people," she says in a weird nonchalant tone, leaving me puzzled and worried. And jealous as fuck.

Does that mean that *she* wants to see other people? I don't want to see *other people*. And I certainly don't want her to see other people. And of course I can't help but wonder whether it has something to do with her ex. Yes, Ryan again, who's just recently decided to move in next door to her, slowly but surely closing the geographical distance. And mostly acting as a giant cockblock.

But instead of protesting or voicing any of my out-of-control concerns, I just play along, hoping to provoke at least a fraction of the jealousy I'm feeling right now in her too. If that works, she's doing a hell of a job hiding it, leaving me in the dust as she steps out of my Land Rover, not even waiting for me to walk her home, and waves goodbye.

Claire

It doesn't take me more than a few hours to realize what I've done. I gave Christian the green light to see *other women*. Not that we ever mentioned exclusivity, so I wasn't really reversing anything, but potentially changing what I'd hoped had been the status quo. Well, I guess, thanks to my big mouth it sure isn't anymore. So why? Why did I do it?

It's the middle of the night and I can't sleep, so speaking to myself feels natural enough. It's been over a month since we embarked on this platonic arrangement, and I don't think it's right to hold Christian back from living his life. Mine is complicated enough, I don't need to keep dragging him into it too. I guess it's all part of trying to give him an opportunity to choose simple. To not choose *me*. But damn, why does not being selfish have to hurt so bad? And now, overanalyzing our last interaction, I realize that maybe deep inside I was hoping to provoke a different response from Christian. One where he objects and claims me back. Or at least says he's not interested in anyone else, instead of... I don't know—looking quiet and reserved, as he did when I finished talking. Like he's thinking it through. Like it's the beginning of an end.

So now I'm freaking out. What if he's already putting my preposterous idea into practice? On the spectrum of all possible reactions, I was not expecting to feel jealous.

And if that's not enough, little Baby here hasn't stopped moving for the past couple hours, as if my little thunderstorm is making him or her restless, or the constant moving inside is making *me* restless, or maybe we just perpetuate each other's restlessness. But I can't sleep, and I can't keep still. I feel like a giant wrecking ball. Metaphorically and physically.

I do the one thing I probably shouldn't be doing. I text Christian.

"Are you sleeping?" Then I hold my breath for his response.

"Very much awake," he responds quickly. "You okay?"

That depends on how one defines *okay*.

"Baby here is asking for you," I write. Go ahead, blame the baby. I expect a funny come back. A laughing emoji. Some sort of response. Any. But instead there's radio silence. Not even the little three—much anticipated—dots. That's what I get for saying things I don't really mean, just because it sounded right. Well, actually it sounded wrong. It just felt like the right thing to say at that moment.

I turn my night light on and grab a science textbook from my stack. At only about ten inches, little baby here is making waves. There are tiny rhythmic flutters, almost like bubble bursts going on in my stomach. Baby hiccups? And some more side-to-side movements. I try to focus on the words in my textbook. I'm about halfway through a chapter, only to realize I can't recall a single word and have to restart. And this is material I know, and have written manuscripts about, yet in my preoccupied state of mind even these sentences make no sense.

"Autoimmunity textbook?" I hear Christian's voice as he enters my bedroom. I may have given him my spare key. The one Ryan used to own. He's leaning on my doorframe, handsome as always.

"Yeah, well, just trying to relax with a good book," I say, trying to hide the smile that's creeping up on my lips. The sense of relief that he's right here with me and nowhere else makes my stray thoughts declare a ceasefire for a bit.

Christian takes off his shoes, picks up the edge of the blanket and settles down next to me. He looks at the heavy book in my lap before studying my face carefully. "It's a science book," he says dryly.

"Yes, I felt like expanding my knowledge on—" I look at the page I landed on, "epigenetic regulation of autoantibody response..."

"That's top-level escapism. And a topic you already know." He smirks and takes my book away, laying it carefully on the nightstand. "Now tell me what's really going on."

"Nothing."

Everything.

"And besides that?" he insists, turning his body to face me.

"Baby here is having a party," I say, pointing at my belly. "And having hiccups. I think."

There's a heart-melting smile on Christian's face as he slides his hands beneath my T-shirt, cupping my baby bump, fingers gently skimming over my skin.

"Hey Baby," he whispers to my bump. My body melts into his touch, muscles instantly relaxing. Baby slows down the riot, as if reacting to Christian's warmth and the sound of his voice. Almost like a "*There you are, finally,*" moment. A few minutes go by and the hiccups disappear as well. We stay like this for a while. An hour, maybe more. In our own bubble, our comfortable silence, basking in each other's touch and warmth. And I wonder about that moving-in proposal we never actually got to discuss, in what seems like ages ago. The one we haven't brought back up since... Ryan.

"You are magical," I tell him, referring to his fetus-calming skills, and maybe a few other skills too. "Baby likes you."

Christian brings his face closer and gently kisses my belly. "I like Baby too," he says. And I want those lips on mine, but he sits back up and says, "I should probably get going."

There are so many words I want to say while he puts his shoes on slowly and then turns back to face me, letting his gaze linger. But instead I just nod, try to come up with some sort of a smile, and let him go.

28

Living not loving

Claire

Mornings. Mornings are the hardest. I can't see why all of life's toughest questions have to come up in my head—uninvited—the minute I open my eyes. In those moments where you're only half awake, still clouded by sleep and the unintelligible parts of forgotten dreams. Where everything seems to mesh together to form a little too much mess. Gray and bottomless. Even if the sun is out, and birds are chirping outside my window, garbage trucks backing up.

That's when I need to remember my purpose, again and again, and as quickly as I can before the darkness pulls me under. Before it gets overwhelming. That same purpose that was pretty clear in my mind up until the moment I fell into a slumber. And lately, it seems to be on repeat. Except for maybe when Christian stays over. Because seeing his smile when I open my eyes has this effect of clearing my clouds away. Or maybe it's keeping my purpose from slipping away.

But it's been a while since he stayed over. Thanks to Ryan and his stupid rule. Thanks to Christian for playing along and following the rules. And mostly thanks to me and my stupid guilty feelings. And it doesn't help that the apartment next door was up for lease and Ryan had to be so annoying and rent it. Official reason: being close in case I needed anything, especially as I get closer to my due date, although that's not going to happen for a while. Unofficial reason: knowing more about my whereabouts, especially as related to Christian. And since Ryan is still paying rent at the place he rented after he broke up with me, that's a pretty expensive way to live just to get metaphorically closer to someone. I guess maybe not just metaphorically. And so I now feel like I'm under surveillance.

Letting Ryan back into my life—even if only part-time and just next door—brings back memories. Some good, but most are ones I would much rather keep dormant. I'm not sure if it's what he does or what he doesn't do. Or the fact he's Ryan and not Christian. But the way he stares into space in silence when we meet for our weekly dinners—that he insisted on—trying to make our situation disappear, the way he blankly looks through me when we speak, unable to stop his mind from wandering. Maybe I'm projecting, having a hard time admitting to myself that if we weren't in this predicament, we wouldn't be where we are now. Spending time together, yet so alone.

We haven't even begun our co-parenting adventure, and already the thought of spending life this way makes me sad. And most of all I can't stop wondering about Christian. The man who's now my *friend without benefits.* The man I stopped spending my nights with almost a month ago, and then topped the situation off by telling him he could see *other people*. Is he spending his nights with another woman in his arms? His attention, his affection, his kisses—are they all being wasted now on someone else? Someone who's not me and would obviously disagree with the wasting part... And I refuse to admit, not even to myself, but the thought of it is enough to make me want to break my own rules, forget about doing the right thing, and let my feet carry me back to Christian. To that little street, the one that seemed so ordinary until I found out he lived there.

But it's Jake who actually calls out my inner battles when I join him and Christian for weekend soccer and ice cream.

"You look sad," he says when Christian walks up to get our order.

"I'm not sad," I say, smiling. A bold lie, but I tell myself that putting a happy face is for the greater good. Jake lifts his eyes to me, tilting his head as if evaluating the accuracy of my statement. Yep, he doesn't buy it. "I'm just ... thinking," I concede.

"That's what my mom says when she's sad." He gives me a smug smile. This kid is way too smart for my avoidance skills. "You should marry my uncle Christian," he whispers before I have a chance to come up with a sophisticated distraction.

"Who told you to say that? Christian?" I chuckle. A simple solution to this complicated issue.

"No," Jake answers. "My brain told me that."

"You are a very smart kid, you know that?" I squeeze this little guy in a bear hug.

"Chocolate ice cream for my two and a half favorite people, coming up," Christian's voice comes from beside us, eyes trailing to my growing baby bump with a grin. "This should be about 40 grams of carbs buddy," he says to Jake, who pulls out his insulin pump for a quick bolus.

I thought I was doing pretty well hiding my declining mood. I thought that if I waited it out, faked it till I made it, the little cloud above me would eventually go away. But the fact that a five- almost-six-year-old was able to call out my bullshit makes me think that maybe it's time for me to go back to therapy. I haven't really thought through the therapy part yet, but I've definitely been overthinking every other part of my life. Because something has to give in my love life, or lack of love in my life.

It's been about fifteen years since my last therapy session. And I thought I had it all together—minus a couple occasions of freaking out over becoming a mom—but maybe it's been too long.

"I'm so glad to finally meet you," Dr. Levine says as we shake hands.

"Heard a lot about me, huh?" I laugh, wishing patient-therapist confidentiality didn't exist and he would just flat-out tell me all that the two men in my life have been talking about for the past few sessions. I could really use that intelligence to make an informed decision.

"So what brings you here?"

It's an open invitation to speak my mind, I think, but instead I just give him a rundown of the basics. Or at least what I see as the basics. Christian, Ryan. Baby. Me. Not loving the current situation.

"So what decision are you working on?" Dr. Levine asks, although I'm pretty certain that I'm already living my decision.

"I'm not sure I still have a choice," I clarify. Because there's no way Christian is just idly waiting around for me. He's surely moved on.

"There's always a choice," Dr. Levine says. I really try, but can't read much into his poker face. And to my quizzical look he adds, "Between the way you feel and what you choose to do, there's always a space to make decisions."

"Hmm." I may have heard a variant of this phrase somewhere. It was as esoteric then as it is now.

"So let's try to tackle this debate together, shall we?"

"Don't you want me to tell you all about my troubled self, my childhood growth pains, my issues...?" I challenge. I know it's been a while since my last therapy session, but has the practice changed that much?

"We could spend hours and hours talking about your past, if that's what you want." He pauses and I shake my head. I always hated this part of therapy anyway, never liked having buried things float back up, especially not my feelings.

"I'd gladly skip it."

"Good, because I'd rather focus on the present. And since you're the one making the decision, I'd like us to focus on what you think and the way you feel about it."

Which tracks pretty nicely with what Christian has been telling me about Dr. Levine and his minimalistic session approach. Hey, if this works, I'm all for it. I'd much rather solve my issues today than work on it for years to come.

Dr. Levine hands me a bottle of water, which works well for buying me some time as I uncap the bottle, take a sip, screw the cap back on, then off again, taking another sip. Until I finally admit for the first time—both out loud and to myself—that "I'm not happy." I expect a surprised reaction from the therapist in front of me, but he looks perfectly at ease. Well, obviously, the man does this for a living. At this point he is probably un-shakable. And since that's the case, I kick back in his couch and continue. "I can't say I was outrageously happy to begin with, but you know—being pregnant with my ex's kid, I don't really have a..." I'm about to use the word choice again, but recalling how Dr. Levine started this entire conversation, I course-correct. "Well, I grew up without a dad. I always wanted to know who that person was, still do," I explain. "Why would I want to put my child in the same situation?"

"Is it really a black or white situation?" he asks.

"It's an all-over-the-place situation. I gave Christian an out, because it just feels too selfish to drag him into my complicated life. It may be the right thing to do, but my heart doesn't seem to agree. And Ryan, I'm pretty sure he hasn't completely dropped the idea of a package deal, even though when he said he was all in or all out, I told him he was out in that case. You'd think him still being here means he's accepted that, but his actions don't exactly match up."

"And by all in, what exactly are we talking about?"

"Back in my life, move in, raise the baby together." I smooth my hand over my baby bump, and decide to rest it there, waiting for the little flutter or a little push, a reaction from the other side.

"Like a spouse?"

"Sort of," I sigh. "A spouse in a very boring, un-talking sort of relationship. I mean we talk—like when one of us runs out of eggs or when we see each other in the elevator, or about what to order when we meet for dinner once a week. But that's about as exciting as it gets. And there's no physical aspect to it either."

"Would you want there to be?"

"I... not with Ryan. There's zero attraction there, and that's not new. That's one of the reasons we broke up to begin with."

"Okay, so what are your options?"

"I guess, tell Ryan that his own all-or-none way to fatherhood is not going to work, and risk a potential shift in his willingness to be in his child's life. Or just stay in this uncomfortable state, but I'm not sure I'm loving it."

"Maybe you should set your own terms to this agreement," Dr. Levine offers.

"Like not being the package in this package deal?" I ask, and he nods. "But then there's no deal. Let me just remind you that he's a lawyer."

"Okay, but in this dynamic you have a dual role. You are also the judge."

"How am I the judge?"

"You have the final say."

"Uh, I'm not sure I'm seeing it."

"Okay, then not a judge, let's leave the court metaphor out," he humors me. "The architect, if you will, shaping your own life. You decide how you want it to look and whether you want to spend it with Ryan."

"Okay, sure." I smile kindly, grateful for the attempt but still not convinced this would do any good. "I'm not sure I'm the concern here," I try to clarify. "It's the baby that I'm making decisions for, and as a future mom I'd like my child to have a chance to grow up with their biological father."

"Okay, so let's look at the pros and cons of this deal," Dr. Levine says. And calling it a deal is spot-on. Because it certainly isn't a relationship. "Let's start with the pros."

I take a deep breath, searching my mind for something. Anything. "Well, the obvious one—my baby will get to grow up with their biological father around. Although Ryan might be a bit of a flight risk, since this whole arrangement is based on us being together. I mean, what if it doesn't last?"

"Then a half pro, half con?"

"Probably."

"Okay, what else?"

"He's a good person. We may not be in the most exciting place, but he has a good and kind heart and I'm sure if he chooses to stick around he'd be a great dad." Dr. Levine nods, waiting for more, but I don't have more. "That's about it for the pros."

"So let's move to the cons."

"We don't love each other. Not in the way a couple should. Not that I know much about parenting, but isn't that a bad example for a kid? And we're pretty bland together. We barely talk, barely smile to each other. Like, I don't even remember how to have fun when he's around."

"Has it been like that all along? Or is it the current arrangement that's weighing you down?"

"It was like that for at least a whole year before we broke up. And I know he can be happy with someone else." I saw how he looked before I broke the pregnancy news to him. And God knows I can too. Because I can't recall a happier time in my life than every single moment spent with Christian. That is, before giving him an out. "How is it fair that I need to make a choice for someone else? One decision could change this unborn baby's entire life. What if I make the wrong one?" I look at the clock above Dr. Levine's head. We're almost at the end of our time. Between thinking and feeling and speaking—time flies.

"Can't wait to get out of here?" he asks good naturedly.

"No, I just have a lot of respect for time," I explain.

"I respect that," he says. "So, now for your homework."

"Can you help me with my homework?" I ask Kate as she hands me a cup of her special herbal tea. The one that's supposed to put me at ease and help me sleep better. It never does, but it tastes good, and it's good for Baby, so I take a sip, burning the roof of my mouth.

"Homework?" She raises an eyebrow at me. Have you gone back to school? One PhD isn't enough anymore?" my helpful sister asks.

"Kind of, I guess?" But Kate looks even more confused so I add, "I went back to therapy, hoping Dr. Levine could fix me. But he's insisting that I'm the only one who can fix this situation. That I'm the architect, shaping my own life. Or the judge. Or whatever profession you find appropriate in this context called my life. I bet there are many."

"You're the judge and Ryan is an actual lawyer. I like that." She smiles widely. "Just send him to jail, no bail. Case adjourned. Did your therapist give you that little gavel?"

"No gavel," I chuckle and Kate sighs in disappointment. "Just homework. I need to come up with—" I pull out the piece of paper from the back of my jeans pocket and unfold it. It has a line in the middle, extending all the way down, splitting the page into two equal parts. The left half is labeled, "What I like and don't like about myself when I'm with Ryan." The right half is labeled, "What I like and don't like about myself when I'm alone."

"Alone? Does it have to be Ryan and no Ryan? Can't it be Ryan or Christian?" Kate protests.

"Dr. Levine says I first need to decide whether I want Ryan as my life partner. Not try to choose between them."

"It should obviously be Christian."

"But that's not part of the homework," I sigh. "There's too much guilt and pleasure in choosing what I want for myself. Which is, apparently, holding me back. Dr. Levine said I need to first eliminate what I don't want in order to clear the way for what I do want." My sister makes a funny face in response. "Will you help me with my homework or not?!"

"Fine," she grunts, pulling a pink marker from her teacher supply drawer, the one she uses to draw smileys on her students' assignments or tests. Because, if you ask Kate, words of encouragement are always more powerful than the opposite.

"So what do I like about myself when I'm with Ryan?" I ask and we both stare into space. Not a single word comes to mind. At least not in my mind. I take a procrastinating sip of my tea. "I'll start with the don't like," I decide. "I'm unhappy. Impatient. Mad. Anxious. Lonely." I read the words I put down. And also sad sometimes. Really sad. But I can't tell Kate that.

"Sexually frustrated," my sister adds helpfully.

"There's no sex, I'm not sleeping with him. I'm not even attracted to him."

"Exactly—which explains the frustrated piece of it."

"Fine," I say, adding frustrated to the list, redacting the sex part. "And I miss Christian," I say, writing the word *longing*.

"That's one of the things you don't like about yourself?"

"I mean, missing someone else when I'm supposed to spend time with Ryan? I'm sure that's almost as bad as cheating."

"Obviously it isn't, seeing as you're still sexually frustrated. Plus, you're not actually *with* Ryan," she reminds me, then grabs my shoulders with both hands and gives them a good shake. "Okay, enough beating yourself up. Now what do you like about yourself when you're alone?"

I bite my lip and give it some thought. "I'm me. I'm independent, and free. And I feel less alone."

"I thought we wanted to keep Christian out of this exercise?" Kate wiggles her eyebrows.

"Still less alone."

"So let me get this straight. You feel lonely when you're with Ryan but less alone when you're... alone?"

I nod. "It sounds crazy." It does. "But it's the truth." How haven't I seen it?

"And yet you're still considering being with Ryan? Remind me why exactly?"

"I need to do what's best for Baby." I sound like a broken record.

"And being unhappy, impatient, mad, anxious, lonely and sexually frustrated," Kate reads from that piece of paper, adding back the 'sexually,' of course, "is better for Baby than being *you*?"

There's nothing I can say to that. So we stay quiet, seated on the couch like this, Kate and I, for what feels like a very long hour. Maybe more. The tea is long gone. Words are too. And no matter how much I try, I can't think of a single thing I like about myself when I'm with Ryan. Because mostly, I realize, when around him, I just can't really be me. This can't be good for any Baby. Biological father or not.

"I need to make sure my baby is happy," I finally say. "And a baby who grows up with both their parents should be happy, right?" I ask my sister.

She gives me her most serious teacher face, then says, "What about making sure Baby's mommy is happy? Who takes care of that?"

29

Lose a War

Claire

A depressing note to self—doing the right thing can sometimes backfire. Especially when the good intentions are coming via Big Boss Joe. Rightly so, he decides to confront Harriett-the-witch Wallington about those worrying findings in our animal studies—the ones she'd been hoping to hide—and maybe also that last clash about insulin not being a cure, the one that made Emily bravely speak up.

As a result, Harriett lashes out, this time not just at me. I didn't tattletale, but Harriett threw a fit anyway. Not in Joe's presence, of course, God forbid she lose her tightly-put-together composure, but she does with me. Granted, there's this thing called non-retaliation written all over our policies and our online HR-based training modules. But as it turns out, Harriett believes in no such policy. Especially where I'm concerned. And so the new orders by her evil majesty are threefold:

1. Steve is no longer my manager. *Subordinates* are not expected to question her decisions. Subordinates. Yes, she actually used that word when referring to me. Bringing yours truly under her direct dictatorship—um, management—will allow her to closely supervise me and ensure I don't go rogue again. Steve isn't happy about it, but when does Steve ever voice his concerns out loud? Not usually, and not this time either.

2. I'm banned from the meeting series in question for the time being, due to my "*inflammatory presence.*" Thankfully, Big Boss Joe will be joining these, so I have no doubt some coveted truths will be uncovered.

3. I no longer support our Type 1 diabetes portfolio. The privilege of working closely with Christian is going to someone else. Harriett made sure to pick Joanna, who has absolutely no experience in clinical development but is the most gorgeous, most stunning human, a badass scientist, but—most importantly—gets along with everyone, even Harriett. And so with Harriett's mission to wreak havoc on my confidence and reduce my joy in work to a minimum—yet make sure her directive claws are everywhere—this is an essential step.

"I may have won one battle, but I have lost the war," I tell Christian during our regular—for now—weekly work catch-up meetings. I'm slumped into a beanbag in one of those tiny brainstorming rooms on a video call, Christian's eyes studying me from the other side of the screen. We've spent the past hour going over our design and concepts, but now I've changed the subject. I may be overly dramatic these days, but Christian being far away from me is making everything seem unbearable. I know it's only been a few days since he left for the conference, and that

Boston is really only about an hour's flight from DC, but that's the longest and farthest we've been apart so far. And there are just too many things not to my liking happening in his absence. I haven't lost my job, but I might as well have.

"This is ridiculous!" Christian determines. "Does Joe know about all of this?"

"I can't keep running to Joe with every tiny issue," I sigh. Besides, getting him involved is what got me into this less-than-stellar situation to begin with.

"I'm going to have a word with her," says my knight in shining armor.

"I can't let you fight my wars." Although it is tempting. I can already envision him pulling out his metaphorical sword, demanding to have me back on the project or he's out. But I can't let that happen. The stakes are too high. If not for the entire population of patients with Type 1 diabetes, then for Jake. Whether I'm part of the revolution or not. I won't let Christian jeopardize this over my stupid childish fight with Harriett. "And besides, Joanna is one of our best scientists, and I'll make sure to bring her up to speed on everything. Plus, she's a much nicer person than me, so she's not going to criticize your theories," I promise, feeling a knot forming in my stomach. Am I... *jealous?*

"I don't want Joanna on this project, I want you," Christian says, making an unintentional smile stretch over my face. "And you don't criticize my theories, you challenge them. As you should. That's how true science is done. Working with someone who always agrees with me? I might as well work alone." His gorgeous eyes look at me through his glasses. And despite the two sets of screens and the miles between us, he knows exactly what's going on in my mind, as if my thoughts are physically written all over my forehead in a secret language that only this man can read. "I'll be back on Thursday, and I'm going to fix this." And before I have a chance to resist, he adds, "Not taking no for an answer."

Gosh, I wish he was here right now. I don't bother answering as he's already said he won't take my no. Plus, my throat feels tight, and I know that if I try to speak, he'll notice. I quickly divert my eyes from his, afraid to let him read more of my stray thoughts. But it's already too late. I usually pride myself on having a poker face, but nothing escapes Christian's radar. Not when it comes to me.

"What else is going on?" It's not really a question, more like a demand for information.

"Not much." Just counting the hours until Thursday. Questioning my latest reactions to Harriett, despite my own personal sense that I did the right thing. Wondering how the Christian-Joanna collaboration will work out and whether the fact that him and I won't be working together anymore will distance us outside of work too. Will Christian still want to be my *someone to run with?*

"I can see the wheels turning inside your head," he tries to joke, but I'm so deep in my own head that by the time I acknowledge it and smile back, his concern has already escalated. "When is Ryan picking you up today?"

"Picking me up?" The last thing on my mind right now, by far, is Ryan.

"For prenatal class," Christian reminds me. We've graduated from prenatal yoga and signed up for another, more advanced session, with Janet. Christian hasn't missed a single one so far, always holding my hand when we walk in, looking like a proud father, making conversation with the other dads. I count the seconds until the moment we settle onto our yoga mat, my back to Christian, my thighs snug against his. I love the way he pulls me back to rest on his chest, letting one hand sprawl protectively across my bump in his special kind of way, while Janet walks the group through some imagery exercises. I feel calm knowing he's there with me.

But since Ryan wants to be part of it too and Christian is in Boston, they both agreed—via our stupid tri-member WhatsApp group—that I was to have a new-old partner in class today.

"He'll meet me there after work," I say. I don't need Ryan to pick me up. I don't need Ryan. Period. And the only reason that he's still in the picture is the baby. "He's in court today, and those things can go long," I explain. And Christian knows, if there's one thing that bothers me—with a passion—it's being late.

"Will he make it in time?" I can see a renewed sense of concern forming on Christian's handsome features.

"Sure," I say, even though I'm quite certain he won't, which is why I've already asked Kate to meet me there. But Christian doesn't need to know all that—he has a major presentation to give in a couple of hours.

"And tomorrow?" Tomorrow... I was trying to—very unsuccessfully—not think about tomorrow. The anatomical scan. By all means a potentially exciting moment for the majority of people, where they also find out the sex of their unborn baby. But me, just being me... I'm freaking out, because my mind is fixed on all the alarming findings that could potentially be seen on an ultrasound. So many things could go wrong during embryonic development and could come to light tomorrow. I'm just hoping everything is okay. "Claire?" Christian frowns on the screen, insisting on pulling me out of my spiraling.

"Let's focus on today," I say, trying to convince myself that I can store these thoughts for the time being. It doesn't work, but I make an effort to slap on a smile, for Christian's sake.

"Is Ryan still planning to be there?" Ryan had seemed excited to take Christian's place at the ultrasound. But that excitement lasted for a whole of five minutes. Then he looked a little nauseated and maybe like he was getting cold feet. But whether he's planning to bail or not, the thought of him being there does very little to ease my concerns. Or calm my nerves. So I just nod. "Everything will be okay, Claire," Christian says softly, tilting his head. "Stop thinking about every possible pathological scenario that you found on Google."

"I did not read anything on Google," I say, offended. "I went straight to PubMed." A.k.a the ultimate source for well-studied, peer-reviewed scientific publications. My findings led me to the conclusion that statistics are very much on the positive outcome side when it comes to something the human body has been naturally nurturing and producing for over—what's the latest estimate?—three hundred thousand years? But I'm still worried.

Christian chuckles. I can feel the tight hold to my jaw loosen a bit; I hadn't even noticed I was clenching it. This man's smile is like sunshine and air to me. "Anyway, enough about that," I pivot. "Are you excited for your presentation?" This isn't some lame attempt to change the subject. I really do want to know. I'm well-aware that he's presented in large, thousands-of-people kinds of forums, multiple times, and may already be immune to the rush that comes with it. But even if he isn't excited, I very much am for him.

"I am," Christian admits, rubbing the back of his neck. The man still keeps a humble outlook despite his professional achievements, and I love that about him.

Did I say love?

"I'm excited for you. Can't wait to hear how it goes and what questions people come up with." Christian's scientific theories are provocative, but he has strong data to support them. I wish I could be there right now too, but Harriett has banned conference travel this year. At least for me.

"Thanks," he says modestly. "I can't wait to tell you all about it." Talking about something else other than my impending pregnancy-related appointments feels good, and for a moment I'm able to almost completely relax. And breathe. Christian's voice is soft and comforting, and I miss being able to touch him.

"How's Jake doin—" I begin to ask when the glass door to the little huddle room opens.

"There you are!" comes the chastising voice of—you guessed it. The witch-bitch. "Haven't you seen the sign?" She points to the small, cartoonish-like "No camping" improvised note on the wall.

"I'm not camping," I say, offended. "I'm on a conference call with Christian." I turn my screen toward her annoyed face, but with all the commotion she doesn't give it a second look.

"Well, there's work to be done. I don't appreciate people wasting company's time and resources on private conversations." And even though this was a pre-scheduled work meeting and we did spend most of it talking about our project, I've admittedly used the last ten minutes to rant about her, so I can't really find the words to counter.

"Harriett, this is a work meeting," Christian says from behind the screen, a crease in his forehead, not something I see often.

"Oh, Chris!" The speed this woman can go from sour to saccharine is unbelievable. "Didn't realize you were on. Are you traveling?"

"It's Christian," he corrects her for what may be the gazillionth time. "And yes, I'm at a conference," he says, his patient voice stretching, not even bothering to say which conference. Or maybe that's just him being modest. "Be back in a couple days. In the meantime, Claire was walking me through the latest developments in the office."

"Yes," Harriett snickers, "we've decided to make a few changes to the line-up, we can talk about them when you're back."

"I've heard, and I don't like it," he counters.

"Once you meet Joanna you will, trust me." Her words, and worst yet—her tone. It makes me want to throw up. Not literally this time, thank God, because no way I'm running away from this conversation.

"Harriett, this does not seem like a professionally wise decision," Christian objects.

"Funny you should say that," she says with a smug face before her eyes leave the screen to address me. "Because sleeping with our academic consultant is also not a very *professionally wise decision*, now is it?" And I can only wish I was still sleeping with said academic consultant.

30

Broken promises

Claire

"Of course he wasn't going to show up in time." I kick my foot into the sidewalk. "I'm done waiting."

"Shall we go in?" Kate gestures toward the little building where my prenatal class is about to commence, trying to keep her cool, but knowing her she's already plotting how to get back at Ryan for doing the exact thing I suspected he would. It's not that he isn't punctual. He has never once been late for work, or court, or a business meeting. The guy certainly has his priorities clear. It's just that in the two years we were together, I was never one of them. So it shouldn't come as a surprise that I'm still not one of them now.

"We shall," I say to Kate, and link my arm with hers. Thank God for my loyal sister who doesn't like to leave things for chance.

"Hello Mama and special friend," Janet welcomes us with a cheerful smile. Her vibrant, colorful outfit today is almost like staring into a painting by Afremov, and given that my childhood home had one hanging in our living room, I find it calming. Or at least the memories that come with it. For a second, I almost forget about Ryan.

"I'm Kate," my sister introduces herself, seeing as my mind is busy walking down memory lane. "Claire's sister and soon to be a proud aunt."

"Oh, that's wonderful!" the woman squeals. "I'm Janet. I love seeing family support. It's so important." I was expecting some quizzical looks regarding Christian's absence, but I see none of that in the Janet's eyes.

"Take a seat mamas, partners and special guests," she says, elevating the already positive atmosphere in the room. "Today, we're going to learn some relaxing breathing techniques, some stretches to help keep pain away from your joints, and for dessert I have an imagery exercise you're going to love." Janet walks around the room, making a point to split her smiles amongst participants. "Exciting evening ahead."

Kate looks around and follows the way the other couples are sitting, positioning herself behind me. I look around too, observing the collection of happy couples that will soon make happy families, which breaks my Afremov painting spell and sends my mind spinning again, questioning my abilities to live up to my own expectations.

We practice some breathing that feel more like hyperventilating than anything, or maybe it's just me. "Slowly," Kate chastises, noting the others around us, but I can't seem to recall what this word means.

This is when Ryan decides to make his appearance, storming into the room like he's about to save the day. Fifteen minutes late. Fashionable, but seriously getting old.

"What did I miss?" he whispers as he lowers himself beside us, a dent in his brow at the sight of Kate's murderous face.

"And you are?" Janet walks over to us, eyeing him suspiciously.

"I'm the father," he says proudly, like he's just won a complicated case in court. Kate rolls her eyes.

"No," the woman responds, quietly so only our little dysfunctional family could hear. "You're late. And look at Mommy's body language—you're making her tense."

Ryan turns his head to me, hoping to dispute the accusation. I shrug. What can I say? The Afremov woman is spot on.

"I'm sorry, I tried to be here in time but had a shitload of work. I'm a lawyer—" He's apologizing, I'll give him that, but our fearless instructor waves him off mid-sentence.

"Explain that to your partners," she says. And although I'm not done being mad that this is Ryan's *trying,* Kate and I exchange a funny look about Janet's use of multiform for my selection of life partners. "And by the way," she lowers her voice again, "I recommend sticking to no more than one or two partners for the duration of the course. Reliable ones."

"I'd recommend the same," I whisper to Kate once Janet is out of earshot, "only life doesn't seem to take my recommendations into account." Although that's not entirely true. The fact that Christian is slowly breaking away is mostly my doing. So is the fact that I'm pregnant. But I'm here to work on my breathing, not beat myself up. So I get in position, supported by Kate on one side, and Ryan on my other.

During the break, Janet pulls me aside to make sure I know she thinks highly of Christian, who "makes your face shine and your eyes sparkle." And lowly of Ryan—"No judgment of course," are her exact words, "but this guy," she says, pointing at Ryan, "drains the happiness right out of you."

Well, it certainly doesn't help when Ryan lets Kate and I know that he thinks the breathing exercises are "bullshit." Or sighs dubiously throughout the imagery session, because he's "not *seeing* it," before he gets his final red card for the day and has to wait outside.

I've spent two years of my life with Ryan, and while I can't say I truly know everything about the guy, I can at least say that he's not trying to be inflammatory, or skeptical. He's actually making an effort. Whether it's the right one though... that's debatable. It *is* him trying. At least where I'm concerned.

"What?" He shrugs as my sister and I emerge from the building once class adjourns. "Breathing and imagery aren't for everyone," he defends, rising from his spot on the brick wall outside the front garden. He does tend to suffer from over-practicality. Although if he'd bother to read the literature, those things can actually make a difference.

"*You* wanted to be here." Kate feels the need to go to war for me, poking his chest with her finger. Ryan better watch out, my protective sister is turning into an aunt, which makes her all the more dangerous. "If you're not having it, at least don't ruin everything for everyone else."

By nighttime, my next-door neighbor stops by to let me know he's taking the night off, as if he's already been put on daddy duty, or as if I care where he spends his time. Ryan's conflict resolution cave, if such a thing were to exist, is his best friend Harris's basement. The man is happily married with five kids already, including two sets of twins. It's a mad house, and in the few times I'd been there with Ryan, I felt pretty compelled to wait a few years to have kids of my own. But Harris is as happy as can be, the epitome of the perfect father and the perfect buddy, and always on speed dial for Ryan. He's a good guy, although he tends to come up with the most atrocious ideas of how to improve any situation. Like—guys-only trip to the Sahara on Baby's potential due date, or a couples-exchange retreat in California. That one was actually his wife's idea. And yes, five-month pregnant me was propositioned to be included. Well, NOT happening. I politely killed that initiative.

Tonight, though, is probably men-camping-under-the-stars, or drink-yourself-to-oblivion night, or whatever else Harris comes up with, but Ryan has already given me the heads up to not expect him back before tomorrow. Not that I was, but he may have felt the need to disclose that information since tomorrow is Baby's ANATOMY SCAN, only the most stressful part of this pregnancy so far—at least for me, until the actual birth. Kate offered to go out for ice cream, but since becoming pregnant, stress-eating hasn't worked well with my food retaining abilities, so I decided to skip.

And now, unrelated to Ryan and his whereabouts, or ice cream-no ice cream, I can't sleep. The clock on my nightstand insists on moving slower than ever. I grab my phone, knowing all too well that blue light is probably not the best choice in such scenarios, but I'm at a loss.

"How did the presentation go?" I text Christian. I should have dropped the idea of communicating with him hours ago, given I'd already attempted a phone call to which he did not reply. And a second one. It actually went straight to voicemail, as if he'd purposely turned his phone off. I know he isn't in any of the scientific sessions at that exact moment; I have the agenda. And I'm sure there are plenty of smart, sexy, un-pregnant women there to choose from. After all, who would stick around with a pregnant girl who lets her ex move next door and pushes the one good thing that ever happened to her away? Telling him he could start seeing other women... what was I thinking?

There's a light knock on my front door followed by the sound of keys and the turn of a lock. There are only two people in this world who have a spare key to my apartment these days. Kate and Christian. Which is why I don't bother with more decent clothing than my underwear and bra-less T-shirt. But I still get up to see who's the offender who has decided to disturb my lack of peace and quiet at—I glimpse at my watch—almost 11 p.m. And there he is. The man who takes my breath away. Face to face with me.

"What are you doing here?" I probably could have said that in a more appreciative way, but surprises put me on alert. Christian chuckles in response and lets himself in. "But your presentation..."

"Went very well, thank you," he says, resting his carry-on beside the shoe rack and loosening his tie, a motion that still sends electric currents through my body, even in our current tor-turous platonic situation. "Then I headed straight to the airport and took the first flight back. There's no way I'm going to miss the ultrasound tomorrow. That is, if you still want me there." I probably should confirm that yes, of course I want him there. I'm not sure how in my right mind I thought I could do any of this without him.

"When you weren't answering my calls, I kind of thought you moved on." I'm not sure why I feel compelled to share this info with him, but I can't seem to stop. "You know, since we said we could see other people. Maybe you're seeing someone else. Sleeping with someone else..." I shrug, as if that would be perfectly okay with me. Just crushing my heart and feeding it to a food processor, that is.

Christian considers me for a moment. I should be grateful that he dropped everything and came here. Other women and all. But that's the thing with thoughts. Once they pop in my head—unfounded as they may be—I can't just fold them back neatly and shove them in the back of my closet.

"I'm not seeing anyone, not sleeping with anyone," he finally says, a bit amused. "You're underestimating the time it would take me to *move on*."

"I thought a whole entire month and a half—" I may have counted the days since the last time we held each other tight. That fervent skin-to-skin contact, his lips on mine, the feel-ing that nothing could keep us apart. "Would be more than enough."

"Are you kidding me? A lifetime would not be enough."

And I know I shouldn't be standing so close to him. Shouldn't be challenging my ability to keep my hands to myself. I know I should go back to my bedroom and put some pants on.

But now, basking in Christian's light, the thought of giving him an out seems impossible. Did I really think that being *friends without benefits*, or letting Christian *see other people* would get easier with time? I can't take it anymore.

"I missed you," I say, letting my body take that one last step to obliterate the distance between us and wrap my arms around him. A sigh of relief escapes me when my head finds its place against his chest, the familiar sensation of his heartbeat reverberating through me.

"I missed you too," he whispers, smoothing a gentle hand around my growing baby bump. "Both of you."

Christian

Claire is pressed tight against me in a hug, wearing nothing but her "I hate my boss" white off-the-shoulder T-shirt that barely reaches her mid-section and a pair of underwear. She has this cute round pregnant belly, and I don't know how it is for other men when their girl is pregnant, but mine is HOT.

Did I just say *mine*?

I'm so fucked.

"Is that how you open the door for everyone?" I whisper into her hair, jealousy and lust hitting me hard.

"No, just you," she answers, her tone turning playful. She takes a step back, breaking the hug to give me a good once-over.

"Will you put some goddamn pants on?" I tease.

"It's my house, my rules," she answers, turning away from me, pulling the shirt over her head and dropping it to the floor. I only see her backside, but can barely control myself.

"I take it your next-door neighbor is not home." I swallow hard, following her to the living room, but she doesn't stop there—she walks into her bedroom, and as the fool I am, I follow her there too.

"No. He's having a sleepover with his friend Harris," Claire says over her shoulder. And as I get closer, she stops in her tracks and leans back into me.

My body instantly responds. "Christ," I groan, hands instinctively sliding to her waist and up her ribs. "We made him a promise," my voice says, but my conviction and will to resist are quickly draining away.

Claire turns in my arms, her naked body covered only by her tiny pair of underwear. "I can't do this anymore." She takes my hand, sliding it across her skin, all the way to her breast. I'm having trouble controlling myself as it is when she guides my other hand down her back and beneath the soft band of the fabric, letting my fingers do the rest. A soft moan escapes her. I'm hanging by a thread.

Goddamn it, I want her so bad.

Claire sheds that last bit of fabric, then pulls me by the tie, and before I know it my lips are on hers, finally kissing her again, tasting her again. She melts in my arms like nothing else matters anymore. Giving me her whole self.

"I've missed this so much. Us," she breathes. "I need you." And I know how hard it is for her to admit. Her hands reach for my belt, undressing me greedily. There are times in life when the responsible adult in you needs to show up, take control. Recall the agreement made with your girl's ex. But as Claire's naked body meets mine again, as our legs tangle together and we're all hands and tongues and out of breath, I can't seem to remember anything else. It's muscle memory from here on out. Every part of my body knows what to do. How to hold her. How to touch her. How to kiss her. How to love her. And there's nothing I can do to stop myself from falling. Deeper and deeper to a place of no return. There's no coming back from here. Not without her.

31

The scan

Christian

There are not enough words in the English language to describe the way I feel as I hold Claire's hand and watch the grayscale sonogram on the screen. I'm awed, and speechless; it's unlike anything I've ever known before. So is the stark realization and jealousy growing in me as Ryan takes her other hand, also fascinated by the creation. *His and Claire's creation*. And I can't help feeling like a third wheel. I know Claire wants me there, needs me there—she made it very clear when Ryan objected to walking in together and told her to choose. Claire refused the ultimatum with a warning that *he* might be the one waiting outside. So reluctantly, he ended up swallowing his pride and followed suit.

But it's not about me, it's about Claire and the baby. So I choose to be in the moment. Something I can't really say about Ryan, who's busy pouting like a toddler on the verge of a tantrum. I guess, despite being the biological father, he too might be feeling like a third wheel. The technician is doing her best to ignore the scene, chatting up Claire, who is growing tense with every swipe of the transducer, especially when the tech stops to study the image on the screen.

"Just tell me everything is okay," Claire pleads, her chest rising and falling quickly. Her grip on my hand grows tighter.

"The doctor will be in shortly and will go over everything with you," the woman in scrubs says, but seeing Claire's terrified face, she nods in reassurance. Claire gives a soft sigh of relief, but the tense expression between her eyebrows doesn't dissolve. I smooth a strand of hair off her face and her eyes flicker to me. It's fleeting, but I can see the fear. The worry. The feeling that things are out of her control.

"Do you want to know if it's a boy or a girl?"

"Of course we do," Ryan responds, completely oblivious to the little storm around him, much too used to being the voice of his clients. Or maybe just being an inconsiderate prick.

"Speak for yourself," Claire reprimands. "I want it to be a surprise." Her gaze turns to me for affirmation. "Do you want to know?" she asks me, like I'm truly a side in this story. This makes my heart swell with some parental pride I don't deserve to own. Not in the current scenario.

"I want what you want," I say, voting Ryan out. I'm curious, of course, but the victorious smile on her face is worth it all.

"Okay, then just tell me quietly," Ryan says, and I get this urge to punch him. "Hopefully a boy."

"Sorry," the tech says. "Mommy is my patient, going to respect her wishes."

"Man..."

"You can tell him after we leave the room," Claire concedes. "As long as you don't tell *me*, Ryan."

Fast-forward thirty minutes, and now he knows. And we don't. But I don't care, because Claire is smiling ear to ear, concerns alleviated. Once the doctor stepped inside the room and confirmed that in fact all was good, she was finally able to let go and admire the wonder. Now she's holding the stretch of print-outs like a proud mom. I'm still holding her hand when we step out of the building, and as we round the corner, she stops to kiss me.

"We're breaking all the rules," I whisper into her lips.

"Just for today."

"And last night," I chuckle.

"That was technically still today," she counters before I pull her close, deepening the kiss.

Claire

Seeing my baby on the screen this morning was one of these transformative moments. You come in with certain thoughts and ideas, then come out completely different. I'm fully aware that this may just be one of many of those moments in parenthood, but as Christian drops me off at the office, headed to his lab, I decide it's time to make it known.

"Do you have a minute?" I half-ask, half-knock on Big Boss Joe's doorframe. The door to his office is wide open, as it typically is, his eyes focused on his computer screen.

"For you, always," he says warmly and gestures to the chair across from his desk. I walk in, close the door behind me and plop into the chair. "What's up?" he asks. An invitation to jump straight into it, so I take it.

"I'm pregnant," I say. "And it's okay, you don't have to act surprised, I know I'm already showing, I just... it didn't feel quite as real until now."

Big Boss Joe gives me his best happy smile, but seeing my somewhat—I assume—wary expression, he rethinks his reaction and asks, "Are congratulations in order?"

"Oh, they are," I say. Because he doesn't need to know that I'm falling for Christian while trying to pretend we're platonic friends in order to give him space and keep Baby's biological father in the picture. He doesn't need to know that I'm worried that once my pregnancy becomes fully known in the office, Harriett is probably going to somehow find a way to use that against me. He doesn't need to know that my mood has taken a dive and that I'm really worried about the possibility that it might get worse as the pregnancy progresses. So I plaster on a big smile. And when he congratulates me with an excited tone, I try to make my "Thank you," match his positive energy. And when he asks my permission to have Charlene throw a baby shower for me, which is so kind and sweet I say, "Of course." Because I still feel the post-scan's everything-is-okay high.

"Okay, now tell me what's really going on," Big Boss Joe says. Not because announcing my pregnancy is not big enough a topic, but because he knows me better than that. "If you're worried about maternity leave, please let me assure you—"

"It's not that," I cut him off. I already have the company's truly generous parental leave guidelines fully memorized. "Were you involved in Harriett's decision to assign Joanna to work with Dr. Copeland on the Type 1 diabetes project instead of me?"

This takes him by surprise. "Claire," he says, "it's none of my business, which is why I haven't brought this up, but people do talk." And by people I'm sure he means Harriett.

"About Christian and me?" I pitch in, already realizing where this is headed. I don't try to deny it. I could say we're going for platonic, but based on last night's events, this no longer holds true. "Let me assure you, it won't impact my judgement."

"I'm not concerned about your judgment, more about the optics."

"But Joanna?" I challenge. "I mean, other than the fact that she has no clinical development experience..." Did Harriett have to pick the most attractive woman in the office while I'm slowly but surely growing to expanded dimensions? Is she purposely trying to make me jealous? Well, no need to answer that question.

Big Boss Joe chuckles, making me wonder what part of my last sentence I may have accidentally said out loud. "I don't think you have anything to worry about," he says, "considering the way Christian looks at you. But I do agree that Joanna may not be the best choice based on her specific experience. I've already told Harriett that. Steve will be Dr. Copeland's partner instead, and you can stay on the project. Your hard work is not going to go to waste. So one less topic to worry about." Then he gives me a fatherly, knowing smile. Or at least I assume that's what a fatherly smile would look like. And despite having to endure a party thrown for me in my near future—yeah, parties are more of a Kate thing—all in all, I think this conversation can be marked as a success.

32

Gratitude

Claire

The weeks go by quickly. Faster than what would be deemed comfortable for a future mother trying to figure out her best path before actually becoming one. Faster than what I'm able to process. Some days are fine. Some not so much. Between trying to keep Christian as my someone to run with, despite the guilt that surrounds it—he truly deserves something simpler than being with me—and keeping Ryan as a stakeholder in my life, I mostly just feel confused.

"Sometimes, especially when I wake up in the morning," I tell Dr. Levine, who agrees to see me on an ad-hoc basis, "I feel like I'm sinking. Like I'm lodged in quicksand. Only it's not really quick. It's slow-sand. There's no advance warning, you just find yourself in it, and it slowly tightens around you, pulling you in until it's hard to breathe. And I desperately try to fight it, but things that typically cheer me up don't work anymore. And I go through the motions, go through with my day. I show up. But no matter what I do, every morning I wake up a little deeper in it. And I can no longer remember how it feels to breathe freely again or smile. Or how to get there. How to get back to my reasonable happy place. Am I going crazy, doc?"

"No Claire," he says warmly, as if the side of myself I've just exposed is the most normal thing that people experience daily. "I think you just need a map."

"A map?" I can't lie, his reaction casts a spark of optimism in my slow-sand sinking heart. Like maybe it's fixable.

"To help you get where you want to go. That 'reasonable happy place' as you call it. Maybe even more than that—let's aspire for more than just reasonable."

"I like you, doc," I say kindly. "But I think you're not being very realistic."

"Also, I'd like you to tell, what you've just told me, to one other person, whoever you choose."

"Uh, doc, I'm fine with making a map, but I don't see how telling my innermost secrets to someone else would help..."

"Wouldn't hurt to take my word for it and give it a try, would it?" Then he pulls out a piece of paper from his desk and a few markers and spreads them on the coffee table next to me. "Now, how are your drawing skills?"

Christian

It's 2 a.m. I'm not really asleep, but not awake either. One of the questionable joys of getting your heart set on a woman who's carrying someone else's child. My phone rings and I pick up, my vision so blurred I can't make out the jumble of letters and image that indicate the caller's ID. "Hello?" I'm sure my voice is an accurate drowsy depiction of the way I feel. Tired.

"Oh, you're awake." Claire's voice attacks my ears, and all at once I am awake. Wide awake.

"Is everything okay?" I ask, thousands of emergency scenarios are spinning through my head. "Are you having contractions?" She shouldn't be sleeping there all alone, now that she's entering her third trimester.

"No, nothing like that," she says, and I mentally let my pulse know it can slow down. "Hey, I didn't mean to wake you," she spits out. "I mean I was hoping you wouldn't be asleep so I could talk to you."

"Do you need me to come over?" I ask, hoping she'll say yes.

"*Need* is a big word," she backs down. "It's not like I'm going into labor right now or any other sort of emergency, just..."

"*Want* me to come over?" I correct myself.

"Yes." I can hear the relief in her voice. There's no hesitation. No thinking-it-through pause. And I'm already putting my jeans on and walking down the hall to wash my face and brush my teeth. "I mean, if you're not busy or trying to go back to sleep." I chuckle. She has no idea how far gone I am for her.

"Where's Mr. I know the baby's gender and you don't?" I inquire twenty minutes later when I walk into her apartment. Ryan has been seriously annoying, trying to prove we're not adhering to his *friends without benefits* rule. I hope he's not planning to use that as an excuse to bail out of his future baby's life. I'll be damned if I let that happen, even if it means I have to be patient, settle for what Claire can give, for as long as she needs, until I can finally—one day, hopefully—make her officially mine.

"Spending another night at Harris's," Claire scoffs. "But even if he was next door, I don't care about his stupid rules anymore. He barely even talks to me. And Baby won't let me sleep."

"I might not let you sleep either," I warn, pulling her into me.

"Hmmm, already better," she purrs. "But I need to tell you something. My therapist said I need to share it with at least one person. And you're it. And it has to be at—" she glances at her watch, "2:25 a.m., because I might not be brave enough to do it during normal business hours."

"Okay." I sit down on her couch and pull her into my lap, letting my palm rest on her tight pregnant belly, enjoying the feel of Baby stretching and reacting to my touch.

"I've been a basket case lately," she says.

"What?" I chuckle, thinking she's trying to make me laugh.

"I'm serious." Claire takes a deep breath, bracing herself, the look in her eyes devoid of any trace of playfulness she may have had when I walked in.

"That's what Dr. Levine told you to say?" Because from the little I've had a chance to become familiar with his style, the guy is unusual and can be bleak sometimes, but he's optimistic, and this... this isn't—

"Of course not," she supplies. "But he would if he fully appreciated the extent." There's humor in her voice, but it's a darker kind. "I may seem okay from the outside, going about my day, doing my thing, living my reasonable life. No one knows. Not even Kate. But inside, at least on some days, I'm falling apart. And I wish I could pinpoint what it is that makes some days okay and some not. But I can't. This is like so stupid on any possible scale," she sighs. "Okay, I said it. But I swear if you tell Kate I'll kill you."

"It's not stupid," I say. "Have you always felt this way?"

"I did as a kid. Then I sort of grew out of it. And now in the past few months it's coming back again, and I don't know how to make it go away. This time it seems it's here to stay." Her words come out quickly, and she stops to take a breath. "Life feels so complicated and overwhelming that I don't even know where to start. Sort of like the feeling one gets when they need to sleep on things, only I sleep plenty, and it doesn't seem to do the trick."

In the past few months, it's coming back... I can't help but feel like I have something to do with it. Especially now that Ryan is trying to gradually increase his part in her life, and I'm stuck between them like a sore thumb. I know Claire says she wants me here, but maybe I'm the one making things complicated for her. I don't know the right thing to say or do, so I just let my arms wrap around her, and she holds on, burying her head in me.

"Weird part is," she continues, speaking into my chest softly, "that the nights are fine. But mornings... they are the worst. It's like there's a sad song stuck in my brain the second I wake up. And that's putting it lightly. Waking up in my head feels like I'm being hit by a tsunami of anxiety. Then I drag my sorry ass out of bed, drink some strong tea—because of course coffee still makes me sick—load up on sugar, and by the time I get on the metro it's usually better."

Claire

I told Christian. Just like Dr. Levine instructed. I sat him down and shared my deepest darkest secret. Only it doesn't feel so dark anymore. Not when Christian pulls my chin up gently with his fingers, his eyes staring straight into my soul. "Hey," he says. "Thank you for trusting me, and telling me how you feel."

Then he goes and gets us ice cream—God only knows where he found ice cream in the middle of the night—and makes a promise, just as he did that time in the restroom stall, that everything will be alright.

"That's ridiculous," I tell him, even though I'm willing to take his word for it. "You can't promise something like that."

"Really? I just did."

"Well, okay, technically you can." I can't avoid the smile creeping into my face, combined with the cold, sweet chocolate ice cream in my mouth. "But you can't possibly keep such a promise. It's not up to you." Although the ice cream is definitely helping. "You know, my mom used to take Kate and me for ice cream when we needed something to cheer us up." And it worked every single time. Ice cream is magical.

"Your mom sounds like an amazing person."

"Yes, she is," I say, realizing that it never really was about the ice cream at all. It was us being together, sharing our thoughts and feelings, supporting each other. Laughing out loud to lighten up the mood. And I realize how fortunate I am to have grown up with such a mom and sister by my side. And how lucky I am to have Christian right here with me. How grateful I am to have these incredible people in my life.

33

Braxton Hicks

Claire

A few more weeks go by. At some point, Christian decided to spoil me with a weekend in New York City and a trip to The Ripped Bodice, a romance-only bookstore in Brooklyn, recommending that I get myself accustomed to uncomplicated happy endings and guaranteed happily ever afters. To make his point, he made the owner do a rundown of popular tropes and authors and refused to leave until I picked at least ten colorful paperbacks to call my own. And now, having read two of them and midway through the third, I can unequivocally say that I like grumpy-sunshine, forbidden romance and friends-to-lovers, and can't wait to check out the other tropes. Me. The ultimate skeptic when it comes to romance, laughing out loud with a book in my hand as I sit at Ryan's favorite restaurant, waiting for him to wrap up a complicated case in court and show up for our weekly dinner. No, he's not late yet, I just showed up early so I can sneak in a few pages. Immersing myself in feel-good, happy-ending romcoms does so much more for me than any therapy session or mood-boosting supplement ever could. It's a natural anti-depressant if you're willing to clear up some real estate on your bookshelf or eReader device, and some time in your schedule.

"Hey honey," is Ryan's greeting as he spots me at our table. Lately he's been trying out endearments for me—inspired by some marriage advice from Harris, I gather—not sure where he's going with it, but I don't really mind. Then, noticing the book in my hand he adds, "Why are you reading this shit?" He picks up my little guilty pleasure with the tips of his fingers, holding it as if he just found it in a pile of dirt.

"Christian got it for me," I say, not caring one bit what he thinks of my new and increasing fondness for the romance genre.

"So you're into smut now?" He quirks an eyebrow.

"Apparently, I've found out I'm into things that put a smile on my face and make me laugh. And smut—yeah, that too. I can't believe there's this great big world out there and I had no idea, until now."

"I see," he says, as if this is a personal insult directed right at him. It wasn't. But that was the reality of our relationship. "Well, it takes two," he says.

"Can't argue with that, I'm equally guilty," I agree. It was always a struggle when it came to the two of us and I didn't fight to keep him. I thought I just didn't have it in me—fighting to keep someone. But now I think I had it all wrong. Because who-ever said loving someone needs to be a struggle? It's so different with Christian. Like my entire being was just meant to love him. Uncontrollable, all-consuming. In fact, I don't know how to do anything else *but* love him. And where did that word come from? These romantic books are really getting the better of me.

"Maybe we should give ourselves another chance?" Ryan offers while I take a cooling sip of water. The last scene in my book was HOT, and I feel a bit guilty thinking about shirtless Christian while Ryan is talking about second or third chances. We would never be having this conversation if it weren't for Baby. My mind drifts into other places, like one where Christian is sitting next to me, gently skating his fingers over my very pregnant belly.

But then—and something tells me it has nothing to do with the smut scene I've just read—something shifts. There's a weird and unfamiliar sensation coursing through me. It's like a wave, crossing and hardening my stomach muscles all at once, then it's gone.

"What?" Ryan asks, still on the last topic we talked about. I can't really recall what it was anymore.

"I..." My hand finds my stomach, as if asking Baby for answers. *Was it you?* "I think I had a contraction."

"You *think*?" Ryan looks puzzled. Or more like I must be delusional. Either that or he's panicking, I can't really tell.

I nod. "I mean, it's gone now, but it felt like one."

"Can't be," says the lawyer who's now apparently a trained obstetrician. "You look completely fine, shouldn't it be like unbearable?"

"How would I know? It's my first time." And while he mulls it over, I pull out my phone to text Christian.

"And it's too early, you're like—"

"Thirty-two weeks pregnant," I chime in, because no way he's been counting, while Christian has a calendar in his kitchen with cute drawings that Jake adds each week. Wow, time flies.

"You can't have the baby now, it's too soon!"

"Oh, thank you, that's helpful," I say, rubbing a hand on my belly as it hardens again, just for a few seconds. Then gone.

My phone rings with a video call from Christian, who's probably worried about my *I think contractions started* message, likely with some typos.

"How are you feeling?" Christian's handsome-worried face appear on the screen. Ryan groans in the background. He's asked several questions already, but interestingly, wondering about the way *I* felt wasn't one of them. "Does it hurt?" Christian's head tilts, trying to assess through the phone.

"I'm feeling fine actually. No, doesn't hurt. Could be Braxton Hicks, I'm not sure."

"I think we should get you to the hospital, just to be on the safe side," he says through the phone, keeping his voice even. I know he's suggesting it because it's early, too early, and if it's not Braxton Hicks and I'm actually going into labor—maybe it can still be stopped.

"No way, they'll just send us back in shame," Ryan objects. As if he's seen thousand births other than that one clip they showed us at that one prenatal class he attended, right before he's got thrown out by Janet for being too... Ryan.

"They probably will," I agree. The two earlier contractions are now long gone, and it almost feels like the whole thing was just a figment of my imagination.

"Let's hope they do," Christian says.

Then my stomach hardens again, so I decide not to risk it and just go check it out. "Yeah, you're right," I breathe.

"Get your ass off the chair Ryan," Christian commands. "I'll meet you guys there."

I insist on not bringing my pre-made delivery-day bag with us. The one with my overnight supply, some books—romance of course—and lots of baby stuff Christian bought and packed for me—I'm not really sure what I might need. Ryan puts it in the trunk and I make him leave it there—not wanting to appear presumptuous and also hoping to not have to stay—as we cross the parking lot leading to the ER. There's a bud of anxiety in my chest, and spiraling thoughts starting to form in my brain with every step. But then I see Christian, getting a head start on signing us in, and my feet feel grounded again.

You okay? his eyes ask as he turns to me, concerned and unsure if he should dial down his affection around Ryan. I'm too worried and scared right now to care about Ryan or any of his games, so I just let my body make a beeline to Christian and nestle into his chest, breathing him in like oxygen supply. Even with my very pregnant belly I still fit perfectly between his arms, in his comforting, nerve-calming hug. "It's going to be okay," he says as he buries his face in my hair and takes a deep inhale, like maybe I'm his oxygen supply too. And I decide to take his word for it, grateful he's here.

Ryan may be less so. "She needs an epidural," he tells the nurse once we get behind a curtain.

"You decided?!" I turn an annoyed face in his direction. "You know I want to have a natural birth, which means *no epidural*."

"But why suffer when you can just have it easy?" is his argument. And it sounds like a plausible argument. Only, the thought of getting an epidural scares me a million times more than an actual birth. We've touched on this topic before. Ryan didn't get it then, as he wouldn't now.

"I don't think anyone's *having it easy*, epidural or not. Plus, it's too early to have the baby!" My voice is a tad louder than needed, perhaps, but I don't care.

"I'm not sure you're thinking straight right—" Ryan starts, but Christian's hand is already landing on his chest. It's a warning. A gentle reminder that he may want to shut up now.

"Let's not get ahead of ourselves," the nurse intervenes, thankfully. "When it's time, we'll go by Mommy's wishes." Her tone is even but she gives Ryan a quick glare. "An epidural is totally optional, but since she's the one having the baby—she's the one who gets to choose." I love this nurse already.

And from that moment on, Ryan doesn't say another word.

Dehydration. Is what the doctors decide as the most plausible cause for my non-labor inducing—thankfully—contractions.

It's 4 a.m. when we walk back out to the parking lot and come to a stop somewhere between Christian's and Ryan's parked cars. The two men in my life are busy fussing over who gets to take me home and who gets to do a strawberry run. Yeah, that's what my pregnant self is craving at the moment, and probably not a bad idea as an extra fix for dehydration.

Right now, I just want to get home, take my shoes off, munch on my strawberries in peace, and hopefully do all that with Christian next to me, because that's the only thing that makes the world fall away and quiets my brain down. I don't have the energy for pissing contests or broken egos, so I walk into Christian's car and get in. But neither of the men in my life move or attempt to go into their respective vehicles. They just stand there, talking with large hand gestures about God knows what. Like they're having some kind of an argument. And I can't make out a word of what they're saying.

Christian

"I need you to take a step back man," Ryan pleads as we stay back in the parking lot before returning to our cars. Claire clearly chose mine. She's sitting there waiting for me, and I can see why Ryan feels like a spare tire in this situation. Because that's what he *is*. A useless spare tire.

"Why would I fucking wanna do that, Ryan?" I ask, trying to calm myself down before my fist takes the initiative to collide with his face. Taking a step back is the last thing I want to do, especially tonight, when Claire needs me. Ryan gives me a tired look. His eyes are bloodshot. He seems worried and unnerved, and I'm not sure where he's going with it.

"I'm going to propose to her," he says. And from this point on it's a daze. Like a bad trip. "She's going to be my wife. I'm going to make it right." I hear his voice, but my brain's refusing to let the words in. "But there's no way she'll say yes if she thinks you're a possibility. She clearly wants you more."

It's like a giant pendulum, swinging fast and heavy, headed toward my chest and I know I have to. I have no choice. I need to do the right thing for Claire and the baby. I can't be the one breaking up a family. I can't be the reason. The one preventing a kid from growing up with his own dad. Ryan is clearly trying to make an effort here. My body protests, and my hand comes to grab him by his fucking dress shirt. There's nothing I would like more right now than punching his smug face.

"It's a girl," he says, right into my burning eyes, shaking my trance away.

"What?"

"The baby. My daughter," Ryan clarifies, twisting a dagger right inside my heart. "Now it's time for you to step away."

I want to fight, obliterate this guy from existence. My hand lets go of his shirt to wrap around his neck. But then ... I let go. Deciding against breaking his fucking teeth, for the sake of his future daughter and probably—the thought makes me shudder. His future wife.

"Understood." What comes out is a foreign sound. I don't even recognize my own voice. Or actions. This quiet agreement to walk away without a fight. Something I'm going to spend the rest of my life regretting. "But not tonight," I ask. "I need to make sure she's alright."

Claire

"What was that all about?" I ask Christian when he finally joins me in the driver's seat. His face looks strained, like he's enduring physical pain, jaw clenched as he takes the front seat.

"Just usual Ryan stuff," he grunts. Even his voice sounds different. The usual melody that carries his words is gone. But maybe this has nothing to do with Ryan. Maybe it's me. A sad, toned-down version of Christian is sitting behind the wheel, steering us into—possibly—a new territory. One that I'm not liking one bit.

And unlike everything else with Christian that always seemed to feel like a first, the following week feels like the last. The way he stays by my side, holds me through the nights. The way he looks into my eyes, as if trying to savor every word, every kiss, every touch. I've been so absorbed in feeling guilty about wanting to make him mine that I never actually tried to define what it is between us. Never stuck a label onto it or discussed our direction. Which is why I have no right to demand anything else when I open my eyes one morning—only one day after we're done setting up the nursery, gender-neutral colors and all—to find a letter on the pillow where Christian's head once rested.

"I couldn't bring myself to say the words out loud." His written sentences are bound together in a melancholic version of his handwriting, messy and scattered and sad. Like he changed his mind a thousand times from the first word to the last. "I have to get away. To do the best I can to give you and Baby a chance to be a family." It doesn't make any sense, or maybe makes total sense. And I can't really blame him. I mean, I'm a real piece of work. And I opened up. I shared my most guarded secrets. The ones about my mood, the noise in my head, the anxiety. I've let all these shades of me show. I bet that in his mind it all became too familiar. His mom who had slowly faded away, leaving Christian and his sister to fend for themselves. Why would anyone in their right mind want to get themselves into a possibly similar situation if they don't have to? He took it all quite well, but maybe he had some time to think things over and realized there isn't really a reason for him to choose complicated if he could just find a normal partner to spend his life with. Someone who isn't pregnant with some other man's kid. Someone who isn't me. Something simple.

That's what I try to tell myself. But I can't help feel that despite all that, he is no better than Kate's dad. Or Jake's dad. Because he promised. Promised to be my someone to run with. Promised that everything will be alright. And now that he's extricated himself from my life, nothing feels right anymore.

34

Baby shower

Claire

I've been to quite a few baby showers in my life. Enough to know that the common theme in these parties is a collision of colors and sugar and happiness. None of which I'm feeling at the moment. Looking at the list of invitees that Charlene shared with me—because she knows my take on surprises—I'm already hoping Harriett will decide to skip the occasion. I have too many things to deal with as it is. My eyes skim through the names and come to a halt when I spot Christian's. My mind is reeling as I try to imagine the scene. Just reading the letters that constitute his name knocks the air out of me. What will he say? What will he do? What will I do? How will seeing him again make me feel? It's been a long, painful week since he wrote those words that pierced a hole through my heart. I miss him in meetings, I linger on the tiny image of his face on the company's chat, and I walk by his old temporary office imagining that maybe he just happened to stop by. I can barely go a single day without him, let alone an entire life.

I spend way too long planning what to wear, what to do, how to interact with him again. But nothing prepares me for what comes next, which is not seeing him at all. I stand in the large conference room, the place we used to bicker about scientific facts and misconceptions, let our eyes meet, share knowing smiles and ideas. Now it's decorated with pink and blue balloons and creative flower arrangements handpicked by Charlene, plus a giant cake and a full table of fancy-looking appetizers and sweets. People, so many people that I didn't even know gave a damn, show up just for me, bearing gifts and good moods. Or maybe it's the free food, but either way they're here, and I should be grateful. And happy. Or at the very least a semblance of happy. I definitely shouldn't be fussing about one specific name on the list who did not bother to show up. And I definitely shouldn't let my gaze gravitate to the door constantly, hoping he'll walk in, even if he's late, despite knowing my relationship with being on time. Late Christian is still Christian, and right now the need to see him, hear his voice, feel his touch again, overshadows everything.

"Please know that I'm here for you." Charlene corners me once the party is done, and I feel guilty, because I mentally missed the whole thing. I was here, making conversation, giving out polite smiles and thank yous, but at the same time I was not here at all.

Charlene is munching on leftover cake. It's a good cake, or at least it looks like one. I didn't take any though, not having much appetite lately. I read it could be a late pregnancy thing, although I'm pretty sure it's a longing thing.

"Thank you," I say, "for everything." And I mean it, I really do. But my eyes water and the tears are out before I have a chance to stop them.

"I'm sorry," she says, taking my hand and giving it a squeeze.

"Sorry? You've done so much for me," I say, quickly wiping my face. "I'm just being overly emotional. Well, the pregnancy hormones are not helping." Go ahead, blame it on the pregnancy.

"And the fact that Christian didn't show up is not helping either," she adds.

"Well, that too," I admit.

"He gave the temporary office back. Said he won't be coming here in person anymore, his interactions with the team are now switched to virtual only."

"Well good," I say. "It will make my life easier if I don't have to see him again." But it's a lie. A hopeful aspirational lie.

"He asks about you every day, you know?"

"What?" This doesn't make much sense.

"He calls, every morning, 10 a.m. sharp. He wants to know you're okay," Charlene explains. As if this additional piece of information can help me understand.

"You can tell him I'm just fine. Living the dream."

And I'm sure there are worse things than having the one you love walk out of your life. But I can't think of any right now.

Love. What a strange situation it is to realize you love someone when it's already too late. I had so many opportunities to say it. Would that have made any difference?

Christian

"Dude, I've known you since kindergarten, and this has to be the most ridiculous thing I've ever heard you say," Derek, the man who's supposed to be my best friend, supplies. Lately, he's been seeing someone more seriously, I think, which is slowly but surely transforming his take on love.

"Thanks for the support, man," I sigh, turning my eyes to Aiden, hoping he'll pour some sense into this conversation. By the quizzical way he stares back at me, I can already tell that salvation is not coming from him either.

"Can you please enlighten us as to why you think you're doing the right thing?" he deadpans.

"Okay, I get it." I raise my hands in surrender. "I'd been certain that there was nothing Ryan could say or do that would change my mind, but then he goes for a marriage proposal. And that clearly changes everything," I scoff. "Because I'm not going to stand in the way of a dad trying to be there for his child, or tear apart a happy family."

"You know, there is more than one player in this equation for it be considered a happy family," Aiden challenges. And despite him being the one close friend I have who has actually settled down and is now a very fresh and proud father, I consider dismissing his claim.

"He asked me to stay away. To give him a fair chance at fixing things with Claire," I say.

"Bullshit," Derek, the eternal bachelor—or maybe not any-more—chimes in. "He had his chance long before Claire even knew you existed, and he blew it. He doesn't excite her. He doesn't love her the way you do. Believe me, we've been working together for quite some time now. I'd never seen her so content as she was with you."

"Derek, you talking feelings? I'm impressed," I try to joke, but I'm also kind of touched by what he's just said. Is that true?

"And you know what else I can tell you?" He seems to be on a roll. "There's nothing Ryan can do that will make her love him half as much as she loves you."

"Well, let me just remind you that he's the biological father of her baby."

"That has nothing to do with love," Derek counters.

"Derek, I'm not sure who the new girl in your life is, but I like her already," Aiden quips.

They're laughing, thinking there's still a chance to turn things around, but Claire's wish to have her child grow up with their biological father, her sad confession that some days she feels like her life is falling apart, I'm sure the constant struggle of trying to find room for me, with Ryan clearly pressing her to choose—all of that isn't making it any easier.

"I've only been making things more complicated for her," I say. "She needed to get Ryan back in her life, we both know it's the right thing to do. I don't want her child to grow up knowing their real dad wanted nothing to do with them. I know what it's like. This kid has a chance to have it better, and who am I to take that chance away? I'm happy for Claire and Ryan." Well, at least I should be. And maybe with time, one day, I will be.

"Right." Derek smacks me on the back and hands me another beer. "So happy."

"I just think it's fucking great," I say. "He's all about getting them back together, no matter what problems they have or what the stakes are or what each of them has to lose."

"Finally, you're making some sense," Aiden takes a swig of his beer, studying me in the process. "Keep going."

"I want to be in *his* shoes," I say. "I want to be able to love her, uncomplicated. *I* want to be the one asking Claire to marry me." I have no idea how to live my life without her. Without breathing her in, hearing her laugh, seeing her smile again. I guess I'll have to learn.

"You don't want to be in his shoes," Derek cuts in. "She might be pregnant with his kid, but there's no spark between them, no passion. Listen to me: she doesn't love him, she loves you."

And I love her. And it's stronger than anything I've ever felt before. Stronger than how I thought love should feel. "Yet I am here and Claire is there, with him." I let my head fall between my hands. Since leaving that letter on her nightstand, I haven't been able to stop obsessing about the *what if*. I can't sleep. I can't think. The highlights of my day, every day, are the updates from Charlene on Claire's whereabouts. I'm hoping she's doing better, now that I'm not part of the equation.

"That's on you," Aiden says. "Because you haven't found the courage to go out there and tell her how you really feel."

"Courage?" I ask, narrowing my eyes at him. "You have no idea how much courage it takes to give up what you truly want and do the right thing," I argue, maybe a bit more forcefully than called for.

But from the looks on their faces, it doesn't appear they agree.

35

A proposal

Claire

Ryan and I are standing by the entrance of a restaurant on M street. Georgetown at night is beautiful, romantic even—if you ask other people, I suppose. Couples are walking hand in hand, looking at each other with heart eyes. Unfortunately, all I see when I look at them are shadows of Christian and me. Memories of an unrealistic fantasy. My mind is so focused on the past and the what if that it doesn't even register the rest of our surroundings. Or the name of the restaurant. Or the fact that Ryan is beside me. Because when we walk inside and he pulls out a chair for me, hearing his voice giving our drinks order almost takes me by surprise. Or maybe it just pulls me back to reality. There's a pressed white tablecloth and a flickering candle between us.

"Christian wasn't serious after all," Ryan says, peeling off that last security blanket that's been covering my heart. This is the third time he's mentioned Christian in a single evening. We're in a fancy place with, I bet, fancy food, but after Ryan's opening statement, I don't think I'll be able to bring myself to eat.

Ryan, on the other hand, looks relieved to have ditched the competition. Like he's been waiting for this moment to swoop in. He was a bit too quick to make plans for the two of us to "*start over*" after I told him about Christian.

Starting over with Ryan is the last thing I want to do. And the last person I want to do it with. I could barely get myself out of bed this morning. Mornings before Christian or with Christian after Ryan's comeback weren't easy. But the days got better with every text, or phone call, or a reassuring word from Christian. Now nothing is easy anymore. Every single thing I do, every thought, reminds me of Christian. Of what I thought could be us. Only I never actually said that to him, any of it. I just shared some of my other deepest secrets and drove him away. I had to make sure he knew what he was getting himself into. Raising a kid who's not his own is one thing; dealing with my mental state, especially given what had happened with his own mom, his own childhood, is another.

But it's not just me anymore. There's Baby on the way. And I have to push through for the sake of us both. So tonight I dried my tears away, washed my hair, put on the only dress that could contain my very pregnant self, and walked out into Ryan's car. To a somewhat romantic dinner, sipping ice-cold water, trying to drown the constant urge to break down and cry or bury my head in a pillow and stay in bed until HR calls from work to ask me to clear my stuff away and—if I'm lucky—discuss a severance package. The only reason it hasn't happened yet is this little baby inside of me—or maybe not so little, as he or she is kicking my ribs in a growing frequency, a reminder that I can't let things break down. Not anymore. I have responsibility.

"We should get married," Ryan says. It's so out of the blue that I choke on my water.

"What?" I cough. Ryan pushes his water glass in my direction—more water for my drowning self, but I'm buying time.

"We should get married," he says again, louder and slower this time, like he would to someone with severe comprehension issues. Me right now. "We'll move in together, raise the baby together. Like a real family should." There's nothing romantic about it. A passerby might think we're discussing a merger deal. One that's not truly beneficial to either side, but maybe meant to minimize negative consequences, possibly avoid bankruptcy. A dream proposal.

"Ryan, we both know this would be a mistake," I tell him.

"A mistake?" Ryan gives me a surprised look. Like he's just offered me an out from a life sentence and I refused to take the deal. And I'm sure he sees it this way. And I do too, only in reverse.

"This is a big deal, marriage shouldn't be taken lightly."

"We both know it's the right thing to do," he says. "To raise this baby together. I've been thinking about it a lot. Believe me, this is not *taking it lightly*." He reaches for his pocket and produces a little black velvet box. A ring?

It's one of those almost cinematic moments, where a jumble of childhood memories and fragmented snapshots of life come rushing through my mind. Not in a confusing way, more like in a you-know-the-right-thing-to-do kind of way. And by the *right thing* I don't mean noble or admirable, I mean selfish and simple and guilt-worthy. The right thing for *me*. It's like a blur filter was covering my eyes, but now I can suddenly see clearly.

"I really appreciate what you're doing here Ryan," I tell him. "I really do. But I can't marry you."

"I thought raising this baby together was what you wanted," he says slowly, as if trying to dig out past moments, pieces of conversation from his memory.

And he's not completely wrong. I do want him in my baby's life. And that means my life too. But committing to marrying someone I can't possibly give my heart to feels wrong. Wrong for me. Wrong for Ryan. Not that the one person who stole my heart wanted to keep it, but like Dr. Levine said— thinking about what I want for myself might carry too much guilt for me to dare choose it. Starting with crossing-out what I don't want, as a first step, might be easier.

"There's nothing I want more for this baby than to grow up with his or her biological father around," I say, taking Ryan's hand in mine to stop him from opening that box. "But do we really have to be together for that to hold true?"

"The way I see it, Claire," he says, pulling his hand away from me, "you have two options. It's a package deal. We're either all in, or I'm all out."

"I'm sorry," I say. "You said it yourself, we don't love each other in that way, which is why we broke up in the first place." I'm not sure he means to, but he nods in agreement. "You deserve to be with someone you're crazy in love with." And I do too, only that person doesn't seem to want to be with me anymore. Not after I made sure he knew what that entails.

"Love is overrated," Ryan says.

"No, Ryan. It really isn't."

"You've been reading way too much of those happily-ever-after romance books that Christian gave you."

"Maybe I have. Maybe you should too. I mean, look at us—this should be one of the happiest moments in a couple's life, and we both look miserable."

I think back to Christian. That night after the hospital. How he stayed by my side, wouldn't move an inch. Every time I opened my eyes he was right there, wide awake, studying me with a gaze full of emotion. There was love in there, or at least that's what I was thinking at the time. Rethinking those moments now, maybe he was already contemplating when the best time to disappear would be. Because there was something else in there too. Sadness. An emotion I hadn't seen before, not on him, but I was so tired and drowsy that I pushed it away. Had I known, would I have done anything different?

36

A roadmap

Claire

I don't regret saying no, even as Ryan packs the last of his stuff from the apartment next door and walks out in a rush, this time for good—or bad—because with that goes our baby's last chance at knowing their biological father. Well done, I tell myself. I've inflicted a future on a child that hasn't been born yet. A future quite similar to my past. To my childhood.

"Can you come over?" I text Kate, adding an ice cream emoji.

"You okay?" she writes back a few minutes later. She's never been that person to live with a phone in her hand, but since I officially crossed over to the ninth month of my pregnancy, she's been on her toes. My mom has too, actually making sure to charge her phone and stay in areas with reasonable reception. Texting me every day to see how I'm doing and ask for a baby bump pic, front and side, certain she can predict my delivery day based on the shape of my belly.

It doesn't take too long for Kate to show up on my doorstep equipped with two ice cream tubs—chocolate, my favorite, and peanut butter, hers, a family pack of Cheetos—recalling my first trimester predilection that hasn't truly gone away—and a box with freshly baked brownies that she somehow managed to make before rushing over to me.

"You've been avoiding me for like three weeks!" she admonishes.

"Guilty," I admit. I mean, we still text regularly but I may have canceled our last few weekly lunches with some lame busy-at-work excuses. She's Jake's kindergarten teacher after all, I didn't want her to have beef with Christian. Plus, I was trying to trick myself into thinking that he might still change his mind.

"Ryan asked me to marry him." I give her a partial rundown of the latest events, omitting some key moments.

"God no! Please tell me you said no!" That's Kate, ladies and gentlemen. A strong woman who has all her priorities straight. Plus, she knows me well.

I nod in agreement and she squeals and hugs me with way too much excitement. Someone watching us from the side might have thought I'd said *yes* to a marriage proposal.

I can't help the tears that come streaming out, like a full-blown attack. "This baby is going to grow up never knowing his or her dad," I mumble. Kate pulls me into a hug and I sniffle into her hair. "Just like *we* did. And it's all my fault."

Kate lets go of her hold and pulls away to get a good look at me. "Was that so bad?" she asks honestly.

That sweet and comforting smell of milk and warm brownies and cold ice cream hits my memory, and for a moment, I'm a kid again, huddled closely with Mom and Kate on our old living room couch. We're all watching a movie, but not really paying attention to what goes on the screen as we're too deep in a light, funny conversation about whatever it was that time; work, school, life. My mom knew how to put a positive spin into any topic, and Kate is certainly living up to this legacy. Sure, I had my sad moments. But there were happy moments in there too. So many more happy moments.

"No, it wasn't," I say. Although, in hindsight, I may have spent way too much time dreaming of what we could have had or what we didn't have, rather than what we did.

"Exactly. And you have me, and Mom and Christian. And that's plenty."

"You and Mom are plenty," I agree.

"Uh oh, what did you do?" My sister gives me a suspicious look.

"I didn't do anything," I say. "Or maybe I just said too much and chased him away."

"That doesn't sound like Christian," she objects, and the stream of tears returns. And this time I can't make it stop.

It doesn't take more than a few days for the news to spread all the way to South America and for my mom to take the first flight home. "I was planning on coming back this week anyway," she explains. "Plus, I wanted to make sure I'm here for the baby!" Based on her prediction during our last conversation, there may still be a full month until that moment, but she doesn't want to throw Kate under the bus and admit she already knows every-thing. Well, regardless, my mom always knows everything by default. Always has. It's her special mom sense.

As a special treat for her first night back, we all go for din-ner and ice cream, and it's like she never actually left. Whether she's thousands of miles away or physically near, she's always there by my side. And after two scoops of ice cream in a choco-late-and-coconut-coated cone, the three of us are fully up to date on most of the important parts of our lives. The said and also the unsaid pieces. Words are not always needed with these two.

"Parental love should be unconditional," my mom says. "Ryan may have contributed half of the gene pool, but that doesn't automatically make someone a dad. Being a parent is not just about having a kid, one needs to own it." Then she studies me for a second before adding, "If you want my tried and tested approach to a happy baby," she plays with my hair, "the first step is making sure *you* are happy."

"I don't know," I sigh. "It feels selfish to think about that right now."

"There's nothing selfish about wanting to be happy," Mom says. "And it's very normal to wake up feeling uncertain, or that you're missing direction when you think that things are out of your control." And all of a sudden, it all makes sense. The struggle with making a choice I didn't want to make. The fear of the unknown.

"How about that map that Dr. Levine was recommending?" she asks. Uh, yes, the map I was trying to avoid. I completely forgot I'd told her about that too. "Time to pave your own path. Take things into your own hands." Trust my mom to focus on the solution. "Sounds like a hell of a therapist. My kind of guy," she laughs.

Apparently, there are art supply stores in DC that are open pretty late into the evening. A short hour later, we're back in my apartment with a pack of poster boards—my mom thought it would be fun if she and Kate made their own roadmaps too, and certainly reduces the pressure—some colorful markers, stickers, glitter glue... My living room now looks like Kate's kindergarten class.

"So what're the rules for our roadmaps again?" Kate asks like we're in the midst of an arts and crafts workshop. She's laying on the floor between Mom and me, a pink marker in hand. She's spent the first hour drawing random color bursts. It looks more like a version of a Candy Land board game than a roadmap. Mom's, on the other hand, looks like a map to an exciting treasure hunt.

"Dr. Levine said to focus on where we are now and the way to where we want to be." I feel like our tour guide. "Road signs and landmarks are the difficulties or obstacles along the way," I explain.

"Or fun things along the way," Kate counters, pointing at a rainbow on her board.

"Sure, if you want to look at life that way."

"Need to enjoy the journey, no?" Mom winks at us, and I realize I may have forgotten that sometimes the journey is the entire point. As much as I don't like surprises, the unexpected doesn't have to be all bad.

"What are these?" Kate asks, glancing at my artwork. "Winding roads?"

"Uh, yeah."

"And these?" She points to my many road signs.

Well, I haven't had a chance to add color yet. "Stop signs, no entry, bumpy road, detour, speed limits, sharp curve warning, no outlet..." I name some of the signs on my roadmap. "It's a simple sketch."

"You've added a surprising amount of detail to your sketch," Kate admires, seeing as I drew the entire road system leading to Christian's address from mine. "I don't think that when Dr. Levine told you to draw a map, he meant a literal map. Plus, I don't think maps typically have street signs."

"Girls, no criticizing the artwork," my mom reprimands, but we ignore it. The critiques are the fun part when it comes to Kate and me.

"Well, they should include street signs," I argue, adding another stop sign. I've memorized every single junction, every crosswalk between my apartment building and Christian's.

"Truck escape ramp?" Kate reads the label of one of my signs. "Is that a thing?"

"It is, this was my escape route, from a life with Ryan."

"Are you comparing yourself to a truck, sis?" Kate's laugh fills the air, making my mom grin.

"In my current state, yes." My lips curve up as if on their own. It feels good to smile again, like settling close to a fireplace after coming in from the cold. "Do we have another board?" I ask, because now that I'm getting my smile muscles up and working, I have the urge to start over.

Luckily we do have another board. And this time I put away the black marker and use other colors. I draw my best depiction of forests and scenic paths. My signs now include "Artist viewpoint" and some restaurant signs and a lake. And Christian is there too, but there are no roads or buildings, just stick figures of him and... me.

"I like this new unpaved map," Kate says.

"Well, that's not really a map, it's a parallel universe," I explain. "One where I wouldn't have been so confused, or scared about the unknown. One where I would have been open to letting life surprise me, expecting good things to come my way. And would have said yes to Christian when he had asked me to move in with him." A world where I'm not scared to admit how much I want him in my life. And how much I love him.

"It's not too late," my mom says. As if her mind-reading skills extend to other people, and not just her two offspring.

I give a wistful laugh. "Well, it's an imaginary parallel universe. And I bet Christian has already moved on, enjoying his uncomplicated life without me."

"I wouldn't be so sure," Kate pitches in. "Jake's drawings still feature you in them, holding his uncle's hand." She pulls out a piece of paper from her back pocket and unfolds it.

"You've stolen your student's artwork?" I clutch my chest, feigning shock.

"Borrowed it, with his permission."

"You don't know that it's me," I say, studying the strokes of crayons. "I mean, his characters are pretty detailed, but this could be any other woman."

"With the same hair color and that stupid plaid shirt you like to wear?"

"Sure."

"And a baby bump?"

Hmmm.

37

Knocked up and single

Christian

I can't take it anymore. I miss Claire like crazy. I know the point was to step aside, back up, give Ryan a fair chance for the sake of their baby and Claire's much-dreamed-of traditional family. But when I call Charlene, like I've been doing every single morning since my stupid damn letter, to ask how Claire is doing, she gives out a worried sigh.

"Not amazing," she tells me.

The typical response so far has been on a more positive note—she'd say things like "She's getting there," or "She's strong," or "She has lots of work to keep her busy," and "Don't worry, we're all here for her." Although it's done very little to ease my mind. Shouldn't doing what's right feel at least a bit easier? Charlene is the type of person who takes care of everything and everyone. She called me up on the morning of Claire's baby shower, asking me to be there for her. And God knows there's nothing I wanted more... But I couldn't do it. I couldn't face walking out on Claire again. And I couldn't stay in her life either, complicating her choices. I made a promise to Ryan. It was the right thing to do, even if everything about it still feels so wrong.

But today is different. "Claire's not doing so well," Charlene says. "I'm worried about her."

And this... this is my breaking point. The moment I stop playing fair. I have to see her. I *need* to see her. To make it okay. Even if she's marrying Ryan, even if all I can offer is to be her friend. I'd rather be Claire's friend than not have her in my life at all. Be her someone to run with, like I fucking promised. Well, a platonic form of it, I guess.

But I can't just show up in the office or at her doorstep—those places are filled with so many memories, and I'm definitely not looking to make things harder. Or come face to face with her husband-to-be, not at the moment when it's all still so raw.

"She's going out with her sister and mom tonight," Charlene whispers. "Her sister called earlier and asked me for a restaurant recommendation." I can hear the smile forming on Charlene's face as she speaks. "I'll text you the address."

Claire

"We're taking you out tonight," is my sister's bright and shiny idea.

"I'm not really in the mood for going out."

"Well, based on your roadmap, you need some scenic views and nice restaurants."

"You mean my imaginary parallel universe drawing?"

"Yes, that one," Kate winks at me. "It's a nice restaurant, and not one of these places you went with Christian or *Ryan*." I don't miss the usual disdain in the way she says Ryan's name but not Christian's. "I got a recommendation from Charlene, you know she's never wrong." Yes, somehow during my pregnancy, Charlene and Kate have formed a secret bond, plotting to take care of me.

"Fine," I grunt.

"It's a date," my sister says. It sounds like a regular figure of speech, but coming from Kate, the genius app designer, it raises my suspicion. Especially since she doesn't usually use this atrocious word unless she means it.

"This sounds awfully like a set-up."

"Ah," is her response, and that's telling.

"You said you and Mom were taking me out," I protest.

"We are, a triple date. Mom has graciously agreed to join the prestige group of beta testers for my app," she chirps.

"But I've retired."

"Well, you're being re-enlisted."

"Kate, I'm about to have a baby in like two weeks." I look down at my giant baby bump to make my point.

"That's great, because your date loves kids!"

"How do you know that?"

"Uh, I just do."

"He may like kids, but that doesn't mean he wants to date a nine-month pregnant woman."

"Hey," she warns, "you look amazing, he'd be lucky to date you!"

"He's going to run away as fast as he can when he sees how pregnant I am."

"No. He. Isn't." Kate's sing-a-song tone is alarmingly confident.

"Don't tell me," I sigh. "We're going to test another app feature? Knocked Up and Single?"

"Oh I LOVE that!" My sister jumps up excitedly, grabbing her phone to take notes. "Claire-bear, you're brilliant."

"No, sis, it sounds awful. No one will actually select that feature willingly. It sounds like a kink—"

"No, I'm thinking it could be a checkbox, they'll need to choose if they want to eliminate that option."

"They'll probably miss the checkbox," I say.

"Well, then, people should pay attention." My sister is relentless.

"So, I'm guessing that this guy knows I'm pregnant?" I dare ask.

Kate nods enthusiastically. "C'mon, it'll be fun! It's a triple date, Mom and I will have dates too."

Oh boy.

Christian

I step inside the restaurant. It's like someone blurred the background and everything else in between, because all I see is her. The woman who took my breath away. Her eyes spot me and her face falls. I see the hurt. The pain. And I hate knowing that I'm the one causing it. There's nothing in this world I wouldn't do to take that pain away, to hold her in my arms again and tell her how I really feel. How fucking crazy I am about her. How much I love her. How I can't even breathe without her. But I gave up that right when I walked out and cleared the way for Ryan. She's sitting there between her sister and another woman who looks just like an older version of her. Knowing that her mom is back warms my heart a bit. I know how much Claire missed her.

There are two guys sitting across from them, and too many unknowns in my equation. Who are these guys? Did Kate know I'd show up here, or was Charlene acting on her own? Where is Ryan? And what was the outcome of his marriage proposal? I assume positive, for Ryan, or else Charlene would have said something. But maybe she doesn't know? Claire rarely shares personal information with anyone.

I walk over to their table, my legs feeling heavier with each step, my chest squeezing harder. The world around me disappears. The only thing my mind seems to know is Claire, and that special smile she used to have just for me that's no longer playing on her lips. Will I ever see her smile like that again?

"Hey," I manage to say when I finally make it, holding my breath for her reaction.

There's silence. Not just around their table. It feels like the entire restaurant has gone quiet. Heck, the entire world has stopped, awaiting her response.

"Mom, this is Christian," Kate says, trying to break the painful silence. "Christian is—"

"Just a guy I used to run with," Claire fires off, all at once diminishing every moment we've ever shared. Her voice is broken and splits at the ends. And I can't blame her. She clears her throat and gets up. "Excuse me," she says, not giving me a second look before disappearing into the depths of the restaurant. This is when I start running, this time—to her.

"Claire, wait," I beg. She stops. Her face solemn and distant. "I'm sorry," I say, getting ahold of her hand, trying to ignore the buzz created by our skin-to-skin contact. God, I missed her so much. Her eyes flicker to me with hesitation. "I had to do the right thing. For you. For Baby," I start.

"You don't need to apologize. I understand," she says, her voice catches. "You're better off without me."

"That's not true," I protest. "God, Claire, you have no idea how much... I love you." I'm not sure what good it'll do to make it known now, when it's already too late, but I can't help it. "I know you've already made your decision." I do wonder why her future husband is not here with her, but I hope she'll stop and correct me if that's not the case. She doesn't, unfortunately, so I go on. "I'm not here to change your mind, but I was hoping that maybe you and I could at least be... friends. I need to know that you're okay."

"*Okay?*" she asks. Her incredulous tone is unmistakable. "How can I possibly be okay?! You promised. You fucking promised. Promised that everything would be alright. You walked away."

My heart falls at that. I did walk away. I was trying to do the right thing, despite the pain, but ended up hurting her too. "I was worried that I was confusing you, weighing on your decision, when you knew you needed to choose Ryan. I was trying to make things easier for you."

She gives out a sad laugh that twists my gut. "I wasn't *confused* about whether or not to choose Ryan. I was terrified. Fucking terrified of losing... you."

Me? Had I been reading this entire situation wrong? My brain goes on rewind mode, reanalyzing every situation, every conversation and decision made in the past few months. Had I known, would I have let Ryan swoop in and ask her to marry him? Would I have fought to make her mine, first? But my fucked-up brain still thinks that a chance at a traditional family should come first.

"I'm so sorry, Claire. I never meant to hurt you..." is all that comes out. Because I know it's too late.

There's a small tear in the corner of her eye, but she wipes it away quickly. "Well, you did. Hurt me. More than I care to admit. And I don't ever want to relive that moment. I don't want to ever have to feel that pain again the next time you decide to walk away."

"I will never—" I try to say, shaking my head, but she shuts me down. Her eyes are red now, filled with unshed tears. Her words cut me like knives. "Was that what you meant *by someone to run with?* Someone who shows you how great life could be together, and then runs away? Thank you very much, I'd much rather run alone. I never liked running anyway." She shakes her head on a sob. "Plus—you really don't need me running along with you, it will just slow you down."

"No, that's not true," I cry out, trying to hold on to her hand, but she pushes me away.

"Please respect my decision," she asks. "And just leave me alone."

Then she snaps that old, feisty expression I remember so vividly from our first days at Amarinex Bio, the one I'd worked so hard to transform, and goes back to her table.

"I don't want to talk about it," I hear her say to her party before I walk away.

38

House visit

Claire

Surprises sometimes come from the least expected places. I guess that's why they're called surprises. And that's why I don't like them. Was I surprised that Charlene and Kate were the masterminds behind a hopeful second-chance meet-cute with Christian? Not really. My sister is not known for giving up easily, and Charlene could be easily crowned the fixer-of-all-things queen. But when Derek stops by my cubicle, informing me that he's going for a much overdue house visit to Ellie and Aiden, now the proud parents of a two-month-old baby girl, and that he's dragging me along? Well, I have to admit, this does take me by surprise. Not the fact that they had the baby two months ago—obviously, Ellie was pregnant, further along than I was—which also made her a very good source of recommendations for everything from prenatal classes to baby stores and pediatrician selections—so that part was expected. I'm also not surprised that Derek is planning to go for a visit—after all, he's one of Aiden's best friends. But I'm a bit confused as to why he wants to drag *me* along.

"Is Christian going to be there?" I ask, trying not to sound suspicious at all. It doesn't work.

Derek chuckles. "No, I don't do that sneaky shit," he says on an honest note. "Ellie asked me to bring you along. She said she has the urge to talk science with *someone who gets it*, as if Aiden and I don't? And that she has a few questions for you."

"Do you think she's also planning to *talk science* with Christian at the same time?"

"Claire," he promises, "there will be no Christian involved."

And so the most surprising part of this all is that I nod my head and tell Derek that "Sure, I'll come." Then make him stop at a toy store on our way there, to get Ellie and Aiden's baby a giant teddy bear.

Ellie greets us with happy squeals and hugs, and infectious positive energy, and introduces baby Romi to us, who mostly cries and makes unhappy gassy expressions. Something I'm sure I'll get to experience firsthand soon. Aiden, she says, "Is at the lab, catching up on both my, thankfully, and his experiments, but should be back soon."

She asks if we want to hold the baby, which almost gives me a heart attack—both because she's so tiny I might break her, and because I'm still waiting for that magical moment where I'll be able to love babies who are not mine. I mean, she is very cute, in her mom's arms. But Derek seems excited by the prospect, and so for the next twenty minutes he walks around the living room with a baby cuddled in his arms, a big smile on his face, rocking her to sleep, and I follow Ellie into the kitchen, where she insists on baking cookies for us and making homemade iced tea.

"So what's it like to be a mom?" I ask, interested to know where I'll be in a couple weeks.

"Amazing, but also scary." Ellie gives a good-natured laugh. "I'm scared I'll make all the wrong choices and mess everything up. But Romi here has been pretty patient with me. Just need to figure out how to get her to sleep—I mean, other than in her dad's or now Derek's arms." She looks tired, but even happier than the last time we spoke.

"Do you miss work?" I ask, assuming she's been on maternity leave since the baby was born.

"I love my work, don't get me wrong," she says with her funny accent and a big smile, "and I'm a known workaholic, but babies grow so fast, and Romi keeps me busy and constantly on my toes. I decided it's okay to take a break for a bit and enjoy the time with her. There'll be plenty of time to work later. I hope you're planning to take some time off too, when the baby comes." She pushes one of the iced tea glasses in my direction and takes a sip from the other one.

"Well, so far your recommendations were spot on, so I think I'll take this one as well."

"Well, good. And how's work treating you?"

"It's fine. Some disappointments there. Things don't always turn out the way you hope them to. It's part of science, isn't it?"

"It is, and it's okay, as long as you don't give up."

"It's hard to stay on target when the target keeps slipping away. And I have a new manager." I think about Harriett. "She's a science killing witch-bitch," I add and Ellie bursts out in laughter.

"I'm sorry, it's not funny," she says snorting, "but I *love* the nickname. I bet she deserves it."

"She really does. She's making my life there miserable, I'm not sure how long I can keep doing it."

"A shitty manager can really make a good place suck." The passion and fast rhythm of her words bring a small smile to my face, and I try to suppress it. Ellie goes on. "Have you tried to speak with HR about her?"

"Not really," I say, not having the energy to make a big deal out of it. And somehow thinking about the office makes me think of Christian again. I miss him so badly.

"Well, you know what they say," Ellie adds, sensing the shift in my mood, I bet, "the people who are your worst nightmare at work either quit or get promoted." And yes, I guess both scenarios would distance Harriett from me, so I'd take either. "But if you feel like going back to the lab, there's a position in my group that's going to open up in a few months, epigenetics research in Type 1 diabetes, and I would love to tell you everything about it." She pauses to let me respond.

"I would love that," I say, taking another sip of her home-made iced tea, trying to wash away images of Christian from my mind.

"But first, let me digress." Ellie gives out a sneaky, deliberate smile as her eyes study my face, confirming my suspicion that there's some sort of a pre-made plan here. "I need to ask you something off topic. Or actually on topic. *The* topic."

"I knew Derek was up to something." I smile despite the possible set-up.

"No, he was just following orders. That guy has no manipulative bone in his body. It's all on me," Ellie smirks.

"Uh oh," I sigh. "What do you want to know?"

"Would it be too forward of me to ask why you and Christian are not standing here together right now, arms around each other, living your happy life, together?"

"Probably," I say, chuckling. But it sounds sad. "There's no sophisticated explanation." My mind trails off. "He's better off without me."

"We're talking about Christian, yes?" Ellie asks, surprised. "You know, the guy who's *crazy* about you? Definitely not doing well without you. Insanely in love with you."

"No he isn't. He's made his choice. He loves me as a friend, he doesn't *love* love me."

"I'm pretty sure he *love* loves you," Ellie corrects me. "And I'm pretty sure the man can't live without you."

"Well, he has a very weird way of showing it, walking out of my life, leaving me with this vague explanation letter that he had to get away, what does that even mean? And then he comes back asking for us to stay friends?" I'm not sure why I'm telling Ellie all that. Something about the way her head tilts as she listens and her eyebrows raise, like she feels the urge to correct my facts or my interpretation, or maybe my words shed new light on what she thought she knew.

"He broke up with you in a letter?" she asks, scrunching her nose. Her accent becomes even more pronounced with every word.

"I mean, we weren't really together, we were actually supposed to be just friends." And failed at that miserably. "I was trying to give Christian an out from my complicated life," I explain. "And because Ryan, my ex, the baby's dad," I smooth a hand over my bump, "was trying to get back into my life. Not in a romantic way, but he didn't want to feel like a third wheel." I pause to think about it for a moment. "Maybe I got that part wrong, because Ryan did ask me to marry him in the end..." I shake my head, "now Christian just wants us to stay friends. I can't do that. There are too many feelings involved. I don't think my heart can take another hit the next time he decides to up and leave. I'm much better off alone." I shake it off and take another sip. "Anyway—"

"Wait, what do you mean alone?" Ellie gives me a confused look.

"Alone, like I'm done with men. I don't need a guy in my life to make me happy. I can take care of myself and this baby." I feel Baby kick, like he or she has a thing or two to say as well. "And I'm definitely not going to marry my ex to make him own his responsibilities, especially not when I'm in love with someone else."

A huge grin appears on Ellie's face at that. "Does Christian know all this?"

"No, but I doubt he'd care."

"Oh believe me, he will." Ellie wiggles her eyebrows and I take the opportunity to change the topic.

"Now tell me about this job opportunity."

When Derek and I get back to the office, I'm already contemplating whether I should mention Ellie's idea to Big Boss Joe. Sure, talking about potentially leaving your job before securing another position is never a good idea, especially with the big Boss. But this wouldn't be the first time I've gotten career advice from Big Boss Joe. He's not just a boss, he's a mentor, and so far he's been able to give me good advice, putting my best interests first, even if it meant he'd be letting me go. This time though, he beats me to it, as Charlene stops by my desk with a "Have a minute to chat with Joe?"

I walk over to the C-suite, a bit wary that maybe Harriett has been doing a little too much work behind the scenes this time.

"Hey," I say, walking in and plopping into a chair. Maybe plopping when I'm nine months pregnant is not an accurate depiction, but hearing Ellie's idea of a brighter professional future makes me feel lighter. "Did you ask for me?"

Big Boss Joe's expression brings me back to earth pretty quickly, and also pushes my potential discussion topic to a later, better, timing. "Yes," he says. And I brace myself. "I'm afraid some of the repeat of the animal study results came back today. You had a good hunch there, it appears that our drug is causing some issues in the animals. We'll be getting the pathology report soon, but for now we're going to have to put all of our clinical plans on hold. This includes the Type 1 diabetes project. I wanted you to hear it from me first, before Harriett announces it at the meeting tomorrow."

"Oh..." I say, not sure I can deal with any more bad news. "Put a hold on the entire project? We have other drugs in our pipeline..."

"Just for now," he sighs and I already know Harriett—and her connection with the board—had something to do with this unwelcome decision. "But please know, you did the right thing. It's better we know now and take the required precautions before we take this drug into patients," he assures me. And yes, I definitely agree, but it still sucks. And the first thought that comes to mind is Christian. And how he's going to feel about it.

Then I text Ryan. He may not be the best ex, but he *is* a lawyer. This can't be Harriett's first rodeo, and there's no way I'm letting this project go down without her going down with it.

And since this day is full of the unexpected, I guess I shouldn't be surprised to find Aiden on my doorstep when I get home. I open the door for us and he walks in. He has his little daughter bundled in one of those cuddly fabric wrap carriers, a bright pink one, sleeping peacefully. It's amazing what parenthood can do even to the most serious, grumpy, almost-intimidating of people. He looks so mellow and blissfully happy with his new baby girl in his arms.

"Congratulations!" I say. "She's adorable! Sorry I missed you earlier when I visited Ellie."

"Thank you," Aiden nods. He has this cute proud-father tone, but his face means business. "There's something important we need to talk about."

"Did Christian send you?" I jump right in.

"God no, he'd kill me if he knew. Ellie sent me," he explains. And I think about the resume I emailed her a few hours ago, the one that has my address in the header. "Apparently romance stories with misunderstanding-related conflicts annoy Ellie deeply. She seems to think this translates into real life too. So I'm here to tell you the truth."

"I appreciate the attempt," I say. "And I know you're just trying to help, but let me just remind you—Christian left." I sigh—I can't believe how difficult it still is for me to talk about him. My throat feels like it's going to implode any moment, my lungs can barely recall how breathing actually works. "He promised. Promised he'd be there for us." I smooth a hand down my giant baby bump. "Yet he left. Just like that, disappeared. As if this whole thing—" My arms spread out to try to explain how big this was. Bigger than me, bigger than anything I could have possibly plan or allow myself to feel. "As if this whole thing was one-sided. A figment of my imagination. Well, maybe it was." I let out a shaky breath, trying hard not to break in front of Christian's best friend.

"He didn't leave," Aiden says, his voice even, as if expecting what I just said.

"Well, he's not here, is he?"

"That's because he stepped aside."

"I don't see the difference—the end result is the same."

"He stepped aside to give you a chance at a happy ever after or some shit with your ex."

"He knew I didn't love Ryan, why on earth?"

"Because Ryan asked him. Said he was going to propose, but that he'd never be able to deal with the competition. He asked Christian to take a step back and give him a fair chance. And Christian—although I think this idea was total bull-shit—thought he was doing the right thing for you and the baby. Giving this baby a chance to grow up with their real dad. A traditional family. Something he thought you wanted more than anything. Even if he had to pay the price. But, Claire, I must say, he's out there missing you like crazy, and he has no idea that you're not marrying Ryan."

"I appreciate the effort," I say. "Ryan may be the biological dad, but to me he's no more than the guy who's responsible for half of the genetic material of my baby. That's not a dad. And Christian—as I've already come to conclude—is better off without me. He's made the right decision, and I've already made mine."

Baby Romi stirs in his arms and starts to cry. "Looks like," Aiden says on a half-smile, planting a gentle kiss on top of her head, "both Romi and I disagree."

39

Dig deep

Christian

I'm not sure how to go on from here. It feels like everything is falling apart. Claire won't talk to me. I tried face to face, which obviously went haywire. I tried calling and texting her, which she's so far ignored. I've been walking by her street every night since that stupid letter, looking up to her bedroom window, contemplating whether to go up, ring her doorbell and try again. It's a constant battle between the need to see her, talk to her, hold her, and the need to let her live the life she's chosen for herself, with Ryan. Respect her wishes, like she asked. And as if that wasn't enough, the work at Amarinex is now being put on hold. Although, this time for a good reason—safety should always come first, even if it means that it's going to take longer to keep my promise to Jake. To find a cure. We're going to have to start all over again, because I'm never giving up. Wish I could say that about Claire and me though.

My phone buzzes in my pocket. I get a glimpse of hope, but only for a second, until I see the message is from Aiden.

"Meet me up for beers tonight?" he writes.

"Not today man, I'm tired," I text back, not feeling like talking to anyone, and definitely not interested in drowning my current shitty self in alcohol. Something that—from the few recent nights I've tried—only seems to bring about more sorrow.

"Have some new data," he insists.

"Sorry, not into science tonight either." Atypical for me, but when you realize you'll never be able to be with the person you love, everything else seems to get pushed into some distant mental parking lot.

"Let me rephrase. New *intel*. Compliments of my wife. And if you say you're not interested I'm going to come over and drag your sorry ass out."

But I call him instead. I need to know now. "Spill it," I say once he picks up.

"Claire is not marrying Ryan," he says with a happy tone. I swear, since he became a dad... "She's in love with someone else."

"What the fu— Who?" I have no patience for a guessing game.

"What do you mean *who*?" he snickers. "And I thought you were smart. Just do yourself a favor and talk to her already."

"Well, news flash, she doesn't want to talk to me."

But there's this shiny glimpse of hope starting to climb up my chest, and those gray clouds covering my sun are starting to clear as I quickly put my shoes back on, not willing to spend another moment without Claire in my life.

"Is it true?" I text Ryan. Fingers flying over the screen. "She said no to you and you didn't even bother to fucking tell me?!"

I wait as the three dots appear. And disappear. Then reappear again.

"Shit. I'm sorry man... She didn't tell you?"

"NO!" I write back, wishing I could punch him through the phone. Until I see his next line.

"I've been wanting to apologize to you both... Don't even know where to begin. She's so fucking in love with you."

Claire

Everything should hurt less when you convince yourself that you don't care anymore. When you give up. Or at least that's what I've been telling myself since I decided to attempt to let go of the possibility of... Christian. But it doesn't make me any less broken or less indescribably sad. It certainly doesn't make this hole in my chest any smaller or the pain any less piercing. Maybe because my self-convincing skills are not that good. Maybe because truly not caring should have lowered the stakes. But that's not what's happening here. The stakes, in fact, have never been so high before. And forget about me, the inept convincer. Even the most adept talented team of persuaders would not be able to talk my heart out of its own carefully dug trench. Or rather—giant sinkhole. Or maybe it's my unborn baby, reminding me that promises were made, and even he or she is not willing to let go. I know this doesn't sound like a coherent scientifically sound explanation, but really at this point—nothing makes sense anymore anyway, so I might as well.

And maybe it's a late pregnancy nesting instinct, or something my mom said the other night, after our encounter at the restaurant. Right after she'd asked if I'd taken up running. *"Christian seems like a nice guy,"* she said. *"Easily the love of your life."* And I looked at her with wonder, because how could she tell based on a two-minute interaction? And plus—wasn't she supposed to be on my side? Or was that what being on my side meant?

Or maybe it's the protocol synopsis for that—now probably canceled-clinical trial—Christian and I worked on. My level of missing Christian has driven me so far as to read his old comments on our shared work documents. There's a question there from me, tagging Christian—"Which of these endpoints has a better chance of success? We can't do everything." And he commented back, tagging me—"Together we can do everything." Surely not an appropriate response in a company shared document, but all of a sudden it feels like a sign. Or a secret message just for me?

Ellie seemed surprised to learn that I didn't choose Ryan. Or maybe just surprised because she didn't *know* that I didn't choose Ryan. Well, Ryan may be the rightful owner of half of my baby's gene pool, but nothing else felt right about it. And that's putting it lightly, because marrying him would have been totally, unbelievably wrong. He may have contributed to the initial conception, but he does not get to take credit for anything from that moment on. It wasn't him who held my hair while I was busy throwing up an entire day's worth of lame food consumption.

Wasn't him who held my hand at all those doctor's appointments, reminding me to breathe, whispering "five things" in my ear. Wasn't him who helped me put together Baby's nursery. And certainly wasn't him who smoothed his hand over my belly, excited for every little kick. Or sang silly songs to this baby. Or kissed me, or held me through the night, or said these words that made me feel so loved, and cherished and cared for.

So yeah, Ryan had one half-drunken night with me that included less-than-mediocre last-resort breakup sex, and a sperm that was found acceptable by one of my eggs. But other than that one single moment, everything else, and I mean EVERY-THING—has been Christian. He was there every step of the way. Through the good and the bad. The fun and the challenging moments. And he never once looked back or turned away or questioned this incredible thing we had. Except for when... Ryan asked him to step away.

My baby knows nothing else, my body knows nothing else. My heart—well, and this is probably why I can't fool myself into thinking I could possibly let him go—my heart knows nothing else. No one else. And as I climb the stairs to Christian's apartment—because it felt like a good idea to do that when I'm nine months pregnant—determined to convince him this is all but a massive mistake, I question my decision—not about Christian, of course, just the part with the stairs. As my climbing-stairs determination starts to break, along with my water.

"You have great timing, Baby." I rub my very pregnant belly, which hardens all at once, currents traveling through my spine—not *those* kind of currents. More like someone is tightening a belt around my waist. A very large and heavy belt. Electrically operated, if such thing exists, making all my muscles twitch and harden. I brace myself, holding tight to the railing, letting this one giant— fuck, is this how contractions feel?—pass. Then I take the last stretch of stairs, barely reaching the top. Breathless, messy, dripping amniotic fluid through my pants—well, really there's not a single graceful or sexy detail in the way I hurl myself into Christian's front door. I ring—more like violently smash—his doorbell, praying he'll be home, because for one—I want to see him so badly. Yes, now. And two—

"I can't go through life without you," I breathe out, possibly very loudly, as the door swings open and Christian appears on the other side, looking like he was just about to go somewhere. "I don't want to *run* without you. Baby doesn't want to come into a world without yo—" Another belt-tightening takes ahold of my entire mid-section as I get to the "you" part. I'm not done with my make-up speech, so I hold my hand up and push through this giant contraction. "I lo—" I exhale, "I love you, Christian." I try to keep my composure but the thunderstorm in my body is taking over my attention.

I think Christian is trying to smile, I think he likes my confession, but it's hard to tell through his concerned expression and the understanding that takes over his handsome features when he realizes that—"Jesus Christ. You're having a baby."

"It appears so," I laugh, because in between these crazy contractions, I almost forget more of them are coming.

"I mean, right now." Christian, admittedly, looks a little shocked. I'm not sure if it's my striking little monologue, or that it's his first time seeing someone about to have a baby on his doorstep, bodily fluids dripping down my thighs and all. But he quickly recovers and regains control. "How far apart?" he asks, settling into the man who sat behind me through all of those prenatal classes, smoothing my hair and encouraging me to breathe.

"Huh?" Thank God he listened to the instructor—Janet was it?—and took mental notes, because right now I can't recall a damn thing. Other than Christian's warm embrace, his undivided attention, his much-needed and welcomed presence around me.

"The contractions. How far apart? And your water broke."

I did notice that part. "Four. I think. Minutes." I feel another one coming, and I think it may be less than four, but I don't want Christian to worry. He might need to drive.

I'm not sure when he came closer or when he wrapped his arms around me. Not sure if he carried me to the car—I hope not, because with all the extra pregnancy weight, I must be heavy. My mind is completely grabbed by what's happening in my body as I try to find the right posture in the passenger seat, watching Christian rushing through traffic while reminding me to breathe, not forgetting to sprinkle affectionate and encouraging words along the way. This man is unbelievable. I can't fathom why it took me so long to—well, no. I've actually known it all along. Just needed that little push to remember I may need to fight for what I want. There was never a doubt that this is what I want. That he is who I want.

I think we're way over the speed limit, but as another contraction rips through me, I let go of that thought and release some vocal expletives to the confines of the car, along with a full bag of worries, almost surprised they didn't show up earlier. Guess I was busy getting Christian back.

"Almost there, I promise." Christian's voice pulls me back. It's like a magic spell, reversing my spiraling thoughts, grounding me. His hand finds mine, creating that little squeeze that reminds me that everything will be all right. He's here with me.

"I love you," I say. And—"I'm scared."

"God, I love you too, Claire. And I'm here, right beside you, every step of the way." His eyes flicker to me for a second before he brings his focus back to the road. But I see it—the love. The exhilaration. He looks unbelievably happy. And excited. And terrified. Like a true dad-to-be.

People say women tend to forget. That if we remembered how giving birth to a human being felt like, we wouldn't want to do it again. I disagree. I don't think this is something I'll ever be able to forget. I definitely don't want to forget. Breathing alongside Christian, squeezing—okay, more like bone-crushing—his hand, watching his face transform all at once, from worry to wonder, several long hours later, when I finally gave that last push and got my tiny, screaming baby delivered back into my arms for the first time.

"I'm sorry," Christian whispers once he regains his ability to speak, watching our newborn trying hungrily to latch onto my nipple. "For thinking I could ever let you go. For thinking there could possibly be a scenario where you and I weren't together in it."

"Well, you have plenty of time to make it up to me." I smile at him, blissfully exhausted.

"And I will," he says, smoothing my hair gently and planting a kiss on my lips. "Now, please don't be mad, but there's one more person who owes you an apology."

There's a soft knock on my door. My eyes open slowly, trying to recall the last few moments before I fell asleep. Christian is resting on a recliner beside my hospital bed, a bundled newborn sleeping peacefully in his arms.

"Thanks for... uh, letting me know." Ryan steps inside. He seems insecure—probably for the first time since I've known him—as he splits an embarrassed, apologetic stare between Christian and me. He walks over slowly, handing me a small box. "It's a cake," he says quietly. "Not lemon cake this time, I promise." It's a peace offering of sorts. "I'm sorry," he adds, rubbing the back of his neck. "For trying to come between you two. For—" his eyes lock on the baby. "For completely missing the point."

"Do you want to hold her?" I ask. Too tired and too happy to say anything else.

"I—" he hesitates again, but Christian is already by his side, gingerly transferring the little bundle into his arms. There's a shift. A complete transformation in Ryan's demeanor, in his gaze, followed by a long moment of silence, and words that come out rusty—as if it's been a while since he's last used his voice—when he asks if it's too late. If it's too late for him to be part of this baby's life. Under my own terms.

40

My someone to run with

Claire

I am not one to jump into moving in with a guy I met less than a year ago. With a newborn. Most definitely not. Even my sister Kate may not be that brave. But when it comes to Christian, I happily made that exception. Since we moved in together, when we wake up in each other's arms, he makes sure to ask about my song. The one that fills my head when I open my eyes every morning. The one that has been a happy song since becoming a mom, and since I stopped feeling guilty for taking what I want, living my life the way I want, and made Christian my official boyfriend.

We're sitting in that cute, small coffee shop at the mall near Jake's school. That same mall where Christian and I shared our first kiss, when I was trying to make Ryan jealous. The biological father of my baby girl, Brie—named after Brianna, the baby sister Christian lost so many years ago. He cried when he saw me filling out that form for Brie's birth certificate. I wouldn't have it any other way. She's currently napping happily in Christian's arms, unaware of how surprising life sometimes turns out to be.

"More coffee?" Ryan asks his new girlfriend, Inna, who shakes her head with a warm smile. They met and fell in love shortly after I rejected Ryan's marriage proposal. When he thought he'd never want any part in Brie's life. It took one visit. One look at this sweet little baby girl who shares half of his genetic material. One long moment of cuddling her in his arm. One tiny little hand closing tight on his finger. One pair of eyes that gazed trustfully into his. For Ryan to change his mind and realize that actually, things don't have to be all or none. There are so many amazing parts in between. And different kinds of families, and different kinds of dads.

It's been two months since I went on maternity leave, enjoying my time with Brie and Christian without interruption. Two months since we moved in together. I can't believe I'd waited so long to just say yes to this man.

I'm also too busy and too happy to worry about the *what's next*. Big Boss Joe stopped for a house visit to tell me we'll be moving forward with our clinical trial design, with a new asset—a safer and better drug—and without Harriett, the science-killing witch, who will likely not work in this industry ever again. Yeah, the smile on my face was unbeatable. I haven't decided between going back to Amarinex, or maybe taking Ellie's offer and joining GERI. But I'm optimistic that whatever path I choose, with Christian, Brie, Kate and Mom by my side, it's going to be awesome. And either way, I'll have the opportunity to continue working with Christian, and be part of the revolution, to find a cure. For Jake. And for all the other superheroes out there living with Type 1 diabetes. Because we are not giving up.

Christian gets up slowly, handing baby Brie to Ryan, and the two men exchange a conspiratorial look. Ryan nods his head, a wordless permission of sorts.

Christian clears his throat, turning his gaze to me. "Now that I'm fully aware of your reputation when it comes to marriage proposals," he says with a crooked smile, "I need to ask you something."

"Reputation, huh?" I laugh. I'm not sure where he's going with it but there's this wave of bliss washing over me.

"Don't laugh. You're supposed to say—*what would you like to ask, Christian.*"

"Okay." I decide to play along. "What would you like to ask, Christian? And in this specific family-wide forum?"

Christian bends over to plant a small kiss on Brie's head, who's now sleeping peacefully in Ryan's arms. Then turns back to plant a kiss on my lips. "How soon is too soon for someone to ask the love of his life to marry him?"

"Hmmm. It depends," I say, fighting a smile. My heart speeds up, my face heats all at once. I hope my cheeks are not as red as they feel. Well, actually, they probably are, but I'm getting too excited to care. "They're going to have to get a ring first."

Christian gives me a content look. "What makes you think they haven't?" He comes to kneel in front of me, pulling a small box from his pocket.

"Claire, from the minute you jumped me right here at this mall, trying to make your ex jealous—no offense Ryan," he says, not taking his eyes off me.

"None taken," I hear Ryan chuckle from somewhere in the background.

Christian clears his throat. "From the first moment you came into my life, even without my glasses on, I knew I was going to make you mine." He stops for a second, awaiting my reaction. There are tears, happy tears, streaming down my face, and my voice is completely gone—excitement does that to people. Especially to very hormonal, freshly made moms who've only recently delivered a baby and are being asked to marry the love of their life.

I nod enthusiastically, turning my gaze to Brie. It's not just me anymore—any decision I make is hers too. "I know you wanted Brie to grow up with both her parents," Christian says, easily reading my mind. "Ryan will always be her biological dad, and I hope, will continue to be part of her life. But there's one more thing I need to say, and just a disclosure—since we're dealing with a lawyer here," he gestures with his head to Ryan, "this language has been pre-approved by him." Ryan nods in confirmation and Christian takes my hands in his. "Putting aside the genetic realm for a moment, a child can have more than one dad. And more than two parents. And I promise to love Brie like she's my own. Because she *is,* and I hope you'll agree—Brie is one hundred percent yours, which means the two of you are *one hundred percent mine.*"

It's goofy logic but I love it. I love him. I love us. "Claire Marie Bellingham, I can't imagine a life without you and Brie. There's nothing in this world I want more than for us to become a family. Will you do me the honors and marry me?"

It's a yes. Of course it's a yes!

The End, but actually also—a very bright beginning.

Overprotective Mom
Blog Entries

Pump Party Part I

January 26th, 2012

The idea of throwing my daughter a pump party came to me while going through online chat rooms of parents of kids with Type 1 diabetes. The parents discussed the first introduction of the insulin pump to their kids through a party, as a way of making it more attractive and appealing to them. For me, at that time, it seemed like a sweet dream, the day we would finally get my daughter an insulin pump. We were waiting over 5 months to get approved for a pump. A time period that took forever for me and my husband, having to give our daughter insulin injections at least four times per day for the first time in our lives, realizing we will have to do it every single day until there's a cure, and knowing there is an alternative, in the shape of an insulin pump. A small beeper-looking device that delivers the insulin 24/7 for you, all you have to do is tell it how much and when. No, it doesn't check your blood sugar and make its own decisions (that's what the artificial pancreas project is all about), but it replaces the four shots per day with one infusion site change or port change every 2-3 days. And it allows you to live your life the way you want it (so I thought) and adjust your insulin accordingly, while on the shots it seemed the other way around; no sleeping late on weekends since the long-acting insulin had to be taken at the exact same time every morning, no skipped meals or else blood sugar goes low etc. Doing all that as an adult could work if you like to follow a schedule and enjoy routines. For kids and especially young children, this could be practically impossible. Especially if they fit into the food troublemakers profile (but really, can you blame a five-year-old for wanting to munch in small portions around the clock, instead of three larger traditional meals on a schedule?). We desperately needed our life back, our spontaneous way of living, our sleep (through the night, and late on weekends), and I especially hated having to tell my Ms. *I'm Not hungry* (that also desperately needed food to get above the 2.5 weight percentile, yes out of 100...) that she couldn't eat anything that had carbohydrates in it until the next meal, since she had already gotten her insulin shot. Of course she always had the option of getting another shot, but somehow, for someone who doesn't like to eat anyway, it didn't seem too attractive.

So we decided we had to get her an insulin pump. Only it didn't take too long to realize it was going to be a laborious and exhausting process. We had to take various training sessions, health assessments for my daughter and undergo psychological evaluations for ourselves, as her parents and main caregivers, just to make sure we are psychologically competent for that. No one had assessed whether we were psychologically competent to raise a child with diabetes before she was diagnosed, yet they made us go through those evaluations in order to be approved to give our child the best medical treatment possible. So after going through all that, how could we not celebrate getting the pump? There was no happier than us that day when the $6,000 pump arrived in the mail, we longed for it so much that somehow we got ourselves under the impression that this would be the end of all our problems, quite a lot to ask from a machine, even from a $6,000 machine. But we were determined to give our daughter her normal life (with diabetes) back, and this small device, we hoped, would make a huge difference.

***

Finally Arrived, Pump Party Part II

January 31st, 2012

The day the big box with the pump and all necessary equipment arrived was a day of celebration, as if our normal lives were waiting in that box to be unfolded. After 5 months of waiting and longing, I was holding this pink (my daughter's choice) beeper-looking device in my hand, finally. But this was only the beginning of a new journey, and I realized that the next step would be to make my daughter like it and feel confident and comfortable enough to wear it. And so I emailed her teacher and asked to reserve a slot on their busy kindergarten schedule for a party.

Somehow my daughter's Pump party was a lot about carbohydrates, coming to think of it, just like diabetes... I wrote down some words; to teach the class a little about Type 1 diabetes, about how brave my daughter was, about her new cool pump, which they had all decided was actually a Nintendo DS. And basically, I stretched almost exclusively the positive aspects of having diabetes; like having to eat candies to increase blood sugar when needed and knowing your body's signs better than any physician. Next, we went on to some arts and crafts. I made pump models—that my husband and I cut out from colorful, thick craft paper—and let each child decorate their own crafted insulin pump with stickers and colorful glue markers. Now it was my daughter's turn to teach her friends a thing or two about how to use it. We made up a game in which each child was holding their pump creation and a bag of gummy candies (Fruit Snacks in individual small packs work best for us in bringing up low blood sugar pretty fast—considering our kid doesn't like juice—and it worked great for the party too). My daughter proudly explained that when her blood sugar was high, she needed to press some buttons on her pump, but when her blood sugar was low, she needed to eat some gummy candies. Therefore, in our game, whenever she said "high," the kids would press the buttons on their crafted pump, and whenever she said "low," the kids would eat a few gummy candies. Whoever gets it right wins. Well, actually, in our game we made sure everyone won. Especially our daughter, who got to be the star for a day.

And finally, there is no real party without a cake, so we all had cupcakes. It turned out to be a pretty cool (well, at least for kindergarten-aged kids and the school staff) successful party, and we also made up a great game. The kids LOVED it! Especially the part where they 'had to' eat candies. In fact, they have been asking me ever since, at every opportunity, when we would play this game again or have another Pump party.

Blog Source: Overprotective Mom—Living Our Normal Life with Diabetes www.overprotectivemom.com

These two blog posts have been approved for use and adaptation in this book. And for future pump party planning, if you wish.

A Note from the Author

I first started my Overprotective-Mom blog over 14 years ago. It was a place to share bits and pieces of our family life, about juggling between kids and a science career, and about raising a child with Type 1 diabetes in the most normal way—we hoped—possible. I never thought any of these blog entries would one day be included in my future books. Nor did I think I would ever write a full-length fiction novel and get it published. Although this hadn't stopped me from spending a significant amount of time dreaming and trying. Fourteen years, one children's book, 63 blog posts, three romance novels later, and here I am, finding that a few of these old blog posts blend so naturally into Claire and Christian's story.

Like Jake (Christian's nephew), my daughter was diagnosed with Type 1 diabetes shortly before her fifth birthday. Her dad and I learned very quickly that insulin, while it keeps patients alive and helps with the symptoms, is NOT a cure. I'm a scientist, and up until that moment, my research had been devoted entirely to genetic and epigenetic mechanisms of diseases. Type 1 diabetes, however, had never been one of those diseases, and other than a few simple facts, I knew nothing about it. I remember sitting next to my daughter, scared and confused, questioning everything I'd known, trying to find a purpose again, or some semblance of a new normal. I also struggled with the thought of ever being able to go back to work, go back to researching mechanisms of other diseases when—all of a sudden—there was one so close to my heart. And oh so personal. But at five years old, my daughter climbed up the sofa and jumped in front of me. Looking me dead in the eye, she commanded—as she still does, because she's a natural leader—"go back to the lab and find me a cure."

So I did, at least the first part of it—I went back to work and switched my entire research to studying Type 1 diabetes. But the second part, finding a cure—well, this part still needs work, and there are so many incredible scientists, researchers, physicians, non-profit organizations, patient organizations, advocates, communities and families that are hard at work trying. In the meantime, there are many misconceptions that accompany this disease and make patients' lives harder, maybe even slow down some of the progress (of finding a cure). Christian, Claire and Jake uncover a very small portion of it. And by sharing that small part of me in their story, I hope to help bring some awareness, while these superheroes living with Type 1 diabetes and their loved ones are still waiting for a cure.

Acknowledgements

This book has truly taken a village. But first and foremost, I'd like to thank my family - My husband, for his un-relented support, no matter what it is that I want to accomplish; no dream is ever too big or too out of reach or too impossible. To my kids, for cheering me on and for letting me bring stories about Christian and Claire to our dinner table as if they were real people (well *they are* real people, in my head). To Lia, my own superhero with Type 1 diabetes, for letting me share that small fraction of her in Jake. To my sister, Shiri, for always being ready to go to war for me since childhood—whether playground politics, teenage drama, or anyone who dared roll their eyes at me, even though you're the younger one, I couldn't ask for a fiercer warrior in my corner. To my parents, grandparents, extended family and friends, for your endless love and support, and for being the first ones to order my books online, in every single format.

To my amazing book club, for making me step out of my comfort zone and read stories outside the romance genre. But ladies, enough with the sad-ending books, please, I can't keep crying in public with a book in my hand.

To my story development team, my beta readers and ARC team, for their insightful comments that helped make this book so much better. And Orly, for putting her therapist hat on in between book chapters to provide professional comments and suggestions. To my editor - Julie, yes, I'll keep coming back, you're never getting rid of me. To the talented illustrator and cover artist - Mitxeran, for having that special talent to know what I want before I even know it.

And finally, to Steven King for his "On Writing, A Memoir of the Craft," my favorite book about writing.

I'd also like to thank all the scientists, researchers, physicians, the JDRF and other non-profit organizations, patient organizations, advocates, communities and everyone else dedicated to accelerating life-changing breakthroughs to cure, prevent and treat Type 1 diabetes. We are never giving up.

About Me

Emma Aiseman is my not-so-secret pen name, devoted to writing happily-ever-afters.

I live in New Jersey with the loves of my life – my husband and our three children (and our tiny yet mighty puppy who firmly believes he's human).

I am a scientist by day – a biochemist, spending my time in the biotech world, questioning dogmas and working to develop medicines for incurable diseases.

I am a writer by night – (actually early mornings), diving into the fictional romance world, swapping pipettes and scientific manuscripts for plotting swoony characters, sizzling chemistry, positive twists and happy endings.

When not managing teams of scientists or writing fiction, you can find me reading (romance, of course), cooking or playing pickleball with my kids.

If you enjoyed *One Hundred Percent Mine*, please leave a review (Amazon, Goodreads or anywhere else). I would love to know!

Hope to meet again on my next book.

Yours,

Emma

emmaaiseman.com

Also by Emma Aiseman

The GERI Labs Series – Nerdy scientists romance
A Symptom of Love
GERI Labs Book 1
Available in Paperback and eBook formats

Let it Love
A contemporary romance novel
Available in Paperback, eBook and Audiobook formats